Cassie Miles, a *USA Today* [author] Colorado for many years a[nd] Her home is an hour from the rugged Pacific Ocean and an hour from the Cascade Mountains—the best of both worlds—not to mention the incredible restaurants in Portland and award-winning wineries in the Willamette Valley. She's looking forward to exploring the Pacific Northwest and finding mysterious new settings for Mills & Boon Heroes romances.

Charlene Parris has been reading books for as long as she can remember and romance stories since high school, after discovering her mother's cache of romance books. She loves smart, sharp-witted, independent heroines; strong heroes who respect them; and of course, happy endings. Charlene writes for the Mills & Boon Heroes series because she loves adding twists and turns to her stories. When she's not writing, Charlene is working her full-time job. And for fun, she reads, walks, and is learning yoga.

Also by Cassie Miles

Mountain Retreat
Colorado Wildfire
Mountain Bodyguard
Mountain Shelter
Mountain Blizzard
Frozen Memories
The Girl Who Wouldn't Stay Dead
The Girl Who Couldn't Forget
The Final Secret
Witness on the Run
Cold Case Colorado
Find Me
Gaslighted in Colorado
Escape from Ice Mountain
Shallow Grave
K-9 Hunter

K-9
MISSING PERSON

CASSIE MILES

DEFENDER
AFTER DARK

CHARLENE PARRIS

MILLS & BOON

First Published in Great Britain 2024
by Mills & Boon, an imprint of HarperCollins*Publishers* Ltd
1 London Bridge Street, London, SE1 9GF

www.harpercollins.co.uk

HarperCollins*Publishers*
Macken House, 39/40 Mayor Street Upper,
Dublin 1, D01 C9W8, Ireland

K-9 Missing Person © 2024 Kay Bergstrom
Defender After Dark © 2024 Charlene L. Lokey

ISBN: 978-0-263-32227-9

0424

MIX
Paper | Supporting
responsible forestry
FSC™ C007454

This book contains FSC™ certified paper and other controlled sources to ensure responsible forest management.

For more information visit: www.harpercollins.co.uk/green

Printed and Bound in the UK using 100% Renewable Electricity at CPI Group (UK) Ltd, Croydon, CR0 4YY

K-9
MISSING PERSON

CASSIE MILES

For all the fantastic, talented K-9 dogs.
And, as always, for Rick.

Chapter One

At the base of a seven-hundred-foot granite cliff, Shane Reilly adjusted his sunglasses and stared at the rock climbers from the Aspen/Pitkin County Search and Rescue team as they made their descent. On the way down, they scrutinized every inch, looking for a scrap of material, a blood smear, a hair clip—anything, any trace of the woman who had gone missing four days ago.

To get to this position at the foot of the cliff, Shane had driven down a steep one-lane service road. His assignment was to search this wide flat canyon where a scrawny creek wound through leafless shrubs, scruffy pines, rocks and patches of October snow that glittered like diamonds in the afternoon sunlight. If the missing woman had dared to hike through this desolate terrain, she must have been desperate to make her getaway. If she'd fallen…he was looking for a dead body.

Head tilted back, he studied the jagged rock face and mentally mapped the route he would have taken if he'd been hired by a group for a day of extreme skiing in the areas outside the groomed slopes. A decade ago, when he was still in his teens, Shane loved being dropped by helicopter into uncharted mountain territory and maneuvering his way down. Then he turned pro and had to be more careful. Skiing had been his life. Until the crash.

He lowered his gaze. The rugged territory had already been surveyed by drones. This effort was a more detailed search—the specialty of Shane's partner, Elvis. The seventy-two-pound, black Labrador retriever kept his tail in the air and his nose to the ground, moving purposefully, searching. His sense of smell, which was ten thousand times more effective than a human, alerted him to the presence of skittering voles as well as elk, coyote and mountain lion. *Layers and layers of scent.* Using a T-shirt that belonged to the missing woman, Elvis could track her through an old-growth forest or across the Colorado high plains. With minimal instruction from Shane, the Lab had divided the wide ravine into quadrants as soon as they arrived. So far, Elvis hadn't shown any indication of a find.

"How are you doing?" Shane glanced over his shoulder to his backpack, where he carried a water jug and collapsible bowl for Elvis. All that sniffing could be dehydrating. "Thirsty?"

Without pausing, Elvis chuffed impatiently as if to say, "Hey, I'm working here."

"Yeah, yeah, don't mind me. I'm just the guy who buys that pricey kibble you like."

Shane always talked to his Lab and, frankly, wouldn't have been too shocked if the dog answered back. Elvis had been his best friend since they were introduced at the physical therapy clinic after the skiing accident. The doctors had told Shane he might never walk again, but Elvis—his assigned service dog—never gave up on him.

When Shane strode out the door from rehab, he brought Elvis with him. For the past two years, they'd undergone SAR training together. Shane had started skiing again. Not professionally, just for fun. And he'd opened his own business. Most of the time, life was good.

Elvis raised his head, went into high alert and shook all over. His feet scrambled in the gravelly dirt, and he bounded toward the cliff face. At the edge of a tall arched boulder, he sat and froze in place, which was his signal for a find.

Shane dashed toward Elvis. Was this the missing woman or something else? If the dog had sensed danger, he would have been in attack mode. This find was probably harmless. Nonetheless, Shane was glad for the Glock 17 in the holster clipped to his belt. He drew his weapon. Couldn't ignore the possibility that the woman who had disappeared might have been kidnapped.

Gun in hand, he stopped beside Elvis. "Heel."

The black Lab stood at his left hip, ready and waiting for the next command from Shane, the alpha of their little pack.

"Whoever is behind that rock, step out," Shane said. "Show me your hands."

The woman who emerged with hands raised had long blond hair cascading past her shoulders almost to her waist. Even though she wore jeans and an oversize flannel shirt, she looked like an angel. *Thank you, Elvis, for finding her.*

Shane peeled off his Ray-Bans and asked, "Who are you?"

"Mallory Greenfield. The person you're looking for is my mother, Gloria."

Though she spoke clearly, he barely made sense of her words. Consumed by inappropriate desire, he yearned to tangle his fingers in those silky blond strands and kiss those full pink lips. *Get a grip, Shaney boy. Been too long since you've had a date.* "Why were you hiding in the rocks?"

"I didn't want to disturb your search. I'm wearing Mom's shirt, and I thought your dog might smell it."

"Which he did." He holstered his Glock. "You can put your hands down."

"Thanks." She jammed her fists into her pockets and frowned.

She was still beautiful, but her unhappiness disturbed him. "What's wrong?"

She glared, and he realized what a dumb question that was. Of course, she was upset. Her mother was missing. "Who wants to know?"

"I'm Shane Reilly." He reached down and patted the Lab. "This is Elvis."

"Why do you call him Elvis?"

"For one thing, he ain't nothing but a hound dog." Shane tried on a disarming grin. "And take a look at his mouth."

She leaned close to study the handsome dog's upper left lip. Elvis the dog mimicked the sexy sneer of his rock star namesake. Mallory looked from the Lab to Shane and back. Then, she gave an enthusiastic laugh that made the world seem brighter. "Does he sing?"

Shane gave a command that wasn't in the regular training manual. "Give us a song. And-a-one-and-a-two-and-a—"

Elvis tilted his head back and yipped.

Mallory applauded. Her scowl was gone. "Can I pet him?"

"He'll be disappointed if you don't."

After a few gentle pats on his round noggin and scratching under his chin, she fondled his floppy ears, then stroked from head to tail. She hugged Elvis, and he gave a happy murmur in the back of his throat. *Some dogs have all the luck.*

Without letting go of her new best friend, she glanced up. "I've heard of you, Shane Reilly. You were a pro skier, competed in the Olympics in downhill and slalom."

"And now, I'm retired."

"What do you do?"

"For one thing, I volunteer with Search and Rescue. Me and Elvis are getting pretty good at SAR." He gazed into her wide-set eyes, which were an incredible shade of turquoise blue. "And I'm a full-time licensed private investigator."

"Really?"

"Elvis was learning how to be a crime solver, and I figured I should do the same. Plus my father and brother are cops in Denver."

"Why didn't you join them?"

"I wanted to have free time for skiing, and you'd be surprised by how many people in Aspen need my services."

She stood, looked him up and down and stuck out her hand. "You're hired, Shane. I want you and Elvis to find my mom."

He grasped her small delicate hand in his and lightly squeezed. "Where do we start?"

"She left a note."

"What did it say?"

She reclaimed her hand and dashed a tear off her cheek. "It said, I'll be back."

Not much to work with, but he'd do anything to find Gloria Greenfield and bring a smile to Mallory's beautiful face.

TWO AND A half days later at the bitter edge of dawn, Mallory turned off her alarm before the buzzer sounded. She'd barely slept. Her mom was still missing. During the past six days, her mood had alternated between elation when a clue arose to panic when she feared Gloria was gone forever, and then to despair and exhaustion. *Where the hell has she gone?*

In thick wool socks, Mallory padded to her bedroom window and threw open the curtains. Snow battered the beveled panes. This marked the first real storm of the season, a cause for celebration in Aspen where the fiscal well-being of the town meant at least twenty-five inches of base and a fresh supply of champagne powder. Mallory's fortunes weren't directly tied to the weather, but her business also depended on tourists and skiers. She was a part owner of Reflections, an art gallery and coffee shop perched at the edge of the cliff where she'd met Shane and Elvis at the bottom. Though Gloria had founded the gallery, she delegated much of the responsibility to Mallory.

For the past several months, Reflections hadn't been doing well. They'd barely survived the COVID shutdown and were still struggling toward recovery, relying mostly on the sale of baked goods, coffee and tea. Though tempted to close the doors and devote herself 24/7 to searching for her mother, Mallory suspected that would be signing a death warrant for Reflections. She couldn't take time off for grief. People depended on her, and the business wasn't going to run itself.

After a quick shower, she plaited her hair into a long braid, tossed on her clothes, shoved her feet into snow boots and donned her parka, hat and gloves. She lived close enough to the gallery that she was able to slog through the knee-high drifts and unlock the rear door. In the mudroom outside the kitchen, she changed from her boots into green slip-resistant clogs, and then she started the early morning prep work—mixing, kneading and proofing the dough for fresh breads and pastries. With muffins and scones in the oven, she took a caffeine break and pushed through the swinging kitchen door into the coffee shop adjoining the gallery.

Sipping her favorite dark roast brew, she peered through a window at the unabated snowfall on the sculpture garden at the edge of the cliff. Was her mother out there, freezing and lost? Suffering from a delusion? Hiding from someone or something that would do her harm? Mallory pinched her lips together to hold back a sob but couldn't stop her tears. *Don't give up.* She had to keep believing that Gloria would come home safe and sound. Living without her was unthinkable.

Given her mom's eccentric and unpredictable nature, her disappearance could be based on a whim or a half-baked scheme. That was Uncle Walter's opinion. Not really a relative, Walter Pulaski had been in Mallory's life for as long as she could remember. Not only was he internationally known as a sculptor who worked primarily in marble from a local quarry, but he also provided Mallory with grandfatherly guidance, ranging from bedtime fables to advice on creating wood carvings of forest creatures and totem poles. The end products were inexpensive and sold well. Not that Mallory considered whittling to be a viable career.

Walter hadn't known where Gloria went. Nor had any of her other friends, employees or ex-boyfriends. Everyone had said, "You know Gloria. She'll turn up."

Mallory wasn't so sure.

She glanced down at her cell phone. *Call Shane.* She'd begun to look forward to their frequent talks and seeing the singing dog with the Elvis sneer. Right now, she wanted reassurance, needed to talk to a kind-hearted, understanding person. She flashed on a mental picture of Shane, who was big—about six feet two inches—and comforting. His sunstreaked brown hair fell across his tanned forehead. He had stubble on his chin. When he grinned, dimples bracketed his mouth. *Call him.* It was after seven o'clock, not too early.

She tapped his number on speed dial, and he answered immediately in a clear, wide-awake voice. "Are you at work?"

"Where else would I be at dawn?"

"You might find this strange, but there are people who actually sleep until eight. Sometimes even later."

"Mom always says there's plenty of time to rest when you're dead." *Not dead, oh, please, not dead.* Another spurt of tears spilled down her cheeks. "This weather has me worried."

"I understand," he said. "You're right to worry. But I got to tell you, I love snow."

Of course, he did. He used to be a pro skier. Before they'd officially met, she'd seen him on the slopes and admired his form. He looked good on skis and even better close up. His hair was perpetually rumpled but not messy. Thick black lashes circled his caramel-brown eyes. Thinking of him gave her a much-needed distraction. "Can you come over today?"

"How about now? I bet you've got fresh muffins in the oven."

"Now is fine." Better than she'd hoped for, but she didn't want to come right out and tell him that she was smitten. There were already enough complications to deal with. "And why are you awake at this ungodly hour?"

"Doing cyber research on your mom. It's two hours later in NYC."

"Why are you researching New York?"

"An art connection to your gallery. I'm always working. A great PI never sleeps." He paused for effect. "Just ask Elvis."

At the sound of his name, the Lab gave a bark.

Shane responded, "That's right, isn't it? You're a great detective."

Mallory imagined the dog spinning in a circle, chasing his tail and wiggling his hindquarters. "Be sure to bring him along."

"You hear that, buddy? She can't help falling in love with you."

She groaned at the song reference. "Come to the kitchen door. It's unlocked."

As soon as she disconnected the call, she stared at the silent phone and wished she'd hear from her mom. The only texts she'd gotten this morning were from employees who would be late. On a typical weekday, at least one of the bakers would have shown up by now. Not that she needed help. The gallery and coffee shop didn't open until ten o'clock, and the monster snowfall would keep people away. Despite the need for paying customers, she hoped for a quiet day. No sooner had that thought registered in her brain than she heard loud thuds. Someone was pounding on the hand-carved doors at the entrance. A woman called out, demanding to be let in.

Mallory pocketed her phone, got to her feet and clomped across the gray-and-brown travertine tiles that reminded her of river rocks. She patted her cheeks, erasing every trace of moisture. Why had this person—this woman—come here? Did she have something to do with Gloria? *Oh, God, I hope so.* About time she'd catch a break.

The voice shouted, "It's cold. Let me in."

Mallory unfastened the dead bolt, unlocked the door and opened it. Outside, partially sheltered from the heavy snowfall by an overhanging eave, stood a tall woman in a black parka. A fur-trimmed hood hid her face.

She shoved against the door and stormed inside. "Thank God, I got here in time. He intends to kill you."

Chapter Two

After nearly a week of fear and confusion, Mallory didn't think she could be taken off guard, but this strange woman had hit her with an unexpected gut shot. Off-balance, Mallory staggered backward a step and bumped into an easel advertising the showing next week for the kindergarten through to fourth-grade classes she taught in the afternoon. She caught the poster before it fell and turned to the stranger. "Who wants to kill me?"

"Conrad Burdock. Actually, he's looking for your mother." The way her voice dropped when she said *mother* made the word sound like a curse.

Nascent hope shot through Mallory. Maybe something could be gained from this bizarre encounter. "What do you know about Gloria?"

"Quite a lot, actually. I'll tell you later. Right now, we've got to run, Mallory."

How does she know my name? "I've never heard of this Burdock."

"I'm trying to tell you. Don't be so stupid." The tall woman slammed the heavy door with a crash that echoed all the way up to the open beam ceiling. She adjusted the shoulder strap on a large leather messenger bag and focused on Mallory. "Listen to me. Do as I say and maybe, just maybe, you'll survive."

"Tell me what you know about my mom."

"First," the woman said, "you come with me."

"Into the blizzard?"

"Unless you can sprout wings and fly."

Now who is being stupid? Mallory pointed to her froggy green clogs. "I'm not dressed to tromp through the snow. If I agree to go outside with you, I have to change into my coat and boots. They're in the kitchen."

"Is anybody else in the kitchen?"

"I'm here alone. And I have muffins in the oven." When the woman unzipped her parka and pulled off her gloves, Mallory's gaze riveted to a gun holster clipped to her belt. The intruder's rude attitude took on a more sinister aspect, and she was grateful that Shane and Elvis would be here at any moment. She decided to stall until her backup arrived. "I want more information, okay?"

"We don't have time to play around. Get your damn boots."

Mallory had grown up dealing with difficult artists and angry customers and various other people her mom rubbed the wrong way. Her tone of voice took on a soothing tone, and she arranged her features in a conciliatory expression. She led the way along the carved half wall that separated the coffee shop from the gallery itself. "Back here, through the swinging doors."

"Nice place you've got here. Lots of polished wood and excellent sculptures."

"By Pulaski." Even under threat, Mallory couldn't help bragging about Uncle Walter.

"Walter Pulaski? I'm impressed."

"Reflections used to be a restaurant. All open space with

the kitchen in the rear. Setting up the partitions and the lecture area took some work, but the end result was worth it." Over her shoulder, she said, "Doesn't seem fair. You know my name, but I don't know yours."

"Amber DeSilva."

"Like the gem?"

"Amber is a fossilized resin, not a gemstone." Though her voice oozed disdain, she stopped short of accusing Mallory of stupidity, again. "Don't you know me?"

Was she supposed to recognize this person? "Sorry."

At the kitchen door, she caught Mallory's arm and turned her around so they were face-to-face. "Look at my face. My eyes."

The color of her chin-length blond hair nearly matched Mallory's long braid. The symmetry of their features—upturned nose, wide mouth, square jaw—was similar. When Mallory gazed deeply into Amber's eyes, the green-blue color of her irises astonished her. An exact match to Mallory, but that was impossible. Nobody else had eyes like hers, nobody except her mom. The most notable difference between them was height. Mallory stood five feet four inches, and Amber had to be nearly six feet tall in her high-heeled boots.

Cautiously, Mallory admitted, "I see a resemblance."

Amber gave a snort. "Ya think?"

"Let's have a cup of coffee before we rush into anything." When she pushed open the kitchen door, the comforting aroma of baking breads and muffins wafted over them. "I really don't want to go outside again. It's freezing."

"You're not listening, damn it." Amber followed her into the huge kitchen. "This is a matter of life and death. We have to find your mother before Burdock gets here."

"We're on the same page. I'm really worried about her

and want to find her. Have you heard anything? Do you know where she is?"

Amber gave a short harsh laugh. "She didn't tell you that she was leaving, did she? Whisked away like magic. She's the queen of hocus-pocus. Ha! Doesn't feel nice to be left behind, does it?"

What was she talking about? "How well do you know my mom?"

"Oh, my God, you still don't get it. Look at me again. Look close."

Mallory took another glance and then shrugged. "Sorry."

Amber DeSilva framed Mallory's face between her hands and stared with her turquoise eyes. "Mallory, my love, I'm your sister."

Stunned, Mallory gaped. *Her sister?* Not possible! According to Gloria, her father died before Mallory was born, and they had no other living relations on either side. Either Amber had fabricated a weird, complicated lie or Gloria had a whole different life before she met Mallory's father. Conceivably she'd been married before and had other children. But why hadn't she mentioned another family?

"You must mean that you're my half sister." Mallory leaned forward, trying to get closer to the truth. "From an earlier marriage."

"Wrong! We have the same father, Raymond DeSilva, and the same mother, Ingrid DeSilva, who you call Gloria Greenfield. You know, I'd love to sit down for a sweet little chat with tea and crumpets, but we damn well don't have time. Get your buns out of the oven and put on your boots."

"How long have you known about me?"

"Only a few days. Once I had the name you were using, tracking you down was easy."

"I don't have a fake name."

Amber gave her a smug grin. "I'm sure Gloria filed all the fake paperwork. She spared no expense, stole enough to get the two of you started on a lovely new life. How sweet. How lovely. How selfish."

"How old are you?"

"I'm four years older than you."

My big sister. A strange feeling—a jumbled combination of joy and fear, happiness and dread—surged through her. She wasn't alone anymore. And her life was completely different.

Most of the mountain roads and streets hadn't been cleared, but Shane drove his Lincoln Navigator SUV, a deluxe 4WD gift from a former sponsor, through the steadily falling snow with no skids, no slips, no problems. The full force of the storm was subsiding, and he guessed they'd get only eight to ten inches—significant but not crippling for Aspen.

In the rear of the SUV, Elvis rode in his specially designed pen where he could watch the snow from windows on both sides. He'd already been out this morning and raced around the fenced area behind Shane's cabin, tunneled into high drifts and buried himself under the glorious snowfall. Before Mallory called, Shane had taken the time to rub dry the dog's shiny black coat. Elvis still smelled doggy, but Shane didn't notice anymore. The Lab was his best friend, and it seemed rude to complain about his natural odor.

In the rearview mirror, Shane saw Elvis staring toward the front of the Navigator. His pink tongue lolled from one side of his mouth while the other side smirked. "We're going to see Mallory. You like her, right?"

A happy bark followed a shoulder shimmy.

"You understand, though, she's more my type than yours."

Elvis growled. He wasn't buying that logic.

"We could find a lady friend for you. Maybe a French poodle."

"Yip. Yip. Yip."

"Okay, three French poodles."

The Navigator rounded a final curve where snowplows had scraped off the parking lot in front of a strip mall and gas station. The art gallery came into view. Lights were on. A glow came from the north-facing windows nearest the entrance. The soaring eaves of Reflections resembled the bow of a clipper ship churning through the snowstorm toward the edge of a treacherous cliff that had claimed the lives of at least five rock climbers. A thick layer of snow piled on the slanted roof and on dozens of heavy marble sculptures in the garden.

Shane had visited plenty of museums and elite galleries around the world while on ski tours, and Reflections impressed him. Mallory's mom had done an outstanding job redesigning this structure, curating the displays and building a reputation. From what he'd heard, artists competed aggressively to be granted a showing here in Aspen, where ski bums rubbed elbows with rich and famous mountain residents.

He frowned to himself. Mallory wasn't going to like the information he'd unearthed in his latest online research. Much of his investigating happened on the computer, and he was skilled at navigating the ins and outs. Gloria Greenfield—art gallery owner and boho-chic free spirit—kept a relatively low-profile on social media with very few photographs. A cause for him to wonder what she was hiding.

Her life before Mallory's birth twenty-six years ago was sketchy. Her hometown in Texas had no records of her. The high school didn't have a photo of her in the yearbook, and the same held true for the art school she attended. Granted, computer data from that era wasn't always efficient or reliable, but he'd expected to fill in some of the blanks. The more questions he'd uncovered about her background, the more Gloria's disappearance smelled like something illegal and dangerous.

Outside Reflections, he saw an SUV parked near the front entrance. It seemed out of place. Shane doubted that the vehicle belonged to an employee. They usually entered through the kitchen where they could hang their coats and scarves in the mudroom before getting started. Tire tracks were still visible in the parking lot, indicating that the SUV hadn't been there for long. Too early for a customer or a friendly visit.

Shane followed a road at the edge of the parking lot and drove around to the rear where he parked. Mallory's car wasn't there, which was no big surprise because she often walked to work. He unlocked the compartment under the center console, removed his Glock 17, checked the clip and slipped the weapon into a belt holster. Not knowing what to expect, he needed to be prepared for anything.

Before entering through the kitchen door, he glanced down at Elvis. In spite of the Lab's high spirits, he was obedient. "Elvis, heel."

Instantly, the dog transformed into a SAR professional, sitting at Shane's side and waiting for further instruction. Shane placed his index finger across his lips. "Elvis, hush."

Confident that the Lab wouldn't make a sound, Shane entered the mudroom, shucked off his parka and drew his gun. *Ready for action.* Hearing voices from the kitchen at the back of the restaurant, he crept closer to the door that separated the mudroom from the kitchen, pushed it slightly open and listened. Elvis sat beside him, silent and alert.

The voice of a stranger said, "Your coffee smells good."

"I can make you a travel mug." That was Mallory.

"We don't have time. Besides, I don't expect your mountain coffee to be anywhere as delicious as my special brew in New York."

"This is an Ethiopian blend, fair trade and dark roasted."

"Don't care," said the stranger. "Hurry up and don't try anything cute. I don't want to hurt you, but you should know that I'm an excellent markswoman. Learned to shoot in Sierra Leone."

"Didn't you say just say you're from New York?"

"I often visited Africa with my father. He was a gemologist."

In his cyber research, Shane had learned that Gloria sold precious gems several years ago. A possible connection with this stranger from Africa. He recalled what he knew of conflict diamonds, also called blood diamonds, which were used to finance insurgents and warlords.

"I'm not going anywhere with you." Mallory's tone rang with determination. "Even if we are sisters…"

Shane swallowed his surprise. *Sisters?*

Mallory continued, "Why should I believe what you say? Why would some guy I've never heard of want to find Gloria and kill her?"

"Oh, my sweet, stupid Mallory. He doesn't care about Gloria or about you. Burdock is after the African Teardrop."

"What?" she gasped. "What do you know about the Teardrop?"

Supremely confident, the stranger continued, "A 521-carat, pale blue diamond that went missing at just about the same time my mother, Ingrid DeSilva, was killed in an explosion."

"What are you saying?"

"My mother—sorry, I guess that's *our* mother—faked her own death, disappeared and stole a small fortune in gems from *our* father, including the Teardrop. She couldn't sell or fence that particular diamond because it was too famous. Does any of this sound familiar?"

"Mom said the Teardrop was cursed."

"Well, she might be right about that. Conrad Burdock has already killed people in his search for that stone. He'll kill again."

Shane had heard enough. He stepped into the kitchen with his Glock braced in both hands. "Don't move."

Beside him, Elvis bared his teeth and growled.

When the tall blonde reached for her holster, Shane snapped, "Don't try it. Raise your hands over your head. Do it."

Though this wasn't the first time he'd faced off with a dangerous adversary, Shane did most of his sleuthing online or by interviewing witnesses. He'd taken training courses to get his license, and his brother, the Denver cop, had given him lessons on how to apprehend and subdue, but he was uncomfortable threatening a woman, especially a woman who looked enough like Mallory to be her actual sister. Still, he kept his Glock aimed in her direction as she lifted her hands over her head.

"It's okay," Mallory said. "She's not here to hurt me."

"Then she won't mind if you disarm her." He nodded toward the woman. "Take her weapon."

"Honestly, Shane. You're overreacting." Still, Mallory followed his instruction and approached the woman. "I'm sorry, Amber. I need to do what he says."

"Who the hell is he?"

Mallory unfastened the safety strap on the holster and carefully removed the Beretta. "His name is Shane Reilly, and he's a private investigator I hired to find Mom. Shane, this is Amber DeSilva, and she claims to be my sister."

"You never mentioned a sister."

"Because I didn't know about her," Mallory said.

Amber exhaled a frustrated groan and pointed toward her leather messenger bag. "I brought a laptop with me. You can look me up."

That would have been Shane's next move. Computer research didn't count as an infallible source for verification, but it gave something to start with. "Okay, sis. Are you carrying any other weapons?"

"I'm not. Trust me?"

"No."

She cocked an eyebrow. "Then I guess you'll just have to do a full body search."

If Mallory had issued that invite, he would have responded in a flash. He'd been longing to slide his hands over her body from the first moment he saw her, but she hadn't given him the okay signal.

"Quit fussing at each other," Mallory said. "Listen carefully, Shane, because I'm not going to repeat this."

She repeated the unbelievable story about Gloria stealing a fabulous gemstone and faking her death during the Civil War in Sierra Leone. He knew her Mom was eccentric, but this was over the top.

"Come on," Amber urged. "We need to hurry."

"Why?"

"I was careful to make sure Burdock's men didn't follow me from the airport, but they're smart enough to figure out the address of this place. It's not safe to stay here."

Or maybe she led these supposed bad guys directly here. Or maybe they didn't exist. He hadn't seen another vehicle out front. Shane lowered his weapon but didn't slide it into the belt holster.

"I should go," Mallory said. "If we don't, she's going to keep harping on it."

"Damn right, I am."

When Amber glared, Shane noticed the unusual turquoise color of her eyes—another indication of a sibling relationship with Mallory. Her story was bizarre, but it might be true. He had questions for her.

Amber dropped her hands and concentrated all her attention on her alleged sister. "This is important, Mallory. Do you know where the Teardrop is?"

"I only saw it once. I was probably ten and didn't realize it was real or valuable." Mallory ducked into the mudroom. "Let me change into my boots. If we hurry, we can get this figured out and be back here by opening time at ten."

"I'll drive," Shane said. "My car is more comfortable for Elvis."

"I'm guessing Elvis is your dog." Amber sneered. "Cute."

Hearing his name, the Lab perked up. But he didn't bounce over toward the tall blonde or even wag his tail. Apparently, Elvis didn't trust Amber, either.

Mallory emerged from the back room wearing her boots and parka. She carried ski gloves in her hands. "Let me lock the front door, and we can get going."

Shane heard the heavy front door crash open. Then came a shout. And the clatter of boots on tile.

Chapter Three

Amber's dire warning had come true. Or had it?

Was this a setup? Shane glanced past Mallory, who stood frozen in the middle of the kitchen and concentrated on Amber. Her haughty expression succumbed to panic. Tension and fear distorted her features. Amber was damn scared, and the people who'd charged through the front door had to be the ones who frightened her. Shane still didn't trust her motives, but he believed her terror was real.

They needed to move fast, before the intruders figured out that they were in the kitchen. While he kept his Glock trained on the swinging door from the gallery, Shane herded the women and Elvis toward the rear door. "Get in my car."

"Key fob?" Mallory held out her hand.

"It's unlocked."

"What if I want to start the engine?"

He handed over the fob. "I'll drive. Wait for me."

As soon as the women disappeared into the mudroom, he braced himself. For a brief moment, he considered stepping into the gallery and attempting to work out some kind of compromise, but the continued shouts and crashes indicated violent intent. These guys hadn't come here for a negotiation. This was a hostile assault.

The door from the gallery swung wide. Two men wearing

black ski masks and heavy parkas charged into the kitchen. In a quick scan, they spotted Shane. Handguns raised, they aimed and fired. Four shots. Four misses.

He raised his Glock and returned fire. The taller guy yelped and fell to the floor.

Before his brain had time to process the fact that he might have killed a man, Shane pivoted and dove through the door into the mudroom. Grabbing his parka, he dashed outside.

Mallory hadn't waited for him to take the driver's seat. She sat behind the steering wheel with the windshield cleared and the engine running. *Smart move. He couldn't complain.*

He jumped into the passenger side. "Go."

Even though she wasn't familiar with Shane's 4WD Lincoln, she deftly maneuvered out from behind Reflections before one of the intruders burst through the back door and started firing at them. Bullets thudded against the rear of his car. In the back seat, Amber whimpered and wrapped her arms around Elvis, who had apparently forgotten that he didn't like this woman. He buried his nose in the fur-trimmed collar of her parka.

Looking over his shoulder, Shane saw the boxy outline of a Hummer crossing the parking lot and stopping at the rear door. How many of them were there? He'd seen two in the kitchen, including the guy who'd fallen, and a third must be driving the tank-like vehicle. Were there others? His Glock handgun didn't seem like enough defense. He asked Amber, "Did you pick up your Beretta?"

Her eyes were wide and frightened. "I have my gun."

"And you know how to use it, right?"

She swallowed hard. "I'm not a good shot from a moving vehicle."

"Nobody is," he said. "We might need the fire power later."

"I'll be ready."

Her trembling voice sounded anything but ready for a shoot-out. Oddly enough, Mallory—who appeared to be a peace-loving flower child—was the coolest person in their little combat group. She drove like a champ, skidding at the edge of disaster but not going too far. Her gloved hands rested steady on the wheel. When the Navigator reached the stop sign at the street that had been cleared earlier this morning, she executed a sharp left turn without slowing. Dangerous move but nobody else was on the road. They were headed into town.

Shane took his phone from his pocket. "Drive directly to police headquarters. I'll call ahead and let them know we're coming."

"No."

"Did you say no? You won't go to the police station?"

"Yes, I said no."

Her flat refusal didn't make sense. Mallory had worked with the sheriff and the police chief during the search for her mother, which meant she didn't have a built-in resentment against law enforcement in general. He kept his tone level and calm, which wasn't the way he felt. Shane was, after all, the son of a cop. "When somebody shoots at you, it's wise to tell the police. At least, let me call."

"No." She was more adamant.

From the back seat, Amber called out, "I see headlights following us."

If the thugs who attacked at Reflections were on their tail, they had even more reason to contact the authorities. But Mallory had a different idea. At the next snowplowed road, she took a right and raced past four other cross streets to a stoplight. Through the thick veil of falling snow, he spotted the headlights behind them. At this distance, he couldn't tell if the other vehicle was a Hummer or not. "Why won't you go to the police?"

"Because I love my mother. I'll do anything for her."

"You care about Gloria. I get that." The bond with her mother ran deep and true. "But what does that have to do with police protection?"

"If half of what Amber told me is true, my mother broke the law. She faked her death and stole a fortune in precious gems. If we contact the police, there will be investigations and prosecutions. I refuse to be the person who sends Mom to jail."

She cranked the steering wheel and turned left again. Too fast. The back of the car fishtailed wildly. The moment she got the skid under control, she went left again, then drove back to the main road. She checked her rearview mirror. "Did we lose them?"

In the back seat, Amber and Elvis stared through the rear window. "I can't tell," Amber said. "There are a couple of other cars."

"We might be able to end this right away," Mallory said. "We're going to Mom's place. I remember where she hid the Teardrop after she showed it to me. Maybe it's still there."

"Not likely," Amber said. "Wasn't that several years ago?"

"Sixteen years. It's still possible."

Shane had no comment. Gloria's A-frame house had been their first stop when he signed on to be Mallory's PI. Together, they'd searched for clues in her desk drawers, her closets, her bedside table and even her pantry. He'd learned quite a bit about her mother but nothing that pointed to her location. And he remembered the final stretch leading to the house. The road bordered a rugged granite wall on the left. The other side was a drop of a couple hundred feet. Not the sort of road to be driving on in a storm, especially not with bad guys on their tail. "This might not be the best time," he said.

"Can't hurt to try."

He knew she wouldn't be dissuaded. Mallory could be as sweet as a baby fawn but had the tenacity of a badger when she made up her mind. In that respect, she was somewhat like Gloria. The only way he could keep her safe was if he had control of the situation. Never again would he agree for her to be the one behind the wheel.

She dodged through a couple more changes of direction and circled around until she and Amber felt sure they'd lost the Hummer. Mallory set her course for her mother's A-frame house in a high canyon.

While the morning sunlight fought a losing battle with overcast skies, he peered in the direction of the ski runs on Aspen Mountain, which were obscured by a curtain of falling snow. The chair lifts and gondolas weren't open yet, but in a few short weeks, the slopes would be filled with skiers and snowboarders. Every year since he'd turned eighteen and moved to Aspen full-time, he'd looked forward to opening day. This season, he hoped Mallory would be with him, flying downhill and soaring over moguls. He wanted to hear her laughter ringing in the frosty air, to see the roses in her cheeks and the sparkle in her turquoise eyes.

She guided his Navigator into the series of winding turns that led to Gloria's house. When they entered the stretch with the steep drop on the passenger side, he held his breath and slammed his foot down on the floorboard to press an invisible brake. A treacherous ride but no one appeared to be chasing them.

Covered in several inches of snow, the odd-shaped house—partly A-frame with a couple of gables and a wall of glass on one side—reminded him of a fairy-tale dwelling.

A place where elves and fairies might live. He told Mallory not to park in the driveway where they might get stuck in the snow. "We don't want anybody to pull in behind us and block our way out."

He swiveled his head and looked at Amber in the back seat. "Have you disabled your cell phone so your location can't be traced?"

"How would I do that?"

Inwardly, he groaned. Amber acted like she was tough and worldly-wise. A lot of bluster, but she had very little idea of what it took to be on the run, evading the alleged villain. What was his name? Conrad something? "Give me the phone."

"You're not going to erase my contacts or anything, are you?"

There were several apps to block locators, but he opted for the quick-and-easy method. "I'm turning it off and taking out your battery. When you need to make a call, let me know."

Mallory parked uphill, off the side of the unplowed road. Though their tracks through the snow couldn't be hidden or erased, their position was set for a quick escape.

Shane held out his hand for the fob. "You did good."

"I was born and raised in the mountains. I know how to drive through snow."

He took a moment to fasten his dog's flashy red leather harness with shiny studs. A little bit sexy and a little bit rock 'n' roll, it was perfect for a Lab named Elvis. Shane didn't hook the leash onto the harness, preferring to let Elvis bound ahead while they slogged through the snow to the rear door.

"The dog shouldn't be with us," Amber said. "He'll make noise."

"That's the point." Mallory kicked through snow that came almost to her knees. "He'll alert us to anybody approaching."

Shane didn't need a doggy alert to the danger he suspected wasn't far from them, but he liked having the seventy-two-pound black Labrador on his side in a fight. In addition to training as an attack dog, Elvis had killer instincts and a ferocious growl.

Reaching inside his parka, Shane rested his gloved hand on the butt of his holstered Glock while Mallory used her key to unlock the back door. She entered an open kitchen that was separated from a long dining room table by a counter where a collection of mushrooms—porcelain, wood and clay—were displayed. Doodads and tchotchkes filled every space in a design scheme that could only be described as chaotic but not unpleasant. He liked the house and wanted to meet the woman who lived there. A cozy warmth snuggled around him. The many windows on two sides of the kitchen, which must have been added on to the original structure, made him feel like they'd entered a snow globe.

"It's weird," Mallory said, "to be coming in here without hearing Mom's music. The greatest hits of the '90s."

"I remember." Amber's tone was uncharacteristically pleasant. "Lots of Madonna and Michael Jackson. She loved to dance the 'Macarena.'"

For the first time, Shane sensed that Amber's connection with Mallory might be the truth. Her unexpected appearance at Reflections had seemed too coincidental. And her story about a multi-million-dollar stolen diamond sounded like a fantasy. In spite of their matching turquoise irises, Amber had no proof that they were sisters.

"Watch me now." Mallory skipped into the front room in front of the long dining table. Humming tunelessly, she moved in a horizontal line, clapped her hands and returned in the opposite direction.

Elvis tried to match her steps, but it was Amber who faced her and provided a mirror image. At the end of the line, she said the magic words. "Can't touch this."

They went the other way. Together, they repeated the MC Hammer line. "Can't touch this."

Mallory laughed. "Did Mom teach you this dance?"

"Actually, it was Felix." She whirled, and her parka opened wide, revealing her belt holster with the Beretta tucked inside.

"Who's Felix?" Shane asked.

"A friend from Sierra Leone. He came home with Dad after my mother was supposedly killed in an explosion in Freetown. Their two-story office building burned for over forty-eight hours. Everything was incinerated. Most of the inventory of gems were lost."

"I didn't think diamonds could burn," Mallory said.

Amber stopped dancing. Her voice took on a smug, superior tone as she explained, "Diamonds are made of carbon, like coal. So, yes, they can burn at extreme heat. Dad found a few intact. But the insurance paid for most of his loss."

Shane had another question. "Why didn't he keep the inventory in a fireproof safe?"

"He did," she said coldly. "The door to the safe was opened. Investigators believed that my mother opened it in the hope that she could rescue the gems, but she couldn't escape before the fire overwhelmed her. Before you ask, there was evidence of human remains but no way of identifying the victim. So long ago in a war zone, DNA testing couldn't be counted on. In the back of the safe, they found her wedding ring."

Mallory shuddered. "I know the story is untrue. Mom

survived, and so did I. But it must have been horrible for you."

"It was." She flicked her wrist as if she could dismiss a lifetime of bad memories. "Felix helped. I was the only four-year-old in Manhattan with an extremely tall male nanny from Sierra Leone with tattoos up and down both arms. He told me all kinds of good stories about my mother. But I didn't believe a word."

"Why not?" Mallory gazed at her with deep sympathy.

"If my mother was such a wonderful person, why did she abandon me?"

Shane watched and cringed. If these two were, in fact, sisters, the differences between them made a stark contrast. A walking illustration of nature versus nurture, they shared genetics but had been brought up differently, and they wanted very different things. Heartbroken, Mallory desperately yearned to find and protect her beloved mother who had been the center of her life since birth. Amber couldn't care less about Gloria. She was after a big payoff from the sale of the Teardrop and figured her mother owed her that much.

Mallory sighed. "I wish you could know her the way I do."

"Back at you," Amber said. "If you knew what she was really like, you might be glad she's gone."

"She'll come back. I just know she will."

"Don't be so sure. She might be—"

"Okay." Shane stepped between them to interrupt that thought. The possibility of her mom's death was already driving Mallory up a wall. "I think you ladies agree on a specific goal. You both want to find the diamond. And that means finding Gloria."

"Yes," Mallory said.

"An uneasy alliance," her sister chimed in.

"Let's get to it," Shane said. "Mallory, you said there was a hiding place somewhere in this house. Where is it?"

Returning to the kitchen, she peeled off her parka and got down on her hands and knees. Though her jeans weren't formfitting, her cute round bottom stuck up in the air, wiggling and distracting him. The more time he spent with her, the more common these moments of instant attraction became. Someday, he might be able to act on these urges. In the meantime, Elvis played surrogate for him, snuggling against Mallory, licking her face and bumping his hindquarters with hers.

In the back of a lower kitchen cabinet, she flipped a small latch and removed a fake wood wall to reveal a safe hidden behind mixing bowls and pans. "The combination is my birthday. I know because Gloria used it for everything."

The lock opened easily, and Shane wondered if this somewhat invisible but easily accessible spot was a good hiding place for a priceless asset. After fishing around in the opening, Mallory pulled out a small, square polished wooden box with dovetailed sides. "The Teardrop was in here. At least, I think so. It was such a long time ago. I might not be remembering correctly."

Amber snatched the box from her hand and tore off the lid. "There's nothing in here, not a thing. Damn, it was too much to hope we'd find it so quickly."

When she discarded the box on the floor, Mallory snatched it up. Sitting cross-legged on the kitchen floor, she probed the satin lining of the box, trying to find a clue or a note. A shred of evidence.

"Forget it," Amber snapped. "Your mother must have realized this was a lame hiding place and moved the diamond."

"You're wrong." Mallory peeled back the velvet on the

bottom of the box. She smiled widely. "I knew there was a reason for coming here, a reason for searching."

"What?"

Mallory held up the small object she'd found in the bottom of the box. "A key."

Chapter Four

Mallory held the flat silver key by the cloverleaf top and ran her finger along the teeth on both sides. No logos or other markings, nothing except a six-digit number, which gave no indication of where the key might fit. "A safe-deposit box?"

"We can track that down," Shane said. "Where did Gloria bank?"

"She had personal and business accounts. A local bank where she got wire deposits and another in Denver." She paused and thought. "Oh, and I think there was something in New York that she opened on vacation. I've heard her talk about offshore banking, but that's probably not where she'd have a safe-deposit box. We should check with Uncle Walter. He knows more about her financials than I do."

Before she had finished speaking, Shane stopped paying attention. Elvis tugged at his sleeve and pulled him out of the kitchen toward the front windows of the A-frame section of the house. The interaction between man and dog reminded her of reruns from an old television show about Lassie, a collie with almost telepathic powers of communication. Under her breath, she mumbled the classic line, "What is it, boy? Did Timmy fall down the well?"

Shane rushed back to the kitchen. "We've got to go."

"What's wrong?" Mallory asked.

"The bad guys are here."

She joined him at the window. "Where?"

He patted the black Lab, who was positively vibrating with warning. "Elvis told me."

"Really?" Amber rolled her eyes. "Are we taking orders from the dog?"

"Stay here if you want," Shane said.

He picked up Mallory's parka and dragged her toward the back door. In seconds, they were outside, threading their way through snow-covered lodgepole pines and aspens toward where she'd parked his 4WD Navigator. A layer of snow had already accumulated on the car. With the sleeve of his parka, Shane wiped the driver's side window and the windshield. He got behind the steering wheel while she opened the back for Elvis and ducked into the passenger seat. Using the fob he'd taken from her when they arrived, he fired up the engine.

"Wait," Mallory said. "Amber isn't here."

"Her decision. And who knows? Maybe it's part of her plan. It's possible she's working with Conrad. The thugs in ski masks might answer to her."

"No way. Didn't you see how scared she was?"

"I don't trust your supposed sister," he said, "and I wasn't hired to protect her."

Before he could pull onto the road, Amber threw herself against the back door and leaped inside. "They're almost here. Coming up the front sidewalk."

Shane smoothly accelerated. "So Elvis was right."

"Yeah, yeah, your dog is brilliant." He reached into a pocket of his parka and took out a plastic sandwich bag. "These are bacon treats. He loves them so don't be stingy, but don't give him all of them."

Around a curve about a hundred yards away, Mallory

saw the Hummer that had chased them from Reflections. One man in a black ski mask limped behind the heavy-duty vehicle. He raised his handgun and aimed at them, but Shane was driving too fast for him to take the shot before they zoomed past. Still, he fired at their car as they sped down the road.

When a bullet thumped against the back, Shane winced. She knew how much he liked the Navigator, and the poor thing was taking a beating today. He swooped onto the treacherous part of the route, skirting the perilous drop on the driver's side. He asked, "How do I get to Uncle Walter's place from here?"

"At the bottom of the hill, you'll hit Meadow Ridge. Take a left." Directions to Uncle Walter's lavish château, part of an elite gated community, weren't complicated. She pulled her phone from a pocket and bypassed the apps Shane had installed a few days ago to disguise her signal. "I'll call ahead and let him know we're coming."

Consulting with Walter Pulaski felt like the smart thing to do. If anyone knew about Mom's secret identity, it had to be him. When she'd gone missing, he claimed ignorance regarding her whereabouts, but he confided in Mallory that Gloria—his long-time partner at Reflections—was troubled about the future of the art gallery and told him she had something of great value to sell. The African Teardrop?

She kept her phone conversation with him short, not wanting to give away too much before they talked face-to-face. She needed for him to look her in the eye and be completely honest even if he thought she'd be hurt. Also, she wanted Shane to be there. Not only was he good at asking questions that didn't occur to her—like knowing whether they should trust Amber—but he had investigative skills. He knew about internet searching, interrogations and legal issues.

Glancing across the console at his profile, she noted the sharp edges of his cheekbones, his stubborn jaw and cleft chin. Apart from the dimples at the corners of his mouth that appeared when he smiled, his features were chiseled and hard, almost obstinate. Not unlike his insistence on calling the police. No doubt, that was the right thing to do, and if any other person had disappeared, Mallory wouldn't have hesitated. But this was Gloria! She couldn't betray the woman who birthed and raised her.

While she directed him around the business area of town and into the hills, she made another call and talked to the guard outside Uncle Walter's gated community, warning him that she might be followed by men in ski masks driving a dark-colored Hummer.

"Don't you worry," he said. "I won't let anybody in who doesn't belong."

"Thanks, Henry. And I'd appreciate if you don't mention this to anybody, especially not the authorities."

"Just like your mama." He chuckled. "Don't worry, Mal. Your secrets are safe with me."

As soon as she ended the call, Shane asked, "Why are you dragging this guy in?"

"Into what?"

"Aiding and abetting," he said. "Sooner or later, we have to talk to the police."

From the back seat, Amber groaned. "For a private eye, you're not very adventurous. Why so law-abiding?"

Mallory answered for him, "His father and brother are both cops."

"Well, that explains it."

"Explains nothing," Shane said. "My goal is survival. The odds are better if we have the law on our side."

"Begging to differ," Amber said. "We're talking about a diamond worth twenty million, which opens a lot of doors to bribery. What makes you think the cops would help you?"

Mallory had to agree. Amber had a point—but could she be trusted?

The Navigator approached the tall wrought iron gates at the entrance to Wind Shadow, an exclusive area so high they could look down on everybody else. Mallory saw the road had already been cleared. Henry, the gatekeeper, sat atop a snowplow the size of a Zamboni blocking the way inside.

Mallory jumped out of the SUV and waved.

Henry responded and pulled the snowplow out of the way. As soon as Shane drove through, the obstacle returned to stop any unwanted guests from entering. Mallory waved again and shouted, "You're the best, Henry."

"No problem, cookie. Good luck finding Gloria."

In spite of his encouraging words, he sadly shook his head, which made her think the worst. Mallory responded with defiance, "She'll be back with a story to tell us all."

"That's the spirit."

She directed Shane past several spectacular homes to the swooping, curved driveway, scraped clean of snow, that led to Uncle Walter's stone and cedar chalet. His sculpture studio—the size of a barn with a huge door for transporting massive statues in and out—stood beside his three-car garage. Outside the front door was a massive marble sculpture of a woman in flowing robes and long hair spilling down her back while she reached toward the sky with an outstretched hand that could cradle the stars and moon. Her laughing face bore a remarkable resemblance to Gloria.

Shane parked in the driveway in front of the garage and

turned to her. "You and Amber go on inside. Elvis and I will check the damage to my vehicle before we come in."

"Are you sure?"

"Elvis could use a break." The corner of his mouth lifted in a smile, activating his dimples. "And so could I. It's been a fraught morning, and it's not even nine o'clock."

His comment reminded her that she needed to put in a call to Sylvia who usually opened the coffee shop on weekdays. "We'll see you inside."

Amber had already left the car. She homed in on the entrance that combined natural elements with sophisticated design. An obviously classy and expensive home, Amber was drawn like a magnet. When Uncle Walter opened the door, she set down the leather messenger bag she'd been carrying since she entered Reflections. She gracefully shook his hand and dipped, almost as though giving him a curtsy. "Love, love, love your work," she gushed.

"Thank you."

"I mean, I saw a display at the VanDusen in Manhattan that was fabulous."

The handsome elderly gentleman braced himself on a hand-carved ebony cane and smoothed the groomed line of his white beard. His gray fleece vest and jeans were spattered with clay, which meant he must have been working on the wheel in his back room rather than trekking to the studio in the snow. Keeping busy had always been Uncle Walter's way of dealing with problems. No matter how cool he pretended to be, Mallory knew he was worried about Gloria. He looked away from Amber and turned to Mallory. "Who is this?"

"Amber DeSilva. I'm Gloria's eldest daughter." She swept past him into the front foyer where four niches held small sculptures of the elements—earth, water, air and fire. Hundreds of reproductions of these artworks had been one of Walter Pulaski's greatest successes. Amber shivered and gasped and moaned as though having an art orgasm. "These must be the originals. Fabulous. These are worth a fortune. Can I touch them? Can I hold them?"

"They're not for you," Walter said quietly.

Mallory was more irritated by Uncle Walter's lack of surprise at Amber's introduction. He must be aware of the secrets in Mom's past. Why had he never told her? Everyone seemed to know more about her mother than she did. Shane had his internet research to keep him updated. Uncle Walter had memories of a different time. And Amber? Well, her sources of information were enigmatic.

Mallory needed to get to the bottom of this. As soon as Walter herded them into his dining room where his housekeeper had placed a coffee service with lox, cream cheese and bagels on a side table, she squared off with Amber.

"Before we go any further," Mallory said, "I think you owe me some evidence. You've made a lot of claims but have given me no reason to trust you."

"You want proof?"

"That's right." Mallory stood toe to toe with her sister, wishing she was six inches taller so she could look Amber straight in the eye. "I never saw you before this morning. How do I know you're telling the truth?"

Amber scoffed. "Do you mean to tell me…that the thugs who chased us through a blizzard and put a couple of bullets in your boyfriend's car…aren't proof enough?"

"Not my boyfriend." *Not that I'd mind if he was.* "Shane Reilly is a private eye. The chase and the gunfire happened after those people in the Hummer spotted your rental car at Reflections. Which only proves somebody is after you."

"Me?" Amber rolled her eyes and looked toward Walter

Pulaski, the man she'd been fawning over. She didn't want to offend him. Even by Aspen standards, the internationally renowned sculptor was Richie Rich. Amber tried to look innocent. "Why would anybody chase me?"

"You're the one talking about stolen diamonds." Mallory backed off a step. "Look, I don't want to fight. But I need proof that Gloria stole the Teardrop, and now—twenty-six years later—she's trying to sell it."

Amber stalked to the end of the satin-smooth teak table with hand-carved legs. The heels of her boots clacked on the polished marble floor. She flipped open the flap on her leather messenger bag. "Mommy's art gallery didn't do well during the pandemic, did it? Reflections is running out of cash, and Gloria needs a great big infusion. Tell her, Pulaski."

Grasping a coffee mug in his calloused hand, he sank heavily into the seat at the head of the table. Mallory studied the scowl on his lined face. Why was he hesitating? What secrets did he know? Years ago, he'd taken over the accounting responsibilities for Reflections because Gloria sucked at math and was somewhat irresponsible. *Somewhat? Change that to wildly irresponsible.* In the circus of life, her mother soared like a spangled trapeze artist while Walter Pulaski was the strongman doing all the heavy lifting, leaving Mallory to play the role of a clown. "Uncle Walter?"

Nervous, he stroked his groomed white beard. "Is it warm in here?"

"Not really. There's nearly a foot of new snow outside."

And yet, he was sweating. He rolled up his shirtsleeves, spread his hands and gestured widely with the muscular forearms of a sculpture artist who chiseled beauty from chunks of granite. "The finances aren't so bad. Even if they were, I promise I'll always take care of you and Gloria. Always. And I'll never let Reflections close down."

Mallory caught the painful undercurrent of what he was saying. They were losing money and the gallery might go out of business. "We're broke."

She left the table, went to the wide triple-paned window and stared into the continuing snowfall. She should have paid more attention to the business end of the gallery. Her mom had never turned down a request for a new expenditure and had run up outrageous costs of her own by bringing in exhibitions from Chihuly, the glass blower, and a graffiti show featuring Banksy, who Gloria claimed to have dated. Maybe she really did have sex with the famously anonymous artist and many, many others. Mallory wasn't often shocked by anything her mom did, but she expected Walter to be straight with her.

As soon as she found her mom, Mallory intended to hire a real lawyer to replace the current guy who traded legal advice for the opportunity to show his paintings of oddly crossbred animals, like a turtle-ostrich or a camel-zebra. Then she would gently ease Uncle Walter out of his job as an unqualified accountant. Everything would be okay when she found Gloria. If she found Gloria…

Tears tickled the backs of her eyelids. More than anything—the money, the art, the diamonds from Africa—Mallory missed her mother.

"Here's proof." Amber pointed to the screen of the laptop she'd taken from her bag. "This is a screen grab, shot three days ago from surveillance outside a pawnshop in Brooklyn. The owner of the shop, Ben Hooker, is a well-known fence, specializing in blood diamonds from Africa."

Staring at the screen, Mallory saw a red-haired woman on the sidewalk. She wore a long beige trench with a scarf in a vivid blue, orange and green pattern—a scarf just like it should be hanging in Gloria's closet. In the screengrab photo, the redhead had just taken off her sunglasses and was staring directly into the camera. There was no mistaking her identity.

"Three days ago," Mallory said.

"That's correct."

Mallory had found her mother.

Still missing but not dead.

Chapter Five

Shane tramped up the neatly shoveled sidewalk with Elvis bouncing beside him, trying to catch snowflakes on his long pink tongue. They paused at the sculpture of the giant woman in a turban rising from the earth and reaching for the sky. Though snow draped across her brow and the bridge of her nose, he saw Mallory in her ecstatic expression. Loving the sky. Open to nature. Had she been the model for this statue? Or had it been Gloria?

Elvis had the good taste not to pee on the artwork. Instead, he went to a clump of leafless aspens near the entrance.

From what Shane had learned online over the past few days, he saw beyond the similarities of mother and daughter and recognized their differences. Both possessed vitality, willingness to take risks and joy in living, but Mallory was more mindful. Though reaching for the stars, her feet remained firmly rooted. She'd organized the search for her mother with the skill of a general deploying troops for battle. Mallory set goals and fulfilled them. Unlike Gloria, she avoided being the center of attention and hid from the spotlight. During the time he'd spent with Mallory, Shane hadn't heard her talk about herself. Not once did she mention her own dreams and desires.

He wanted to open that Pandora's box, to know her on a deeper level, to understand what went on inside her head behind the breathtaking turquoise eyes. But he wasn't sure he could continue along this path, ignoring the glaring fact that Gloria had broken the law when she faked her death twenty-six years ago and stole a fortune in precious gems. Not unless he knew why she'd done it.

For sure, this was the most interesting investigation he'd had since getting his PI license, but he knew better than to sidestep the law, especially since they were being pursued by thugs in ski masks. He had to assume a firm stance, had to take control, to tell Mallory no. He couldn't work for her. Not unless she talked to the authorities. Though he liked to believe he could provide all the protection she needed, he wanted to be able to call for backup.

As he approached the carved entryway, the door whipped open. Mallory jumped out, threw her arms around his neck and planted a powerful kiss on his mouth. Too shocked to do anything but react, his arms coiled around her and lifted her feet off the floor. Not light as a hummingbird but solid and real, her slender body pressed tight against his chest. She was toasty warm and smelled like coffee. He allowed himself to accept and savor her wild burst of passion while it lasted, which wasn't long. She bounced away from him.

Beaming, she said, "She's alive. Gloria is alive."

When Mallory reacted on a purely emotional basis, she was ferocious and unstoppable. He couldn't say no to her. His resolution to immediately talk to the police melted like an ice sculpture in a sauna. He cleared his throat and said, "What brought you to this conclusion?"

"Amber has a photo, taken three days ago."

"And you're sure it's Gloria."

"As if I don't know my own mother."

He stepped into the foyer and closed the door. "I didn't mean to suggest—"

"Never mind." She dashed into a lavish dining room to the right of the entrance where she confronted Walter Pulaski, who stood at a side table filling his coffee mug. Mallory jabbed her finger at his chest. "You knew about Mom. Her history."

"I did," he admitted as he hobbled to the chair at the head of the long teak dining table. "I met her when she was in her teens. We hit it off, stayed in touch. Then she came to me when she was in her early twenties. Right before she changed her name."

"More proof." Amber pumped a fist in the air. "Walter is a witness to our mother's name change from Ingrid DeSilva."

Shane could think of several valid and sensible reasons for a name change. This bit of evidence represented the least devastating piece of the puzzle. He faced the white-haired man whom he'd met once before and liked. "Nice to see you again, Walter."

"Same to you, Shane. A devoted skier like yourself must be happy about the snow."

"The start of the season is always a cause for celebration." He'd think about skiing later. Right now, he concentrated on being a private eye. "What happened all those years ago when you saw Gloria?"

He nodded slowly, remembering. "She came to me here in Aspen and asked for help. I hardly knew her, but I couldn't refuse this fascinating creature. She was a goddess—a pregnant goddess. I might have been in love with her."

"I thought you were gay," Amber said.

"I'm an artist, fascinated by the female form. Gloria was my muse. And we had a good partnership. We both benefited. After she took over the sale of my sculptures, I began to profit royally. And she earned enough in commissions to open Reflections."

"You were royally successful," Shane said. "And Gloria had savings of her own."

"Quite a healthy nest egg."

Shane had heard this story before, but he recalled that Mallory mentioned current financial problems. "What happened to the money?"

"That was twenty-six years ago. Things change." Walter shrugged. "When the economy suffers, the purchase of art is one of the first things to go. I'm fortunate. My sales—especially the reproductions—are still doing well. But gallery owners, like Gloria and Mallory, take a risk with every new artist they spend money on to promote."

Elvis sidled through the door to the dining room. Before the dog could shake, rattle, roll and splatter snow all over the place, Shane dropped a towel he'd been carrying over the Lab's back and gave him a rub down. "Sorry, Walter, I should have done this the minute we came inside. He smells like wet dog."

"Perfectly natural."

Shane turned to Mallory. "In case you're wondering, my Navigator wasn't seriously damaged. Only four bullet holes in the left rear fender. The guys in the Hummer aren't great shots."

Walter Pulaski turned his chair, leaned forward with his elbows braced on his knees and smiled at Elvis. "I've been thinking about getting a dog."

"I recommend it," Shane said. "Forgive me for bringing this up, but the last time we visited I noticed you have a limp."

"Knee surgery."

"I'm no stranger to PT and rehab. That's where Elvis and I met. He was my therapy dog—the only one who believed I'd learn to walk and ski again."

"How does a dog help you to walk?"

"There's a whole range of AAT, Animal-Assisted Therapy. Much of the procedure is based on motivation. Working with a dog makes the boring repetition of therapy exercises less tedious. A larger dog like Elvis can be fitted with a special harness and trained to hold a position and provide a solid base for you to balance. They can help in all kinds of ways. Let me give you a quick demonstration."

Shane waved Elvis toward the chair where Walter was sitting and introduced them. With an expression that seemed both friendly and compassionate, Elvis held up his paw to shake hands.

"After you pet him for a while," Shane said, "have a conversation using his name. Be sure to tell Elvis that he's smart and good-looking. Flattery will get you everywhere."

Amber elbowed her way into their conversation. "Excuse me, but I have more evidence, important evidence."

"Not now." Shane held up his hand, signaling her to stop. Amber had inherited her mother's love of center stage, but he refused to be sucked into a conversation with her as the star, not until he was ready. "We're in the middle of something with Elvis."

"Really?" She huffed. "You'd rather pay attention to your dog?"

So true. Shane nodded to Walter. "I saw your cane hanging near the front door. In a conversational way, tell Elvis to get it for you."

Uncle Walter looked into the dog's attentive face and said, "Elvis, I'd like to go for a little walk. Would you, please, be so kind as to fetch my cane for me?"

"Repeat the important words," Shane said.

"Please. Bring me the cane."

Elvis cocked his head to one side as though logging the information into his brain. Then he turned in a circle, raised his nose in the air and pranced toward the entry where Walter's cane hung on a coatrack. Delicately, Elvis lifted the cane in his teeth, carried it across the room and placed it on Walter's lap.

Mallory, Walter and Shane applauded while Elvis thumped his tail on the polished marble floor, tossed his head and gave his trademark sneer.

"Thanks, Elvis," Walter said. "You're a champ. I'm definitely going to look for a dog like you. Any suggestions for where I should start?"

"I'll hook you up," Shane said. "Not that I'd try to influence you, but Elvis is partial to lady poodles—long-legged standard poodles with curly hair."

Amber groaned. "Are we done setting up a dating service for your dog? Do you think we can get back to the multi-million-dollar business at hand?"

"Fine." Mallory pulled out a chair, set her coffee mug on the table and sat. "It seems that you've had zero contact with Gloria over the years. How did you know she'd gone missing? Why did you come looking for her and for me?"

Amber sat opposite. She reached out with a manicured fingernail and pointed at the laptop screen photograph of Gloria with red hair. "I received this picture with a message to contact Ben Hooker, the pawnshop owner I mentioned earlier. Though I hadn't seen her in person since I was a child, I recognized our mother. She still looks very much like the old photos from Sierra Leone that Felix showed me. I barely knew her. Thought she was dead. The pictures were all I had."

Though he didn't like Amber, Shane was touched by the story of an abandoned child who had lost her mother. When he saw the tears brimming in Mallory's eyes, he knew she felt the same. "Amber, have you stayed in touch with Felix?"

"Of course. He's more like family than my blood relatives. He lived with us almost full-time until I was eighteen and went off to college. As I got older, I realized that he paid for many things that my dad or grandma said were too expensive for a young girl. As if they had any idea what was suitable for me. Felix knew. He gets me. He understands."

"Is he wealthy?" Shane asked.

"He inherited," Amber said. "And he earns a decent amount of money from his original artwork, especially the carved painted masks based on traditional tribal designs."

Mallory's spine stiffened. "Felix Komenda. I know him. We handle his sales at Reflections."

"It's the least our mother could do for him. From what I understand, she never would have gotten away from Sierra Leone without his help."

"So Felix knew all along that Gloria wasn't dead. And he never told you. Or me."

"He was loyal to Gloria."

Walter spoke up. "Your mother was in danger. If certain people found out she was still alive, they would have come after her."

"Like this Conrad person," Shane said. This complicated, intriguing story had taken them very far afield, and he reminded himself that the entire yarn hung on the childhood memories of Amber, who couldn't be trusted as a reliable source. "What happened after you contacted the fence?"

"Ben Hooker promised top dollar if I delivered the African Teardrop to him. After Ingrid or Gloria or whatever she's calling herself visited him, she pulled another vanishing act."

"Did she ever show him the Teardrop?"

"No."

"Did she tell him where it was?"

"No."

This series of events had taken an illogical turn. If Gloria had the diamond, it made sense for her to hand it over to Hooker when she first met with him or make arrangements to deliver the Teardrop shortly thereafter. Was it possible that she'd lost the precious stone? "Did Hooker demand proof? Why look for a buyer if he wasn't one hundred percent sure she had the stone?"

"She showed him photos on her phone with the diamond resting on a newspaper. You know, like kidnappers do with ransom victims."

He wondered if the pictures were taken in New York. "Which newspaper?"

"*USA TODAY.* The date was proof. The location could be anywhere."

Mallory pursued their interrogation from a totally different direction. "You've got me worried again. We know Mom was okay in that photo with the red wig, before she disappeared again. How do we know she's still all right?"

"She calls Hooker. And she sent a photo of herself in Denver to prove she's still alive."

Mallory perked up. "So she's in Colorado."

"I suppose." Amber scowled. "She's doing this wild dance to keep Hooker on the line, but he's not amused. He'd rather deal with me than her or any of the other dangerous people after the diamond."

"So you made friends with Hooker," Mallory said, summarizing. "How did that lead to me?"

"Like I told you before, once I had the name Gloria Greenfield, I tracked you down. Your website is absolutely full of inquiries about your missing mother, which backed up Hooker's story. And there were also pictures of you. Well, I took one look and—" Amber framed her own face with her fingers "—I knew. You were the fetus our mother was carrying when she disappeared from Sierra Leone."

Shane still had questions. Why would Gloria keep checking in with a pawnbroker in Brooklyn? Had she come to Denver? Where was the diamond? He looked to Walter for explanations. "Does this sound plausible to you?"

He gave a slow sad nod. "It's not reasonable but utterly possible. Gloria has never been known for making well-considered plans. She's impulsive."

"If she has the diamond, why doesn't she move forward to sell it?"

"She might have lost it." Walter spread his hands, palm up, as if making an offering to the gods. "It seems inconceivable, but I can think of dozens of other scenarios. Maybe she gave it to a friend to hold. Or buried it and forgot where she dug the hole. She might have decided not to sell it, after all, and return it to its rightful home. At one time, the Teardrop was considered a national treasure belonging to Sierra Leone."

"What?" Amber shrieked. "Give it back? Never!"

"That's what we should do," Mallory said. "Return the stone to the rightful owner."

"Don't be absurd."

"First we need to find it." Shane struggled to bring order to the chaos that seemed to infect Gloria's plans. "We'll start with the safe-deposit box. Mallory, show Walter the key."

She reached into her jeans pocket and pulled out the key

they'd found at Gloria's house. "Uncle Walter, do you know which bank this belongs to?"

Frowning, he studied the key. "She uses Fidelity United Bank here in town. She chose it for the initials."

"FU," Shane said.

"Exactly," Walter responded. "And there's another bank in Denver. Can't recall the name but I can look it up."

"We'll start here with FU." Shane was glad to have some kind of direction. "Then we'll go to Reflections and make a more thorough search."

Amber stood and looked down her nose at them. "Aren't you forgetting something? We have a gang of armed thugs in ski masks chasing after us."

"I sure as hell haven't forgotten." Shane's wary brain sent out constant warning signals, keeping him on edge. "I'm still in favor of calling the police for protection."

"Can't do it," Mallory said. "Mom would end up in jail."

"Absolutely can't," Amber chimed in. "Not that I particularly care about Gloria being arrested. But I'm sure the police would confiscate the Teardrop, and we'd be out millions of dollars."

"One of you stands for love. The other for greed," Shane said. "Two powerful emotions. Neither of you will give in."

"Not a chance," the two women said with one voice.

"I have one nonnegotiable condition." Disregarding Amber, he concentrated on Mallory. "Until this is resolved and Gloria is found, I will act as your bodyguard. All day and all night."

An enticing little grin curved her mouth. "I accept your terms, Shane. It's you and me, together. Twenty-four hours a day."

Bring it on.

Chapter Six

Wondering if Shane was worried about what he'd just gotten himself into, Mallory held his gaze. His dark eyebrows and thick lashes emphasized the honey-brown color of his eyes. His cheeks were still ruddy from being out in the snow. He radiated confidence. No matter what life threw at him, Shane came out a winner.

She enjoyed looking at him, and the prospect of having him with her day and night was super appealing, especially at night when they'd have to stay close together. Sharing the same meals, the same bed or the same shower. Her breath caught in her throat. She had to change her focus before she slid all the way down the rabbit hole into an impossible wonderland. Too many other issues to consider. His undeniable charm didn't count for much when dealing with her mother's disappearance and the loss of the African Teardrop. More than anything, he had to be a good enough detective to solve this puzzle.

The phone in her pocket chimed. When she saw the name *Sylvia* on caller ID, Mallory cringed. Should have called Sylvia earlier. Her good friend and coworker for the past six years tended to be easily excitable, a trait that her new husband found adorable. Mallory wasn't so delighted with semi-hysterics. With a resigned sigh, she answered the phone. "I'm sorry that I didn't—"

"There's blood on the kitchen floor," Sylvia shouted in a high nervous voice, nearly a banshee shriek. "Blood. Both doors are unlocked, front and back. A tray of coffee mugs is scattered on the floor, displays in the front are messed up."

Though Sylvia might be overreacting, a bolt of fear shot through Mallory. What if the bad guys were still there? It hadn't occurred to her that they might stick around or come back to Reflections, but that was a definite possibility. "Listen to me, Sylvia. It's best if you get out of there. Right away."

"Did I mention the blood!"

"Lock up and go home."

"I'm calling Brock."

The police chief. "No, please don't do that."

"Something terrible has happened."

"You're right about that, and it's connected to Mom's disappearance." Mallory heard a string of unintelligible curses from her friend who wasn't one of Gloria's greatest fans. "Getting the authorities involved will only make things worse. Trust me on this. Please."

"I'm not going to turn tail and run, and I won't drag the police into this. But I'm calling Damien. He can be here in ten minutes, and he'll protect me."

Damien Harrison, her husband of four months, stood as tall as Shane and was forty pounds heavier. His extra weight was solid muscle. He managed a horse ranch and was a professional cowboy. He'd won the bronco busting competition two years running at Frontier Days in Cheyenne. For sure, Damien could keep his wife safe.

"We'll be there as soon as we can," Mallory promised.

"We? Who's with you?"

"Shane Reilly, the private investigator." How could she explain Amber? "And someone you've never met before. See you soon. Be careful."

She disconnected the call before Sylvia could ask more probing questions. Explaining Amber was going to be a problem. Uncle Walter had accepted her without hesitation, which might be because he was more familiar with Gloria's checkered past. Sylvia would be judgmental, as would most of Mallory's friends and associates who considered Gloria to be an irresponsible twit. They didn't see her as a single mother who had struggled to establish a business in a highly competitive field while raising a daughter. Mallory couldn't waste time worrying about other people's opinions.

She turned toward Shane and Amber. "We need to get back to Reflections. Sylvia showed up for work, and she's there alone."

"I heard you tell her to leave," Shane said.

"And she refused. Her husband, Damien, is coming to protect her and ought to be there in just a couple of minutes."

"Damien Harrison," Shane said. "He's a big guy and tough as they come, but the men who attacked us were armed."

If something happened to Sylvia or any of her other employees, Mallory would be devastated. "What should I do?"

"Close Reflections until this is over."

Though it went against her instincts as a business owner to shut down, especially after their forced time off during the pandemic, she knew he was right. She immediately called Sylvia back and told her to go home because she was shutting down Reflections for the immediate future. She'd send out an email blast to everybody who worked there, making an excuse for the lockdown. Something about repairs or plumbing. She ended with, "Please don't tell anybody about the blood."

"Not even Damien?"

"Only if he promises not to tell anybody else."

"As if he's some kind of gossip?" Sylvia laughed at the idea of her macho husband chitchatting with the other cowboys at the ranch.

"You're right. My secret is safe with him."

"Before I go, I'll post a closed sign at the door and turn out the lights."

"Thanks, I'll stay in touch."

When she ended her call, she saw that Shane already had his phone in hand. "Just in case, I'm calling Damien. He'll make sure his wife is tucked away safely."

"How do you know Damien Harrison?"

"We've got a lot in common. Until Damien started dating your friend, we were both single guys in Aspen."

Mallory caught the gist of his comment. Many of the hot local guys ran in the same circles, drank in the same taverns and dated the same women. She shuddered. Not a pleasant thought.

He continued, "We're both athletes. Different venues, but we'd run into each other doing weight training."

"Of course." A skier and a rodeo cowboy had more similarities than differences. Maybe they were working on different sets of muscles, but they both needed to stay in shape. Aspen was that kind of town: obnoxiously healthy. Mallory followed her own physical regimen—jogging, weights, yoga and tai chi—even though she wasn't a competitive sportswoman.

Turning away from him, she concentrated on shutting down Reflections for what she hoped would be a limited time. She changed the message on the phone and with the answering service to say they'd be closed for a while and wouldn't be able to return calls for a few days. Next, she contacted her employees. Using her phone she sent out a text and an email saying that Reflections would be closed for a few days, maybe a week, due to repair work. She added that they'd be paid for their time off and ended with, Enjoy the snow.

Collapsing in her chair at Uncle Walter's dining table, she checked the time. It was only 9:52 a.m., but she felt like she'd already put in a full day's work. She glanced toward Amber, who perched on a chair near Uncle Walter and lavished him with praise while he sat sipping his coffee and sketching in a five-by-eight notebook. Mallory really didn't want to drag Amber along with them while they searched at Reflections and went to the bank to check the safe-deposit box. Her complaining and superior attitude were a drag, to say the least.

She looked over at Shane. "Earlier this morning, you said you'd dug up more information on Mom."

"Knowing about her change of identity pretty much explains my online investigating. I found no records for Gloria Greenfield before you were born. A shallow attempt was made to create an alternate background with a high school and art school, but it didn't take much research to figure out that her alleged history was bogus. I'll go back and search for info on Ingrid DeSilva. That might give us a clue for where she's hiding."

"What kind of clue?"

"She could be staying with friends or family she knew before she became Gloria." He went to the side table and poured himself another cup of coffee. "I'll check it out."

"Really? Do you think I have more family that I'm not aware of?"

"Maybe."

The idea shocked her. Finding out about her missing sister had been a major surprise, but a whole family? Mallory had grown up with no reference to grandparents, aunts, uncles or cousins. According to Gloria, the two of them were alone in the world. "Why wouldn't Mom tell me about them?"

"My guess? She thought she was protecting you. The less you knew about her criminal past, the better."

So many emotions churned inside her. Mallory couldn't sit still. She rose from the dining table and returned to the wide bay window that looked out at the giant statue of Gloria reaching for the sky through the continuing snowfall. Elvis sat beside her, and she stroked his still-damp fur. Had Mom lied to her about everything? Mallory paced toward the corner where a white marble statue on a pedestal—Gloria breastfeeding—greeted her. In Uncle Walter's house, Mom was inescapable. She dominated his art and his memories. Had friends and family from her earlier life felt the same way? Would they welcome her home with open arms?

Mallory struggled to regain her balance and pull herself together. When she heard Amber giggle, she turned her head and saw her alleged sister preening for Uncle Walter. Obviously, she wanted him to use his renown and talent to sculpt her. *Too obviously.* If Amber had asked for her advice, Mallory could have told her that nobody coerced Uncle Walter into taking on a project that didn't interest him. Not even commissioned jobs. His last major project was a life-size memorial for his good buddy, Hunter S. Thompson, with a cigarette dangling from the corner of his mouth and a Colt .45 revolver held close to his vest. Mallory loved the statue. The whirling grain of the stone suggested the hazy thinking of the gonzo journalist. The lenses on his glasses were mirrors that reflected the viewer in a disturbing way.

Amber giggled again. "What are you drawing, Walter? Is it me?"

He frowned, ran his fingers through his beard and gave a noncommittal grunt.

"It is." She clapped her hands. "You're making a sketch of me."

"Not you." He turned his drawing pad around so she could see the picture he'd been working on. "It's the dog."

He'd captured the bright intelligence of the Lab and the Elvis-like smirk on his upper left lip. "I love it," Mallory said.

"I have a chunk of black marble I've been itching to use."

His focus on the sketch told her that his attention had shifted to his art, which didn't work well for her. She needed his thoughts and memories tied to Mom. "You knew Gloria when she was Ingrid DeSilva. Did she mention family or friends?"

"Don't think so. And she wasn't married to DeSilva when we first met. Her name was Ingrid Stromberg or something like that. No family. There was a young man with her, but he faded quickly from sight. I don't even recall his name. Why are you asking about long ago?"

"She could be contacting people from her past. People she might have kept in touch with over the years. She did a lot of traveling. Business trips, you know. And she went to New York twice a year."

"Where I live," Amber said without her usual bluster. Knowing that Walter preferred the dog over her had deflated her ego. "I can promise you that she wasn't visiting me."

"What about our, um, father?" Mallory steeled herself for what might come next. She'd spent her entire life believing her father was dead. "Would she turn to him?"

"Not unless she had a death wish," Amber said. "He hated her. Cursed her memory."

Mallory couldn't blame her for the harsh tone. She'd grown up motherless, abandoned by Gloria. "I'm sorry for what you went through."

"Save your pity for someone who needs it. My life wasn't bad at all. I lived with my grandpa and grandma DeSilva in a tall narrow Manhattan townhouse that had been in the family for generations. Like your mother, Dad traveled a lot, but Felix was always there for me. He lived on the fourth floor and had a studio where he did his painting."

Mallory made a mental note to track down Felix Komenda. "What else can you tell me about our father? How old is he? What does he look like?"

"There's not much more to tell." Genuine emotion tugged at the corners of her mouth. For a moment, she showed her grief. "He died in Africa a few years ago. Murdered."

Her voice softened to a husky whisper as though telling this story to herself. But the others were paying rapt attention. Shane, Walter and even Elvis watched her as she continued, "The thug who killed Dad worked for Conrad Burdock."

"The man who's after Gloria," Shane said.

"My, my, you catch on quick." Her hostile attitude was back in full force. "Burdock is a terrible human being, a mercenary who fled to Africa to avoid prosecution in the United States, and I'm certain he was behind Dad's murder. The guy who actually committed the crime claimed he was hired by Burdock."

"Do the police have the murderer in custody?" Shane asked.

"He's dead." She flashed a hard satisfied smile. "The worm got what he deserved."

Mallory had the wretched feeling that Amber had arranged for the death of the assassin hired by Burdock. Maybe she'd even pulled the trigger.

Amber spun the laptop around and tapped on the keys. The screen showed a snapshot of a handsome man wearing a custom tuxedo. His dark hair was combed straight back from his high forehead and streaked with gray at the temples. His eyebrows and mustache were black. His hazel eyes stared with a ferocious intensity that some women would find sexy. Not Mallory. To her, he looked mean.

Amber gestured gracefully as she introduced him. "This is Raymond DeSilva."

Their father. Mallory saw nothing of herself in his features. His mouth sneered. His angry eyes accused her of doing something wrong before she'd even said hello. Still, she wished she'd had the opportunity to meet him, to hear his voice and discover why her Mom had found him attractive.

Amber took the laptop back and punched in a new code. Another photo came up. "This is Conrad Burdock."

This time, Mallory recognized the face on the screen. A few days ago, just before she hired Shane, Conrad Burdock came to Reflections and spoke to her about purchasing one of Uncle Walter's sculptures of Gloria.

Chapter Seven

Their search had swerved into a disturbing new direction, and Shane didn't like the look of the road around that corner. Danger pointed directly at Mallory. Her encounter with Burdock—a man he was beginning to think of as some kind of evil mastermind/supervillain—represented a clear threat. He wanted to bring in the Aspen police, the Pitkin county sheriff and maybe the National Guard—whatever it took to protect her. But she refused. Her logic: Burdock hadn't harmed her when he'd had the chance, which meant she wasn't really in danger. Shane thought otherwise.

With Mallory in the passenger seat and Elvis in the back, he drove his Navigator through the sputtering end of the storm. Fat white flakes fell in batches and swirled through the air rather than joining together in a nearly impenetrable curtain. They were headed toward Reflections to search for the Teardrop among the art displays.

He cleared his throat. "I'm going to call my brother in Denver."

"The cop?" Her eyes widened in alarm.

"Don't worry. I won't tell him about the stolen diamonds or any of your mom's other crimes. I need his help with research."

"What kind of research?"

"The local police and I worked together to track the usage of Gloria Greenfield's credit cards. Not a difficult task because we had access to all her records, identification numbers and passwords. As you know, we found nothing. The day your mom disappeared, she stopped charging her expenses and left no record of buying plane, train or bus tickets."

"You think she might be using an alternate identity, like Ingrid DeSilva," Mallory said. "If not DeSilva, Uncle Walter said her maiden name might be Stromberg."

"If we get a nibble on those aliases, we'd have a clue as to her whereabouts. Unfortunately, I don't have the legal authority to quickly put my hands on confidential records."

"But your brother does."

"Logan has helped me before." And wasn't happy about skirting the edges of the law for his private eye brother. Still, both Logan and their father would do just about anything to encourage Shane's pursuit of a more stable profession than "former professional skier who might be talked into extreme life-threatening adventures." The fact that they considered private investigating to be a relatively safe occupation said a lot about his family's values.

He drove his 4WD Navigator past Reflections where the only vehicle in the parking lot was Amber's snow-covered rental SUV. Fading tire tracks showed where Sylvia had come and gone. There was no sign of the men in ski masks.

After circling a few blocks, he maneuvered the Navigator through the accumulated snow outside Mallory's house where he managed to park in the driveway. In addition to searching, they had a number of other projects, and he was glad they'd talked Amber into staying at Uncle Walter's house. Hadn't taken much convincing; she was delighted to lounge in the lap of luxury while they schlepped through the storm.

"Bring a small suitcase," he said. "Pack enough for a couple of days at my place."

"I still don't understand why we can't stay here."

"Do you have an alarm system on your house?"

"No."

"How about weapons and ammo?"

"I used to have a hunting rifle. But now? *Nada*."

"What kind of search engine do you have on your computer?"

She threw up her hands. "Okay, I get it. Your place is better prepared for detective work and more well-protected."

"Also there's space for Elvis to roam, plus all his food and other supplies."

"Fine," she agreed with a resigned sigh. "We'll stay at your cabin."

He didn't usually have this much trouble convincing women to come home with him, and he very much wanted to have her willing consent. Though she sounded annoyed about spending the night with him, he wondered, *Was she, really?* A couple of times, he'd caught her watching him from the corner of her beautiful turquoise eyes. She often smiled and laughed at his silly jokes. And then, there was that kiss. She'd planted one on him, supposedly because she was happy to discover her mom was alive, but he sensed a deeper connection between them.

"You'll like my house." He made direct eye contact. "And I'll like having you there."

An impatient whine from the back seat reminded him that Elvis wanted out. Pulling his watch cap over his hair, Shane stepped out of the Navigator and opened the door for his dog. Much as he loved the snow, he wasn't a fan of the cold that came with it. Not one of those guys who scampers around in a blizzard wearing board shorts and a tee, his winter clothing—from head to toe—was insulated and flexible, designed to keep him toasty and warm. He followed Mallory up the sidewalk.

Standing under the small gable roof over her front porch, she picked up a snow shovel and handed it to him. "While you're waiting for me, make yourself useful."

He grabbed the handle and muttered, "Shoveling the sidewalk isn't usually covered by my detective fee."

"Don't forget the driveway. Otherwise I'll have trouble getting out of the garage." She pivoted, unlocked the door and darted inside. "Should I bring anything from the kitchen?"

"I have food." His cabin was secluded but only a couple of miles away from an excellent organic grocery, and they delivered. "Just pack clothes and your lady bathroom products. I don't keep lotions and potions in stock."

"No scented candles for the bathtub?"

"I'm a shower guy. My tub is for hydrotherapy." Though the last remnants of the storm tumbled around them, his imagination filled with steam from the bath and Mallory rising naked from the water. Under his layers of clothing and parka, he began to sweat. "Twelve massage jets and a whirlpool. I'd be happy to show you how it works."

"And I'd be happy to let you."

Before she closed the door, she flashed a sexy smile and winked. Definitely, she was flirting. He couldn't be misreading these signals. Mallory liked him.

That conclusion kept him energized while he cleared the snow from the short sidewalk leading to the porch, the sidewalk in front and some of the driveway. Elvis bounded across her yard, burying himself in the snow and then standing and shaking it off. In a sudden change of pace, the dog stiffened the way he did when he'd made a find while doing search and rescue.

"What is it, boy?"

The dog sneered, growled and stared across the street.

Dropping the shovel, Shane looked in the direction Elvis indicated. He didn't see what had caused the reaction but feared there might be a threat. "Elvis, heel."

The Lab moved into position, standing at Shane's left hip and still staring. If the guys in the ski masks were back, Shane was in big trouble. The bad guys had gotten the drop on him, which was why bodyguards didn't do things like shovel walkways.

He should have concentrated on the task at hand, which was to protect Mallory. Should have gone into the house with her. Why was she taking so long? He tore off his glove to unzip his parka and reach for his gun.

Though Elvis stayed in the "heel" position, he wiggled and wagged his tail—too friendly for danger. He wasn't cool and determined like his namesake when he sang the lyric, "Are you looking for trouble?" Elvis the dog yipped. Across the street, a malamute appeared, took a stance and barked a greeting of his own.

"Are you kidding me?" Shane muttered. "Dude, we're not here to make friends."

Elvis gave him a skeptical look.

"You're right, I'm lying. I want to be friends with Mallory. More than friends." He stuck his gun into the holster, picked up the shovel and tramped back to the porch. "Maybe then I'll stop trying to have meaningful conversations with a Labrador retriever. No offense."

Walking close beside him, the dog bobbed his head.

Shane entered without knocking. He'd visited Mallory's

house before and liked her eclectic mix of classic and modern, similar to her mom's decor but not so chaotic. Some of the oil paintings were compelling, rich and beautiful. Others had been done by kids with finger paints and watercolors. In a seemingly unplanned manner, all the pieces fit together and created a charming whole. She was a master at setting up interesting little displays in ignored corners, using ceramics, origami, dried branches and yarn sculptures. Her home felt lived in. "Hey," he called out.

"In the dining room," she responded.

As he and Elvis went through the front room into the attached dining area, he asked, "Did you search for clues in your house?"

"First thing I did." Mallory sat at the head of the table and plucked at the keys on her laptop. "Mom bought this house when I was a baby, and she had plenty of time to hide grown-up stuff so I couldn't get my sticky little fingers on it."

"Find anything interesting?"

"Mostly keepsakes, like a shell from a beach in San Francisco and crystals from a cave on the Continental Divide. And jewelry, lots of costume jewelry."

"The African Teardrop? You were only a kid. Wouldn't know the difference between cubic zirconia and the genuine stone."

"That's not the way I was raised," she said. "Mom knew a lot about precious gems, and she taught me how to tell a real diamond from a fake."

"How?"

"You can tell by looking at it. Diamonds have more sparkle in a brighter spectrum. They don't get scratched but usually have flaws deep inside. You can see through a fake as though it was glass. And there's the water test."

"Tell."

"Fill a glass halfway with water. Drop the naked stone into it. If it sinks, it's a diamond. If it floats, it's fake."

And she'd learned all this when she was a kid. "You had an interesting childhood."

"There are advantages to having a weirdo mom."

On the floor beside her chair was an extra-large, expandable backpack. The thing looked big enough to carry the uniforms for the Colorado Avalanche hockey team, including their skates. "You're packed," he said.

"I should have come outside and joined you, but I had a few emails I needed to send."

He didn't believe that excuse. "More likely you wanted to stay inside while I finished shoveling. Otherwise, you could have taken the laptop with us, and we'd be on our way."

"Or I'm such a good employer that I feel an immediate obligation to the people who work for me and the suppliers who come every day—rain, shine or blizzard—with supplies for the coffee shop. Maybe I'm such a good teacher that I needed to notify the kids in my afternoon classes that we wouldn't be meeting for the rest of the week."

Elvis rubbed his red leather harness against the backpack, which was easily large enough for him to fit inside. Usually Shane was careful not to allow Elvis to drip all over somebody else's house, but he was irritated at her. "You teach?"

"Four classes with different age groups. We have a showing scheduled for next week at Reflections. All the parents come, and the kids show off for their friends from school. We have cheese and crackers and juice while we talk about colors and shadows."

He pointed to a framed picture on the wall that appeared to be a man on horseback who had lassoed a rocket ship.

Everything was painted in shades of blue and purple. "Tell me how you'd analyze this technique."

"An outsize talent. Great metaphor." She grinned. "It's an astronaut cowboy reaching for a blue moon."

While she talked, the tension at the corner of her eyes relaxed, and the tone of her voice mellowed. He could tell she honestly enjoyed working with these kids. "Can anybody come to this showing? Or do I need a special invite?"

"I'd love to have you there. Elvis, too. He's well-behaved, and I know he'd be a hit with the kids." She stood and slipped into her parka. "I guess we ought to get going."

His natural instinct was to pick up her giant backpack and carry it for her, but he needed to be a bodyguard instead of a boyfriend. If weighed down by her luggage, he couldn't reach his gun quickly. And so he straightened his shoulders and walked unencumbered to her front door.

"I'm going onto the porch first," he informed her. "As your bodyguard, I want to check out the neighborhood and make sure it's safe before you come out."

She hefted her pack and nodded. "Whatever you say."

"When we leave here, I think we should go to the bank first."

"I'm with you. Even a total flake like Mom would have the good sense to keep something as precious as the Teardrop in a safe-deposit box instead of a hidey-hole at Reflections."

He didn't point out that the key to the box had been discovered in a secret cache at Gloria's house. "Let's hope so."

"We can only hope that this is the right bank."

On the porch, he stuck his Ray-Bans onto the bridge of his nose and scanned the street from left to right and back again. Two houses up the hill, a teenager shoveled the sidewalk. A Wagoneer chugged down the neighbor's driveway to the street. He saw no sign of the men in black ski masks or their massive Hummer, but he wouldn't let down his guard. It was too much to hope that supervillain Burdock had given up the hunt.

FIDELITY UNITED BANK occupied the first floor of a redbrick building with windows across the front, parking in back and a drive-through. Mallory had been here hundreds of times before. They used FU for deposits from Reflections, and she'd established a savings account for college when she was ten and Uncle Walter had given her a check for two hundred bucks. Several of the tellers and the bank manager knew her by name. Born and raised in Aspen, Mallory's roots went deep. She'd gone to high school here and was prom queen in her senior year. Practically all the locals had participated in the search for Gloria, and Mallory didn't anticipate any trouble accessing the safe-deposit box.

The snowfall had lessened, and people were getting started with their day while the plows cleared the main thoroughfares. According to weather reports, the upper slopes had gotten over eighteen inches of new snow. In town, they were looking at eight to ten inches overnight, which wasn't considered too hazardous. In the high Rockies, a minor blizzard didn't amount to a major threat.

On the other hand, her life was a nightmare and getting scarier by the minute. In the past few hours, she'd learned that her mother faked her own death, stole a precious diamond and was on the run. Mallory had confronted a sister who resented and hated her. As if that weren't enough, she'd been shot at, chased and stalked. At the moment, she could only think of one positive aspect, and that was Shane.

During the drive from her house, he acted like a professional bodyguard, diligently checking his rearview and side mirrors to make sure they weren't being followed. She also kept watch. He drove into the mostly empty parking lot, which had already been plowed, and parked near the entrance. "Before we go inside, Elvis needs a wardrobe change."

"Why?"

"Well, he's wearing his badass studded leather and looks like a tough guy. To go into the bank, he needs his service dog harness."

"Are you and Elvis coming with me to open the safe-deposit box?"

"I'm going to stay in the lobby so I can cut off any threat before it gets close to you. Also, I'm armed and don't intend to hand over my weapon."

He went around to the far back of the Navigator and rummaged until he found a red harness and matching leash, which he handed to her so she could help Elvis get changed. Shane posted himself at the back bumper and kept watch. Though she suspected this extreme level of vigilance might be over the top, Mallory appreciated her bodyguard. Never before had anyone devoted themselves to watching over her. With his dark sunglasses and alert posture, Shane looked like one of those secret service agents who protected VIPs and diplomats. She was neither but liked the attention.

While she unfastened Elvis's leather harness and put on the other, she was impressed with how the supposedly tough, fierce dog behaved. He wagged his tail and licked her cheek. When he was outfitted in his service dog vest, she picked up his leash and slung the small knapsack she used as a purse over her shoulder. "We're ready."

Shane escorted her through the front door and waited by the bank guard's post with Elvis while she strolled past the teller stations and went to an office at the rear of the bank.

She peeked inside the open door and waved to the heavy-set man with thick brown hair and heavy eyebrows. "Hey, Mr. Sherman."

"Howdy-doody, Mallory." The bank vice president bounded to his feet and came around his carved mahogany desk to envelope her in a hug. "Knock-knock."

"Who's there?"

"Could be a skier. Snow telling unless you open the door." He immediately launched into another one. "When the skier's car broke down, how did he get around?"

"Don't know."

"By icicle."

"Good one." She rewarded him with a quiet chuckle. He had a dozen jokes for every occasion, each worse than the one before, but he meant well. Their acquaintance went back several years to the time when she'd dated his son, Josh—a wide receiver for the Aspen High School football team, appropriately named the Skiers.

The banker gave her a concerned smile. "Any news on your mother?"

"Nothing definite."

"She dropped by my office just about a week ago."

To look into her safe-deposit box? Mallory waited for him to continue, but he was silent. She added, "I hired Shane Reilly to investigate."

Mr. Sherman shook his head and frowned. "Poor guy, how's he holding up?"

The clear inference was that Shane's injury and subsequent loss of his career as an Olympic athlete should have left him broken and devastated. She resented the attitude but understood where it was coming from. Josh Sherman blew out his knee in college and ended what might have been a chance to play in the NFL.

Still, she defended Shane. "He might turn out to be a better detective than a skier. Did you know that both his dad and his brother are Denver cops?"

"Well, I hope he finds Gloria for you."

"And that's why I'm here." She dug into the front pocket of her knapsack, pulled out the flat silver key with six digits and held it toward him. "Is this for a safe-deposit box at the bank?"

"Looks like one of ours, and isn't that a co-inki-dink? Your Mom wanted to open the box, too."

This was it! Mallory felt certain she'd solved the mystery of the diamond worth twenty million dollars. Mr. Sherman took the key from her trembling hand and returned to the swivel chair behind his impressive desk. "Let's check the number."

While he searched the screen of his desk computer, she concentrated on keeping her breath steady and her pulse calm. This could be momentous. The air in the bank seemed to press in around her. When she swallowed, her throat felt tight.

"Okey dokey," Mr. Sherman said. "I verified this is Gloria's key. And you are an authorized person to open the safe-deposit box."

Her heart thumped hard against her rib cage. "Can we do it now?"

"Sure thing." He beamed at her. "I need to have you sign a couple of standard forms, and then we can go into the basement."

A terrible thought occurred to her. "If I find something of value in the box, can I take it home with me?"

"That's an excellent question." He rose from his chair and moved toward her. "Since Gloria designated you as an authorized person—a surrogate for herself, if you will—

whatever is in that box belongs to you. I might have even given it to you without the key, being as you're a friend of the family."

After signing a few forms, Mallory followed Mr. Sherman down the stairs into a windowless basement where she'd never been before. In spite of the carpeted floor and cheery yellow walls, it felt cold amid the many file cabinets. The few employees working in this area wore thick sweaters, which wasn't all that unusual considering the weather. At the far end of the room, she saw a metal vault door that required two special keys and a digital code to open. The young woman at the desk nearest the door joined Mr. Sherman while he went through the required procedures and chatted about his son whose real estate business was doing very well. "But he still hasn't settled down, never saw fit to get married and give us grandchildren. I seem to recall that you're single, too."

"Yes, sir, I am."

"Josh's mother and I surely wish something had developed between the two of you. You'd make a handsome couple."

Borderline inappropriate, but she smiled anyway. Though she and Josh had dated for several months, she'd never felt the breath-taking connection to him that had overwhelmed her from the moment she laid eyes on Shane. Mr. Sherman pulled open the door to the safe-deposit vault. Together with the clerk from the nearby desk, he stepped inside.

Mallory caught a glimpse of a large room with floor-to-ceiling lockers of various sizes. "Wow," she said. "I didn't think there'd be so many."

"We have more than average for a bank our size. Aspen is a small but wealthy community. Now, I'll have to ask you to wait here while we retrieve the proper container."

"Can you tell me when Gloria got this box?"

"I could look up the exact date for you, but it was about ten years ago. I remember because you and Josh had just started dating."

When he returned to the vault door, he was carrying a metal container, almost two feet long, which he passed to the clerk who had accompanied him. He relocked the vault and escorted her to a small room with a long table and three chairs. Mr. Sherman centered the long box that looked to be about fourteen inches wide on the table and stepped back.

"I have to lock you in, Mallory, but don't worry. When you're ready to leave, push the button by the door and someone will let you out." He patted her shoulder. "It was good to see you. Don't be a stranger."

As soon as the door closed, she flipped open the lid. The box appeared to be stuffed with nine-by-twelve brown envelopes marked with dates from twenty years ago to the present. *No diamond.* She fished around the envelopes, feeling around at the edges for a relatively small piece of jewelry. *Nothing but paperwork.* Carefully, she lifted each envelope out and felt the inside contents. *Damn it, Mom, what's this all about?*

Mallory opened the most recent envelope and found a letter addressed to Gloria. Dated a week ago, the letter ended with *I will see you in Colorado, my friend.* Signed with a flourish by Felix Komenda.

Chapter Eight

Against his better judgment, Shane gave in to Mallory's wishes and agreed to return to Walter Pulaski's chalet so she could talk to Amber. Driving through downtown, he noted the efficient snow removal from the streets and the sidewalks outside shops and businesses. Everything seemed to be returning to normal after the semi-blizzard. Blue sky peeked through the clouds above the slopes. On a typical weekday in Aspen, it should have been easy to solve the complicated human drama playing out in Mallory Greenfield's life. *Not so.* They had a lot to figure out before they put things right.

From what she'd told him, the letters from Gloria's safe-deposit box had been written by Felix Komenda. Most of them provided a narrative of Amber DeSilva's childhood and early teens, including details a mother would want to know. Apparently, Felix had performed more than nanny duties, and his talents extended beyond his artwork. He was a biographer.

Mallory shuffled through the file box given to her by a bank official to carry the brown envelopes. "The latest letters, especially the one from a week ago, don't mention Amber at all. Felix talks about returning a precious treasure."

"The African Teardrop," Shane said. "Returning it?"

"Doesn't make sense. Seems more like she intended to sell it," she said. "He also mentions a trip to Colorado."

"Has he been to Reflections before? Maybe to discuss the sale of his artwork."

"I've met him once or twice." While she pondered, Mallory absentmindedly twirled the loose tip of her long golden braid. "He's about as tall as you are and very thin. Shaved head. Tattoo sleeves on both arms. Across his chest is a huge tattoo of the famous Cotton Tree in Freetown, the capital of Sierra Leone. His skin is a light mocha, and the orange and green colors of his tats really stand out."

"Impressive," he said. "With that detailed description, I could pick him out of a lineup."

"Yeah, I'm not an artist, but I've got a good visual sense."

"Does the letter say when he'll arrive?"

"It's vague. He also mentioned the Museum of Nature and Science in Denver. Specifically, he talks about the gem exhibit and a guy who works there. His name is Ty Rivera. You've got to admit that these letters are the best leads we've gotten so far."

"The fact that your mother was planning to meet Felix somewhere in Colorado is a whole lot more specific than her cryptic departure note."

"I'll be back?" Mallory chuckled.

Finding the cache of correspondence had brightened her mood. But Shane wasn't amused. Gloria was hiding something from her daughter. In Shane's experience, secrecy led to lies and lies meant trouble. He needed to figure out how to control the threat.

She pulled an envelope from the middle of the box, opened the flap and reached inside. "Seems like I shouldn't look at these."

"Why not?"

"Most of the stuff from earlier years is about Amber. It's intimate and private. She ought to be the person going through them."

"We're not prying," he said. "The letters are evidence. Besides, Gloria wanted you to find them. She designated you as an authorized person to open the box."

"Apparently, I signed a form." Under her knitted blue cap, her smooth forehead wrinkled. "I don't remember. Since I'm a part owner of Reflections, Gloria used to routinely give me a bunch of business-related stuff to review and sign. Did I ever take a look at it? Not really."

"I used to be the same way about paperwork. Not anymore."

"What happened?"

"After my ski accident, I was in a coma for three days. My brother was there when I woke up. As soon as the nurse gave the okay, he hugged me and blubbered like a baby. The first coherent thing Logan said was, 'Dude, you never changed your will.'"

Her eyebrows raised. "I don't mean to criticize your brother, but that's a little bit mercenary."

"No, he was smart to check it out. In the will, I left everything to a former girlfriend. That's *former* with a capital *F*. To say we had a bad breakup would be like calling World War II a minor altercation. I always meant to update the will but never got around to it." Logan was right about a lot of things, and Shane still needed to call him for help in tracking credit cards for his private eye work. "Anyway, don't worry about violating Gloria's privacy. She saved that stuff for a reason."

Mallory lifted a photograph from the envelope. "So adorable. It's little Amber blowing out candles on a birthday cake. Eight candles. Her eighth birthday. I can't wait to show her. She's going to love it."

"What makes you think so?"

"These letters and photos prove that Gloria didn't just turn her back and walk away. She had Felix keeping an eye on her daughter. Mom cared about Amber. When she reads these letters, she'll know. And she'll be happier."

His impression of her prodigal sister was way more cynical. Not once had he heard Amber speak fondly of their mother. She'd come looking for Gloria with a loaded gun, which didn't strike him as the attitude of a person who was longing to make a connection.

While Mallory pored over the letters, pointing out Amber's good qualities, he scanned the winding road leading to Pulaski's château, looking for the Hummer and considering what else they could accomplish today. A search at Reflections was on the agenda. Also, they needed to track down some of Gloria's clients, close friends and former lovers—people she might have told about her plan to disappear. He added doctor and lawyer to the list. The number one, most important contact had to be Amber's former nanny, Felix.

When they approached the entrance where the gatekeeper kept watch, Shane glanced over at Mallory, who chirped a friendly greeting to Henry. He beamed and waved back. Everybody who knew her loved her. Apart from hair color and matching turquoise eyes, she was very different from her sister. Amber was colder than a blizzard and hard as granite, while Mallory was warm, sweet and kind without being saccharine. The best part of his plan for the day would be taking her home with him tonight.

He parked his SUV in the shoveled driveway outside Walter Pulaski's house. The last time they were here, he'd caught a glimpse of the housekeeper who laid out the breakfast spread and coffee before vanishing. He guessed that Pulaski's other employees—like the person who cleared the snow—were also ubiquitous and silent. When Shane first came home after rehab, he'd required that kind of assistance. He'd had a part-time physical therapist and a live-in housekeeper who cooked and cleaned. Both had done their jobs well, but he couldn't wait to get rid of them and have the cabin to himself. Just him and Elvis against the world, that was the way he liked it.

Amber answered the front door as though she was mistress of the house, but she didn't look happy. "Walter locked himself in the small studio at the back of the house," she said.

Smart man. "And left you in charge?"

"No need to sound so surprised. I've been running households since I was a kid. I've just been chatting with the housekeeper about lunch."

"Great," Mallory piped up. "I'm starved."

Shane gestured with the file box from the bank. "May we come in?"

Amber stepped out of his way. "Walter told me that when you returned, he wanted to see Shane and the dog."

A perfect excuse for a getaway. He carried the box of letters to the dining room table, set it down and turned toward the sisters. "I know how to get to the small studio. I'll take Elvis and leave you two with this."

Amber scowled and flicked her fingers against the cardboard. "What's in there?"

"The contents of Mom's safe-deposit box. Something she considered precious." Mallory took off the lid and pulled out one of the brown envelopes. "I think you're going to be happy to see these letters. They're all about you."

"Why would that make me happy?"

"Well, it shows she cares about you."

"Ha! More likely she felt guilty, which is exactly what she deserves. What kind of person abandons her only child? Letters aren't enough."

"In her letters, she mentions seeing you from a distance on her trips to New York."

"And never saying hello."

Shane stepped into the hallway and made his escape with Elvis following close behind. He tapped on the door to the working studio behind the home office and the kitchen. "It's us, Shane and Elvis."

The door opened inward. Braced on his ebony cane, Walter peered around the edge. "Are you alone?"

"Amber isn't with us if that's what you're asking."

Breathing a sigh of relief, the old man stepped aside and let them enter. The rest of the house was pristine and polished. In here, splashes of dried paint decorated the concrete floor, and the walls held dozens of rough sketches. A potter's wheel stood in one corner and an easel in another. Shelves and tables held supplies and models for future work in the big studio beside the garage. The earthy smell of dried clay mingled with the scent of burnt wood from the potbellied stove. Sunlight filtered through the many windows.

On a heavy center table, he'd been experimenting with small canine figures in modeling clay to use as a basis for his sculpture of Elvis. He hobbled to a sink, leaned his cane against it and washed his hands. "Haven't found the pose I want yet. Do you mind if I take photos?"

"Elvis loves being the center of attention, like Amber… but in a good way."

Pulaski settled himself on a special stool with a back he could lean against. "Hard to believe she's Mallory's sister. They resemble each other physically and both have a lot of

Gloria in them, but being with Mallory always makes me happy. Amber's a bitch."

Shane couldn't have said it better himself. "At the bank, a vice president found paperwork showing Mallory as a designated person to open the safe-deposit box. No diamonds inside, but there were hundreds of letters written by Felix Komenda to Gloria and talking about Amber as a child."

"She saved those?" He rolled down his sleeves and buttoned the cuffs. "I knew she kept in touch with Felix and trusted him to take care of the kid. She also sent money and made several trips to New York to see for herself how Amber was doing. Nearly broke her heart to leave that little girl behind."

"Is that so?" Shane still didn't have the impression that Gloria was a caring mother.

"You don't know the whole story," Walter said. "Felix told me that Gloria had been physically and mentally abused by her husband. If she hadn't run when she had the chance, he suspected Raymond DeSilva would've killed her."

His explanation put a different slant on Gloria's motivations, but Shane wasn't sure he could take her friend Walter's word for her mothering skills. "According to the letters, Felix planned to be in Colorado, which probably means Gloria will join him. I'd like to check in with some of her associates and find out if she's contacted them."

"Got any names?"

Shane rattled off the two that Felix had mentioned specifically. "Her lawyer might know something. And her doctor."

"Dr. Freestone." He grinned and reached over to stroke Elvis's square forehead. "He's known Gloria since Mallory was born. Far as I know, she doesn't have any medical problems, but he's a person she trusts."

"And the lawyer?"

"Don't bother. He's barely competent, and we've been talking about replacing him."

From the dining room, he heard the angry voices of Mallory and her sister. So much for the idea that Amber would be pleased about the letters from Felix. Shane took his phone from his pocket and prepared to contact his brother in Denver. "If you'll excuse me, I need to make a call."

Walter rose from the stool and used his cane to walk to the door. "You stay here. I'm going to check with Constance about lunch and have her bring it in here."

"Thanks, I've been thinking about food. Do you mind if Elvis comes with you to the kitchen?"

"I'd be honored."

Shane called his brother's cell phone and caught him at his desk in DPD's Major Crimes Division where he'd recently been transferred. Logan sounded happy to hear from him. After a quick update on his two kids in grade school—Shane's niece and nephew—and his bright, beautiful CPA wife, he tossed out the usual query. "So, baby brother, any closer to finding a lady and settling down?"

"I've been busy." He kept his attraction to Mallory to himself, not wanting to get his brother's hopes up. Besides which, lusting after a client was highly unprofessional. "I could use your help on an investigation."

"Why am I not surprised? Tell me what you need."

Without explaining any of the details about Gloria's disappearance, he asked his brother to check into possible aliases on credit cards or travel documents. "On a related issue, I'm trying to locate a man named Felix Komenda, originally from Sierra Leone."

"Is this about diamonds?"

"What?" Surprised by his brother's conclusion, Shane

cleared his throat and forced himself to remain calm. "Why would you think that?"

"Conflict diamonds, buddy. West African countries are known for using those gems to fund insurrections. Come on, you ought to know that. You're the one who traveled the world."

"But you've got more experience in crime solving."

"Neither one of us Colorado boys need to get involved in international intrigue."

"Felix doesn't have anything to do with that." *At least, I hope not.* "He's been living in the US for over twenty years. He's an artist."

Logan agreed to make the inquiries for him, and Shane ended the call just as Mallory and Amber stormed into the studio like a double-edged blonde tornado. Both were talking. Loudly.

"Where's Walter?" Amber demanded.

Mallory appealed to Shane, "Don't you think it means something that Gloria kept track of Amber for all these years? She loved her daughter."

He recalled Walter's statement about Gloria being heartbroken, but he wasn't about to step into the middle of this sister versus sister argument. "It's hard to know what's going on in another person's mind."

"That's for damn sure," Amber snapped. "Connect the dots on this bit of illogic. She decided to fake her death and steal diamonds. Because she loved me? No way."

"Look at these photos. She kept them all."

Amber picked up the picture of herself and the birthday candles. "I remember my eighth birthday. Felix gave me a two-wheeler. All the DeSilva cousins were so jealous."

"And the bike was probably paid for by Gloria."

"Which doesn't make it right," Amber said. "Tell me about your eighth birthday."

"It was special." Mallory's turquoise eyes took on a gentle sheen and she smiled. "Mom took me and two of my friends for a ride in a hot-air balloon."

"Compare an idyllic balloon ride floating through the clouds with a messy party, surrounded by cousins and family while Felix snapped photos. Doesn't feel special, does it?" She pushed the box of letters away from herself. "I would have traded a dozen bikes for the chance to spend actual physical time with the woman who gave birth to me."

"It's not too late," Mallory said. "You could still have a relationship."

"Don't give a damn about Ingrid or Gloria or whatever she's calling herself this week. All I want is my share of the payoff. I never want to see her or hear from her."

Before Mallory could pipe up with another defense of her beloved Gloria, Shane stopped their argument. "I want to know more about Felix Komenda. Those first letters indicate that he's in Colorado. Amber, has he contacted you?"

"No, and I tried his phone and sent a text. He didn't answer."

"Does Mallory have his number?"

"I do," she said. "When Felix came to Aspen to discuss the sales of his artwork, he usually moved into Mom's extra bedroom. Once, he stayed at the Hotel Jerome. I'll check there and find out if he's registered. In the meantime, we can go to Reflections and look for more clues."

"Seems like a huge waste of time for all of us to poke around at the gallery," Amber said. "Felix used to talk about the gemology exhibit at the Museum of Nature and Science in Denver. I could go into the city and talk to the guy in charge."

"Ty Rivera," Mallory said. "One of Felix's letters mentioned him."

Shane loved the idea of sending Amber off on a quest of her own. "It's a plan," he said. "We'll take you to Reflections where you can pick up your rental car. You go to Denver, and we'll talk to each other tonight to compare notes."

"Can I trust you?" Amber scowled. "If you people stumble across the Teardrop, why would you contact me?"

"Because you're my sister, and I want the best for you."

For a moment, both were smiling. But Shane didn't believe the hostilities were over. They'd had twenty-six years of separation, and that distance wouldn't be erased in one day. Still, he was willing to accept this temporary truce between the two sisters.

Chapter Nine

After they wolfed down a quick but hearty lunch at Uncle Walter's place, Mallory and Shane dropped Amber off at her rented SUV outside Reflections. While he helped her clear the accumulated snow off her vehicle and Elvis dashed around the uncleared parking lot in lopsided figure eights, Mallory sat back in the passenger seat and put through one of the phone calls suggested by Uncle Walter.

Though she'd expected to get the nurse/receptionist Olivia or a recorded message, a familiar male voice answered on the third ring. "Dr. Freestone here."

"Hi, Doc." She'd known him literally since the day she was born, and he always made her smile. "How about this snow?"

"I'm looking forward to hitting the slopes, but the storm played havoc with my schedule. Olivia didn't make it in, and all my morning appointments canceled. Have you heard anything about your mother?"

"I know she was in Brooklyn three days ago."

"New York, eh? She didn't tell you she was going there?"

"She left a note. All it said was, I'll be back."

"Erratic behavior." He hummed to himself. "Even for Gloria, it's erratic."

"That's why I'm calling," she said. "Walter Pulaski suggested that you might know something about her state of mind. Is she sick? Does she have amnesia? Maybe she mentioned travel or visiting a friend."

"State of mind, yes." He hummed some more, and she could almost see him tapping his pencil to the tuneless beat. Freestone fancied himself a musician and had played in a band of nurses and interns called The Infarction in the '80s. "I really can't talk about her medical issues. Patient-doctor confidentiality, you know."

"Of course."

"But I wonder if Gloria had ever spoken to you about, um, you know. About the change?"

"What change?"

"I'm talking about menopause. Some women her age start thinking of rejuvenation and plastic surgery. Maybe breast augmentation. Maybe she'd considered expanding to a D-cup."

Mallory's jaw dropped. *Mom had gone shopping for a boob job, what?* Had she run off to New York to find a specialist plastic surgeon? "Can't believe it."

"In my experience, women who seek augmentation…" He picked up with his humming again. "Well, they often have a new boyfriend."

She stumbled through the rest of their conversation and thanked Dr. Freestone for his insights before she ended the call. Looking through the windshield, she saw that Shane was done helping Amber and making sure her rental car started. Mist from breathing in the cold surrounded him as he returned to the Navigator. He opened the rear door for Elvis and got behind the wheel. "I'll park in that stand of pines around back. The trees will camouflage the car, and nobody will get the idea that Reflections is open."

When she dropped her hand onto his parka above the

wrist, the light dusting of snow melted against her flesh. The cold braced her. No matter how confused she was by Amber's hostility and Gloria's erratic behavior, Mallory couldn't allow herself to go numb. She had to keep her head in the game. "New theory," she said. "Dr. Freestone suggested it."

"Okay."

"Mom took off because she has a new boyfriend."

He started the engine. "That's a hell of a theory. Her disappearance and the search involving every rescue team in Pitkin County is because of a guy she's romancing?"

"The Doc told me Gloria was thinking about having a boob job. In his mind, that particular surgery equals boyfriend. Maybe she'll turn up in a couple of days with a new body and ask why we were worried."

Though they needed to consider every possibility, she doubted this scenario. Gloria was famous for her positive body image, didn't mind disrobing to pose as an artist's model. Uncle Walter had sculpted her nude from dozens of angles.

"There's a quick way to eighty-six that theory," he said as he drove to the back entrance of Reflections. "The Aspen police obtained her phone records. I'll check with them and find out if she's been calling plastic surgeons."

"And Hooker, the pawnbroker in Brooklyn. See if she talked to him."

He snugged the Navigator among the pine trees and turned toward her. "When we get inside, I want you to lead me through the search. Think like Gloria. Don't waste time running around and peeking in obscure corners."

"This won't be the first time I've searched Reflections."

"But now you're looking for a diamond that can be hidden in a small space."

"Got it." She noticed that he already had his door partially open. "Are we in a hurry?"

"Let's just say that I trust Amber about as much as she trusts us, which is not at all. She might be working with Burdock. If she locates the diamond, I doubt she'll share with us. I hope we find the jewel before she does."

She nodded. "I'm ready."

"After we're done here, our investigation will move to my cabin where I can make phone calls and launch computer searches. More crimes are solved by research than by action." He shrugged. "My dad told me that."

"Then you'd better listen."

He shot her a quizzical look. "Why would you say that?"

"I did some research of my own after I hired you."

"And what did you find out?"

"Enough." She'd learned that his father and brother, who he casually referred to as cops, were high-ranking officers in the DPD. His father was a deputy chief with half a dozen commendations including a Medal of Honor, and his brother was a sergeant in the Major Crimes Division. Needless to say, his family wouldn't get along with Gloria. Not a topic she wanted to delve into.

Inside the kitchen at Reflections, she was struck by the faint lingering scent of fresh baked goods: breads, muffins, cinnamon coffee cake and rolls. A shame to let this food go to waste. She put in a call to Sylvia Harrison and arranged for her and her cowboy husband to come over and take the food—as well as anything else perishable—to someone who could use it.

"What's going on?" Sylvia asked.

"Shane and I might have to go into Denver for a few days. I want to leave Reflections locked up tight with the alarm system set. We'll be closed for at least three or four days."

"Don't worry. I'll come by tonight to pick up the baked goods. Over the next few days, I'll check on things."

"Bring your big strong cowboy husband with you." If anything bad happened to Sylvia, Mallory would never forgive herself. "No risks. Understand?"

"I know it's dangerous. Don't you remember? I was the one who found the puddle of blood on the kitchen floor."

And she must have mopped it up because the kitchen was clean and clutter cleaned away. Mallory was lucky to have such a smart efficient person as her second-in-command. After she ended the call, she glanced around the large room with high windows and tried to decide if Gloria would have hidden anything in here. Not likely. There was a distinct lack of privacy. Too many others—employees and delivery people and suppliers—came and went.

Skirting the area on the kitchen floor where she imagined the blood had pooled, she strode through the swinging door into the coffee shop. Shane stood at the cantilevered window, gazing out at the gentle snowfall on the sculpture garden. He'd shed his parka, and his thermal turtleneck and vest outlined his muscular upper body and wide shoulders. His sun-streaked brown hair fell across his forehead in rumpled waves. He was as handsome as the artworks in the gallery. Plus, Shane had the added advantage of being warm-blooded and mobile. When he turned to face her, a spark of electricity zipped through the air and struck her nerve endings like a lightning bolt. Paralyzed, she continued to stare.

Elvis padded toward her and nudged her thigh. When she glanced down, she noticed the dog looking up with eyebrows raised. Never before had she seen a dog roll his eyes, but Elvis managed to convey a nonverbal urging for her to "get it together."

Shane came closer, moving as confidently and smoothly across the travertine tiles as when he whooshed down a ski slope on his way to an Olympic medal. When he was near enough, his golden-brown eyes linked with hers, and the electricity accelerated to a high-intensity whirr. She saw his lips move but couldn't make sense of the words. "What?"

"Let's get started," he repeated.

The sooner they launched into this search, the sooner they'd be finished. Then they'd drive to his cabin where they'd spend the night. Just the two of them, with him guarding her body. They'd be alone, except for the smart aleck dog.

SHANE APPRECIATED THE clever use of space in the gallery. Gloria might be an irredeemable wing nut, but she showed a touch of brilliance in the way she curated art. The walls and partitions on the main display floor kept to neutral tones—soft white, cool gray and beige—to avoid clashing with the paintings. The arrangement of partitions with wide-open areas and sharp corners felt like a labyrinth drawing him deeper into the array of passionate oil paintings, airy watercolors and intense abstracts. Around random corners, sculptures of all sizes and shapes were lurking.

He trailed behind Mallory as she wove through the displays, pointing out the way artists were grouped with several of their paintings together. "On the lower level, we have storage for more of their work. If a patron shows serious interest, we might take them down to the cellar for a more in-depth display of the artist's work."

He paused in front of a huge oil painting of a sunset, five by seven feet. Beside it were two smaller paintings of dawn and high noon. "Tell me about these."

"The artist is local. He only paints sky." She stood in front of the sunset and took a few steps back for a better perspective. "Makes sense, I guess. He's a pilot, Steve Fordham."

"Does he have a private plane?"

"He has several, the Fordham Fleet. Two choppers, three little Cessnas and a midsize executive jet. I think it's a Gulfstream."

"The sort of aircraft that could easily make a flight to Brooklyn."

When she whirled around to face him, her long blond braid flipped over her shoulder. "You think Gloria convinced him to take her to New York. But why wouldn't he tell me? Everybody in Aspen knows I'm looking for her."

Offhand, he could think of several reasons. The guy might still be in New York. Or Gloria could have convinced him that it was a secret. Or he could be in love with her. Maybe he was the new boyfriend. "Put him on your list of people to call. Catching a private flight would explain why her name never showed up on a passenger manifest."

She leaned forward and pulled an orange sticky note from a wall plaque with the name of the artist and the artwork. She held it for him to see Gloria's familiar scrawl.

He read the words. "Out of kombucha."

"It's a health drink. Gloria's latest craze."

"Does she leave many of these notes to herself?"

"All the time. She carries a pad of stickies in her pocket." Mallory exhaled an exasperated sigh, probably thinking of the cryptic note her mother had dropped before she disappeared. "I don't think she'd give directions to the Teardrop in a sticky note, but we should probably try to read most of them."

Once he'd become aware of the notes, he saw them everywhere. The messages ranged from trivial reminders to pick up the dry cleaning to scribbled phone numbers to dinner invitations. Disconnected pieces of Gloria were scattered throughout the gallery. Nothing pertained to the African Teardrop. As far as he could tell, there were no hints about the location of the gem. In the far corner of the gallery, he reached for the doorknob on an office.

"Don't bother," Mallory said. "I've gone over both offices with a fine-toothed comb. Those were the first place I searched."

"You're sure?"

"Absolutely."

She led the way to a circular metal staircase, and he followed. While she lectured about the addition of this narrow loft that was twelve feet above the floor of the main gallery and ten feet down from the open beam ceiling, his gaze slid lower on her body. He focused on the swell of her hips and her delicious, round bottom. Her jeans were a perfect fit. The Vibram soles of her hiking boots clunked on the metal steps, and yet her ascent flowed gracefully. Mallory in motion was a sight to behold.

The displays in the long narrow space beside the wall were small paintings, individually lit, and cases of original jewelry—mostly silver and turquoise—which Mallory studied carefully, peering into corners to find the diamond. He didn't follow her gaze. Instead, his attention riveted to her. He watched every gesture and the way her arms moved. Her slender throat. The tilt of her head when she glanced over her shoulder to make eye contact.

Shane forced himself to look away so he could sever this connection and end his fascination with her body. He rested his elbows on the iron railing at the edge of the loft and gazed down into the displays. Though there wasn't anything in the PI rule book forbidding him from hitting on a client, he knew it would be inappropriate. *Even though she'd kissed me first.* He needed to concentrate on his job, namely finding Gloria.

Mallory joined him at the railing, and he felt her warmth, heard the gentle whisper of her breathing and smelled the citrus scent of her shampoo. Instead of looking at her and being sucked into fantasy again, he gestured wide to encompass the displays on the floor below them. "Someday in the far distant future, all this will be yours."

"The gallery is Mom's passion. Not mine. Don't get me wrong, I love Reflections. But running a gallery isn't my dream."

"Tell me what is."

"I'll show you."

She pivoted and stalked the length of the loft to the metal staircase. Descending, he didn't have the distraction of watching her hips. Instead, he gazed at the swing of her braid and imagined unfastening that gleaming plait, strand by strand.

At the opposite end of the gallery, she paused outside a closed door beside the coffee shop. "When Mom bought this place, it was a fully functioning restaurant with a huge wine cellar in the basement. We transformed that space into storage for artwork."

He nodded. "You mentioned that some of the artists on display had other pieces for special clients' viewing."

"And the former wine cellar can be kept at sixty-five degrees with a humidity level of forty-eight percent. Perfect for maintaining the art in prime condition."

He doubted that primo storage conditions had anything to do with Mallory's dreams. "What else is down there?"

She pushed open the basement door and led him down into her lair. "This is my part of Reflections, which is why

I don't think Mom would hide her treasure down here. The idea just wouldn't occur to her."

Subtle but well-placed lighting illuminated a long room with thick colorful rugs on the carpeted floor. Beanbag chairs mingled with regular seating and tables. The chalkboard had lettering in various hues. Corkboards in a rainbow array of frames, ranging from violet to red, decorated the walls and were filled with lively, imaginative paintings.

He'd seen a similar display at her house and drew the obvious conclusion. "These are from your students."

"Yes."

"You want to be a teacher."

"Yes."

Her dream seemed readily attainable, but he didn't make the mistake of thinking her ambitions were easy. Obstacles arose when you least expected them. He knew from experience that when everything seemed to be going well, disaster could strike.

Chapter Ten

By the time they left Reflections, the sun had begun to dip behind the low-hanging remnants of snow clouds. Roads were mostly cleared, and people were out and about, celebrating the first decent snowfall of the winter season. Mallory gazed through the windshield at the winding road that climbed the rugged hills above the Roaring Fork Valley.

Today's intense concentration on Gloria had been exhausting, and she set aside her fear, frustration and confusion. Instead, she thought about Shane. She'd never been to his cabin and didn't know what to expect. During his pro-skiing years, he must have been raking in the dough from prize money, endorsements and private lessons. He'd been famous for hosting extreme, off-piste skiing trips for wealthy clients. Did he squirrel away every penny? Or spend lavishly on a mountain mansion? Was he modern or traditional? Fancy or rustic? They'd spent a lot of time together, but she didn't really *know* him.

She needed to *know*. They'd be spending the night together and *anything* could happen. Her instincts urged her to take their simmering attraction to the next level, but she needed to figure out what to expect from him on the morning after. A cynical, clinical way of forming an opinion about sex, but she'd been hurt too many times to risk her heart.

After years of dating, she'd come up with guidelines to decide potential compatibility. Her categories for bachelor pads ranged from "elite," which was decorator glam with every detail perfect, to "slob" for apartments with empty pizza boxes as the predominant decor. Elite guys usually picked her apart and found her lacking. Slobs were too cluttered to think of anything but themselves. She hoped Shane fell somewhere in between.

Nearing his home, she checked out the view. *Spectacular.* His property stretched along the edge of a cliff, overlooking a scenic snow-covered valley with snow-capped peaks in the distance. His cabin—twice as large as her house—had log siding, a peaked roof over a covered porch, a partial second floor and a tall stone chimney. Classy but not pretentious.

Was he secretly a slob? Or, equally problematic, obsessively tidy? As he guided the Navigator into a neatly shoveled driveway leading to a three-car garage, she asked, "Did you clear the snow this morning before you left?"

"I've got a guy who shovels in the winter, rakes in the fall and mows in the summer. I hired him when I got back from rehab and all my physical energy needed to go into therapy."

"But you're recovered now."

"It's a luxury," he admitted. "But he's worth it. I've also got a twice-a-month cleaning person and an office assistant who I call when necessary."

He scored another plus by recognizing that sometimes he needed help. Also, she liked the responsible way he took care of the things he owned and didn't have a full-time housekeeper to fuss over him. *Not an entitled rich guy.*

The interior of his extra-large garage was well lit with shelving across the back wall. He parked in the slot nearest the entry to his house. A Ford truck—older model, beat-up but clean—was next to that. The rest of the space was filled with sporting equipment, including an ATV. Not surprising. She'd known from the moment she met him that Shane was the athletic type, which suited her just fine. Mallory loved mountain sports. Hitting the slopes in winter. Rock climbing and kayaking in summer. Jogging year-round.

Before they left the garage, he reset the digital alarm. "This system is separate from the interior of the house. If you come in here, you've got thirty seconds to disarm it."

"Then what happens?"

"A screaming alarm and a security firm is alerted. They call. If I don't give them the correct password, they'll be here inside of fifteen minutes."

He didn't sound paranoid, but still she wondered. "Why separate systems?"

"Some of the equipment in the garage is valuable."

Shane slung the giant backpack over his shoulder and scooped up the box of letters from Felix. In the mudroom behind the kitchen, he hung his parka and stomped the last bit of snow off his boots. She did the same. Elvis scooted past them, and she followed the dog into an efficient-looking kitchen with hardwood floors, walnut cabinets and black granite countertops. Elvis trotted past a circular breakfast table and proceeded directly to his water bowl in front of the sliding glass door leading onto a snow-covered deck. Through the windows, a red and gold sunset streaked the sky.

Elvis nudged her thigh. When she looked down at him, he sashayed over to his water bowl and tapped the empty food dish beside it. "I understand," she said. "You're hungry."

He gave her an Elvis-like sneer and used his snout to push the food dish toward her.

She called to Shane. "I think your dog is trying to tell me that he's starving."

Shane joined her, shot a glance at Elvis and shook his

head. "You ain't nothing but a hound dog, but I'll get your kibble."

"What about you and me?" she asked. "What should we do for dinner?"

She'd already had plenty of opportunity to watch him eat and knew that he preferred healthy options. But a gander inside his shiny double-door refrigerator would tell her if he was gourmet curious or solid meat-and-potatoes.

While he filled the dog's bowl, he asked, "What can I get you to drink? Coffee or tea? Wine or something stronger?"

"Water is fine."

"I've got fizzy and flat, but I usually drink whatever comes out of the tap. One of the reasons I bought this house was the excellent well water."

He earned a double thumbs-up from her. Real mountain people were concerned first and foremost about their water situation. "Tap water sounds great."

"For dinner, I'm thinking honey-glazed pork chops with acorn squash and a balsamic reduction on a caprese salad."

A menu that sounded both delicious and fascinating. *Like him?* "Do you do your own cooking?"

"I got into the habit after my accident. Before then, I never had time. Now, making dinner is how I unwind. I come in here, turn on some music, call up a recipe online and cook."

Music was another area for consideration. Mallory was open to many different styles but definitely had favorites. "What do you listen to?"

"Depends on what I'm doing. I like a heavy beat when I'm running or exercising."

"Are you a country-western fan? Do you prefer classical?"

"Both." He took two glasses down from the shelf beside the sink and confronted her with a steady gaze. "You're asking a lot of questions."

"Just curious."

"Ever since we met, you've been focused on Gloria. Now you've turned the spotlight on me." He turned on the tap and filled the glasses. "What's going on?"

"You're very perceptive." Another point in his favor. But she didn't want to tell him that she'd been judging him. "Have you ever been in therapy?"

"All kinds of therapy. Physical and psychological. And I went to a psychic once."

"You have an open mind. That's good." She took the water glass and swallowed a couple of long gulps. Maybe she ought to abandon her questions. She liked him and vice versa. Shouldn't that be enough to decide where their relationship went? Still, she wasn't sure what skeletons he had in his closet. "Aren't you going to show me around your house?"

He escorted her through the living room, furnished with comfortable modern furniture in shades of blue and gold. The stone fireplace held a long mantel where he'd chosen to display framed photos, Navajo pottery and geodes. He showed her a picture of two kids, a boy and girl. "My nephew and niece. He's seven, and she's five."

"Your brother's children." The warmth in his voice told her that he liked kids. *Another plus.* "How long has he been married?"

"Almost ten years. Cops are famous for having difficult relationships. But not Logan. He and Cheryl are still crazy about each other. They keep trying to fix me up with the perfect mate."

This was a big topic. *Huge.* "Have you been married before?"

"I've come close. Had a couple of long-term relationships, but nothing worked out. In the early years of my career, I was too preoccupied with skiing. After the accident, I had to rebuild myself before I dragged someone else into my messed-up life."

Though she was curious, probing into his breakups was too nosy, even for her. She gestured to the mantel. "I expected to see trophies. Where do you keep your Olympic medal?"

"Another question." He ducked into the kitchen, retrieved her giant backpack and strode down the hallway. Gesturing to an open door, he said, "This is my office."

She peeked inside. The large space held a desk, file cabinets and a long sofa behind a coffee table. The bronze third-place medal in giant slalom hung in a frame on the wall beside a photo of Shane and the rest of the US team in their uniforms. The placement told her that he wasn't egotistical about his win but treated the accomplishment with respect. *Perfect.*

He went down the hall to a bedroom. After placing her pack on an antique-looking steamer chest at the foot of the queen-size bed, he turned to face her. "I usually sleep upstairs but I'm moving down here for the night. I'll be right across the hall."

"You're taking the bodyguard thing seriously."

"Hell, yes." He stepped back into the hall. "We'll be sharing a bathroom."

In addition to the sink, toilet and shower, the outer wall of the pearl-tiled room held a whirlpool bath that was eight feet long. Her analysis of Shane came to a screeching halt as she perched at the edge of the tub. Any guy who owned a whirlpool with twelve—she counted them—jets went to the head of the line. "Loving it."

"The controls are over here. The jets have two different

actions. And this one is for a chromotherapy function that turns on pastel lights."

"Water churning. And lights, too?" Better than a ride at the amusement park.

He leaned against the tiled wall. "About all those questions. What's the deal?"

"Do you really want to know?"

"That's why I asked."

"You've been around me long enough to understand a few things about Mom and the way I was raised." She glided her fingertips along the high-gloss white acrylic of the tub. "Gloria didn't give me many rules. She always said if it feels good, do it. I had to make my own decisions and come up with my own boundaries."

"Okay, but I need more explanation."

"When I get interested in a man, I have a series of questions that tell me if he's a good bet for a relationship."

"You've been testing me?"

"In a way."

The easygoing grin fell from his face, and the light in his caramel-colored eyes faded. The temperature in the bathroom dropped by several degrees. "What's the decision, Mallory? Am I good enough for you?"

"When you say it like that, my perfectly rational process sounds creepy."

"You bet it does." He pushed away from the wall and headed for the bathroom door. "Dinner will be ready in an hour and a half."

BEFORE HE GOT started in the kitchen, Shane grabbed the box of letters, went to his office accompanied by Elvis and closed the door. Didn't slam it, though he wanted to. He dropped the box by the couch, then flung himself into the ergonomic swivel chair behind the desk—a chair which Mallory would probably disapprove of because the design with special back support had cost a bundle. She'd think he wasn't practical. And where did she get off judging him? Why did he have to justify himself? Prove himself worthy? He glanced down at Elvis who rested his head on Shane's knee and waited for a pet.

"Why do I care?" He scratched behind the Lab's velvety ears. "She's a client. It ought to be enough that she's paying me for my time."

He wondered if dogs had the same kind of problem with mating. Did Elvis ever approach a female in heat who rejected him? Probably had. Sooner or later, some hot poodle would turn up her nose at him. Just like a bitch.

That description didn't apply to Mallory. She was different. At least, he'd thought so. Sure, she looked like a typical Colorado blonde with long straight hair, a sun-kissed complexion and a tight athletic body, but she lacked the snotty attitude that usually accompanied that natural beauty. Mallory seemed sweet, hardworking, considerate and genuinely concerned about others. He'd wanted to protect her. Not only from physical danger but from the slings and arrows of gossip. Growing up with someone like her mother must have been a challenge, which still didn't justify her system of making a list of requirements for her friends and lovers. He paused. Had she been considering him for the latter role?

A lover, her lover? Shane felt himself smiling through his anger. Most certainly, he'd been looking at her that way. Was she on the same page? *This had to stop. Now.* He had to quit mooning over Mallory and get down to the business of being a competent private eye. "That's right, Elvis. Isn't it?"

The Lab bobbed his head, which meant he either agreed or he wanted more pets.

Shane rose from his comfortable desk chair and went to the leather sofa by the wall and sat beside the box of letters from Felix. Logic told him that somewhere in that stack of memories was a clue. At random, he pulled out a brown envelope and sorted through the contents, noting Felix's excellent penmanship and his attention to detail. He had described Amber's birthday party dress with incredible clarity. He chatted about weather, writing vivid descriptions of the skies over Manhattan and the foliage in Central Park. When it came to clues, nothing jumped out.

Though not really hungry, Shane needed to get started with dinner. There would definitely be wine, something to take the edge off. Later tonight, he'd check in with his brother and launch into computer research into Gloria's possible aliases. If she'd used a credit card, he could analyze where she'd gone and what she was doing.

For now, his only reference points came from these old letters. Felix had mentioned Ty Rivera in the gemology displays at the Museum of Nature and Science in Denver. And there were references to other friends who Gloria might contact. He and Mallory might need to take a trip into the city.

Shoving the letters back in their envelopes, he rose from the sofa, stretched his arms over his head and yawned. As long as he concentrated on detective work, he could avoid thinking about Mallory in a more intimate, personal, delectable way. Just a client, she was only a client. No matter how much he wanted to run his fingers through her silky hair and carry her into his bedroom, that wasn't part of their bargain. All he owed her were answers about her mother.

Chapter Eleven

When she took her place at the table, Mallory inhaled the rich aroma of perfectly grilled chops and vinaigrette. The stoneware plates were caramel and slate blue. Stemmed wineglasses held an enticing splash of ruby pinot noir. Streaming music in the background featured lovable divas, like Adele, Lady Gaga and Elton John. A perfect dinner, except for one thing. Shane's mood was stiffly polite, almost cold.

She hadn't meant to make him angry, but that was the end result of her questioning and judging. Did that mean he was too proud or too sensitive? Or was it a reflection on her? The first time she'd met him, she'd been attracted. Who wouldn't be? He was a handsome, athletic man with a good sense of humor who talked to his dog. *Adorable.*

But she had to be cautious when it came to relationships. The therapist she'd gone to for a while suggested that because she'd never known her father, she had subconscious daddy issues that made her crave attention from men. Whatever the reason, she often fell too hard, too fast.

She couldn't stand to be hurt again. And so, she accepted the awkward silence that fell between them, making his cozy dining area seem as dismal as a dungeon.

After dinner, Shane retired to his office to do computer research on Gloria. Mallory also had phone calls to make, but she insisted on cleaning up the dishes, which only seemed fair because he'd cooked. While she tidied the countertops, rinsed and stacked the plates in the dishwasher, Elvis kept her company. The black Lab's attentive gaze encouraged conversation, and she said, "I hope Shane doesn't stay mad."

Elvis gave a snort.

"Yeah, I deserve it. I should have thought of how insulting it was before interrogating him. Is it really such a big deal? People judge each other all the time. It makes sense to base decisions about relationships on past experiences."

When the dishes were done, Elvis followed her down the hallway to her bedroom where she grabbed her basic toiletries and a long flannel nightgown. Hoping to sweep the broken fantasies about Shane from her mind, she ducked into the gleaming white bathroom, started the hot water and found a fluffy blue bath towel that she placed within easy reach beside the tub. Before she disrobed, she scampered back to the kitchen and poured herself another glass of red wine, which she took to the bathroom. Elvis followed her inside.

With a barrette, she fastened her braid on top of her head, undressed and slid into the water. Steam rose in thick clouds that fogged the corner windows overlooking a cliff. No one could see inside unless they had the ability to hover like a helicopter. Even with all this glass, the bathroom wasn't cold. Shane had assured her that the panes were triple thick for good insulation, which also meant bulletproof.

Tapping buttons and turning dials on the control panel, she adjusted the high-pressure action on the jets, starting a swirling, churning motion around her legs and feet. With her upper arms resting on the smooth edge of the tub, she positioned her back against the jets and sighed contentedly as the water pummeled and massaged. Her muscles relaxed, releasing the tension she'd been carrying since Mom ran away.

The heat from the bath opened her pores, and the earthy red wine warmed her on the inside. She fiddled with the control panel, discovering that she could dim the overhead lights and then turn them off entirely. In the dark, she gazed through the windows into the snow-covered forest. Distant mountains framed a cloudy night sky sprinkled with stars. She sipped the wine and tried to forget her worries, but as soon as she erased one crisis, another arose, then another. *Stop thinking.* She programmed the lights to sequentially go through the colors of a spectrum from blue to green to yellow to red. The tub water changed from a deep magenta to purple. *More wine.* Her art classes of elementary school kids would love this whirlpool.

She heard a knock at the door and bolted upright in the tub, nearly sloshing the pinot noir into the pulsating light show. She pressed buttons on the control panel. In her confusion, she plunged the bathroom into total darkness.

"Mallory, do you mind if I come in?"

"Maybe later." She didn't want him to see her wallowing in the dark and sucking down wine. "Not right now."

"Don't worry." He sounded irritated. "I promise not to look."

As if I care about modesty. She couldn't figure out the controls. Another button sent the jets into high speed like the mythical zx threatening to swallow her whole. Water splashed out of the tub, and the room was still dark. "Just a minute."

Elvis tilted back his head and howled, which she supposed was better than having the dog burst into laughter.

"What's Elvis barking at? What's going on?" Shane asked. "I'm coming in."

The bathroom door cracked open, and light from the hallway spilled inside. She saw his tall silhouette. Still wearing jeans, he'd changed into a long-sleeved flannel shirt rolled up at the cuffs. Elvis trotted over to his master and sat, thumping his tail on the floor. The two of them exchanged a glance, then looked in her direction. She'd never felt so utterly, totally naked.

"Before you come any closer," she said, "I just want to tell you that I'm sorry for prying and judging and not trusting you."

"Can we turn on the lights? I won't peek."

"There's nothing shameful about the human body." She'd been posing in the nude for art classes since she was sixteen. "I didn't mean for it to be dark in here. I was hitting buttons and accidentally turned off the lights."

"It's kind of nice like this." He crossed the bathroom and approached the tub. "There's just enough moonlight from the window to outline the shape of your head and shoulders."

"Do you forgive me?"

"Oh, yeah." His husky voice soothed her fear that he'd despise her, but she was still tense. He hunkered down by the tub so he was eye level with her. "I can't stay mad at a water sprite, if that's what you are. More likely a wood nymph."

Or a wood nymphomaniac. His nearness combined with the wine, churning water and her nudity set her hormones on fire. Looking away from him, she watched Elvis come closer with his toenails clicking on the tile floor. She gave the dog a fake scowl. "Now you're my friend, huh? After setting up a howl and making Shane think I was in trouble. You threw me under the bus."

The dog raised his eyebrows as if to say, "Who, me?"

"Yeah, you." She splashed him, and Elvis stepped back.

"Hey, don't take out your frustration on the dog."

She aimed a second splash at Shane. "Who says I'm frustrated?"

He wiped droplets of water from his cheek and forehead. In the glow of moonlight through the windows, he looked cool and calm, almost businesslike. As for Mallory? Not so much. She was nude and her pulse was racing—the opposite of unperturbed. "Why was it so important for you to come in here? Is there something you wanted to tell me?"

"I heard back from my brother and have information. Your mother has been using a credit card and identification from her youth when her name was Ingrid Stromberg."

"Whoa." *More wine.* "She went back in time."

"Ingrid Stromberg is a legitimate person. She has a bank account in Denver, files taxes and uses the credit card often enough to keep the account active, usually during her travels to New York and beyond."

"Why would she do that?" Mallory managed to dial the whirlpool jets back to a reasonable level. "What's the point?"

"A second identity can come in handy. Makes it easy to go incognito."

Which made her think that Mom had been planning all along to disappear and start another new life by selling the Teardrop. Her work at Reflections was only a stopping point along the way and Mallory could be abandoned...like Amber. "What else?"

"She also has a cell phone in that name. My brother tracked the numbers she called and those who called her."

"Is anybody from Aspen on that list?" Mallory wanted to know if she'd been played for a fool. "How about Uncle Walter?"

"The only names I recognized were Ben Hooker, the

fence, and Felix. I tried calling them both and leaving messages mentioning your name. Neither has returned my call."

"I almost hate to ask." A shudder wriggled down her backbone. "Has she been in contact with Conrad Burdock?"

"Her supposed enemy?" His fingertips dangled in the water, and she fought the urge to grab his hand and pull him into the tub with her. He continued, "Actually, he's the first name I looked for. We only have Amber's word that Burdock engineered the attack on Reflections, and I thought he might be one of your mom's phone contacts. But no."

"Can't your brother trace her whereabouts using her phone?"

He gave her a questioning look. "For somebody who doesn't want police involvement, you seem very willing to take advantage of their resources."

"Hey, I watch crime shows on TV. I know about tracking phone signals."

"Not as easy as it looks," he said. "My brother tried, but Gloria has a very old model and has either figured out a way to turn it off or she's thrown it away. There's been no activity on that phone since she got to New York."

Thanks to modern technology, they'd located her, but she'd slipped away before they could catch her. Mom had spent a lifetime evading notice and had gotten good at it. "What about travel? Did Ingrid Stromberg make plane reservations to New York?"

"He couldn't find any of her aliases on passenger manifests," Shane said. "I'm guessing she used her friend the pilot. What's his name again?"

"Steve Fordham."

"The good news," he said, "is that early this morning her credit card pinged at a restaurant in Denver. She's in Colorado. Didn't Amber say that she'd sent Hooker a photo of herself in Denver?"

"She did, and I guess I should call her with this new information." But it might not be wise to share with her sister. Though Mallory didn't want to imagine a conspiracy, it was possible that Gloria and Amber and Felix were working together and not telling her. If so, why would Amber contact her in the first place? "I'm confused. Too many secrets. Too many lies."

"I know."

"I should finish my bath and start driving to Denver."

"Not tonight. We're both tired. And we need a game plan."

"Smart. Logical." Denver was a four-to five-hour drive and a huge city. They couldn't just wander up and down every street calling her name. "I guess we need to do more research. Make a few more phone calls. Check the computer."

He pushed up his shirtsleeve, stretched his long arm across the whirlpool to the control panel and adjusted the overhead lights to a dim glow. From his vantage point, he had a clear view of her naked body in the lightly swirling water, but she didn't care. In fact, she welcomed his gaze. They'd been ogling each other since the moment they met. It was time to take it to the next level. She was ready. Or was she?

She rested her forearms on the side of the tub and looked into Shane's eyes. Only inches from his face, she studied the pale brown, burnished gold and hazel facets of his iris beneath his dark brows. Light stubble shadowed his cheeks and emphasized the cleft in his chin.

Gently, he caressed her cheek and tucked a loose strand of hair behind her ear. Reaching up, he unhooked the barrette holding her long braid out of the water. The blond plait fell across her shoulder. "What are you doing?" she asked.

"Helping you unfasten your braid."

"Okay."

She swiveled around in the tub and sat with her back against the side while he took her braid in hand and gave a light tug. "Soft."

"Well, sure. It's hair."

"How long did it take to grow this length?"

"A while."

She covered her breasts with her palms, not because she was embarrassed but it seemed like a comfortable position. What else was she going to do with her hands? As he untwined her braid, she felt the length of it tickling her back and shoulders.

"I've got to admit," he said, "I'm kind of obsessed with your hair. It's mythic, like a mermaid."

"And what does that make you?"

"The hapless dope who can't resist your siren song."

She turned her head to face him. The whirlpool swirled around her legs, but he wouldn't let her float away from his grasp. Shane lifted her from the water and enclosed her in his arms. His kiss was liquid and sensual. His tongue slid between her teeth, exploring and then demanding. When she pressed her wet body against him, he rose to his feet, pulling her from the tub. Cool air raised goose bumps on her backside. He draped the fluffy blue towel around her shoulders.

"Wait," she said. "I have to wash my hair."

"Let me help. It'll be easier in the shower."

"Yes."

Though the distance from the tub to the shower was only a few feet, he guided her protectively across the white-tiled floor. Inside the glass enclosure, a rainfall showerhead splashed a steady flow upon her long hair. She turned her face up toward the hot water and allowed the rivulets to sluice down her throat and over her breasts. The dizzying effects of the wine lingered in a gentle buzz.

Then he was beside her in the shower, naked and muscular. She pushed the rising steam aside for a better view of his hard athletic body. He did not disappoint. Shane could have been one of Uncle Walter's sexy marble sculptures, except for the scars on his legs from his many surgeries after the skiing accident.

They soaped and rinsed and kissed. He paid particular attention to her hair, ending the shower by piling the long tresses under a towel on top of her head. After they dried off, he carried her—still naked—into the guest bedroom. When he tried to place her onto the comforter, Elvis had already claimed the bed and sprawled possessively across it.

Shane dropped her feet to the floor and shooed the dog. "Sorry, buddy. Off the bed."

Elvis sneered and grumbled under his breath.

"You heard the boss," she said.

The dog hopped down and slouched out of the bedroom. Shane closed the door behind him and turned to her. "Do you really think I'm the boss?"

"Of the dog."

She threw aside the comforter and slid between the dark blue sheets. He joined her and they embraced until their damp flesh was warm. They made love throughout the night.

THE NEXT MORNING, Mallory wakened slowly. She replayed the night before, remembering one amazing climax after another, crashing like waves against a distant shore. She recalled a gentle moment when Shane had sung to her, and she to him. Elvis had returned to the bedroom and joined in. Happily exhausted, she'd slept.

Through the window, she saw blue skies. Elvis danced between the bed and the bedroom door as if heralding the arrival of breakfast. The aroma of fresh brewed coffee rose from a large bed tray table where Shane had placed two mugs and a plate of cinnamon rolls. His wide smile emphasized his dimples. Oh, my god, he was handsome.

Before she could even say good morning, her phone rang and she answered. The voice on the other end was light and cheery. "Have you missed me?"

Mallory stared at her phone screen in disbelief. Caller ID showed the name Hannah Wye, an attorney and a mid-talent watercolor artist from Denver, but the voice definitely belonged to her mother. Mom's chuckle rippled through Mallory's memory, sparking the recall of a million jokes and sweet, silly games.

"What's the matter, honey pie?" Gloria asked. "Cat got your tongue?"

"Mom, where are you?"

"I'm so sorry if I upset you. It was never ever my intention to hurt you. You understand, don't you? That's why I left a note."

As she recalled the scribble, Mallory clenched her jaw. The note read, *I'll be back.*

"Mom, that's a tag line for a movie. Three damn words aren't an explanation for why you took off and disappeared for over a week without any other communication."

"A dear friend needed my help, and I simply couldn't say no to him."

"What friend?"

"Felix. You've met him. Tall, skinny, shaved head and tattoos up and down both arms. He's Black."

"Felix Komenda. Is he here in Colorado? Can I meet him?"

"Don't worry. Everything's going to be all right."

Just like that. Gloria expected the intense efforts of an all-out search to be forgiven. Never mind the risks and the long hours put in by the sheriff's office, Aspen police and Aspen/Pitkin County Search and Rescue teams. Mallory forced herself to remain calm. "Tell me where you are, and I'll pick you up."

"Not yet, munchkin. There's one more thing to do, then I'll come home."

"When?"

"Gotta run." Another musical chuckle. "When I get back, I'll answer all your questions."

"Will you? Will you, really?" Mallory had a lot more to say, but her throat choked up. She shoved the phone toward Shane.

He turned the volume up so she could hear, then he spoke into the screen. "May I ask a few questions?"

"Who the holy heck are you?"

"Shane Reilly. I'm a private investigator your daughter hired to locate you, Mrs. Greenfield."

"There's no need for further conversation. I was lost, but now I'm found. Like it says in the song." Her tone had changed. Mallory could tell that she was on the verge of an argument. "And I'm not a Mrs., for your information."

"Okay." Shane's shoulders tensed. "Would you prefer I call you by your maiden name? Or your prior married name? Ingrid DeSilva."

"How did you know?" Rage underlined her words. It went against her free-spirited, live-and-let-live attitude to get angry. But when she did, the effect was terrifying. "This is none of your damn business."

Mallory grabbed the phone. "Please don't hang up."

"How could you hire some creepy private eye to poke around in my life?"

"I was desperate, scared that you were hurt or even dead."

"I'd never die without letting you know."

"Please, Mom, tell me where you are."

"I'm so sorry, but I have to do this my way."

"Wait!"

"Goodbye, Mallory."

She couldn't let her go, couldn't let it end like this. "When were you planning to tell me about Amber? Did you fake your own death? Answer me, Mom. What happened to the priceless African Teardrop? Did you take it from your safe-deposit bank?"

The phone went dead.

Chapter Twelve

Gloria needed to put distance between herself and Hannah Wye's downtown Denver art studio/law office on Blake Street before her daughter and the private investigator sent someone to find her and drag her back to Aspen to face the consequences. Why were all these people getting in her way? She was trying to do the right thing, damn it. Ben Hooker in Brooklyn had turned out to be a Greedy Gus, which made her grateful that she hadn't brought the diamond with her to New York. Felix had been annoyingly uncooperative, and she could only hope that Ty Rivera at the museum would have better contacts. Then there was Mallory. How had her daughter discovered the theft of the Teardrop and how had she deduced that the diamond had been in her safe-deposit box at the bank? Worse, how had she learned about her sister?

Amber, dear little Amber. At the remembrance of the spunky blond child with turquoise eyes, an unexpected pain stabbed Gloria so hard that she doubled over. Her first baby, her darling Amber had been bright, athletic and strong. Even at four years old, she'd known her mind. Leaving Amber behind was the greatest regret of Gloria's life. She never could have done it if Felix hadn't been there to protect the child and keep her safe.

She stepped away from the landline phone, slung her backpack over her shoulder and stalked out the door, grateful that Hannah Wye had seen fit to give her a key of her own so she could pick up artwork even if the artist was out of town. Gloria hadn't been ready to return to Aspen last night, especially after she heard about several inches of snowfall in the mountains.

The city sidewalks had been spared from the storm. The air felt dry and relatively warm on this October morning. There was something good to be said for living at a lower elevation.

As she strolled past Coors Field and headed toward Larimer Square to the bistro where she'd meet with Felix for a breakfast of chai tea and muffins, Gloria remembered when she had lived at sea level. It had been twenty-six years ago...

AFTER SIX O'CLOCK, she had shuffled through the open-air marketplace of Freetown in Sierra Leone. The sunlight had begun to fade, and the night violence commenced. Tall modern buildings loomed over the colorful street where most of the stalls were vacant. The few people she saw shouted at her and told her to find safety. A futile warning.

The dangers of a civil war that had been ongoing since the early '90s seemed distant compared to the daily threat of living with her husband, Raymond DeSilva. Whenever his diamond-brokering business took them to Sierra Leone, he drank Jameson like it was water. And he blamed her for every little thing that went wrong. Even now, when she was seven months pregnant, he lashed out.

Thinking of his latest assault, she stumbled in her ill-fitting leather sandals. Raymond had shoved her to the floor, bruising her knees. That dull ache was nothing compared to the throbbing pain in her left wrist from when he'd twisted her arm and demanded that she admit to mishandling a computer entry about their inventory.

To end the pain, she admitted to a wrong she'd never committed and decided, at the same time, to leave the abusive monster. His violent attacks came more and more frequently. And he'd started drinking when they were home in Manhattan where Amber was being cared for by Raymond's parents. The thought of her daughter spiked tears. She hadn't asked to be dragged into this life, watching her father inflict painful punishment on her mother, hearing her mother's sobs. True enough, Raymond adored the child. His love for Amber was the only reason she'd stayed with him during these long painful years. She'd endure anything, absolutely anything, to be certain that Amber was protected.

Her long dress in a bold pattern of dark green, orange, yellow and brown flowed over her pregnant belly and brushed the pavement. Her long blond hair was piled on top of her head and wrapped in a yellow-and-green-striped turban. In spite of the tropical heat, she pulled a shawl around her shoulders, trying to become invisible and unnoticed. She wished she could disappear. Not for the first time, she wished she was dead.

At the end of the street, she saw a dozen young men with rifles. They shouted wildly and fired into the air. If she stood right here and faced them, she might be killed. Her nightmare would be over.

But that was not to be. Her friend Felix emerged from an alley, caught hold of her uninjured wrist and guided her away from the crossfire on the street. In his soothing accented voice, he said, "Come with me. This shall not be the end of you."

"I can't stay with him." She staggered down the narrow alley between sunbaked brick and stucco walls. When she protectively cradled her belly, pain knifed from her wrist down to the tips of her fingers and up to her elbow. "I can't bring another child into this hell."

"Divorce him."

A bitter laugh fell from her lips. Raymond would never agree to a divorce, and not because he loved her. "He'd rather kill me than pay alimony or child support."

"Your husband has enemies. They seek to destroy him."

According to Raymond, the aura of hatred surrounding him was her fault. Though she sat quietly in a corner and said not a word, she had offended people and turned them against him. "Felix, do people hate me?"

"Not at all."

"But I don't have friends."

"My country is at war. Friendship is a luxury few can afford."

He was a kind man, the only person she trusted. And she believed him when he told her about the plans of Raymond's enemies. They intended to set off a bomb in the dingy two-story office building where DeSilva Gems kept a small office in Freetown.

She knew they were close to the plain ugly building with bars on the windows and double locks on every door. They needed to go there, to warn her husband. She hated Raymond but wasn't a murderer.

"He is not there," Felix said. "He does not work late."

She knew as much. She knew he was at their rented apartment where she'd left him with his half-empty bottle of whiskey. He'd ordered her to go out into the streets where she was supposed to go to the office and pick up one of the ledgers. Her husband had sent her directly into the line of fire.

In the destructive orange flare of multiple explosions

on the streets of Freetown, she saw her future. The cries of victims and attackers urged her forward. This was her chance to run.

If she could clean out Raymond's diamond inventory before the building was destroyed, she'd be presumed dead in the explosion. There would be no reason to come after her, to chase a ghost. With the sale of the precious gems, she could finance her escape from Africa.

Raymond wouldn't care that she was gone. Insurance would cover his loss from the stolen gems. And she would disappear into a new life of freedom and safety...and heart-wrenching sorrow. She would have to leave her beloved Amber behind.

Chapter Thirteen

Shane approached Mallory carefully. Fragile as a porcelain statue, she sat motionless in the center of the bed with her legs tucked beneath her and her head drooping forward. A curtain of straight blond hair hid her face. Still naked, she clutched the dark blue sheet over her breasts and shivered. But when she lifted her chin, he didn't see tears. Though the call from Gloria had obviously left her shaken, her eyes remained dry. How could a mother treat her child with such callous disregard? So wrong, so very wrong.

Carefully, he moved the tray with two mugs of coffee off the bed and placed it on the floor. Then he reached for her cell phone. From the corner of his eye, he saw Elvis sneaking toward the tray and warned him off. "Don't even think about eating those cinnamon rolls."

The dog sneered.

"I mean it," Shane snapped. He didn't have time for games. "Don't touch. Step away from the breakfast pastries."

With a shrug, the dog obeyed. Shane joined Mallory on the bed and glided his arm around her. She melted into his embrace and exhaled a sigh. "I shouldn't be surprised by Mom's refusal to talk to me. Everybody has secrets."

No wonder she didn't give her trust easily. Her father

couldn't be counted on; he'd never been around. Her sister was hostile, cold and completely out for herself. As for her mother? Her mom's whole life was a lie. He wasn't inclined to let Gloria get away with this. If she didn't face the illegality of her actions, she should at least acknowledge the damage done to her children. He whispered, "We'll find her."

"Yeah, sure." She nuzzled her head under his chin. "Please don't tell me everything is going to be all right. I can't take another lie."

"No promises, but I'll do whatever I can."

She tilted her head back and looked into his eyes. The line of her cheekbone and chin formed a delicate silhouette. "We need to get moving," she said. "And that's kind of a shame."

"Why?"

"Another disappointment. Like the fact that you're completely dressed. You know, I'd hoped we'd have some time this morning...time for us."

"I'm glad you feel that way." Last night had been outstanding, both in the shower and in the bed. Did he want more? Hell, yes. But they had to wait. He dropped a light kiss on her forehead and on the tip of her nose. "Before we go, there's something we need to do."

"Something fun?"

"Something necessary." He picked up her phone. "We need to turn this thing off and take out the battery."

"But you already made the signal untraceable."

"This is an extra precaution."

"Just let me call Sylvia and check on Reflections." She clutched the phone to her breast. "Then you can turn it off."

"Don't forget. Those guys in ski masks who chased after us in the Hummer worry me." He stroked her silky hair. "I don't want them to be able to find you. So, call Sylvia and hand over your phone. We'll have our coffee and get rolling."

When he reached down to pick up the bed tray, he saw that the coffee mugs were undisturbed but the pastries were gone, and Elvis had smears of frosting on his nose. "Bad dog."

"What did he do?"

"Ate the cinnamon rolls, didn't you?" The Lab ducked his head. His brow wrinkled, and he looked totally ashamed. "Oh, man, I can't believe you."

When she leaned forward, the sheet slipped lower and gave him an even more enticing view. She reached toward the dog who crawled toward her, rested his chin on the bed and whimpered. "It's okay, sweetie. Shane's being mean."

"I can't let him get away with stuff like this." And he couldn't indulge her by allowing her to keep her phone. His job was to protect both of them. "It's not good for him to eat sugary stuff, especially rolls with raisins."

"Then you shouldn't have left the cinnamon rolls so close. You can't blame Elvis for giving in to temptation."

Shane handed her the coffee mug. "Have some caffeine."

"You're right. We have to get going. It's a long drive to Denver."

"Who said anything about driving?"

She cocked her eyebrows. "What did you have in mind?"

"I know a guy," he said. "We used to work together when I took rich tourists on extreme skiing excursions to remote terrain. Long story short, he'd drop us off in the backcountry."

"By helicopter?"

"We're supposed to meet him at nine thirty, which means we've got to hurry. I've already contacted SAR to let them know I'll be out of town. And my answering service."

He left her to get dressed and drink her coffee while he dashed upstairs to his primary suite, grabbed a dark blue cashmere sweater from his closet and pulled it over his but-ton-down shirt and khakis. His brown leather jacket could transition from snow in Aspen to the warmer weather in Denver, and his lightweight hiking boots worked for either climate. After he slid his second Glock into a shoulder hol-ster, he went downstairs to get his laptop.

Before they joined his friend at the Roaring Fork pri-vate airfield, they needed to make a stop at Uncle Walter's place, where Shane had already arranged to drop off Elvis. He couldn't very well drag the dog into town. Though his black Lab had a harness proclaiming his training as a ther-apy dog, a lot of places didn't make exceptions for any ca-nines. Besides, the only other time he'd taken Elvis on the chopper, the dog had been "all shook up" for a week.

It felt like he'd covered all the bases. Since he'd kept Mal-lory safe overnight, he figured he was doing a decent job as a bodyguard. His phone calls and PI investigating had made progress toward finding her mom. Best of all, he and Mallory had gone deeper in their connection. *To the deep-est level, the mermaid level.* He imagined her long silky hair streaming behind them as they joined together in a warm soothing sea. No more need to wonder if there was a future for them.

At the foot of the staircase, Elvis dashed toward him, nervously woofing and panting and spinning in a circle.

"What's wrong, dude?"

Then he heard Mallory shout, "How did you get my phone number?"

Shane charged past the dog and went into her bedroom. She'd promised to hand over her phone after one more call to Sylvia—a promise that came too late. She held up her phone and hit the speaker button so he could hear both sides of the conversation.

"How, indeed. You gave me your card and your personal number when I visited Reflections." The speaker had a baritone voice with an unusual accent, a combination of British and Middle Eastern. "You sound upset. Why is that?"

"You've had dealings with my family in the past. You should have told me." She looked at Shane and whispered, "It's Conrad Burdock."

"I fear you have drawn some unfortunate conclusions, young lady. I mean you no harm. In fact, I have a proposition for you."

"Why would I ever hook up with you? Your thugs charged into my gallery with guns blazing. They chased us through the streets in a Hummer and put bullet holes in my friend's car."

"Do not be absurd. It was never my intention to injure you or frighten you. The opposite is true. I hope to catch more flies with honey."

"What are you talking about?"

"Listen to me, Mallory. I believe, sincerely believe, we can work together. You and I can find the African Teardrop and return the gem to the people of Sierra Leone."

Shane noticed a softening at the edges of Mallory's turquoise eyes, and he could tell that the idea of returning the stone to its rightful owners appealed to her. In spite of Burdock's melodious voice, he recognized the words of a con man who'd say anything to get what he wanted.

"Why should I trust you?" Mallory asked.

"I have lived in Africa for most of my life. I love the land and the wildlife. I understand the people, their customs and their ways. With proceeds from the sale of the Teardrop, we could fight the extreme poverty afflicting Sierra Leone. We could provide wholesome food and medicine for the children. We could build schools."

Shane gripped her free hand and whispered, "Don't fall for his pitch."

But her tender heart had been touched. "Suppose I agree to go along with you, what do you want me to do?"

"We must get your sister out of the way. I am sorry to inform you, but Amber DeSilva is a liar and a cheat. If you and I talk to your mother, she will see things my way. She will want to do the right thing."

"Give me a minute." She muted the phone and made eye contact with Shane. "I believe what he's saying. Mom would want to help the starving children."

"Hey, I'm the last person to say your sister is trustworthy, but I believe her more than this crook. Don't forget the guys in ski masks with guns."

"Right." She unmuted the phone. "You said the men who attacked us at Reflections weren't connected with you."

"Correct."

"If they aren't working for you, who sent them?"

"Once again, I must be the bearer of sad tidings. Forgive me." He cleared his throat. "I have every reason to believe that the culprit is none other than Raymond DeSilva. Your papa."

"But he's dead."

"And so is your mother, Ingrid Stromberg DeSilva." A low chuckle. "Yet, she appears to be extremely active."

Was he suggesting that both Mallory's mother and father faked their deaths? Not a chance! The odds against two faked deaths in one family were astronomical. Shane vigorously shook his head and gestured for her to mute the call again.

"Please excuse me," she said.

"I am out of time. Must dash. Think of all I have said."

"Wait!" Mallory's voice rang with urgency. "Amber said you killed my father."

"Consider the source," he said darkly. "Farewell, Mallory. I shall be in touch."

The call ended. She sank onto the unmade bed and waved the blank screen of the phone in Shane's direction. "This is a perfect illustration of why I need to keep my phone with me."

"So you can get calls from murderous international liars?"

He took the phone away from her and pulled out the battery, hoping he had disabled Burdock's ability to trace their location. They needed to get rid of the phone as soon as possible.

"What if he's telling the truth?" She'd already dressed in jeans and a forest green sweater. Sitting on the edge of the bed, she stuck her feet into her hiking boots. "I like the idea of giving the Teardrop back to Sierra Leone."

"Let me look into the background for Raymond DeSilva. When Amber told us he was dead, I crossed him off my list of suspects."

She flopped back on the bed. "When I was just a kid, I used to dream about having a real father. A handsome prince or a dashing explorer like Indiana Jones or a rock star. In the screen photo Amber showed me, he's almost handsome with his black hair and mustache. Maybe I can still meet him."

And maybe that wasn't such a good idea. If her father was still alive, he had a stronger motive than anyone else to come after her mom and reclaim the Teardrop. Twenty-six years ago, Gloria had faked her death and stolen a fortune in precious gems from him.

Shane knelt before her and finished tying her bootlaces.

When he stood, he pulled her into his arms. Keeping Mallory safe was becoming more complicated by the minute.

AT THE ROARING FORK private airfield outside Aspen, the runways and tarmac surrounding several hangars were cleared of snow. Sunlight glistened on the white wings of the small aircraft and the blades of helos. Mallory and Shane had been rushing since they left his house. She looked down at his laptop, which she held on her lap. The minute when Burdock had claimed her father was still alive, she'd wanted to do a computer search for Raymond DeSilva. As soon as she got a chance…

First, they'd dropped off Elvis. Not an easy task. Though the dog had politely accepted treats from Uncle Walter and allowed himself to be petted, he kept firing sad pathetic looks in their direction. She'd assured him that they'd be back. If he was a good boy, he'd have a lovely time with sweet, kindly Uncle Walter. Then Shane had taken her phone away and given it to Walter for safekeeping. She felt naked without it.

When they'd returned to the Navigator, she'd used Shane's phone to make a few calls and ascertained that Steve Fordham, the pilot who might have given Mom a ride to Brooklyn kept his fleet at the Roaring Fork facility. He wasn't in his office, but she hoped she could talk to someone who worked for him.

They were making progress. Slowly.

Shane parked the Navigator outside an arched metal hangar that was the size of a small warehouse. Under the curved roof, she could see two helicopters with green bodies and striped yellow and black blades. Though she'd gone on helo rides before, Mallory wasn't really comfortable with flying. Not that there was anything to fear with Shane at her side.

She looked toward him, appreciating his confident grin and steady gaze. Once again, he held his phone toward her. "Give Amber a call. Find out where she's staying and if she's uncovered any new information."

"I don't want to talk to her."

His smile didn't falter. "Don't tell me you trust that Burdock weasel more than your long-lost sister."

"Okay, I won't tell you." She snatched the phone from him. "After this, I want to run over to Fordham's hangar and see if somebody can verify his trip to New York with Mom."

"I can do that while you talk to Amber."

She patted his cheek, not intending to notice how fine-looking he was in the clear, sunny morning light. But she couldn't help herself. A warm sexy feeling started in her belly and spread through her body. "Fordham's office staff will be more willing to talk to me because I'm Gloria's daughter."

"And I'm an Olympic skier." He stroked her hair, tucking a strand back into the messy bun on the top of her head. "In most places, nobody cares about my rep, but here in Aspen I'm kind of a superstar."

"You might want to check that ego before you talk to anybody."

"I think Fordham's people will understand." He gestured to three nearby hangars with the name Fordham written in oversize wildly egotistical letters. He opened the car door and stepped out. "Wish me luck."

"Don't break a leg."

Watching him jog toward the Fordham hangars, Mallory decided that Shane had made a full recovery from his injuries. No limp. No hitch in his step. He seemed to be a man at the peak of his physical powers, but she knew that wasn't true. Before his accident, he'd been an elite world-class athlete. Being merely "above average" had to be disappointing. Last night, she'd been blown away by the perfect proportions of his naked body. Never would she forget the way he strutted across the bedroom like the king of the castle. But she'd noticed the scars from operations on his legs. Were they imperfections or badges of courage that came from overcoming adversity?

She hoped to have a long time to figure Shane out, but now she had more pressing issues. She flipped open the laptop. Though it would probably be best to wait until she had some quiet time to explore on the internet, she just couldn't wait any longer. She typed in the codes he'd shown her to bypass his cyber security and access the Internet. The browser lit up. Entering her father's name brought up several possibilities. While she sorted through them, she called her sister, hoping to be able to leave a message. Unfortunately, Amber picked up after the fourth ring.

"It's me," Mallory said. "Did you find a place to stay?"

"Brown Palace Hotel in downtown Denver. It's old-fashioned, surprisingly charming."

"Why surprising?"

"Well, it's Denver, after all. Not a place I associate with class."

"You're showing your ignorance." Mallory hated the way some people put down the city. Denver hadn't been a backwoods cow town for decades. "Denver is very sophisticated."

"Whatever."

She sounded like a spoiled eye-rolling teenager. Amber epitomized many attitudes Mallory disliked, and she'd already decided not to tell her sister about Burdock. There was no problem sharing her conversation with Mom. "She called earlier this morning."

"Ingrid?"

Mallory didn't bother correcting her. "It seems that Mom stayed with a Denver artist. Her name is Hannah Wye."

Amber verified the spelling and promised to look her up. "What else?"

"She mentioned her good friend Felix." Only half concentrating on her talk with Amber, she sorted through computer entries until she found a likely thread to follow. "Have you contacted him?"

"Matter of fact, I have." There was a hesitation in Amber's voice. Was she lying? "Felix and I made an appointment for a one o'clock lunch at the Ship Tavern at the hotel. Too bad you won't be able to get to Denver in time for that meeting."

Mallory smiled to herself. *Oh, yes, I will.* "What about the guy from the museum? Ty Rivera. Have you spoken to him?"

"I left a message. I'll check back later. When do you expect to get here?"

"We haven't left Aspen yet," Mallory said truthfully. The laptop screen filled with a photograph of Raymond DeSilva—a dashing gent with distinguished silver streaks at his temples. "I'll call when we're near the Brown. I have a good feeling about our investigation. We might find her today."

"Forget her," Amber said. "We might find the diamond."

At least her sister was consistent. Her priority had always been to find the Teardrop, and she'd never pretended to care about their mother. For her, the investigation was all about the money.

When she ended the call, Mallory concentrated fully on her internet search and read her father's biography. Raymond DeSilva was very much alive, living in Johannesburg. Why had her sister lied to her? Amber had to know about Raymond DeSilva. He didn't seem to be making any attempt to hide. Photos of his estate showed a gleaming modern mansion constructed of geometric shapes, similar to the facets on a diamond. His trophy wife couldn't have been much older than Mallory.

She had a father. Should have been good news. She should have been excited, happy, fascinated. Truthfully, she just didn't care.

Chapter Fourteen

Shane couldn't say she hadn't warned him. Mallory had told him about her phobia regarding air travel. During the hour and a half helicopter flight from the airfield outside Aspen to a small airport south of Denver, she'd gone from clutching his hand in a finger-crushing grip to a somewhat more relaxed state of panic. Two or three times, she'd peered through the plexiglass bubble of the helo at the earth below. Together, they'd watched the snow-topped mountains recede into valleys and rocky foothills, which morphed into houses and streets and highways packed with vehicles. Her momentary fascination faded quickly, and her eyelids squeezed shut. Not sleeping but denying the queasy fear that churned in her gut.

Her phobia might have been worsened by the unsettling discovery that Amber had lied and Mallory's father—the father she'd never met—was alive. When Shane saw the computer article about Raymond DeSilva, he kicked himself for not taking the time to research the guy when his name first came up. But it didn't make sense for Amber to pretend she didn't know he was alive. Why tell them a fairy tale that could be so easily disproved?

He wondered if Amber arrogantly assumed he and Mallory were idiots and would never figure it out. Or she might be keeping Raymond DeSilva out of the picture to protect him from his enemies like Burdock. Speaking of that devil, Burdock had offered a reasonable explanation for Amber's deception: she and her father were working together to get the Teardrop. By claiming he was dead, she'd hoped to divert suspicion from them both.

When they climbed out of the helo and stepped onto the airport's tarmac, Mallory flung herself into his arms and squeezed with all her strength. "Sorry to be such a baby."

"You did fine." He held her close, pleased by the way they fit together. He enjoyed being her rock—the guy who protected her, even though she was far from helpless. "All the same, I wouldn't mind driving back to Aspen when we're done here. Instead of flying."

"I'd like that." She pivoted, gave their pilot a less emphatic embrace and thanked him for the ride.

"No prob." He shrugged his narrow shoulders and adjusted his aviator shades to deal with the brilliant Denver sunlight. "I've got a couple of things I need to do in the city, and I already lined up a vehicle. You guys need a ride into town?"

"I've got it covered." Shane had ordered a rental car to be delivered to the small terminal with attached offices, a lounge and coffee shop. "There's somebody I need to talk to before we head out."

While Mallory and the pilot walked to the terminal, Shane made his way to Hangar D where Steve Fordham rented space for his planes when he was in Denver. His assistant in Aspen had told Shane that Fordham would be at this airport from ten o'clock until noon, and he wanted to meet this guy in person. It seemed obvious that Fordham had given Gloria a ride to New York, but Shane sensed there was more to the story.

In the small lounge attached to the hangar, he found the CEO of Fordham Aviation sprawled on an uncomfortable-looking love seat with metal arms. His long legs stretched out in front of him, and a blue baseball cap with his logo—a huge *F* and smaller *ordham*—shaded his eyes.

Shane sat in the chair opposite. "Steve Fordham," he said.

"Who wants to know?"

"Shane Reilly. I'm a PI working for Mallory Greenfield."

"And you want to know if I gave Gloria a ride to New York." Fordham sat up straight, took off his cap and stared at Shane with intense blue eyes that contrasted his dark leathery tan. "I took her there. She called me about a week ago and asked if I could give her a lift. It's a trip we've made a couple of times before, and I don't mind helping her out."

The aviator didn't seem like the sort of guy who did favors out of the goodness of his heart. "Are you and Gloria dating?"

"I wish." He flashed an over-whitened smile and licked his lips suggestively. "She's a fine-looking woman. A little old for my taste but still hot. Like her daughter. Am I right?"

Shane wasn't amused by the creepy playboy attitude. "You must have heard about the search for Gloria in Aspen. It's big news."

"Yeah, I guess. Everybody thinks Aspen is so sophisticated, but it's really just a small town where everybody gets up into everybody else's business. Some of my passengers are movie stars and royalty, but they're no different than you or me. Do you remember that Swedish supermodel who plays a space cop? Bang, bang, bang, she's a real tasty meatball. And then—"

Before he could list all the famous people who had flown with Fordham Aviation, Shane got back on topic.

"Why didn't you notify the police? Let them know Gloria was okay."

"She asked me not to tell anybody."

"You don't seem like the kind of guy who lets somebody else call the shots." Shane took a jab at Fordham's ego. "I'm guessing Gloria has some kind of leverage over you."

His gaze slid sideways, evading direct eye contact. "She's my agent."

Shane had all but forgotten the artist-to-agent part of their relationship. "Gloria must have a lot of contacts in New York."

"You bet she does." He stood and stabbed at Shane with his index finger. "The woman represents Walter Pulaski, and he makes big bucks. If she could get a couple of my paintings into galleries in Manhattan, my work might catch on. I'm a pilot who paints the sky. That's a good hook, right?"

"Not exactly unexpected."

"As if you're an expert." He took two angry strides toward the exit. "Besides, I figured the guy who drove her to the airfield would be responsible and talk to the sheriff."

Finally, he'd said something interesting. Shane jumped to his feet. "What guy?"

"You know who." He reached for the doorknob.

Much as he hated chasing Fordham, Shane dodged around the chair and blocked the exit. Gloria's disappearance might be a joke to this flyboy who was a legend in his own mind, but Mallory was nearly devastated. And there was a twenty-million-dollar diamond involved. He pinned Fordham with a gaze. "I want a name."

"Okey dokey." He scoffed, mocking the lighthearted word. "That's how he talks. Howdy-doody and diddly-do and great googly-moogly."

"A name."

"The vice president at Fidelity Union, Drew Sherman."

Everybody in town knew Sherman. The husky man with heavy black eyebrows had a smile for every patron of the bank and an encyclopedic memory for jokes. He played Santa at the Christmas Carnival and was known as a family man. "What was he doing with Gloria?"

"Not sure," Fordham admitted. "He didn't come into the hangar to say hello, but I saw him arguing with her outside his car. When she came inside, I asked about Sherman, and she told me that they'd been associates for years."

His inflection when he said *associates* made Shane wonder if there was more to the story. It seemed like Gloria had a lot of male friends, ranging from Uncle Walter to Fordham to Felix to the local banker. "Do you know anything else about their relationship?"

"I'd say they were palsy-walsy." He smirked at the cornball phrase, which he obviously intended to make fun of Sherman. "She's known him for years, ever since Mallory dated his son in high school. Get your mind out of the gutter, Shane."

"Occupational hazard." Private investigators tended to see the worst in everybody, and they were often correct when it came to cheating spouses and lying businessmen. Shane missed the more straightforward world occupied by his police officer brother and father.

"Anything else?" Fordham asked.

Shane figured he might as well tie up loose ends. "You flew Gloria back to Denver from New York."

"That's right."

"Will you be taking her back to Aspen?"

"She's not on my schedule. I dropped her off a couple of days ago and haven't seen her since. I suppose if her timing worked out, I'd give her a lift. No point in alienating an agent, right?"

His body language didn't indicate deception, but Fordham had folded his arms across his chest, which usually meant a closed-down or unfriendly attitude. No surprise. The pilot walked a shaky tightrope between civil and hostile. He never actually said anything offensive but implied a lot.

Figuring he had nothing to lose, Shane introduced the multimillion-dollar question. "Did Gloria mention a special object that she was taking to New York?"

"Like what?"

His gaze turned shifty. Shane wondered how involved Fordham was in Gloria's disappearance. Was he more than a hapless dupe who wanted to get on his agent's good side? "Forget I said anything."

"Come on, man. You can tell me. Are you talking about some kind of artwork?"

"You might call it that." Again, Shane studied the other man's body language, looking for clues. "When I think about this object, I want to cry. To shed a teardrop."

Fordham looked confused. Apparently, the word *teardrop* meant nothing to him. "Have it your way. I don't care what kind of game she's playing. Are we done here?"

"Afraid so."

After this little talk with Fordham, Shane didn't feel much closer to finding the elusive Gloria Greenfield or the diamond she'd stolen twenty-six years ago. He'd ask Mallory about Drew Sherman but doubted there was anything more than a friend giving another friend a lift to the airport. Maybe they'd have better luck with Amber.

AT TEN MINUTES past one o'clock, she and Shane dropped off their rental car at the valet station and strolled into the

Brown Palace Hotel in downtown Denver. As she crossed the luxurious lobby, Mallory flashed back to her junior year in high school when she attended the Rocky Mountain Debutante Ball at the Brown. The event was an unaccustomed splash of glamour in her super-casual lifestyle. For her, getting dressed up meant wearing clean jeans, which was what she had on right now—black jeans, hiking boots and a cashmere sweater set in deep burgundy. Her simple pearl necklace was a gift from a boyfriend and couldn't have possibly come from the stash Mom had supposedly stolen.

"The first time I came into this hotel," she said as she fingered the pearls, "I was wearing a coral chiffon gown. Long and ruffled in the back. Short in the front. With a halter neck because I didn't have the boobs to hold up a strapless. Still don't."

"There's nothing wrong with your boobs," Shane said. "Was it a debutante ball?"

"How'd you guess?"

"I got roped into escorting girlfriends to a couple of those things. Always wore the same black suit."

"Men have it easy when it comes to fancy events. My date for that dance was Josh Sherman, the football star."

Her family had known his for nearly ten years, and it came as no surprise when Shane told her that Mr. Sherman gave Mom a ride to the airfield. But why hadn't he mentioned it to her when she stopped by the bank? Or to the sheriff when he was involved in the search? Mr. Sherman wasn't the sort of person who kept secrets unless he had a very good reason. The obvious inference was an affair, but she couldn't imagine the straight-arrow banker cheating on his wife of thirty years.

She straightened her shoulders when they paused at the hostess desk in the Ship Tavern. Like the prow of a galleon, the restaurant was located at the front of the triangle-shaped red sandstone hotel. The decor and the long bar suggested a vintage pub with polished wood and leather booths. The ship fixtures—such an odd metaphor for Denver—included a thick mast and crow's nest with an old-fashioned ship's clock. She spotted Amber and Felix at a table halfway across the floor. Her sister was blithely sipping a margarita.

Amber's carefree attitude lit the fuse on Mallory's anger. She felt a red flush rising on her cheeks, and she clutched Shane's hand, needing his self-control before she confronted her sister, who had lied about the death of their father and had done nothing to help in the search for Gloria.

"Hey." Shane summoned her attention. "Don't explode until after we find out what she knows."

"Don't worry. I can control myself."

He looked doubtful. "Maybe I should do the talking."

"I've got this." She set her mouth in a rigid smile as she approached Felix Komenda, who rose politely from his chair to shake her hand. "We met at Reflections in Aspen. I'm Mallory."

"Of course." He was as tall as Shane—slender, poised and graceful. Under his blazer, Mallory knew he had full-sleeve tattoos. "Even if I did not remember our first meeting, I would know you ladies are sisters."

True, they resembled each other. Today, they both happened to be wearing similar shades of mauve. Mallory had pulled her long hair up into a knot on top of her head. Amber's neatly styled hair was a nearly identical blond. The sisters glared at each other with matching turquoise eyes.

Amber stated the obvious. "You're here."

"Surprised?"

"I thought it would take longer to drive."

"Which is why we decided to fly," Mallory said. "Shane's friend runs a helicopter service."

The two men shook hands like civilized human beings while the sisters faced off like a couple of lionesses sizing each other up before going in for the kill. Mallory had never been this furious. Her sister had done more than subtly betray her trust. Amber had outright lied.

"I am so very pleased to see you," Felix said in an accented melodic voice. "Please sit down. Would you care for a drink?"

When Shane pulled out her chair and guided her into it, she was grateful for his assistance. Her legs and arms were tense and stiff, nearly immoveable. "I'll stick to water."

"An upset stomach, perhaps?" Felix regarded her with what appeared to be genuine sympathy. "Your mother mentioned that you are an anxious flyer."

Not allowing herself to be distracted from her outrage, Mallory's glare at her sister intensified. "I'm fine."

Under the table, Shane took her hand, holding her back from the hostility that simmered so near the surface. "We have a few questions."

"Right," Mallory snapped, ready to get down to business. They had an investigation to pursue, and she didn't intend to waste time. "Mr. Komenda, have you spoken to my mother recently?"

His gleaming smile highlighted his mocha brown skin. The last time Mallory had seen him, his head was shaved. Now his hair was closely trimmed, and he wasn't bald. His onyx eyes held a depth of unreadable expression. "Gloria and I met for brunch."

"Her name is Ingrid," Amber said. "I don't know why you people insist on using her alias. She is now and has always been Ingrid DeSilva."

"For purposes of clarity," Felix said, "I will refer to her as Gloria, the name she chose for herself rather than the one she was given. I believe it is a woman's right to name herself."

"Absolutely," Mallory said. "I like the way you think."

"You would." Amber turned to Felix and stuck her tongue out at him like an angry kindergartner. "You're never on my side."

"My dear child, I have watched over you from when you were an energetic four-year-old. I documented your life in hundreds of letters to Gloria and—"

"Ingrid," she interrupted.

When he stretched his long arm and touched her hand, his collar—which was open four buttons—spread wider, and Mallory caught a glimpse of the topmost branches of the Cotton Tree in Freetown tattooed on his chest. When he spoke to Amber, he was gentle. "You must trust me, child. I will always do what is best for you."

"Then tell me..." In contrast, her voice was harsh. "Where is the African Teardrop?"

"I do not know."

"Don't know?" She flung his hand away from her. "Or won't say?"

"I speak the truth."

"You've always been on Ingrid's side. Never on mine," she snarled. "You've been lying to me since I was a little girl."

Mallory surged to her feet. "You're a fine one to talk about lies. You claimed my father was dead. Not so. Raymond DeSilva is living with his new wife in South Africa."

"She's a bitch. And so are you." On the opposite side of the small table, Amber stood to confront her. "I never should have contacted you. You and your broken-down-skier-turned-investigator have been useless. He and his ugly mutt are a joke."

"I can believe that you think I'm a bitch. Making an allowance for rudeness, I can accept your snide comment about Shane. But nobody, and I mean absolutely nobody, insults Elvis." Mallory snatched the water glass from beside Felix's place setting and flung the contents into her sister's face.

Gasping, Amber stared as water dripped down her chin onto her silk blouse. She huffed and puffed, unable to speak. Nose in the air, she stalked away from the table.

Mallory had no regret for what she'd done. In fact, she wished she'd ordered a cocktail to throw. Something big and messy like a Bloody Mary.

Chapter Fifteen

When Felix took a step toward the exit from the Ship Tavern to follow Amber, Shane gestured for him to return to the table. "Stay with us."

"I must be certain that she is all right."

"She'll recover. It was only water."

Much as Shane might have hoped that Amber had been drenched in goop or splashed with permanent dye, Mallory's attack had been benign—wild and a little bit shocking but still harmless. It was time for him—the so-called broken-down skier/investigator—to take charge and start tying up loose ends. He waited for Felix to sit, then signaled the waiter who had been hovering nearby, waiting for their drama to fizzle. "I'll have a Guinness on tap."

The waiter nodded to Mallory. "And for the lady?"

"A Bloody Mary."

"Very well." The waiter glanced at the vacant chair. "Will she be returning?"

"Don't know," Shane said. After the waiter left, he leaned across the table toward Felix. "We have questions that will be easier for you to answer without Amber hanging over your shoulder."

Felix nodded. "Perhaps."

"From what I understand, you've been watching over her since she was four and her mother faked her own death."

Felix affirmed the somewhat outrageous statement, and Shane had to wonder why this seemingly sane, sophisticated man would accept Gloria's criminal intentions. Why would he agree to watch over a child he barely knew? There must be some way he benefited from this relationship. "Why?"

"Of course, I cared about the child. Amber can be endearing. However, she has not outgrown a habit of throwing tantrums and making ridiculous demands."

A lovable child abandoned and needing help was a partial explanation, but Shane sensed a more compelling, more personal reason. He couldn't believe that Felix—a man of the world—would dedicate his life to Amber because he liked the kid. Maybe he was looking for a way to escape Sierra Leone. "You stayed with her family in New York. Was it difficult to get a green card?"

"I have United States citizenship. I was born in Atlanta, Georgia. My parents moved to Sierra Leone when I was a toddler. I consider both countries to be my home."

Immigration hadn't been an issue, but there were other advantages to living in America. "When you came here, did you go to college?"

"Oh, yes, I attended several art schools and academies in New York. Also, I worked in galleries, like Reflections." He beamed at Mallory. "I was pleased when Gloria told me what she was doing in Aspen."

Everything he said made sense, but Shane wasn't close to satisfied. The story lacked important connections. "Tell me about Amber's father. Are you close to him?"

He exhaled a weary sigh and shook his head. "Raymond DeSilva paid me to act as Amber's nanny and bodyguard—"

"Excuse me," Mallory interrupted. "Why does she need a bodyguard?"

"Much as I hate to bear more bad news, your father has enemies, legions of enemies. Need I remind you of Conrad Burdock?"

"I guess not," she said.

"I worked for DeSilva, but we were never friends. His lying, cheating, thievery and violence disgusted me. I hated him for the way he abused Gloria."

"Physically?" Mallory asked in a voice shaking with anger or grief or both. "Did he physically hurt her?"

"Yes," Felix said. "Gloria tried to make her marriage work, but she could not change her husband. Leaving him was the best decision she ever made. She is a strong, wise woman."

Shane heard the anger in his voice when he talked about DeSilva, which was counterbalanced by affection when he mentioned Gloria's name, and that explained a lot. The puzzle pieces were falling into place. Felix had taken care of little Amber because he had deep, intimate feelings for her mother, maybe even loved her.

A familiar pattern began to form. Shane couldn't explain, but he recognized intuitively what was happening. *Gloria Greenfield is magic.* As she floated through life being irresponsible and creative, she cast magical spells that drew people, mostly men, to do her bidding. Walter Pulaski called her his muse. Fordham, the misogynist pilot, rearranged his schedule to fly her to New York, free of charge. And Felix Komenda had devoted over a decade of his life to babysitting her daughter.

When the waiter returned with their drinks, he glanced over at Mallory as she tucked a long strand of gleaming blond hair behind her ear. The crimson flush of anger that colored her cheeks had faded to a pinkish hue, and her mouth curved in a smile. *She's magical, too.* He'd do anything for another taste of those soft full lips.

They tipped their glasses toward each other and sipped. In unison, they turned toward Felix. Shane hated to leave the relationship part of this complicated story behind, but they might not have much time before Amber came charging back into the Tavern. "I have to ask about the Teardrop."

Felix laced his long slender fingers together and rested his hands on the tabletop. "This story covers many, many years. I shall try to condense my narrative. At 521 carats, the African Teardrop ranks among the finest stones found in Sierra Leone. The pale blue gem—with the color and glitter of a perfect teardrop—is worth more than twenty million and symbolizes the dichotomy between the natural wealth of the nation and the poverty of the people who live there. Shortly after the Teardrop was discovered in 1968 and displayed to the world, it disappeared. Everyone assumed it was stolen and sold as a blood diamond or hidden in the private vault of a wealthy collector."

Shane knew a little bit about the tragedy of blood diamonds, also called conflict diamonds. During his prime, he'd skied off-piste in the Atlas Mountains of northern Africa and had been approached by warlords and terrorists who offered to sell him gems at cut-rate prices—a heinous, tragic bargain. The real cost came in the suffering of the people who were forced to give up these treasures and barely had enough to feed their families. The United Nations and the Kimberley Process system were involved in regulating the sales of gems and marketing them as "conflict-free."

This history didn't explain what had happened to the Teardrop. "How did the gem fall into the hands of Raymond DeSilva?"

"We will never know," Felix said. "When Gloria scooped up Raymond's inventory before his shop in Freetown was bombed and burned to the ground, she did not know the Teardrop was among the other stones. After she left Sierra Leone, she discovered the treasure. And this is where I come into the story."

"You had an interest in the gem," Shane said.

"Of course." He winced at a distant but still remembered heartache. "The African Teardrop is a national treasure in addition to the monetary value. Gloria was aware of this heritage. She wished to return the gem, making sure that it went to the right people. I offered my help, and she accepted."

"A hell of a huge responsibility."

"Yes."

"How old were you at the time?"

"Twenty-six." He nodded to Mallory. "The same age as you."

"And my mom when she left Africa," she said. "I hope I can step up the way you both did and make things right. The Teardrop could provide funding for hospitals and schools, alleviating suffering and truly helping the people of Sierra Leone."

"The opposite is equally true," Felix warned. "For decades, conflict diamonds have financed warlords and terrorists. The Teardrop might be used to pay for a slaughter. This is a most delicate political situation."

Shane wanted to get back to his narrative. "When you realized that Gloria had the Teardrop, what did you do?"

"I was young and needed guidance. My parents had many contacts, but they were spending more time in the United States because of the civil war in Sierra Leone. Government officials were corrupt. Some of the rebels were admirable.

Others were pure evil. No one seemed worthy. None could help me. I didn't know who I could trust."

"I understand," Mallory said. "Not knowing who to believe can paralyze you."

"When it came to the Teardrop, you and Gloria were faced with difficult decisions," Shane said. "You didn't want to make a mistake."

Felix paused to take a sip of his beer. "And so, we did nothing."

"You told no one about the Teardrop?"

"Gloria's escape from DeSilva seemed to be successful. No one knew where she had gone. They weren't following her. They believed her to be dead."

A miracle. Again, Shane thought of Gloria's secret weapon—a magic that caused criminals to provide her with perfectly forged identification and gemologists, like Ty Rivera at the Museum of Nature and Science, who helped her sell the precious stones. Uncle Walter got her settled in Aspen, which couldn't have been an easy proposition. And she'd made a living for herself and her infant daughter with an art gallery. Not the most lucrative or stable occupation.

Felix continued, "She hid the Teardrop. For twenty-six years, we kept the secret."

With rapt attention, Mallory asked, "What changed?"

"DeSilva."

"Did he find her?"

"To be honest, I do not know." Felix lifted his beer mug to his lips and took another taste. "She started receiving odd emails and texts. On the street outside Hotel Jerome, she thought she saw him. More than once, she heard his voice, threatening her. And she found objects in her house missing or misplaced, including mementos that DeSilva would know were important to her. Frightened, she believed she must return the Teardrop before DeSilva got his hands on it."

The new revelation opened other doors for investigation, namely he needed to track the location of Raymond DeSilva. Shane had several questions, but he caught sight of Amber at the entrance to Ship Tavern, and knew they were about to be interrupted. He asked Felix, "Who is Hannah Wye and how does she fit in?"

"She's a watercolor artist."

"And also an attorney," Felix added. "Her services might be needed while dealing with the return of the Teardrop. And she offered Gloria use of her downtown loft last night."

Shane pressed forward. "Why did Gloria go to the fence in Brooklyn?"

"A mistake." Felix shook his head. "I suspect she planned to easily sell the gem and be done with it. Instead, her actions alerted Amber and Conrad Burdock."

"What can you tell me about Ty Rivera at the museum? Can he be trusted?"

"I hope so. Gloria went to see him at lunchtime. I wanted to accompany her, but she insisted on talking to Rivera alone."

"Mallory has an appointment with him," Shane said. "In less than two hours."

"Rivera has excellent contacts in Sierra Leone. His advice would be highly beneficial."

Keeping his voice low, Shane asked, "How can I reach Gloria?"

"I fear you must wait for her to contact you."

"Is she returning to Aspen?"

"I do not know."

"Stay in touch, Felix. I'll do the same."

Amber stormed around the table and returned to her seat.

With a nasty smirk, she stared at Mallory and lifted her stemmed margarita glass. The tip of her tongue licked salt from the rim. Mallory did the same with her Bloody Mary, which was a much more destructive drink than the water she'd flung before. It seemed apparent that neither of these women was inclined to apologize for the prior argument. He would have liked to probe into Amber's relationship with her father but doubted she'd tell him the truth. When the people in this dysfunctional family took sides, she was firmly on Team DeSilva.

He pushed back his chair and stood. "We should be going."

"Oh, I don't think so," Amber said. "You won't get away from me that easily. I want to know what you've found out about the Teardrop. I've waited a lifetime for that inheritance, and I deserve every penny."

Mallory stood tall and straightened her shoulders. "You and your father stay away from me and Gloria. We owe you nothing."

Shane tossed a couple of twenties on the table and took Mallory's hand. Together, they left the Ship Tavern and went to the valet station on the street. He glanced over his shoulder at the charming old hotel. "Should I make a reservation? We could stay here tonight."

"With Amber down the hall?" She shook her head, and another strand of hair slipped out of her loosely knotted bun. "This hotel isn't big enough for the both of us."

"Still, I hate to pass up a night without Elvis. Just you and me."

"I miss the dog."

When their rental car pulled up to the valet station, he held the door open for her. "We're early for our appointment with Rivera, but I wouldn't mind taking a walk around Ferril Lake at City Park."

"Perfect." She turned her face up to the sun, unfastened her bun and let her silky golden hair cascade down her back. "When we get back to Aspen, we're looking at snow and cold. While we're here, it's nice to enjoy the autumn."

He slipped behind the steering wheel and drove east on Seventeenth Avenue. Brilliant sunshine glistened on the red maples and golden aspens that still had their leaves. He'd grown up in Denver and loved the temperate October weather, perfect for jogging, biking and football.

After he parked near the lake, he noticed a commotion in the parking lot outside the Museum of Nature and Science that overlooked a fountain and rose garden. Though there was no sound from sirens, red and blue police lights flashed against the granite walls of the four-story rectangular building that housed dinosaur skeletons, dioramas of hundreds of animals and impressive rocks and mineral displays.

"I have a bad feeling about those police lights," he said.

"Me, too."

His cell phone jangled. A call from Logan.

His brother got right to the point. "Last night, you asked me to research credit cards for Ingrid DeSilva, Ingrid Stromberg and Gloria Greenfield."

"And I appreciate your help." Already he didn't like the direction of this conversation.

"Did you find the woman?"

"I haven't laid eyes on her," Shane said truthfully. "What's the problem?"

"This woman—let's call her Gloria—had a lunch meeting at the Museum of Nature and Science with the gemologist in charge of the precious stones exhibits. She was last seen in his company at the café in the museum. His name is Ty Rivera. Do you know him?"

Once again, Shane could be completely honest without implicating Mallory or her mom. "Never met the guy."

"I have another name for you," Logan said. His voice sharpened, and Shane recognized the tone from when they were kids and Logan was about to give him a hard time. "Mallory Greenfield."

No way to sidestep that one. "I know her. Why do you ask?"

"I made some phone calls to the cops in Aspen and found out that Mallory is the daughter of Gloria, the woman you asked me to trace. She's been missing for seven days."

"Right."

"I was thinking that maybe, just maybe, Mallory hired you to find her mother. Is she your client?"

As a cop, his brother ought to recognize the confidentiality issues involved in being a private investigator. "Can't tell you," Shane said.

Life would have been easier if he could have honestly talked to Logan, confided everything they'd learned about Gloria and the African Teardrop. He wanted his brother's help in tracking down Gloria and DeSilva and Conrad Burdock. But he couldn't betray Mallory. He refused to be the person responsible for sending her mom to jail.

"Your friend Mallory also has an appointment scheduled with Ty Rivera. At half past three." Logan paused, waiting for him to fill the silence. When Shane didn't speak, his brother continued, "If you have contact with her, you can tell Mallory Greenfield that Mr. Rivera won't be able to meet with her."

Dreading the answer, Shane asked, "Why is that?"

"Your client is knee-deep in a stinking pile of trouble,

buddy. I know you're trying to protect her. I get it. But you're both going to get hurt. You've got to tell me whatever you know."

"Why can't she meet with Rivera?"

"He's dead. Murdered. His throat slashed by an ancient Mesoamerican obsidian blade from one of the museum exhibits."

Chapter Sixteen

A loud disorderly gaggle of Canadian geese waddled along the paved path encircling Ferril Lake at City Park. Mallory tried to disregard their raucous honking and eavesdrop on Shane's phone call. His part in the conversation sounded noncommittal, but still she worried. His brother was a cop, an occupation which represented a heavy-duty threat to Mom. Never mind that her crimes didn't hurt anyone except her abusive husband. For twenty-six years, she'd paid her taxes and been a model citizen notwithstanding her eccentricity. None of that mattered. Because she'd faked her death and assumed a false identity, she was considered a criminal, and it was Logan's job to arrest her.

When Shane ended his call, he stood for a moment, staring at the screen on his cell phone, giving her a chance to appreciate his tousled sun-streaked hair and tanned complexion. His ridiculously long eyelashes drew her attention to his caramel-colored eyes. The way he'd looked at her last night set off a chain reaction unlike anything she'd felt before. If he wanted to turn Mom over to the police, Mallory didn't think she could bear it.

He tried to smile, but his mouth was tense. "I just got a

text from Pulaski. Gloria called your phone, and he's passing on the message."

Her heart skipped a beat. "Is she all right?"

"Yes."

"What did she say?"

"She wants you to call her back. But before you do, I need to tell you something. Let's walk."

"Why?"

"I can't think when I'm standing still." As he moved along the paved path beside the lake, static energy fizzed around him. "We were right to be worried about the police lights at the museum."

She kept pace with his long-legged stride, fearing the worst. "Is this about Ty Rivera?"

"He's dead."

Shocked by the unexpected news, she sucked in a sharp breath. Though she'd never actually met Rivera, she'd spoken to him on the phone and had an appointment this very afternoon. "An accident?"

"His throat was cut."

"How did—"

"You don't want to know," he said. "I don't mean to be blunt, but there's no time for a sensitive explanation. And you might want to brace yourself. From here on, the story gets worse."

When he unintentionally started walking faster, she nearly had to jog to keep up with him. "I'm ready."

"According to Logan, your mom met Ty Rivera for lunch. It's likely Gloria was one of the last people to see him alive." He shook his head. "Logan recognized her name from when I asked him to trace her credit cards. And he knows you have an appointment with Rivera."

She digested the information and immediately recognized the possible consequences. Gloria could be a murder suspect. "Is your brother going to arrest her?"

"He wants me to put him in touch with you and with Gloria."

She came to a halt, gazed across the lake where geese and ducks swooped and chased along the calm water. At the eastern end was the Band Shell and Pavilion, sunlit and glowing amidst a canopy of trees and lawns, which were still green in October. The scene was idyllic, but she was gripped by dread. This was the moment she'd feared, the moment when Shane had to choose between his law-abiding up-bringing and her edgy family. "What are you going to do?"

"He's my brother, Mallory. I can't lie to him."

"What did you tell him?" She shot a nervous glance over her shoulder at the museum where police lights continued to flash. Shane had been guiding her in that direction. Did he intend to leave her in his brother's custody? Had he already decided to abandon her?

"I didn't lie," he said.

When he clasped her hand, she jerked away from him. Last night, she thought she'd finally found a man she could trust, but she was wrong. He'd betrayed her. "Let me go."

"I'll never hurt you, Mallory. Sure, I'd feel better if I could tell my brother the whole truth. And I'd welcome the police for backup. We're talking about murder here and need all the help we can get. You and I are running around with nothing but my Glock for protection, and I'm not a great marksman."

"But we have Elvis."

In spite of his tension, he laughed. "The dog is fierce."

She met his gaze. "What exactly did you say to Logan?"

"I sidestepped. When we were kids, I got out of fights by telling nothing while using a barrage of words. Here's how it works. One time I borrowed his favorite baseball glove without asking and left it at the park. I never actually lied to him but never admitted that I lost his dumb glove. After dinner, I crept out of the house and found it. All was cool."

The current situation was far more complicated than a piece of missing sports equipment. "How much did you say about Mom?"

"I could honestly say that I've never met the woman. Then I tap danced around the topic, avoided telling him about the Teardrop and our investigation. I didn't even mention that I was in Denver, probably standing a couple of hundred yards away from where the murder took place."

A gust of relief whooshed through her. She stepped toward him and collapsed against his chest, welcoming the shelter of his arms. "What did you tell him about me?"

"He already knows about your search for Gloria and has spoken to the Aspen sheriff and the Pitkin County sheriff. Until this is over, we've got to avoid all the local cops."

"I wish it didn't have to be like this. I had hoped that the first time I met your family, we'd be sharing a dinner, reminiscing over pot roast and mashed potatoes."

"Wrong picture. My family are decent people, but we're not a wholesome Norman Rockwell painting."

"Who?"

"As part owner of an art gallery, you ought to know." He tightened his embrace. "We'll head back to Aspen. Gloria mentioned to Walter that she was returning home."

"Should we drive?"

"Yeah." He kissed her forehead. "I want to keep my Glock with me, so we can't fly commercial. And I can't count on my buddy with the helo."

She glanced back at the museum. "It's probably for the

best that I can't talk to your brother. I mean, there isn't really anything I can tell him about the murder."

"Begging to differ." Using his thumb and forefinger, he lifted her chin so she was looking up at him. "Tell me, Mallory. Who do you think killed Ty Rivera?"

"Conrad Burdock is a shady character. And Felix told us that Mom suspected my father was following her. He could be a murderer."

"Those are two suspects my brother doesn't have. You know a hell of a lot more than my brother."

But she didn't want to know. She wished her mind could be blissfully empty of all these terrible details of what had happened long ago before she was born. Her lighthearted mother had been an abused wife. She'd stolen a fortune in precious gems and changed her identity. Mallory had to wonder if she'd ever contacted her birth parents. Did Gloria have brothers and sisters? Someday, Mallory might wake up to find she had a dozen cousins. *But I can't complain.* Throughout her life, Mallory had enjoyed being with Mom, who was fun and funny, always attentive and encouraging. She'd made a great single mother. The best. And she wanted to stay in that world where they were happy and…innocent.

She wanted to build her future with sweet, sensual fantasies about her and Shane, joined together in the shower, talking and laughing. She longed for a real relationship, maybe more, maybe children. Ironically, she knew that Gloria would adore him—the man who claimed that he'd never hurt her. Deeply, deeply, deeply, Mallory wished she could follow this beautiful new path.

THE RENTAL CAR wasn't nearly as comfortable as Shane's Navigator, but Mallory was glad to be leaving the city and zipping along I-70 into the foothills, leaving rush hour behind. Denver was great, but Aspen was home. Before she made her phone call to Gloria, she needed to organize her thoughts. First, she needed to know what kind of arrangements Mom had made with Ty Rivera. Second, Gloria was undoubtedly returning to Aspen to pick up the Teardrop, and Mallory needed to know where she'd hidden it.

She glanced over at Shane. "You're sure Fordham recognized Mr. Sherman."

"Absolutely. Fordham even did his own parody of the way Drew Sherman talks. Phony-baloney, if you know what I mean."

"Are we thinking that she left the Teardrop with him for safekeeping?"

"It's a place to start looking, assuming she won't tell you."

The third thing she ought to bring up with Mom was Hannah Wye, the attorney. Mallory didn't know if Hannah was a legit lawyer or a flaky artist who dabbled in lawsuits. Gloria was going to need a criminal attorney to defend her against possible murder charges as well as the whole faking-her-death thing.

Last but not least, Mallory had to convince Mom to tell her where she was. She and Shane could pick her up and eventually turn herself over to law enforcement. Though Gloria had spent the past twenty-six years hiding from the authorities, that had to change. The murder of Ty Rivera sounded an alarm that couldn't be ignored. *Danger, danger, danger.* Someone—possibly Burdock, possibly her father or maybe even Amber—was willing to slash a man's throat to get what they wanted. If they got ahold of Gloria, it would be light's out.

In the meantime, she and Shane would keep Mom safe. Again, she looked toward him. Though she didn't trust him one hundred percent, she was beginning to depend on him.

"Somehow, we've got to make her come with us so we can protect her."

"I have an idea."

"Shoot."

"Back in the old days when I had fans and groupies, especially in Aspen, I sometimes needed a place to go where I could be totally alone. I bought a tiny cabin in the middle of nowhere. It came in handy when I was in recovery and didn't want anybody to see me limping around."

"You have a secret hideout?"

He shrugged. "Call it a safe house. We can take Gloria there and barricade the doors."

With her seat belt fastened, she couldn't lean close enough for a real kiss. So she settled for stroking his cheek. "You're a genius."

"I know." Shane handed her a phone. "Call your mom. I already plugged in the number that Walter gave me. You can talk as long as you want on this. It's a prepaid mobile phone."

"A burner. Why do you have one?"

"I have several. They came with my how-to-be-a-great-private-eye kit," he said. "Burners are handy for all sorts of things. Use it. Then pitch it. Untraceable."

She dialed the number and listened to six rings before Gloria answered with a squeaky, nasal voice that wouldn't fool anybody. *"Bonjour,"* she said, "this is zee wrong number."

"Mom, it's Mallory. We need to talk."

"Me first," Gloria said without the phony voice. "I called to let you know that I finally have everything worked out. By this time tomorrow, I'll be able to explain everything."

Tomorrow might be too late. Hoping to get Mom's attention, Mallory held her reaction and switched focus. "Does Mr. Sherman have the Teardrop?"

"How on earth did you figure that out? I'm impressed or, as Drew Sherman would say, I'm hob-nob-gobsmacked." She gave a raucous chuckle. Clearly, Gloria thought she'd solved all her problems and was sitting pretty. "Did his son tell you? I didn't know you and Josh were still friends."

"Are you going to pick up the diamond from him?"

"Well, I can't do that until tomorrow morning when the bank opens. He put it into his personal safe-deposit box, and it requires two keys to open the vault."

"And then what happens?"

"I made arrangements with a guy at the Museum of Nature and—"

"Ty Rivera," Mallory said. "He's a friend of Felix's."

"Well, you know everything, don't you? Anyway, Ty set me up for a meeting with an important person from Sierra Leone to hand over the Teardrop."

"I need details, Mom." Rivera hadn't been killed for a vague indication of a handoff. "What is this important person's name? Does Felix know him or her? Where will the meet take place? When?"

"None of those things are any of your concern."

As if she could keep from being concerned? Late afternoon was fading into twilight, a hazardous time to be on the road. "Are you driving, Mom? Maybe you should pull over while we talk. I have some bad news."

"Not about Amber, I hope. I've always felt terrible about leaving her behind. Do you think she can ever forgive me?"

Not unless you give her the diamond. "Just pull over."

"I could say the same to you, Mallory. Are you driving?"

"I'm not behind the wheel."

"Who is?"

Now wasn't the time to introduce her to Shane, though she'd technically already met him by phone the last time they talked. "Please, listen to me. I don't want you to drive while you're distracted."

"I'm hanging up now."

"Wait, wait, wait. Okay, we'll do this your way." *Was there ever any doubt that Gloria would wear me down?* "So, Mom, answer this for me. After all these years of hiding, why are you suddenly willing to trust the word of Rivera?"

"Recommendations from other gem dealers," Gloria said.

"Like who?" Despite an effort to stay cool, Mallory's temper was rising. "Fences? Thieves? Conflict diamond warlords? Criminals?"

"Don't be overdramatic, dear. Felix knows Rivera and can vouch for him."

Mallory didn't want to lapse into a futile argument but needed for Gloria to understand. "I want to help you. There's no need to do this by yourself."

"I have everything under control."

"Ty Rivera is dead. Murdered."

"No."

Gloria gasped. Mallory cringed. Maybe, just maybe, she finally realized what kind of risk she was taking. "Are you okay?"

"We had lunch together. I thought he might be flirting with me but more likely he was thinking about the Teardrop. Damn that stone. It brings nothing but pain and sorrow." She rambled, avoiding the difficult topic. "The food wasn't even that good. Some limp salad. Ty had the vegetarian chili."

"I get it. You ate at the T-Rex Café in the museum." Gently, Mallory reined her in. "There were witnesses. You were one of the last people to see Rivera alive."

"You make it sound like I'm a suspect."

"It might be smart to put a good attorney on retainer. Does Hannah Wye handle criminal cases?"

"Don't be ridiculous. I'm not a murderer."

"You can't pretend like this isn't happening." Desperation crept into her voice. "Mother, you're in danger."

"I can handle it."

"Let me help." She glanced over at Shane. "I know a safe house where you can hide out until this is settled. Where can we meet in Aspen?"

"That's not going to happen, especially not now. I'm not going to put you in danger."

Mallory flopped back against the seat. *Talk about a giant reversal.* All this time, she'd been protecting Gloria. Now the tables turned. "Trust me."

"You listen to me and pay attention. It's true that I messed up with Amber, but I did a good job raising you, and I'm not going to let a murderer attack you. Stay away from me. I forbid you to contact me again."

Taken aback, Mallory stared at the phone. Her mother wasn't the type of parent who forbade her from doing anything. When Mallory wanted to go on an overnight trip or skip school or try vodka, Mom had stepped aside and allowed her to make her own mistakes. Gloria was a cool mother, not the type to tell her she couldn't do something.

Gloria continued, "My way of parenting worked. You graduated at the top of your class with scholarship offers for college. You were popular, mostly drug-free and strong. Now, I'm giving you an order. Leave me alone."

"Don't you dare forbid me. I'm not going to stand around with my thumb up my nose while some diamond hunter attacks you."

"Goodbye, Mal. I love you."

The phone went dead.

"She hung up on me." Not a big surprise. Mom had decided not to cooperate and nothing would change her mind. Mallory looked to Shane. "Now what are we going to do?"

"Gotta find her," he said.

"In Aspen? Offhand, I can think of dozens of places she could hole up until tomorrow morning when the bank opens. Not to mention that there might be a killer tracking us down. As if that isn't enough, the police are going to be looking for us." One complication piled on top of another. "How are we going to search?"

"We have a secret weapon."

"What's that?"

"He ain't nothing but a hound dog." Shane tapped the side of his nose. "But Elvis can find anybody, anywhere."

Even when they don't want to be found.

Chapter Seventeen

By the time they drove the rental car into Walter Pulaski's gated community and parked in his triple driveway, twilight had merged into dark. The huge marble sculpture of a woman emerging from the snow in his front yard with her head tilted back and her arm extended was artistically lit. Revolving lights created the illusion that her long hair rippled in the breeze as her delicately sculpted hand reached for the stars. The effect mesmerized Shane. He thought the statue's impossible quest to grasp the heavens made her oblivious to the mundane concerns of everyday creatures. Much like Gloria, Pulaski's muse.

Starting twenty-six years ago, Mallory's mom had made a series of bad decisions. The latest—refusing their help—was risky for her and for them. Though he understood her pride and her unshakeable belief that she had life under control, her current decision impacted Mallory. He couldn't let things slide or pretend nothing was wrong, which seemed to be Gloria's default position. He needed to find her and the Teardrop.

Right now, things were about to get a whole lot better because Elvis would be rejoining the team. While in Denver, Shane had missed his canine partner. As he and Mallory walked up the shoveled sidewalk to the front door, he saw the black Lab bouncing up and down as if his feet were on springs. At the high point of each bounce, he peeked through the beveled glass window in the door.

As soon as Pulaski unlocked the door, Elvis leaped outside. Though the dog was trained not to jump on people, Shane had a signal to override that command. He went down on his good knee and held out his arms, which meant it was okay for Elvis to dive into his embrace, to lick his face and make all kinds of weird growls and joyful yips. His sleek furry body wriggled happily against Shane's chest. Was there anything better than the greeting from a loyal dog after being apart? Still excited, Elvis danced in a circle, shaking his shoulders and wagging his tail like a metronome gone wild.

Mallory copied Shane's pose, and Elvis pounced on her. Since she wasn't very large, the dog toppled her into the snow beside the shoveled walk. She let out a giggle and a shriek. Unapologetic, he stood over her, nudging her with his nose and licking while she laughed.

"I missed you," she said to the dog. "Our trip to Denver was terrible."

"Sorry to hear that," Pulaski said. "Come on in. I've got a pot of beef stew and homemade bread."

On the front stoop, Shane caught a whiff of the stew from the kitchen and realized that the sisterly fight had caused him and Mallory to skip lunch. "Great timing. I'm hungry."

She gave Pulaski a giant hug. "I'm so glad to see someone I can trust."

Could she? Shane had slotted Pulaski in the "good guy" column but intended to be careful in what he said and did. The multi-million-dollar diamond made a powerful incentive for switching over to the dark side.

Before he entered the house, Shane glanced over his

shoulder at the street and considered the imminent threat. Though Pulaski's house featured top-notch security and he employed two husky assistants who could also act as body-guards, danger still existed. Pulaski's friendship with Mallory's mom was well-known. He'd been pulling that lady out of trouble ever since she moved to Aspen.

Following him inside, Shane asked quietly, "Any other contact from Gloria?"

"Only the one phone call to Mallory's number. You?"

While Mallory and Elvis went to the kitchen to dish up bowls of stew, Shane confided, "I suppose it won't come as a shock to you that she's being unreasonable."

"I'd expect no less." In a thoughtful gesture, he stroked his white beard. "Can you give me a recap?"

"She made an arrangement with Ty Rivera at the Museum of Nature and Science. Gloria was the last person to see him before he was killed—his throat slashed by an ancient Mesoamerican obsidian blade from one of the exhibits."

Pulaski exhaled a sigh. His eyes were weary and worried. "Are the police looking for her?"

"My brother's a cop. The Denver PD views her—and Mallory—as persons of interest in the murder. The Aspen police and Pitkin county sheriff have also been informed."

"Sounds to me like you and Mallory have nowhere to turn." He took his usual seat at the head of the table where a half-full snifter of brandy awaited his return. "What's next?"

"First, we eat. And then we locate Gloria and try to talk sense into her."

"Good luck with that."

When Mallory returned to the dining room with a bowl-ful of stew and a chunk of fresh bread, Elvis made his presence known. He rubbed against Shane's leg and looked up at him with a happy smirk as if to say, "Glad you're back.

Don't ever leave me again." Then he went to Pulaski and rested his chin on the old man's knee.

As soon as she was seated, she asked, "Uncle Walter, how well do you know Felix Komenda?"

"The guy who sent those letters to Gloria? We've met. On one of his visits to Aspen, I spent some time with him. A lean handsome man," he said with a sigh. "And a sophisticated artist who modernizes themes and colors from folk art. On his chest, he has a tattoo of a kapok tree that stands in the middle of Freetown. When I asked about it, he told me the Cotton Tree is over two hundred years old and symbolizes freedom for the Black settlers of Sierra Leone."

Shane didn't ask how Pulaski knew what tattoo imprinted Felix's bare chest. These guys were entitled to their privacy, and Shane liked both of them. But he couldn't ignore the many connections Felix had with the Teardrop. He raised Amber, worked for her father and corresponded with Gloria. With roots in Sierra Leone, he might know Burdock, Ty Rivera and the mysterious person who would help Gloria deliver the diamond to those who needed it.

Felix seemed like a "good guy," but Shane had to wonder. He looked toward Mallory. "Why are you asking about Felix?"

"Trying to get my bearings and figure out what we do next. I'm thinking we should first visit Mr. Sherman."

Pulaski gave her a disbelieving look. "Drew Sherman the banker?"

In the kitchen, Shane filled a bowl with chunky beef stew containing potatoes, carrots, onions, parsnips and peas. He listened to Mallory explain how Fordham had seen Gloria with Sherman at the airfield. It seemed obvious that she'd given the Teardrop to the banker. But why hadn't he contacted the police when Gloria was reported missing? At least he should have told Mallory. Why was Sherman keeping that secret? Though it was hard to believe a man who claimed everything was hunky-dory could be part of a plot to steal the jewel, Shane needed to treat Sherman with the same level of suspicion as everyone else.

He took his place at the table opposite Mallory and dug into the hearty stew. He gave a long low moan that must have sounded like one he'd make while having sex because Mallory was staring at him with her eyebrows raised and a smart-aleck grin. He allowed pleasant memories to penetrate his mind and arouse his senses before speaking. "I don't think we should bother with Sherman tonight. Gloria said that he promised to keep the Teardrop in his personal safe-deposit box at the bank. Which means he can't access it until tomorrow."

"He might have lied to Gloria."

"Sure, but if he's being a loyal friend and hiding it for her, why lie? On the other hand, if he's aware of the danger associated with the gem, why keep it at his home?"

She dipped the heel of her bread into the last of her stew, soaking up the dark, rich mushroom gravy. "Where should we start searching?"

Though he wanted to drive out to the airfield and pick up his Navigator, the anonymous rental vehicle offered more protection. "Your mother mentioned seeing Raymond DeSilva at the Hotel Jerome. Let's go there and show his photo around."

"Hold on." Pulaski waved his hands. "I thought DeSilva was dead."

"So did we," Mallory said. "Amber lied."

"A terrible deception. I'm so sorry, dear heart."

"It's just as well." She tossed her head and lifted her chin. "Amber and I want very different things. She's after the big payoff for selling the diamond, and I feel that it ought to be returned to Sierra Leone to benefit the people."

Elvis circled the table and sat by her, offering a sure signal of approval. Shane agreed. As far as he was concerned, the Teardrop was cursed until it was used for good.

THE MIDSIZE RENTAL sedan didn't meet with Elvis's approval. Shane had spoiled the diva dog by refurbishing the back of the Navigator into a cozy nest with an excellent view. Though he'd spread a couple of towels to protect the rear seat upholstery, Elvis couldn't get comfortable. Growling to himself, he paced from one side to the other and nudged the windows, an indication that the only way he'd like this mode of transportation was if he could hang his head out the window.

"Not gonna happen, buddy." Sitting behind the steering wheel, Shane craned his neck around to see into the back. "It's too cold to drive with the windows down, and we're supposed to be incognito. Everybody in town knows you."

Mallory reached between the seats to scratch the parallel worry lines between the Lab's eyebrows, if he'd had eyebrows. "You're too famous for your own good."

Elvis already wore his harness emblazoned with the words *service dog*, which ought to be enough to get him in the front door when they reached the downtown hotel. Shane had already called ahead to make sure his friend was working tonight and would be willing to talk about current guests. This interview couldn't be conducted over the phone since Shane had identification photos to show from his computer. The bad guys probably checked in using aliases.

He'd debated with himself about whether or not Mallory should be involved in this part of the investigation. His number one priority was to protect her from certain danger. If the police were involved, she'd be tucked away in a safe house with armed guards protecting her. Instead, they were on their own with little more than Shane's two Glocks to hold off the threat.

Leaving her with Pulaski hadn't been an option. Not only would she have refused to sit quietly on the sidelines, but Shane didn't feel right about putting her trusted old friend in peril. As he drove through the plowed but still snow-covered streets of Aspen toward Hotel Jerome, he considered asking her to stay in the car while he went inside. *Not a good solution.* If Mallory was alone, she made an easier target.

"I have a question," she said.

"Shoot."

"Well, I would. But I don't have a weapon." From the corner of his eye, he saw her smile before she said, "Har-de-har-har."

"Are you channeling Drew Sherman?"

"Making a point," she said. "You have two guns. One in a shoulder holster and the other hooked to your belt. I should have one of those in my pocket."

Inwardly, he groaned. "You told me Gloria didn't approve of firearms. Have you ever even held a gun before?"

"I'm not a hunter, but I know the basics."

"I'll keep that in mind. For right now, I need you to concentrate on managing Elvis." Actually, the dog made a more intimidating weapon than a Glock. "His attack command is *g-e-t-e-m.* Drop his leash, point, give the command and watch this handsome rock star turn into Cujo."

At the hotel, he pulled up to the valet station, handed the guy a twenty and told him they'd be back in fifteen. Mallory held the leash as they entered the lobby. Hotel Jerome didn't have the high ceilings and ornate design of the Brown Palace, but the historic Aspen hotel had a uniquely Western charm with polished wainscoting, heavy furniture and mounted trophy heads of elk and deer on the walls. With Mallory and Elvis at his side, Shane approached the reception desk and nodded to his friend Kevin, who motioned for them to come around the desk into the office area. The front-desk clerk stood taller than Shane's six feet two and had an athletic build. Years ago, he'd come to the mountains as a ski bum. Now this was his home. He greeted Shane, gave Mallory a hug and hunkered down to shake paws with Elvis.

"We appreciate this," Shane said.

"Always happy to help my favorite private eye and his fur-ball sidekick." Kevin straightened his vest and stood. "What do you need?"

"These guys might be registered under fake names." He opened his tablet screen and showed the first photo.

"That's Felix Komenda. I don't remember seeing him recently, but he stays here often. He's friends with Gloria. Good tipper." He gave Mallory a skeptical look. "I can't believe he did something bad."

"Neither can I," she said. "We're just covering all the bases."

Shane held up a photo of Raymond DeSilva, a handsome older gentleman with a groomed mustache and silver streaks at his temples. "How about this guy?"

Kevin nodded. "Yeah, he was here for a couple of days. Checked out this morning."

The timing struck Shane as being too coincidental. Amber and her father had arrived in Aspen at approximately the same time. "What name was he using?"

"I remember because it was an obvious alias. Raymond Chandler, like the guy who wrote the detective books. You know, Phillip Marlowe."

"I didn't know you were a reader."

"At night, it gets boring," Kevin said. "And I like a good *noir*."

Shane pulled up a snapshot he'd found of Conrad Burdock. Since Mallory actually saw Burdock, she had verified the identification. Hadn't been an easy search. Supervillains, like Burdock, didn't like to have their pictures taken. He showed the screen to Kevin.

"Whoa, you know him?" Kevin's surprise was genuine. "The ambassador?"

"Tell me more."

"He checked in five days ago with an entourage—all big guys who looked more like bodyguards than butlers. The ambassador is all class but friendly. Nice to the little people. He stopped at the desk himself to pick up a special delivery package and opened it right there. A bunch of muffin-type things from a bakery in Denver. The ambassador called them street cakes and offered me one."

"Nice," Shane said. Was Burdock a supervillain or a superhero?

"Totally delicious. And he's a handsome dude. In this job, I see a lot of beautiful people, but the ambassador was right up there at the top. His dark brown Versace jacket fit perfectly, and he had a humongous diamond pinkie ring."

"A diamond?"

"Huge diamond."

Shane exchanged a glance with Mallory before looking back at Kevin and asking, "Where is the ambassador from?"

"Someplace in Africa. He has a lapel pin with a blue, white and green flag. And a circle pin with a stylized picture of a tree."

"Freetown," Mallory said. "The Cotton Tree. And those are the colors of the Sierra Leone flag."

"Is he here?" Shane asked.

"Not on a Friday night. He and his entourage are out and about. The guy who pays all their bills asked where they could hear jazz and eat sushi. I made reservations. He tipped me a hundred bucks and passed on his thanks from the ambassador. Like I said, a class act."

And maybe a murderer.

Chapter Eighteen

Back in the rental car on their way to pick up the Navigator from the airfield where Shane had left it, Mallory hunched over the computer. In spite of occasional jostling in the passenger seat, her search of the internet quickly led to the ambassador to the United States from Sierra Leone. His multi-syllable British-sounding name wasn't Conrad Burdock, but his face belonged to the guy she'd met at the gallery.

"Everybody's got some kind of false identity." She leaned back in her seat and stared through the windshield at the cloudless night. "My father is pretending to be somebody else. My mother faked her death, and I can't begin to guess where she came up with the Gloria Greenfield name."

"Suits her," Shane said. "I've never met her, but the name makes me think of something bright and natural."

"That's her, all right." She continued her list of phony names. "The ambassador from Sierra Leone—with the last name of Lewiston-Blankenship—has his own alias."

"The first time we heard about Burdock was through Amber, right?"

"She claimed that he'd killed our father. Obviously, not true. She also said the guys who chased us away from Reflections worked for him which he denied. Another lie?"

"Absolutely," Shane said. "Kevin's description of an entourage built like bodyguards fits the thugs in ski masks who came after us and made bullet holes in my car."

"An ambassador." She shook her head and sighed. Truly, there was no one or nothing she could trust.

"The fact that Burdock and your father were both staying at Hotel Jerome at the same time is suspicious. They might be working together."

"How does Amber fit into that picture?"

"She doesn't." He shrugged, but his tense grip on the steering wheel told her he was anything but nonchalant. "I think Amber is about to get the rug pulled from beneath her feet. One or both of those men are going to cut her out of the profits when they sell the Teardrop."

Mallory almost felt sorry for her sister. Amber dreamed of a vast fortune, enough wealth to live like a princess. Not much chance of that. By placing her trust in her slimeball father, she'd bet on the wrong horse.

Not that Mallory's loyalty to Gloria had paid off. "Do you think the ambassador is the person Ty Rivera arranged for Mom to meet?"

"I do."

She noticed how he kept checking the rearview mirrors, making sure they weren't being followed. Fortunately, there weren't many headlights on the road to the airfield. The major activity on a weekend would be in town with everybody yakking about the new snow and wondering when the slopes would open. The Hotel Jerome had just been starting to get busy when they left. "If Ty Rivera was working with the ambassador, why was he killed?"

"Loose ends," Shane said. "Rivera was a witness. Maybe he knew the ambassador was after the Teardrop and expected to receive a payoff. Or maybe Rivera honestly believed a high-ranking official from Sierra Leone would do the right thing. Either way, he'd be a liability…if and when these crimes come to light."

"What do you mean? What crimes?"

"Let's start with fraud. Who owns the diamond and how can they prove it? There's smuggling involved to get the jewel in and out of the country. Don't even get me started on political ramifications. In the worst-case scenario, violence erupts and somebody else gets killed. I don't need to remind you that the ambassador's thugs shot at us."

"Do you think they'd hurt Mom?"

A long moment of silence stretched between them. In a quiet voice, he said, "Yes."

Deep in her gut, she knew he was right. Her mother could be killed. Mallory's eyes squeezed shut. She turned off the computer and clenched her fingers into fists, holding onto fragile hope. Sensing her distress, Elvis poked his nose between the front seats and bumped her elbow, demanding a pet. She loosened her hand to stroke the soft fur on his head. The warm friendliness comforted her, though she was far from calm.

From the moment Gloria went missing, Mallory feared dire consequences, even before she knew the whole story. Mom shouldn't have gone off half-cocked, should have looked to Mallory for help, should have engaged a lawyer. Was it too late to make things right? "What can we do?"

A few more ticks of silence passed. "I know you don't want to hear this, but the murder of Ty Rivera makes the threat to your mom even greater. We should call the police. I can coordinate their actions through my brother."

"Sensible."

"Safe."

But she couldn't betray Mom's confidence, couldn't be

the person to send her to prison. "Before we call in the cops, we have to find her."

"The cops can make our search easier. When you first discovered she was missing, you activated the entire town of Aspen, from forest rangers to the Pitkin County sheriff."

"That effort didn't turn out well," she reminded him. "I know Mom better than anybody else. With a little help from Elvis, I can find her."

He turned left onto the road that led to the hangars at the airfield. "I'm worried about you, Mallory. You could be next on the list of people who need to be eliminated."

Once again, his reasoning made sense. Another complication she didn't want to face. "I hadn't considered the threat to myself."

"I have." He parked beside his Navigator and killed the engine on the rental sedan. "You're the main thing I think about."

She unfastened her seat belt and twisted in her seat to embrace him. The midsize sedan had insufficient room for maneuvering, and Elvis got between them. But she managed to join her lips with his. His mouth tasted warm and familiar but exciting at the same time. Fighting the dog for Shane's attention, she pressed her upper body against his.

Though she didn't agree with everything he'd said, she understood his logic. And she actually appreciated his law-abiding attitude. Gloria had taught her the difference between right and wrong. "She's not really a criminal."

"A lot of decent people step outside the rules from time to time." He kissed her again. "Most of them don't get involved in international intrigues with twenty-million-dollar gems."

"Go big or go home." That was what Mom always said.

Elvis disentangled himself from their threesome, bounded into the back seat and ran to the window. Peering through the glass at the Navigator, he raised his chin and howled like a coyote seeing the moon.

"I think he wants to go back to your car," she said.

"You bet he does. It's cozy, and he's got a great view. The Navigator is like home on wheels." He unfastened his seat belt and opened the car door. "Let's go find Gloria."

SHANE POINTED THE 4WD Navigator—a vehicle both he and Elvis loved—back toward town. Their starting place had to be Gloria's house. Neither he nor Mallory thought her mom would be dumb enough to make that her hideout, but they needed to pick up an article of her clothing for Elvis to sniff before he got into serious tracking.

In the passenger seat beside him, Mallory was making plans, listing places her mom liked to hang out, including the back room of her favorite restaurant, an ex-lover's house and a mountain cave at the bottom of the towering cliff beside Reflections. She mumbled, "I doubt she'll go there in this weather."

"Probably not, but don't scratch anything off the list." If they found Gloria, he could convince mom and daughter to abandon the lone-ranger act and go to the police. His brother would be hacked off at him for not leveling with him, but Shane's loyalty rested with his client. Even if he wasn't falling for Mallory, he'd follow her wishes, which seemed to be coming into sync with his. Finally, he'd almost convinced her to seek help from the police. With full-on protection from law enforcement, they might all survive.

As he drove into the hills outside Aspen, he watched Mallory in a series of quick glances as she combed her fingers through her hair, pulled it together in a long tail and twisted it into a knot on top of her head. He looked forward to the moment when he would unfasten her barrette and allow her blond hair to tumble over her creamy white shoulders.

"Almost there," she said. "You remember the house, right?"

"Hard to forget."

"Mom has wild taste, and that's an understatement. She claims to be utterly nonjudgmental with a unique ability to recognize when an art object or a painting is inspired or skillfully done."

Gloria's logic was shaky, but she must be doing something right. Reflections had been successful in a competitive market. "Tell me more about the house."

"When she bought the half-acre property twenty-six years ago, she got a great deal. It was just a small A-frame in a clearing surrounded by pines."

"You were a newborn."

"And she was raising me by herself. A single mother starting life over with a new identity. You'd think that would be enough for her to handle, but noooo. Gloria never could sit still. Almost immediately, she started adding rooms to the house. A totally new kitchen. A playroom for me. A giant bedroom with a walk-in closet for her. The A-frame was always under construction."

He remembered his first impression of Gloria's house. Chaotic but warm. "How did you feel about the constant renovation?"

"Why are you asking? Are you my psychotherapist?" She shrugged. "I don't mean to sound defensive, but it seems like I've spent most of my life explaining Mom to people."

Taking care of Gloria. He didn't say those words out loud because he wasn't a shrink and didn't want to criticize or analyze Mallory. If she was okay with her Mom revamping the house, so was he. "Home improvement and DIY is a way of life for a lot of people."

"Nothing wrong with that."

After he drove the scary stretch of road at the edge of a cliff and rounded a few more curves, they arrived. The porch light was on as well as other strategically placed lights to emphasize the multilevel architecture that sprouted with inconsistent styles, materials and colors. A deep purple wall melted into a rock silo bordered by a modernistic cedar cube. A barn-sized structure with a southwest wall of glass looked like an artist studio. The overall effect, even at night, was kind of breathtaking.

More than the wild design, he noticed light shining from one of the lower windows and most of the second floor. "Somebody's here."

She pointed to a rental car. A black SUV. "The ambassador?"

The other car had parked in the driveway, which had been shoveled earlier in the day. Shane pulled in behind the other vehicle. Moving cautiously in case anybody inside was watching, he approached the SUV and slashed the rear right tire with a four-inch blade he kept in his glove compartment. This time, nobody would be able to chase them. Then, he went to the back of the Navigator, opened the door for Elvis and gave a single command. "Quiet."

The Lab hopped out and stood beside him in a silent alert stance. In the brief time he'd been separated from Elvis, Shane had missed this level of unflagging obedience. "Good dog."

When Mallory stepped out of the door, he warned, "Don't slam it."

She carefully closed the door and tiptoed through the

snow toward him. "Now might be a good time to give me a weapon."

"Not yet. You're in charge of Elvis. Do you remember the command for attack?"

"It's *g-e-t-e-m.*"

"Follow me."

Reaching inside his parka, he drew the Glock from his shoulder holster and held it at his side as he followed a shoveled sidewalk to the front porch of what was probably the original A-frame. The front door showed no signs of being broken into, and the handle twisted easily. Unlocked.

Mallory stayed behind him with Elvis at her side. For her, this had to be a weird way to enter the house where she'd spent much of her life. The black-and-white-tiled foyer reflected another era—maybe the roaring '20s—with deco statues, ornate framed paintings and two small antique oak tables. Shuffling noises could be heard and seemed to be coming from the second floor. The intruder or intruders made a lot of noise, opening and closing doors and drawers. They didn't seem to care about being overheard.

Exchanging a look with Mallory and with Elvis, Shane raised his weapon and ascended the carved oak staircase to the peaked second floor of the A-frame where lavish Persian rugs covered the floors. A dusky rose paint covered the upper walls in a sitting room with a peaked ceiling at the top of the "A" and dark oak trim.

He followed the noises to a door beyond the original A-frame. If he had to guess, he'd say this was Gloria's bedroom with the walk-in closet. Before entering, he assessed the possibilities. With no idea how many people he might be facing or whether they had guns, he wanted to protect Mallory and Elvis. First disarm the enemy.

With a hard shove, he pushed the door. It swung wide

and crashed against the wall. In a two-handed stance, Shane took aim. "Show me your hands."

The man stood beside a long dresser with the top drawer open. He wore a gray parka and a black knit cap. He whirled, dropped to one knee and raised his handgun. Felix!

Before Shane could react, Mallory shouted the command. "Get 'em, Elvis."

The dog flew past him. Though Felix lifted his hands in immediate surrender when he recognized Shane, Elvis had been given his order. He bashed into Felix, knocking him flat on his back. His jaws closed around the wrist that had been holding the gun.

"Down." Shane stalked across the room. "Down, Elvis. It's okay. You're a good boy."

The black Lab released his grip and lowered himself onto the floor with his chin on his front paws. A low growl rumbled in his throat.

Mallory rushed to Elvis and knelt beside him. She cooed and kissed the dog's smooth furry head, lightening his mood and causing his tail to thump. "Such a good boy. You're a star."

Straightening her spine, she glared at Felix. "And you're an ass. Did you break in? You could have been shot and killed."

"The dog is fierce," Felix said.

"Only when he needs to be." Shane studied the sleeve of Felix's parka where Elvis had chomped down just hard enough to tear the fabric. He'd been trained to take down the enemy and neutralize them, not to harm them unless commanded to do so. Shane had never needed to test his dog's lethal instincts.

"I did not break in. Gloria gave me a key a long time ago."

"Which still doesn't give you the right to come and go

without permission." Mallory jabbed an index finger at his chest. "Have you spoken to her?"

"I have not. Many times, I tried to reach her by phone. She will not answer." His gaze darted around the room. "I must warn you. I did not come to this house alone."

Bad news. Shane looked over his shoulder toward the door. Of all the villains who could have accompanied Felix, the most toxic was the woman who strode through the door with her Beretta clutched in her manicured hand but not aimed at him. Her turquoise eyes—so like Mallory's—narrowed in a hostile glare.

"I'm not here to hurt anybody," she said, "especially not your stupid dog, but Ty Rivera's murder freaked me out."

Shane figured he might as well try to get some useful info from Mallory's sister. "Who do you think killed him?"

"That's obvious." She waved her gun impatiently. A gesture that made him nervous. "The killer had to be Conrad Burdock. Or one of his hired thugs."

"You're referring to a man who was staying at Hotel Jerome with his entourage. The ambassador from Sierra Leone."

Felix's expression showed confusion and concern. Amber—who was a much better actress—protested loudly that she didn't know what he was talking about. "Burdock is a thief, a criminal. He followed me here and has been trying to—"

"No more lies." Shane had just about had it with Amber. "The ambassador checked into the hotel five days ago. I'm guessing it was shortly after Gloria visited the pawnbroker in Brooklyn. That's what inspired you to take up the chase for the Teardrop, and it must have done the same for Ambassador Lewiston-Blankenship."

"You're the liar," Amber said.

She pointed her gun at his chest, and Shane had to wonder if prodding Amber was the best strategy. "The man you call Burdock was in Aspen before you."

"Put down your gun and stop threatening us." Mallory stepped into the argument. "We know you arrived in town at almost the same time as your father, Raymond DeSilva."

"He's here?" Amber's fuss and bluster turned into tears. She lowered the gun. "He didn't tell me."

"Maybe you aren't his favorite person, after all."

"I don't have to listen to this." She swabbed moisture from her cheeks. "The Teardrop belongs to me."

"Is that why you're here? To search?"

"Duh! Isn't that why you're here?"

"We came to find something with Mom's scent. For Elvis to use in tracking."

"Cute." Amber pivoted and stalked away.

"She'll be back," Shane said to Felix. "I slashed one of your tires."

He exhaled a weary sigh. "Is it true? Burdock and the ambassador are one and the same."

"You knew Rivera, right?"

"Yes."

"Do you think he intended to refer Gloria to the ambassador?"

"I believe so," Felix said. "But Rivera is a respected gemologist. I find it unlikely that he would associate with Burdock. I fear this mistaken identity was engineered by someone very clever, namely Raymond DeSilva."

Shane had come to a similar conclusion.

Chapter Nineteen

Leaving Amber and Felix to deal with the flat tire at Mom's house, Mallory and Shane set out to track Gloria using a couple of T-shirts from the dirty clothes hamper. One featured a logo for Save the Whales. The other advertised the Jimi Hendrix Experience. Sitting in the passenger seat of the Navigator, she sniffed the unique scent of Gloria Greenfield, a mixture of oil paint, turpentine, the balsamic vinegar she often used on salads, lavender and a hint of patchouli. She hoped these faint fragrances would be enough to do the job. "Do you really think Elvis can find her?"

"Like I told you before, his sense of smell is ten thousand times more sensitive than ours." Shane drove toward a more populated area of Aspen. "I think we should start at your house. Gloria might seek places that are more familiar."

"Agreed. All she needs is a hideout until tomorrow morning when she can pick up the Teardrop from the bank."

"Is the bank open on Saturday?"

"Until noon," she said.

"What's going to happen after she has it?"

She'd been considering possibilities. Mom had held the Teardrop in her possession for twenty-six years and kept it, fearing the valuable gem would fall into the wrong hands. Also, she realized that as soon as her story was known, she had to face the consequences. Mallory didn't like her answer but realized it had to be. "We go to the police."

"My brother can help."

"Maybe."

She appreciated that Shane didn't gloat. Instead, he seemed genuinely concerned about what would happen to Mom, a woman he'd never met. Mallory sighed. "I'll stand by her, no matter what. And I'll make sure she has a terrific attorney."

Though she hoped and prayed that everything would turn out all right, she couldn't count on happily-ever-after. Mom's vanishing act had overturned her life. She didn't know what to believe or which way to go. Nothing made sense. Her carefree mom had been an abused wife who undertook desperate measures to save herself. Unbelievable! Her past held so much sorrow. It seemed impossible for a loving person like Gloria to abandon her child. Which pointed out another big change in Mallory's life. She had a sister! And a father who was still alive and, by all accounts, an evil, vicious, malevolent human being.

She gazed through the darkness at Shane and allowed herself to smile. Meeting him signaled a change in the right direction. For a long time, the idea of a significant relationship didn't fit into her future. She'd put romance on the back burner, allowing it to simmer like an ex-boyfriend stew and never really expecting to find a mate. Then she'd tumbled into Shane's embrace, and she never wanted to leave. Happily-ever-after? Maybe so.

He parked the Navigator in front of her house. The porch lamp lit on a timer as it always did after sunset. Same for a lamp in the dining room. Her sidewalk hadn't been shoveled since this morning but was clear enough to walk on without slipping. There didn't appear to be any indication that Gloria had been here.

When Elvis climbed down from the back of the Navigator, he was all business. Shane poured water into a collapsible bowl for the dog and changed his harness to the search-and-rescue vest he'd been wearing the first time she saw him. He looked to Mallory as though awaiting some instruction.

"Okay, Elvis. Here's the deal," she said. "We're searching for Gloria. She's the person you were looking for at the base of the cliff near Reflections. I have a couple of her shirts. Hope that's enough to give you the scent."

Though she knew the Lab didn't understand most of the words she spoke, Elvis was a better listener than most people she knew. At least he paid attention.

While she unlocked the front door, Shane gave Elvis a chance to get familiar with Gloria's scent before entering the house. He also talked to the dog, much the same way she had. Elvis was the third partner in their little team, their family.

Shane gave the command. "Elvis, search."

Inside her house, she noticed that Shane held the Glock he'd taken from his shoulder holster, ready for return fire if they were attacked. She followed Elvis into the kitchen. On the countertop, she saw a newly opened package of chocolate and macadamia cookies, Mom's favorite. "Good boy, Elvis. That's a clue."

"He's good at his job."

"So are you," she said.

"Glad to hear you say that." He caught hold of her hand and pulled her toward him. "I might need for you to write me a recommendation."

She glided toward him and wrapped her arms around his

middle. With her head tilted back, she gazed into his golden-brown eyes. "I'd definitely recommend you. You're so good at so many things. Maybe too good. Maybe I shouldn't tell anybody else about you and hire you for a permanent position."

He kissed her, starting with a gentle pressure and escalating. At the same time, he tightened their embrace, until she felt like they were joined together. A happy ending and a new beginning at the same time.

The kiss ended, and he loosened his hold on her. With a grin, he said, "I'll take the job."

In the upstairs bedroom, they spotted a note in the same place she'd left her original "I'll be back" message. Mallory picked it up and read, "I love you, Mallie Monster. Don't want you to be hurt. Please, please, please don't try to follow me."

Mallory talked at the sheet of paper torn from a spiral notebook. "Too late, Mom. We're already on the trail, and we're going to rescue you. Whether you like it or not."

Shane signaled to her. "Let's go, Elvis is on the move."

The dog had returned to the front door where he stood, apparently waiting for them to catch up. "What's going on?" she asked. "Does he want to go out?"

"We need to follow him." Shane gave Elvis another whiff of Mom's shirts and opened the door. "I'm guessing Gloria left the house."

"Sharp deduction, Sherlock."

"Just try to keep up."

She found it hard to believe that Elvis could track Mom's scent through the snow, but the dog kept his nose down and his tail pointed straight up. He moved swiftly while she and Shane struggled to keep pace. A gust of chill wind slapped her cheeks. Her boots tread carefully on the cleared but icy sidewalk.

Elvis led them down the street to the corner and from there to nearby Reflections. The parking lot hadn't been shoveled. Tire tracks of various sizes crisscrossed the snow, but no vehicles were parked there. It made sense for Mom to come here. Reflections probably would have been next on their list of places to search.

Elvis stood at the back door, looking at them over his shoulder. He gave a woof, as if telling them to hurry up.

Stumbling across the ridges of ice and snowdrifts, a sense of anticipation ratcheted up inside her. They might come face-to-face with her mother. No matter the final outcome, the drama that had started twenty-six years ago might finally grind to a conclusion.

Shane reached the door first, twisted the handle and shoved. It opened with a squawk, and Elvis immediately poked his nose inside. Mallory was right behind him.

"Wait," Shane said softly. "We don't know who or what is inside. I should go first. Down, Elvis."

The dog obeyed.

Though her heart revved at high speed, she agreed. Shane had the weapon and could protect them. She took a step backward and watched as he entered the mudroom where she'd changed from her boots to her green clogs almost every day. Using the Maglite from a shelf by the door, he checked out the room, then gestured for her and Elvis to follow him into the kitchen, where the overhead lights were already turned on.

Considering all the time she spent at Reflections, the place ought to be as familiar as her own home. But tonight, she saw the kitchen through different eyes, influenced by fear and apprehension. The pans hanging on a circular rack above the butcher-block table glinted brightly. An anxious, ceaseless hum from the refrigerator and meat locker stirred the air. The cutlery betrayed sharp edges. So many things could go wrong.

Elvis circled the prep tables in the kitchen, still sniffing. After a brief pause at the industrial-size oven, he went to the swinging door that led into the gallery and coffee shop. Out there, the gallery display area was huge, filled with nooks and alcoves. Following Mom's path, Elvis had his work cut out for him.

Before going through the swinging door, Shane whispered to her, "Lights on or off?"

"I can find my way around in the dark," she said, "and there ought to be enough glow from moonlight through the windows in the coffee shop."

"Elvis can search without lights, but can you?"

Good point. If Mom was determined to hide, she could make herself invisible in a shadowy corner. And if the bad guys had already arrived, they could be anywhere. "Lights on."

Passing through the swinging door, she flicked the switch that illuminated the coffee shop and the front area. The aroma of fresh brew told her that Gloria had been here. Three used cups sat in the middle of a table by the window. *Three cups.* She'd had company.

Bracing for the worst, Mallory hit the light switches by the front door. At first glance, nothing seemed out of place. Gloria might have already come and gone. If bad guys were here, she'd probably already alerted them by turning on the lights.

"Mom, are you here?" Her voice stayed at a conversational level. She cleared her throat and called out more loudly, "Gloria? Where are you? Mom?"

"Let's keep moving." Shane gave her a hug. "We'll find her."

Following Elvis saved them a lot of time. The dog didn't bother with the basement area where Mallory taught classes and paintings were stored. Elvis skirted most of the displays and went directly to the staircase leading to the narrow upstairs gallery outside the offices. From that vantage point, they could look down on the entire gallery.

With her boots clanging on every step, she charged up the metal stairs with Shane following. He'd moved from the front of the pack to the rear, and she noticed that he held his Glock at the ready and was constantly scanning, looking for threats. On the balcony, she leaned against the iron railing and looked down on the displays of paintings, photographs and sketches. She saw the garish sky paintings by Fordham, the pilot, and dainty watercolors of hummingbirds by Hannah Wye, the lawyer.

Mom was nowhere in sight. Elvis went down the corridor leading to offices but didn't pause outside any of the closed doors. Instead, the dog returned to the staircase and descended. His toenails clicked against the metal. He loped around the edge of the displays and returned to the coffee shop.

"Where's he going?" she asked Shane as she chased after the dog.

"Not sure, but we better follow."

Elvis paced back and forth in front of the tall window panels that looked out on the sculpture garden where several of Uncle Walter's pieces were on display, ranging from an abstract grizzly bear to his trademark goddesses to several baby bunnies. Not that they could see details. The bright light in the coffee shop obscured the darkness beyond the windows, and moonlight didn't provide enough illumination to see anything more than vague shapes of white marble.

Squinting hard, Mallory could make out the two-foot-tall stone retaining wall at the edge of the garden, meant to be a barrier to protect unwary hikers from the seven-hundred-foot drop. In years past, it hadn't proven effective. At least five climbers had fallen to their deaths.

"What is it, Elvis?" Shane hunkered down to talk face-to-face with his search dog. "What did you find?"

The dog stood up on his hind legs and pressed his nose against the window glass. Something must be out there. At the far end of the windows near the coffee maker, Mallory flipped several light switches to activate spotlights in the sculpture garden. Much of the snow had melted on this western-facing patch of land that spread to the edge of the cliff.

She saw Gloria, tied to a life-size sculpture of Artemis, goddess of the hunt. A heavy rope around Mom's waist bound her to the white marble statue, but one hand had broken free. Visibly trembling, she reached toward the window.

Mallory gasped. Paralyzed by shock, her feet rooted to the floor. Her hand thrust forward as if she could break through the glass and rescue Mom.

Gloria's hand fell limply to her side. Her head drooped forward.

Chapter Twenty

Shane squeezed Mallory's shoulders and whispered, "Stay here with Elvis. I'll bring her inside."

She ought to go with him. This was her fight, not his. But it took all her strength to remain standing and not collapse in a heap on the floor. Her fingertips touched the ice-cold glass. Her gaze riveted on Mom. She must be so terribly cold, wearing only a light windbreaker and no mittens. When she raised her hand, her fingers clenched into a grotesque claw.

Stumbling toward a table, Mallory sank into a chair beside the window. Beside her, Elvis paced back and forth, expelling nervous tension, and then the dog halted and stood at attention, staring through the glass. Shane had entered the sculpture garden. Gun in hand, he made his way through the snow toward Gloria. He reached her and enfolded her in a hug. Mallory leaped to her feet, knocking over the chair where she'd been sitting. She couldn't hear what he was saying but knew he was speaking to Mom, offering reassurances.

Gloria nodded. Her eyes opened to slits. Mallory could tell that she was in pain. But still alive, damn it, she was still alive.

Shane had to put down his weapon to untie the knots on

the rope that held Gloria against the sculptured huntress with her bow and arrow. Though his fingers worked quickly, the minutes felt as slow as hours.

Gloria pointed. Shane twisted to look over his shoulder. A shot rang out.

A man dressed in black and wearing a ski mask aimed his handgun at Shane and Gloria. He must have missed because neither appeared to be injured. Shane dove to the ground to pick up his Glock. He rose to one knee, aimed and fired.

The masked man let out a yelp, loud enough for Mallory to hear through the triple-paned glass. He ducked behind a sculpture of a buck with an intricate eight-point rack and fired again.

Shane was on the move, drawing fire away from Mom, who had loosened the ropes and fallen to the snow-covered earth. Shane was in greater danger. From the time they first met, he'd warned her that he wasn't a sharpshooter, but he'd hit the attacker on the first try and now he nicked the antlers on the marble deer.

At the retaining wall on the edge of the garden, Shane angled for a better shot.

The masked man fired three times in rapid succession.

Shane flinched. He was hit.

Helpless, she watched as his legs gave out. His body twisted. He fell over the retaining wall and disappeared from sight.

A guttural scream tore from her throat. With both hands, she banged against the window. Shane was gone. *This can't be happening.* She couldn't believe the cliff had claimed another victim, but she'd seen him fall. The man who shot him went to the retaining wall, looked over and shrugged. Shane's death meant nothing to him.

Elvis took off running. She didn't know which way he'd

gone, couldn't remember the command that would stop him. Her only thought was revenge. If she couldn't have Shane back, she wanted to destroy the men who'd killed him. Under her breath, she muttered, "Get 'em, Elvis. Get 'em."

Through the window, she watched as another masked man lifted her mother and threw her over his shoulder like a sack of potatoes. Did he mean to fling her over the cliff?

"No!" she yelled. "Don't hurt her."

"Calm down," said a smooth baritone voice behind her. "We're not going to kill Gloria. That would be foolish. We need her to collect the diamond."

She turned and faced the man she'd known as Conrad Burdock. "You must be the Ambassador."

"I suppose I am." He went to the coffeepot and poured himself a mug. "It's unfortunate you discovered that connection. I can't have you talking to the Sierra Leone Embassy, can I?"

"You're a monster." Rage overwhelmed her sorrow. She wanted this man dead. "Why would you force my mother to stay out in the snow?"

"As I mentioned before, I don't want to kill Gloria, but I need her to work with me. She was being uncooperative, and I thought the cold might change her mind." He sipped his coffee. "This is a very nice brew."

"Choke on it."

"I'm so glad you're here. Your mother couldn't be convinced to work with me in spite of pain and cold. But I think she'll feel differently about threats to you, her darling daughter."

"You don't scare me."

"Then, you are a fool."

Mallory returned to the window. Elvis had gotten outside and positioned himself at the edge of the retaining wall where Shane had fallen. When one of the men in black approached the dog, Elvis bared his teeth and growled. The masked man backed off.

Elvis sat beside the wall. He tilted back his head and howled, long and low, commencing a loyal dog's vigil for his fallen master.

CLINGING TO THE granite face with one hand, Shane tried to recall details from when he had been here before, standing at the base of the cliff, looking up and thinking about the good old days when he'd guided groups on extreme skiing adventures that sometimes required him to do rock climbing. He had a knack for discovering the best route across a supposedly impassible wall of stone. If he hadn't been shot in the left shoulder, making his arm useless, and had been wearing better shoes for climbing, he could have easily maneuvered his way to the top. The snow didn't bother him. He was a skier and had dressed for the cold.

When he fell over the retaining wall, survival had been topmost in his mind. He'd skidded down the rock face over an outcropping that hid him from view from above. And he slowed his fall by grabbing every rocky protrusion and dangling root until he found purchase on a ledge about twelve feet from the lip and wide enough for him to stand flat-footed. He caught his breath and took stock of his situation.

In the garden above him, he heard Elvis setting up a howl. If he continued, one of the thugs would undoubtedly shoot him. Shane whispered the command, "Down, boy. Get down."

The howl ended immediately. Shane imagined the dog with his belly on the ground and his head resting on his front paws. But when he looked up, he saw the face of the black Lab peering down at him. "You heard me, Elvis. Get down."

He figured Elvis would prevent any of the masked men from coming closer to look for him. If they did, he wasn't helpless. True, he'd lost one of his guns in the fall. But he had another in his belt holster. Not that he wanted to get into a shoot-out. Blood seeped from his wound, and his shoulder felt numb. Plus, he didn't know how many of the enemy he'd be facing. Earlier, they'd encountered four attackers who worked for the ambassador, who made five. And there was Raymond DeSilva to consider.

The best option for his survival and that of Mallory and her mom meant calling for backup. Balancing precariously, he dug into his pocket and pulled out his phone. Activating the screen took some tricky maneuvering, but he got it working only to discover that his phone was fully charged but there were no bars. Not a big surprise. Not many people tried to make calls while dangling off the edge of a seven-hundred-foot cliff in the high Rockies above Aspen.

The irony struck him. Finally, he had a legitimate reason to call in the police, but his phone didn't work. If he hadn't been losing blood and feeling dizzy, he would have laughed.

Only one thing to do. He had to climb up a vertical rock face, crash into Reflections and overwhelm an unknown number of armed thugs. Not the first time in his life that he'd faced an impossible challenge. He could do it. He had great motivation, and her name was Mallory.

MALLORY HUGGED HER MOM, sharing bodily warmth. Cold as ice, Gloria shivered in her arms. Mallory took off her parka and wrapped it around her. Still not enough. Gloria's fingers showed signs of hypothermia.

Mallory snapped an order at one of the men who worked for the ambassador. "Go to the mudroom behind the kitchen and get me a couple of blankets. And take off that stupid ski mask. You look like a joke."

The ambassador nodded to him. "Do it."

She glared at him. "Leave us alone."

He swept a bow to Gloria. "I apologize for the inconvenience, but I must insist on your cooperation. Where is the diamond?"

Obstinately, Gloria shook her head.

"You're stoic when it comes to your own safety. But how do you feel about punishment inflicted on your child?" He snatched Mallory's long hair and yanked her toward him. His arm snaked around her middle, and he squeezed her upper arm so tightly that she yelped.

"Stop it," she snapped. "I'll be happy to tell you where the Teardrop is."

"No," her mom said.

"It doesn't matter. He can't get to it." She faced the ambassador. "In a safe-deposit bank at Fidelity Union Bank. The box belongs to Drew Sherman, a bank vice president. If you threaten him, the police will be involved."

"I don't believe you."

"Call Mr. Sherman. Before you start threatening him, consider the potential charges for bank robbery." She took the blankets from the guy who'd gone to the mudroom and tucked them around Mom's legs and shoulders. "By the way, did you murder Ty Rivera?"

He cleared his throat. "Certainly not."

"I'll rephrase," Mallory said. "Did you or one of your hired goons take a blade from a museum exhibit and slash his throat?"

"Why would anyone do such a thing?"

She knew the answer. "Because he thought you were the

ambassador. But Gloria could identify you as your alter ego, Conrad Burdock, a criminal. I'm guessing you've used your political status to stay out of trouble with the law. Rivera could have ended that deception."

"And now," he said coldly, "you and Gloria know my secret. I arranged for the death of Ty Rivera."

Their chances for survival looked slim. She had to think fast, to come up with something that would cause him to hesitate and allow them to escape. "Earlier, you called me and suggested that we work together against Amber. Do you remember?"

He refreshed his coffee without offering any to her or Mom. "You should have accepted. There was no need for us to be enemies."

"We can still be partners."

She went to the coffee machine. Standing this close to the ambassador, Mallory struggled to restrain herself. There were weapons at hand. Hot coffee. The glass carafe. She might even find a knife in one of the drawers. But that revenge would be a short-lived pleasure. She kept herself under control, dumping the used grounds and brewing a fresh pot of coffee. While learning how to make sales at Reflections, Mom had taught her about bargaining. Wait for the other person to speak first.

"What do you propose?" the ambassador asked.

"In the morning, Mom and I will go to the bank. You'll have to trust us to fetch the Teardrop and bring it to you. After that, we'll trust you to grant us our freedom."

"Why wouldn't you turn me over to the police?"

"Because we'd also go to jail. Mom stole the Teardrop." He still looked dubious, so she added, "And you'll pay us $200,000, which is about one percent of the worth."

The criminal alter ego of the ambassador understood her plan. "You have a deal."

"Now I'd like to take Mom home so she can rest and recover."

Mallory exchanged a grin with Mom. Truly, the acorn didn't fall far from the tree. She had no problem lying and making a deal with a criminal. She'd been born to it.

WITH A FINAL burst of strength, Shane hauled himself over the edge of the retaining wall and lay flat against it, breathing heavily while Elvis licked his face. The spotlights in the garden had been turned off, and he doubted anyone could see them in the shadows. The frozen night surrounded him. Snow permeated his clothing, but his shoulder wound flamed with dark wet heat. He was still losing blood. Not much time left before he passed out.

With his back leaning against the wall, he pulled the Glock from his belt holster. Staggering to his feet, he peered through the windows at the interior of the coffee shop. Mallory served a mug of coffee to her mom, who was swaddled in mismatched blankets. The ambassador, aliás Burdock, strutted through the tables and chairs.

Shane saw two armed men who no longer wore masks. One of them must have been the guy he shot in the garden. Both his right leg and right wrist were bandaged. Shane figured the other two had been assigned to protect the front and back doors of Reflections, which meant he only had to get past one guard. And then what?

He took out his phone, glad to see the screen light up and he had bars indicating he could make a call. He tapped speed dial for his brother. The call went through.

Shane's strength was fading. He had to talk fast while his brain was still working and he made sense. "Logan, I'm at

Reflections in Aspen. There are at least five men holding Mallory and her mom hostage. One of them probably killed Ty Rivera. I need backup."

"I'm on it, bro. I know the chief of police in Aspen. They'll be there pronto."

"Hostage situation," he repeated. "They can't go in with guns blazing."

"Got it," Logan said. "Mallory Greenfield is the woman you're working for, right? You care about her. I get it. Just don't do anything stupid."

"Count on it."

Shane ended the call and headed toward the rear door with Elvis following close behind. He didn't intend to do anything dumb but hoped to disarm the situation before the police arrived and everything got crazy. Mallory needed him. Now.

At the rear entrance, he saw a guy in a ski mask standing under the porch light, almost as though waiting for Shane to sneak up to him and knock him unconscious with the butt of his Glock, which was exactly what he did. Shane dragged the guy into the mudroom. In the masked man's pocket, Shane found a zip tie and used it to fasten his wrists behind his back. He turned the ski mask into a gag.

He crept through the kitchen and stopped at the swinging door. His shoulder wound began to throb. Still bleeding, he needed for this to be over. But he couldn't charge into the coffee shop while outnumbered and outgunned. He needed a distraction.

As if on cue, Amber slammed the front door and entered Reflections. In a loud near-hysterical voice, she demanded to know where the diamond was. "When will I get my share?"

He heard Gloria's faint voice. "My beautiful daughter, can you ever forgive me?"

"No. Never."

"I tried to do what was best."

"Best for you," Amber said. "Not for me."

He wondered where Felix was. He must have changed the tire and given Amber a ride here. Felix would be on Shane's side. He might even the odds.

Shane opened the swinging door enough that he could see when another person entered from the front. An older man, tall and handsome with silver streaks at his temples. Raymond DeSilva.

He swaggered toward the coffee shop and held his arms wide open. "Daddy's home."

Shane needed to take advantage of the chaos, but he didn't want Elvis involved. Even though the dog was trained to attack, he couldn't stop a bullet. "Stay," Shane ordered. "Elvis, you need to stay here."

The dog looked up at him with a wise, patient gaze that told Shane he understood. At the same time, Elvis gave a low dangerous growl. He was ready for a fight.

Shane crept toward the coffee shop where Amber argued with her father about how they should handle the situation. She seemed to think the plan hatched by Mallory and the ambassador would cut them out of the money. He was more inclined to take absolute control. When Gloria piped up, DeSilva whirled and slapped her hard, knocking her from the chair where she'd been huddled in blankets.

To his surprise, Amber responded, "It's true what Felix said about you. You're abusive, a predator."

"I'm the guy who paid your bills, little girl. You'll give me the respect I deserve."

"What happens if I don't? Are you going to hit me, too?" Amber whipped out her handgun. "Don't even think about it."

Mallory helped her mom back into the chair and placed herself in the middle of the argument. "Everybody settle down."

"Don't push me," DeSilva said with a sneer as he drew his gun.

"Go ahead and shoot," she confronted him. "You think you have a lot to lose, but it's only money. Tonight, I had everything taken away. My heart is broken. The man I love is dead."

Shane entered the coffee shop. His Glock aimed at DeSilva. "Drop it."

Before he could react, Amber fired her weapon. The bullet hit her father's gun, causing him to drop it. Amber laughed. "Daddy did an excellent job of teaching me how to handle firearms."

Shane turned his weapon on the ambassador and his men. "I've got you covered. No false moves."

From outside, he heard police sirens wailing. So much for the subtle approach from the Aspen cops. The threat was enough to disarm the ambassador's men, who would all be arrested.

Mallory found her place beside him with his one good arm wrapped around her. Her incredible turquoise eyes filled with tears as she looked up at him. She whispered, "When I thought you were dead, I knew. You're the love of my life. I want to be with you forever."

"Yes," he said.

Forever and ever.

TEN MONTHS LATER in late summer, Mallory made good on her proposal. The wedding would be held in the sculpture garden at Reflections, where she thought she'd lost Shane forever. Mom had served a six-month sentence in a low-security prison in Englewood and would be on probation for five years. The light sentence came as a result of intervention from the Sierra Leone government, which was thrilled to once again have possession of the African Teardrop. The plans were to sell it and use the proceeds for schools. The new ambassador from Sierra Leone planned to attend the wedding.

Amber would serve as maid of honor. She still wasn't happy about losing out on the millions from the sale of the Teardrop but received a regular paycheck for opening a Reflections gallery in Brooklyn and handling uncle Walter's sculptures.

Logan Reilly would act as Shane's best man.

Standing at the edge of the garden, Mallory held Drew Sherman's elbow. He would escort her to the minister whostood before a bower of flowers. He leaned down to kiss her cheek. "You look real fancy-schmancy in that lacy white dress."

"Okey dokey."

Elvis in his red leather harness with the silver studs pranced down the aisle ahead of her, carrying their rings in a pouch. She had to admit that the dog was pretty cute, but her entire field of vision was filled by Shane, who looked amazing in his tuxedo. Shane Reilly was the best thing that had ever happened to her, and it was almost worth going through the tribulation of nearly losing her mother to find him. *Almost worth it.*

* * * * *

DEFENDER
AFTER DARK

CHARLENE PARRIS

To my family, and especially my cousins, Rochelle and Kim, who have cheered me on and demand when the next book is coming out. Gotta love the enthusiasm!

To my darling friend Britt, who is the inspiration for the heroine. Love you! <3

Chapter One

When Detective Mark Hawthorne stepped out of his vehicle, he looked around in confusion and frustration. "What the hell?"

The crime scene was across the street, within the dark bowels of a construction site. Unfortunately, the area in front of it was filling up with curious onlookers, their cell phones held high and lights flashing as if they'd spotted a celebrity.

"Damn it." He looked at both ends of the narrow two-lane street. The intersections were blocked off with police vehicles and bright yellow caution tape. However, the officers were having a difficult time removing pedestrians who had already wandered over to see what was going on. An ambulance was parked a few feet away.

He jogged to the closest officer, who was yelling into his walkie-talkie. "Detective Hawthorne," he shouted, showing his badge. "Are there more officers coming?"

He waited while the officer finished providing instructions. "They're on the way now. Seriously, I don't know how these people found out about this. I got here five minutes after the call."

Mark swore—social media these days was a pain in the ass for stuff like this. "I'm the lead on this case." He spotted a bright light and the silhouette of a crime scene barrier. *Good, Walsh is here already.* "As soon as your backup arrives, get these people out of here."

He'd been notified of a murder while at the precinct, and despite the gruesomeness of the investigation, Mark was itching to get started. Weeks of working on burglaries, car thefts and other minor cases had started to get on his nerves. He wanted what Detectives Timmins and Solberg routinely got—the meatier investigations, ones that made them really think through the clues until they solved them.

And now he was finally going to get his chance.

He observed his surroundings. The building consisted only of stone pillars, some wooden walls and a roof. A chain-link fence encompassed the site, and its front gate stood slightly open. Barely visible within the semidarkness of the building, he could just make out piles of cut lumber, neatly stacked. "Where's the witness who called it in?" Mark asked the officer.

"Over there, just inside the fence with two of my guys. She's pretty shaken up."

"Okay, let me check in with Forensics, see who the murder victim is first."

"Well, that's the odd thing," the officer said, rubbing his forehead. "There's a victim for sure, but he's not dead."

Mark frowned. "Come again?"

He pointed. "He's in the ambulance getting medical attention. The witness who found him panicked and called it in as a homicide. By the time we got here, the guy had regained consciousness, but he's beat up pretty bad."

Mark pursed his lips, annoyed and relieved at the same time. No one was dead, but bringing in police forces across the region… "Thanks."

As Mark headed in the direction of the witness, he noticed that she couldn't be more than twenty-five. She had taken off her hard hat, a hint that she worked here. She was quite pretty, with light brown hair tied up in a bun and blue eyes. He saw the worry and fear etched in her face. "Hey," he called out. When she turned around, he showed his badge. "Detective Hawthorne. Can you tell me what happened?"

"I'm not in trouble, am I?" she asked. The woman was visibly upset.

He gave her a smile. "Why would you think that?"

"Because I thought I saw a dead body—my God, it scared the crap out of me. I managed to call 911 without screaming into the phone and waited outside." She made the sign of the cross on her chest. "When the ambulance and police arrived, the body got up and started walking toward us. I swear, I thought it was a ghost."

"But he's not, thanks to you." Mark looked around again. Construction sites followed strict rules regarding safety. "How do you think he got in there?"

"Oh, he was inspecting the site and chatting with the supervisor about an hour ago."

Weirder and weirder. "Who is he?"

"Mr. Edward Ferguson."

She said the name like he was supposed to recognize it—he didn't, and shrugged.

She raised her brows. "He's the guy who owns the Mighty Big Bakery chain."

Ah, now he was getting somewhere. Edward Ferguson was a conglomerate powerhouse who owned one of the biggest baked goods store chains in southern Ontario.

"I must have really panicked. Maybe he just tripped and hit his head on something," the woman said, twisting her construction hat between nervous fingers.

"I'll see how he's doing. You don't have to hang around,

but I would like you to come to York Regional Police 4 District tomorrow morning to provide a witness statement." He brought out his business card.

"Of course." As she took the card from him, she smiled, which transformed her face. "You don't seem like a cop."

"I try to display the friendlier side of the force. We're not all monsters."

"No...you're not." She stuck his card into her back pocket. "Maybe when this is over, you can continue showing me your nice side."

Mark knew his eyebrow went up. Did she just ask him out on a date? She didn't seem in any hurry now to leave, but he had to get back to work. "How about you get a good night's rest and I'll talk to you at the precinct at nine tomorrow morning?"

"Works for me. Oh, and in case you missed it, the name's Jenny." She sauntered off.

Definitely an invitation.

He turned his attention to the ambulance, where Mr. Ferguson was reclined on a stretcher. However, as he got closer, Mark noticed that Mr. Ferguson was arguing with the paramedics.

"Listen to me, I told you I'm fine. Now will you let me go?"

Mark watched him, surprised at Mr. Ferguson's attitude. He had been beaten pretty badly, his face covered in bruises and a split lip, but now the man was fighting the people trying to help him.

"Sir, you might have a concussion," a female medic told him. "At the very least, we need to take you to the hospital for observation..."

"I'm not going to a damn hospital! I need to get back to my office!"

Mark watched the struggle a bit more, then stepped in. "I suggest you do as the medic advises," he said, keeping his voice neutral.

The man glared at him. "Who the hell are you? And do you know who the hell I am?"

"You're Edward Ferguson."

That shut him up for a hot minute.

"And I'm Detective Mark Hawthorne." He held up his badge. "While you have every right to refuse medical attention, I'm afraid you still have to go to the hospital. The police will need the doctor's help in collecting criminal evidence from you." Mark smiled—he couldn't help himself. "After you're done, I'll interrogate you at the hospital for information. Which means you'll need to stay there until I arrive."

Mr. Ferguson mumbled something under his breath.

"I don't know what you're complaining about. York Region's finest is providing you the fast, courteous assistance I'm sure you'd expect," Mark added.

"Fine, I get it." Mr. Ferguson lay back on the stretcher as the medics strapped him in.

Mark rubbed his face with one hand. It had been a long day, and it was going to be a longer evening. But it wasn't an excuse to talk to Mr. Ferguson like that, even if the man had it coming. He'd probably get an earful from the captain first thing Monday morning.

"The sarcasm is strong with you tonight," an amused voice said. Myrna Walsh, the new forensics investigator with his precinct, was a fiery redhead with a personality to match. "For a second there, I thought you were going to describe how the medical staff would poke and prod him. You managed to restrain yourself."

He sighed. "I'm sure Ferguson will give Captain Fraust an earful, followed by her doing the same to me."

"Cross that bridge when you get to it." She glanced over her shoulder. "Looks like we finally have the place to ourselves. Come on, we've got a crime to solve."

"Yeah, let's go."

The construction site was bordered with an eight-foot chain-link fence. A section of it was slightly ajar. Normally there would be a chain and padlock securing the gate after-hours. Both were nowhere around.

Mark pulled on a pair of thin plastic gloves and pulled the fence wide enough for him and Myrna to pass through. She handed him a flashlight, and when they passed beneath the unfinished concrete pillars, he turned it on.

They stood in a wide rectangular area about twenty feet across, while the rest faded into blackness. "The witness said she saw Mr. Ferguson lying where I've set up the screen." Myrna pointed. "How did she even see him?"

"She must have come this way when her shift was over and spotted his body." Mark followed her to the crime site, lit up by the harsh brightness of a portable lamp. Dark stains smudged the concrete flooring, and several unknown items lay scattered around it. "Are you finished?"

"No, I've got a few more things to look over."

"I'll let you get to it. I'm going to walk the perimeter."

"Here, put these on." She handed him a pair of booties.

After slipping on the plastic coverings, Mark moved farther into the building, scanning the ground with his light. This case was his first significant one as lead investigator, but he wondered if he would have even received it if Timmins and Solberg weren't already involved in other projects.

No, he needed to shut that down—it wouldn't do to let his insecurities get in the way. Besides, Timmins told him he could handle this with no problem and had offered his support if Mark needed a sounding board. Still, that little twitch of nagging doubt persisted...

He stopped. Just within his flashlight's field, he spied the chain and padlock. He knelt down and placed a yellow marker by them, then scanned the area with his light. He could just make out several footprints. "Myrna, I found the security chain and padlock," he called out. "Might have something on them. I also see footprints, probably belonging to the construction workers, but no harm in checking them out, either." He pulled out his phone and snapped some pictures, then marked the prints with several of the small yellow cones.

"Okay, I'll get over there as soon as I can." Her voice echoed across the space.

Mark continued his observations, spying more footprints. He placed his markers as he completed his sweep. "What did you find?" he asked as he approached her.

She sat back on her heels. "Well, I'm sure the blood is Mr. Ferguson's, but I took samples from a number of areas just in case we're lucky and some of it belongs to the suspect." She pointed to a piece of wood in a large plastic evidence bag. "That was used to beat him. I found more blood and hair samples, and I'll see if there are any fingerprints I can lift."

Myrna then gestured behind her. "The suspect tried to sweep away his footprints, but he—or she—didn't get it all. I took photos of a distinctive sole pattern. You said you found footprints, too?"

"Near the chain and padlock back there. Might be fingerprints on those as well."

"I'll bag them." She stood. "Other than that, I haven't found anything else, but I'd like to keep the area roped off for another day, just in case."

"You got it." Mark looked down at the footprints Myrna had found. Streaks of dust and debris surrounded the spot where Mr. Ferguson had been discovered, but on the edge of the disturbed space was a very clear shoe print. He hunkered down to take a closer look at it, until he spied a distinctive logo. He whistled. "This should prove interesting."

"What is it?" Myrna asked.

"See the logo? We can narrow down our search based on this."

She frowned. "Really? How? This running shoe is more than just famous, you know. I've seen babies wearing these!"

Mark pointed. "The tread pattern. Shoe size. And because I know this brand makes limited quantities of exclusive editions every year. This footprint is one of them." He pulled out his phone again and took a few close-up shots.

"Are they the same footprints as by the chain and padlock?"

He stood. "Don't know. Finish up what you're doing, then let's check the rest of the perimeter. I also want to talk to the site supervisor."

The supervisor, a man in his late forties, had nothing to offer. "I gave Mr. Ferguson a tour of the premises and provided updates. That took about an hour. He said he was going back to his office, and the last time I saw him, he was heading for the exit."

"You didn't hear anything odd?" Mark asked.

"No, sir, I didn't. So damn noisy around here."

It was late evening now, and dark within the half-constructed building. "Can you take us around the outside of the construction site?" Mark asked. "I'd like to see if there's anything else that's helpful."

"Yeah, sure. Both of you need to wear these." The supervisor gave them hard hats. "Let me turn on the portable light towers first, and I've got a large flashlight. I'll bring that, especially as you both need to watch your footing."

The powerful beam cut through the pools of darkness the light towers didn't reach as they slowly walked along a narrow dirt pathway. "Is Mr. Ferguson okay?" the supervisor asked.

"He's got cuts and bruises. I told him to go to the hospital in case anything's broken." Mark didn't want to say too much.

"I keep telling him he needs to wear the hard hat and work boots when he's here. Sometimes he'll wear them, but those other times…" The supervisor let out a loud sigh. "The man can be stubborn."

"Do you work with him frequently?"

"This is my first job as supervisor with him. He's very smart, but his common sense needs a bit of work, in my opinion."

As they came around a corner, the supervisor stopped. "What the hell is that?"

Mark looked at the red container, its shape immediately recognizable. "You weren't expecting to see a fuel canister?"

"At a construction site? Hell no." The supervisor made a move to reach for it.

"Hang on." Mark looked at Myrna. "Can you see if you can get any prints off that?"

"You betcha." She crouched in front of the fuel can as the supervisor held his flashlight steady. "You think the suspect might have wanted to start a fire in here?" she asked. "Maybe Mr. Ferguson caught him in the act and got beaten up?"

"What?" The supervisor wiped his brow. "Hey, this is getting to be too much."

Mark had to agree. A plan to burn down a building with

staff inside had just raised the stakes of this investigation. "We'll take it with us," he said, waiting until Myrna finished her analysis. He grabbed the container with a gloved hand. "We'll check if there are any more, then head back."

Thankfully, there were no more fuel cans, but Mark's sixth sense was acting up. "Mr. Smith, I think it best you give your staff the day off tomorrow. I'd like to check the construction site one more time to make sure there aren't any more of these." He held up the fuel canister. "Or any other viable clues."

Mr. Smith shook his head. "Mr. Ferguson won't like it."

"I'll talk to him. In the meantime, don't let anyone come into work tomorrow. But we'll need you here to escort us through the rest of the building."

"Sure, sure."

Mark handed him his card. "Is tomorrow morning around eleven thirty okay with you?"

"Yeah, I'll be here." They had reached the front gate, and Mr. Smith switched off his flashlight. "I hope you catch the son of a bitch who did this."

"That's the plan. I'll be talking to one of your construction workers tomorrow morning as well at the police station. You and I will do a thorough search of the premises. And see if you have another way to secure the site. The last thing we need is some jerk taking videos of himself at the crime scene."

He paused beside the chain-link fence, uncertainty creeping through his skin, gnawing at his gut. This case had taken an odd twist. A homicide was one thing—catch the killer, throw him in jail, give closure to the family. That might be a bit oversimplified, but that was how it seemed to progress when the other detectives worked the investigations.

But this… Someone had tried to kill one of the biggest

store owners in Ontario, and if that gasoline had been spread around and lit, several construction workers might have lost their lives as well. Everyone knew Mighty Big Bakery, and the spotlight would be on Mark, glaring at everything he did until he solved the case. To say that he felt the pressure was an understatement.

"Hey, you okay?" Myrna asked.

"Not really. This investigation is going to be..." He didn't finish.

"Don't sweat it. We'll get it done." She took the fuel canister from him. "I'll do an initial analysis when I get back, see if I can come up with some more answers for you."

He smiled, thinking of a memory. "You sound like Cynthia."

Myrna laughed. "What can I say? Ms. Cornwall is one of the best. She sort of rubs off on you."

Mark talked to the officer in charge about security while watching the few remaining curious bystanders, including a pair of young teenagers. "We can open up the street to traffic," he told him, "but I'd like a rotating shift for tonight. I'm coming back to finish looking around tomorrow." Across the street, he noticed the familiar markings of a television van and groaned. "When the hell did they show up?"

"About ten minutes ago. The interviewer is over there." The officer frowned. "May as well get it over and done with."

With Myrna gone, Mark felt vulnerable, like a team member had taken a hit and he was left holding the ball. But he refused to let that show. His interview was brief and vague, despite the demands for answers—answers he didn't have and wouldn't provide if he knew. Captain Fraust should be okay with that.

He walked to his car, exhaustion making him drag his

feet. It was nighttime now, and the street had been reopened to traffic. Car lights and incessant honking grated on his nerves until he thought he'd yell with frustration. He would need some serious downtime when this case was over. He hadn't been under the impression that he'd pushed himself too hard, but his brain and body were giving him other ideas.

And yet, a tremor of exhilaration coursed through him. This was his first major case as lead investigator. How could he not be excited about that?

He would have a load of stuff to do tomorrow, but for now, a hot shower and his bed were calling him.

He pulled out his key fob and clicked it, hearing the familiar chirp as his car door unlocked. Halfway across the street, Mark let his gaze scan across the pedestrians as they traveled to whatever entertainment awaited them on a Friday night, until he noticed a woman.

She stood on the sidewalk just ahead of his car, so that he had a full, unobstructed, amazing view.

The first thing that caught his attention was her long blond hair, tied back into a ponytail, although some strands had escaped to frame her face. The color was so striking, it looked like a halo around a pale, serene expression. She was tall—about five feet nine inches—and wearing a pair of slim denim jeans and a white T-shirt that couldn't hide the toned body hidden beneath them.

He couldn't see the color of her eyes, but he felt sure they would either be an icy blue or as green as the British Columbia forests that surrounded his old home. A classic Norwegian princess who literally took his breath away. Mark noticed nothing else—only her.

She remained still, watching him, her arms wrapped around a tote bag, one eyebrow raised. He noticed that she was studying him just as intently but hadn't moved. His feet chose to answer for him, drawing him closer, step by agonizing step. That clichéd phrase of moths being drawn to flame ran through his mind. This beautiful vision, only mere feet away, was a flame that lit up emotions Mark had buried so that he could concentrate on his job and claim back the life his father had taken away.

She made a move as if to turn away, and he stopped, holding his breath. *Please*, he thought. *Just three more seconds...*

The sudden squeal of tires, followed by the loud, blaring sound of a car horn, made him jump, his heart pounding in his chest. He turned to look at the white SUV and the irate driver waving her fist at him. "Get off the street!" she screamed. "What the hell are you doing?"

"Sorry," he called out, and got out of the way. But when he turned back to his dream come true, she was gone.

BRITT GRONLUND CLOSED the door behind her, then leaned against it, clutching her purse so tight to her chest she was afraid she might have ripped holes in it with her nails.

The front window of her bakery shop was a wide pane of glass, and unable to help herself, she turned toward it, wondering if the gorgeous stranger had possibly followed her. But after a few minutes, she realized it wasn't the case.

She sighed, trying to decide if she'd made the right choice. When she'd noticed him crossing the street, she believed the Fates had something to do with it. Britt had been late getting to the bank, and the long lineup had tested her patience. It also didn't help that the police had closed down her street to do an investigation. When the area finally opened up, she'd quickened her pace, thinking about the things she needed to finish before closing up for the evening.

But when she'd seen him, thoughts of work had flown

out of her mind. Britt had no way to describe what she felt when he came toward her. He'd seemed distracted, yet his confident stride and aura made her stand at attention. This was a man few could ignore, including her.

She had stopped and stood at the curb, watching as he dug out a set of keys and automatically unlocked his door. As she frantically debated whether to call out a greeting, he looked up, and their gazes locked on each other.

The intensity in his eyes sent shivers through every part of her, and she'd held her breath. Britt had never believed in love at first sight, but the stranger's continued look woke some part of her that she'd believed dead and gone...

The sudden noise of a car horn had propelled her out of her fantasy. Damn it, why was this happening now when she still had her life to get in order? Any kind of intimate relationship would only stall her goals, and Britt had promised herself that she would come first.

So, with one regretful backward glance, she had blended into the Friday-night crowd, memorizing what little she'd seen of the handsome stranger.

Life must still go on.

Blowing out a frustrated breath, she frowned as she stared at the half-constructed building almost across from her, wondering why the police had felt it necessary to shut down the street. She'd seen the barrier and police officers on duty keeping away the curious. Bright lighting illuminated the starkness of the construction site.

That building belonged to Edward Ferguson.

Pursing her lips, Britt carefully wove between waiting customers to get to her office. Betty and Kevin moved around each other like two dancers as they fulfilled orders for those in line, while other customers sat at a few of the half dozen tables throughout the room. One corner held a dedicated free library, where customers could pick a book and read while enjoying a drink and their favorite pastry.

The pace was steady, and her staff were handling it with their usual efficiency and upbeat friendliness. Britt headed toward the back, passing the door to the large well-stocked kitchen and Jacques, her head baker. He waved at her. "Britt! Did you hear?"

Britt hesitated at the entrance. "About what?"

"The assault across the street." Jacques was an older man in his late forties, and had worked with her for almost three years, helping her build the business from the ground up to where it stood now.

"Assault?" She walked into the kitchen, now curious. "Was that what all the commotion was about?"

"Yeah." He was folding dough. "It was Edward Ferguson."

"No way." The CEO had been trying to buy out her store, and she'd told him, using colorful language, where he could shove it. It seemed like karma had paid him a visit. She allowed herself a tiny moment of petty elation before asking, "Do you know if he's okay?"

Jacques gave her a disgusted look. "Should we care? He wanted to shut us down, *chérie*. He's bought a lot of the small bakeries in Toronto already."

"I know. It's just…well, there are other ways to handle a man like Mr. Ferguson."

"I suppose." He portioned out the dough, placed it on a metal pan and covered it with plastic before sliding it into the huge fridge. "However, you and I know that Ferguson is not the diplomatic type. He's a bully."

"Can't disagree on that."

In her office, Britt turned on her computer and checked her email. They had received orders through the week, but there was always someone who would frantically put in a last-minute request for the weekend. This time, there were two—a small order for tomorrow in the early afternoon, and another larger order for the day after, Sunday morning. Thank God they weren't catering events, or she'd have to decline them.

Britt was proud of the work she'd put into Konditori, her bakery and life's dream. The sudden change in direction had been scary, but in the end, well worth it.

She sent the replies, drew up invoices and made notes. She would need to advise Jacques, of course, and have him bring in Thomas, his assistant. She'd leave messages for Jasmine and Oliver coming in for the weekend shift, and she'd be here, overseeing everything.

It's not as if she had a date or weekend plans, right?

Chapter Two

Mark stood in the hospital room that night, tapping his foot impatiently as Mr. Ferguson continued talking on his cell. Ten minutes had already lapsed, and as the man's voice started rising in irritation, he suspected it could go on much longer.

He moved to stand in front of the CEO. "I need to talk to you," he said loudly. "This is a criminal investigation, remember?"

Ferguson gave him a look, but Mark didn't back down. Finally with a sigh, he nodded. "Look, let me call you back. I don't have a choice—there's a police officer standing in front of me." He clicked off the phone.

Mark chewed his lip in frustration but didn't bother correcting his job title—the effort would have been wasted, and he needed to pick his battles with someone as influential as the man lying in the hospital bed before him. "Thank you," he said, trying not to grit his teeth. "So, give me a rundown of what happened." Myrna had arrived earlier to collect the forensic samples taken by the hospital staff.

Ferguson drank from a glass of water, then lay back down. "I have no idea why this kind of shit would happen to me."

I have a few ideas, Mark said to himself. "It can happen to anyone."

"Not to me."

Mark let that one slide and pulled out his work phone. "I just need to record our conversation so that you don't have to come to the precinct later." He placed the instrument on a small table beside the bed and sat down. "What happened?" he repeated.

Mr. Ferguson rubbed his arm, which was bandaged. "I don't know. I had a meeting with the site supervisor at four this afternoon. I was running late and called him to say I'd be there in another fifteen minutes.

"When I got to the site office, he insisted I put on the hard hat and boots. I took off my shoes, and I remember struggling with the boots. I got ticked off and said let's get on with it."

"Do you remember putting on the hard hat?" Mark asked.

"Nah, hate the damn things. I wasn't going to be there long anyway. We went in and did the inspection. That was it."

Mark leaned forward in his chair. "You didn't see anyone suspicious?"

"I wasn't looking for anyone suspicious," he retorted. "As far as I'm concerned, I'm just there to make sure everything's on schedule."

That sounded like him. "Then what?"

"I went back to the office, put on my shoes and got ready to leave. Said I was happy with the progress, and the supervisor confirmed the store would be ready to open by the end of the year."

Mark nodded, more to himself. It sounded like an ordinary day to the bakery owner. And yet… "How did you get lured back?"

Mr. Ferguson turned his head to look at him directly. "I was in a hurry and didn't wait for the supervisor. I got to the front gate and saw someone walking to the back with a gasoline container. He wasn't dressed like a construction worker, either, only had on the safety vest and hard hat, and nothing else. I've been in enough sites to know. And the gate hadn't been locked, so I was sure it was a trespasser.

"I ran after him and started shouting. I actually got my phone out to call the supervisor. I could see the guy was scared, but when my phone started ringing—I had it on speaker—he must have panicked. Little prick ran at me and pushed me over, knocked the phone out of my hand. Next thing I know, I'm getting hit with something hard. I started kicking and yelling, and pretty sure I scored a couple of hits."

Mark was impressed—Mr. Ferguson was an observant man. "Did you see his face?"

He nodded. "For about three seconds. I don't think I can identify him. But you managed to find some clues, right?"

"We have some evidence, yes." Mark decided to keep the discovery of the fuel container to himself, along with shutting down the site tomorrow. He had a suspicion the CEO would throw a tantrum, and he wanted to avoid that.

"Good, I want that asshole arrested, you got that?"

Mark got up and retrieved his phone. He had a theory and decided to confirm it. "Do you think you were attacked because of your…business ethics?"

Mr. Ferguson laughed. "People need to understand it's a dog-eat-dog world, son. If you can't keep up, you'll be run over. Anyone who tells you different is lying."

Mark pursed his lips. Of course, he held a different view, but what was the point in arguing it? "The doctor told me you should be able to go home tomorrow. I'll keep you up to date on my progress, but if I have any more questions, I'll let you know."

He walked out of the hospital feeling gross. There was just something about Ferguson that rubbed him in all the wrong ways. It was one thing to say you wanted to beat your competition, and another when you'd do anything it took to climb on top.

It was one of the reasons he had decided on law enforcement. He believed in defending people who didn't stand a chance against men like Ferguson. Bullying and intimidation didn't sit well in Mark's view.

So it was ironic that he had to defend a bully. "Will wonders never cease?" he muttered as he got into his car.

MARK WOKE AND stretched his arms over his head. He heard birds chirping outside his window, and when he glanced at his clock, saw that it was just past seven in the morning.

He grabbed his work phone and checked the timing on the two interviews he had scheduled. Jenny, the construction worker, was at nine, while Mr. Smith, the site supervisor, was at eleven thirty. Myrna had texted him as well, letting him know she had stayed at the precinct until late last night, and would arrive midmorning.

After a shower and shave, he felt human again. But when he opened his fridge door, he swore. He'd forgotten to pick up some groceries last night after being distracted by the Nordic princess.

Damn it, he wished he'd been more on the ball. Mark had been awestruck by the woman's beauty and hadn't gotten his act together in time to approach and maybe say a few complimentary words to her. Bad luck on his part, and the chances of seeing her or having the same spellbound reaction to another woman again was close to nil.

He slapped the fridge in frustration. He knew that had been a once-in-a-long-time encounter. Maybe, if the stars aligned themselves, he might see her again, but he wouldn't get his hopes up.

An hour later, Mark sat at his desk after grabbing a breakfast sandwich and a large cup of decent coffee from the local takeout store close to the precinct. He read through his notes, though the case was still fresh in his mind. He had an idea of the questions he would ask Jenny, the construction worker, and Mr. Smith, the site supervisor. While he believed Smith would be straightforward, he wondered how Jenny would behave during the interview. It may be a bad habit in his profession, but thinking the worst of witnesses and suspects before they proved their innocence did get him around obstacles. If he fell for her flirting, where would that end up, especially if she was guilty of something?

A phone call from the officer at the front desk confirmed her arrival. Timmins wasn't in the office yet—he had texted, saying he'd be there in ten minutes. Mark grabbed his notepad and headed to the reception area to pick her up. "Good morning," he said. "Thanks for coming in."

"Hey, no problem." She stood, and he immediately noticed that she had put care into her appearance. Jenny wore makeup, had styled her hair in waves that framed her face, and her clothing was more suited for an evening out than a weekend police interrogation. It wasn't hard to put two and two together that she was making an effort to continue flirting with him.

"Come on, we're going to an interrogation room to get a formal statement."

The ride on the elevator was silent. He caught Jenny watching him out of the corner of his eye, but he remained quiet while he led her down the fluorescent-lit hallway and into a barely furnished room. "Have a seat."

She looked around, rubbing her arms. "This looks like a jail cell."

Mark dropped his notepad and phone on the bolted table. "You know what the inside of a jail cell looks like?" he asked. That was an odd statement from her.

"Only from the television shows." She sat down, continuing to take in her surroundings.

"Did you want anything? Coffee?"

"No, I'm good."

He looked at his watch. "Detective Walter Timmins should be here in a few minutes."

She frowned.

"We always need two officers during an interview. Protocol."

"Oh." She sounded disappointed.

That will keep her from trying anything funny.

A couple of minutes later, Timmins walked in. "Sorry I'm late," he apologized, and took the seat at the other end of the small room.

"No problem." Mark lifted his hand toward the camera in the wall to signal he was ready. After introducing himself and Timmins formally and describing the purpose of the interview, he got started. "Can you give me a full rundown of your day up to when you discovered Mr. Edward Ferguson?"

"Yeah, sure." She glanced back at Timmins, then took a breath. "All of us knew Mr. Ferguson was coming by yesterday afternoon at four o'clock. Smith, our site supervisor, runs a tight ship—really organized. Everyone knows what they're supposed to be working on each day. But he wanted me and one other coworker to walk the area and clean up any loose debris, check that everything was in its place, that sort of thing."

"What time did this start?" Mark asked.

"I got to work at my usual time, eight in the morning. I think maybe an hour later?"

He wrote some notes. "And when you finished?"

"The coworker and I started our shift. I was helping with the steel girders on the second floor, but I don't know what my coworker's job was."

"Did you work on that during your whole shift?"

"For the morning, yes, until twelve thirty, then I had lunch."

"Do all the workers take their lunch at the same time?" Timmins asked.

Jenny half turned in her chair. "No, lunchtime is split into two shifts."

"So Mr. Ferguson arrived when all of you finished lunch."

"Well, it's not like he needs us with him while he's inspecting," Jenny retorted. "Mr. Smith was there, and I think he took two of his junior assistants with him."

Mark jotted down the assistants' names—he'd verify that with Smith later. "And after lunch?"

"Got back to work. We were starting the electrical, so I was on hand for that until my shift was over, around six that evening."

"Did you see Mr. Ferguson and your boss at all during the afternoon?"

Jenny shook her head. "Nope. Just kept my head down. We were on a schedule."

"And after work?"

She shrugged. "I headed to the front gate and saw something weird on the ground within the site. That's how I found him."

"It's pretty hard to see that distance when it's dark under there," Timmins stated.

"It wasn't that dark where Mr. Ferguson was."

Mark paused in taking notes. "But it would have been difficult to spot him immediately."

She shrugged. "We're trained to spot inconsistencies. I don't know what else to tell you."

The rest of Jenny's story was almost verbatim to what she'd told him last night.

"Thanks for your help," Mark said, getting up. "If you think of anything else, you have my business card."

"Sooo, I'm not getting arrested for anything?" she said innocently, holding her wrists together.

He almost rolled his eyes, then caught Timmins hiding his face with a hand. His cough sounded suspiciously like a laugh. "No." He opened the door to let her out.

In their office, Timmins mimicked Jenny's failed flirtation attempt. "Are you sure you don't want to arrest me, officer?" Timmins asked, imitating Jenny's voice and doing a bad job of it.

"Knock it off."

"Jeez, you're moody this morning. And I thought your witness might have been your type."

"She's not."

"Yeah, maybe she's too kinky for you."

"You know what? That's kinda unpleasant, coming from you."

Timmins leaned back in his chair. "How's your investigation going so far?"

Thank God Timmins changed the subject. "I have to talk to Myrna to find out what she's discovered, but I'm interrogating the site supervisor at eleven thirty if you want to back me up again."

At the appointed time in the interrogation room, Mark wasn't much further ahead. Mr. Smith verified his assistants were with him when they escorted Mr. Ferguson around the premises. "Did anything seem out of place?" Mark asked him.

Mr. Smith shook his head. "Everyone had been doing a fantastic job, and all on time, too. I gotta say, I'm grateful for this team."

"What time did Mr. Ferguson leave?"

The supervisor pursed his lips. "Between five and five thirty."

So in between the time Mr. Ferguson left and saw the intruder, and Jenny discovering Mr. Ferguson's unconscious body, the gate would have been open. There was about an hour in that time frame where a suspect could have done some serious damage with the fuel canister. Mark wondered if the suspect even knew Mr. Ferguson was on the premises. What if beating up the bakery owner was better than burning down the building?

He jotted down his thoughts. "If you don't mind, Mr. Smith, let me do one more sweep of the building with you before you bring your employees back."

"Yeah, sure."

More than an hour later, Mark was satisfied there was nothing hidden around the construction site that could blow up. The supervisor had given his employees the day off as Mark had suggested. The police tape was still up, and one officer was on duty. After thanking Mr. Smith and watching him head to his car, Mark approached his colleague. "Hey," he called out, and showed his badge. "How's everything?"

"Quiet, which is how I like it. There were some kids hanging around when I came on duty, but they took off."

"I'm pretty sure we've collected all the evidence we

need." Mark looked around, thinking he'd need to reconfirm that with Myrna.

"I heard it was some big shot that got beat up. The guy
who owns those big-box bakery stores."

Mark nodded.

"Probably had it coming to him."

He frowned. "Why are you thinking that?"

The officer's eyes widened, and his face flushed red.
"Sorry, sir, that was out of line."

"Not from what I've heard." No one had anything good
to say about Edward Ferguson, and Mark now wondered
if there was more to this beating than the CEO was letting
on. "Tell me why you said that."

The officer shrugged. "My cousin worked for a well-
known chain in the Italian community out in the west end.
This guy bought the business and promised my cousin and
the other workers they'd have jobs when the changeover
was finished." He turned and spat onto the ground. "Lied
through his teeth."

That seemed to be a consistent trait of the conglomerate.
"I'm sorry about your cousin," Mark told him.

"It's okay. She found a job she really loves now." The
officer glanced up at the building. "I guess he's gonna try
and force out the couple of little businesses along this street.
What a douche."

Mark eyed the stores opposite him—a bank on the corner,
a variety store, a small grocer's and, at the far end, a bakery
painted bright pink with the word *Konditori* spelled out in
dark blue letters above the large window. Several customers waited outside to get in.

He decided to skip the bank and started with the variety
store, since it and the other stores faced the construction
site. An older gentleman sitting beside the front counter

barely spoke English, but after Mark pulled out his badge, the man yelled something, and a young woman appeared from the back of the store. A few questions came up empty.

He moved on to the grocer's, where several employees kept busy stocking produce. This time, he got some interesting information from another older gentleman, who spoke perfect English. "That Ferguson man, he tried to buy the stores on this side of the street," he said, his accent thick but understandable. "We all told him no and to get out."

Mark wrote that down. "He wasn't nice?"

"He has plenty of stores. Why does he want more? I told him to leave us alone and don't come back."

Mark pointed out the door. "But he bought property from someone across the street?"

The old man nodded. "Nice people. Butcher shop, fruit and vegetable grocery, and clothing store that also sold flowers. The grocery and butcher owners sold with no argument. But the lady who sold the clothes and flowers refused. Always busy. But I heard bad things happened to her."

He frowned. "What bad things?"

The man leaned forward, and his voice dropped. "Bad people destroyed her store, tore up the merchandise. Broke windows and painted awful words on the building. I'm sure it was Mr. Ferguson who did this. After two weeks, we found out the owner sold her store. That was late last year. She moved back home to Europe." He frowned. "Now all we see is Mighty Big Bakery. No one is happy."

Mark wandered down the street, thinking on what he'd heard. Ferguson had given the impression he'd do whatever it took to get what he wanted, yet somehow, he didn't get the stores on this side of the street first. He jotted that down, intending to question the CEO about it.

The last store, called Konditori, was a quirky-looking

bakery. Inside, the space was well lit and bright. Pale gray walls were the perfect background for the colorful wall art. Tables and chairs made of thick white oak were set up neatly to one side, while a tall bookcase covered half a wall at the opposite end.

Two employees—a man and a woman—were behind the long counter, taking orders and moving around each other with a practiced ease born of experience.

"Welcome to Konditori," the man greeted him with a wide smile. "How can I help you today?"

Mark couldn't resist—the smell of fresh-baked goods surrounded him, making his mouth water. He selected a pastry and a large coffee. "I wanted to ask if the owner was here," he said as he paid for his meal.

"Sure is. She's in the back office."

"Could you let her know that Detective Mark Hawthorne is here? Just wanted to ask if she knows anything about what happened across the street last night."

"You bet. Give me a couple of minutes."

"Thanks." He took his snack to a table nearest the front window. The day was turning out cloudy and gray, and as he watched, the sidewalk glistened from a light sprinkle of rain that sprang up out of nowhere.

From his seat, he had a clear view of the half-constructed Mighty Big Bakery. At this angle, he noticed how large the building was, about a half block in length. When it was completed, it would overshadow the stores on this side. Hopefully, the store owners had a plan for that.

Mark heard a gasp behind him, and when he turned around in his seat…

Oh my God, it's her.

Her golden presence slammed hard into his chest—he was glad he was sitting down. Her thick blond hair was braided today and hung over her shoulder. Instead of the casual look from last night, today she wore wide-legged pants and a loose blouse. But he only noticed these things because he was trained for that.

What held him in his chair was her eyes, so green he imagined that he was swimming in them. The ocean off the British Columbia coast had nothing on this woman's gaze. Sparkling, bright, its depths a tantalizing mystery.

Her eyes were wide with surprise, and while he didn't dare to guess, Mark hoped her thoughts were in sync with his.

The temptation to just sit and look at her was overwhelming. But he finally remembered to get his bearings and scrambled out of his seat. "Hello," he managed to say in a normal voice, although there was nothing normal about seeing her again—someone was smiling down on him today.

She blinked several times, as if refocusing. "Good afternoon."

Her voice only enhanced her beauty. Smooth and low-pitched, it had a European accent that gave her voice a musical lilt. Although it could also be her luscious full lips that made her voice sound so delectable.

Crap, don't stand here staring at her like a drooling twit. Inhaling a deep breath, he held out his hand. "Detective Mark Hawthorne. Thank you for seeing me."

Her handshake was firm and warm. "Britt Gronlund."

He pulled out a chair for her. "Please join me."

As she sat down, her hair brushed against his hand. It was silky soft, almost a caress, and his body tingled with heightened awareness. He took another deep breath to calm himself before sitting down across from her.

But looking at Ms. Gronlund this close increased his urge

to talk to her about everything else except work. *One day.* Mark paused, surprised at the unexpected thought.

"I suspect you're here to talk to me about Edward Ferguson?" she asked.

"Yes, that's right." He pulled out his work phone, hit Record and placed it on the table between them. "This saves a trip to the police station," he explained when she glanced down at it.

"Makes sense."

Mark deliberately sipped his coffee, allowing him a few moments to figure out how to start. Her comments had been short and to the point, which wasn't a problem. However, to own a bright, cheery bakery like Konditori, with friendly staff and customers who seemed to know each other, Ms. Gronlund's mannerisms seemed off-balance. Maybe she was nervous.

He held up his cup. "This coffee is amazing. I think I'm wired for the rest of the day."

She smiled, but it didn't quite reach her eyes. "Thank you. It's a special coffee roast I get from my supplier in Ethiopia."

"And the Danish? Was it made fresh this morning?"

Her eyes widened in shock. "How did you know?"

"My family had friends who owned a bakery in British Columbia, and I could guess when they had freshly baked goods ready." He pointed to the store name located above the cashier. "What does Konditori mean?"

She glanced over her shoulder. "It's Norwegian for cake shop."

"I like that. It feels authentic."

She was starting to look more relaxed. "It reminds me of home."

He nodded, then looked around the bakery. There was still a lineup, although he knew at least a dozen people had come and gone. "Is it always this busy?" he asked. "It's what, about two o'clock now? I've never been to a bakery that had so many people in it."

This time, her smile lit up her face. "It's always busy, but especially on the weekends. Customers like to pick up dessert for their weekend events. It makes the days go by faster."

Mark wasn't sure how to take her comment. Did she want her days to fly by because she had nothing else to do? "Sounds like my schedule, sometimes."

She raised an eyebrow at that.

"Speaking of schedules, I don't want to take up too much of your time, Ms. Gronlund. Can you give me a rundown of what you did on Friday?"

Mark loved listening to her voice. She was methodical and precise, describing everything until she reached the evening.

"After I left the bank, the police had stopped pedestrians from entering the street. They mentioned there was a police investigation. A lot of people took alternate routes, but I decided to wait. It gave me a chance to catch up on work emails."

He watched her face, wondering what she would say next. "And when the street reopened?"

"I hurried back to the store, as we were closing in thirty minutes. I'm very strict on that. My employees' well-being comes first, and I wanted them to enjoy their Friday night."

Ms. Gronlund lowered her gaze, as if thinking. But then she slowly propped her elbows on the table, linked her fingers together and rested her chin on her hands. When she looked up, her eyes had darkened. "Then I saw you."

THERE WERE NO words to describe the strange vibrating pulse that coursed through her body when she saw him.

Britt half suspected that the police would pay a visit to see if she knew anything about what happened Friday night. When Oliver had told her a Detective Hawthorne was here to talk to her, she'd been ready.

She'd stepped out of her office, then slowed to a complete stop. The detective was half turned while looking out the window, and she had a clear view of his profile. A strong square jaw, straight nose and a muscular neck swept up from the collar of his shirt. His hands and manicured fingers were agile as he fiddled with the mug. And despite the looser cut of the shirt, Britt caught glimpses of well-defined muscle beneath the material as he moved.

Her hand came up to her chest, and she released a sigh that was louder than intended. He turned around, no doubt hearing her, then held still.

And Britt experienced the same damn uncontrollable emotions that hit her last night.

When he stood, she almost had to take a step back. There was something about him that demanded respect, but it wasn't threatening, a trait that made her want to know more about him. In retrospect, Britt thought it was his eyes. They were a warm brown with flecks of gold, and she wondered if they changed color depending on his mood. And his voice... deep with a hint of roughness. She could spend all day listening to him recite a damn dictionary.

That in itself excited and scared her at the same time.

Detective Hawthorne had asked for a summary of her Friday activities, which didn't take long to discuss. However, she was more interested in talking about another topic. "Were you at the crime scene last night?" she asked.

"I was." He turned off his phone and stuck it into his pants pocket.

"Do you think it'll be a complicated case?" Britt knew

He started to organize his information, moving the pieces around until they resembled a timeline. Mr. Ferguson's and Ms. Gronlund's statements were still on his work phone, and Mark tapped the necessary buttons to transfer them to his computer.

"Hey there." Myrna walked through the open door, her arms laden with several folders and her laptop.

"Hi." He watched as she dumped her stuff on the small meeting table. "How late were you here last night?"

"Oh, until about two in the morning."

"Myrna, you didn't have to do that."

"I know, but I wanted to because I knew it would be quiet. Besides," she added as she opened her laptop, "this case is a big one. You and I need to get a decent report together to present to Captain Fraust first thing Monday morning."

Mark groaned. "I'm surprised she hasn't called me yet."

"Be careful what you wish for, Hawthorne."

He sat opposite her. "We can cross-reference with my evidence," he told her, pointing to his desk. "But I want to find out what you've got first."

She tapped a few keys. "So the blood and hair in the area all belonged to Mr. Ferguson, along with the footprints that led from the site's entrance to that particular spot. I managed to lift the suspect's fingerprints from the fuel canister and the piece of wood used as the weapon. But when I ran the prints through the database, I didn't get any hits. The canister is a common brand sold at Canadian Tire stores—it'll be hard to track down the location that sold it."

"Guess I can't be surprised at that." Mark leaned forward. "What about the sneaker prints?"

"Ah yes, you hit the bell on those. The majority of this brand's shoes have the recognizable circular pattern on their sole, with the logo located in the middle. This one, however, is different." Myrna turned her laptop so that he could look at the screen. "The distinctive logo is at the top of the sole this time. There's another symbol under the heel of the shoe."

"Yeah, I know this edition. There was a stink a few years ago about that symbol. It resembled an Arabic word."

"And as a result, the company had to stop selling that particular shoe, but not before the initial 225 pairs were sold in Toronto."

Mark knew his brow went up in disbelief.

Myrna nodded. "That's it. We can get a list of buyers."

"That's it? Myrna, that's a lot of customers to get through." Mark envisioned the amount of time and manpower involved in that task. "What if the suspect sold off his shoes?"

"Do you really think that? Those shoes are worth a lot of money, especially after that debacle. I don't think he'd sell them."

"So you know they're men's shoes. Good work."

"Not only that, but we won't have to go through the full customer list." She tapped a couple of keys. "Take a look at that."

He stared at a photo with two different-sized prints. "We're looking for two suspects?" he asked.

"No. These were the only prints in the immediate area."

He thought hard, wondering what the investigator was trying to show him. He pursed his lips and shook his head. "You've lost me."

Myrna grinned. "Our suspect's feet are two different sizes."

The stroke of luck that Myrna provided him had Mark feeling they would be close to nailing the bastard. "What size are we looking for?"

"That's even better. According to my measurements, he's wearing a size 14 on his right foot, and a size 12 on his left. Average height would range from five foot ten inches to six foot three inches."

So a man wearing two different-sized shoes of a limited edition. How much luckier could they get? "Myrna, I could kiss you."

"Now, now. No office hanky-panky, please." Her grin was contagious.

HE PARKED HIS car at a lot within the Queen and Yonge Street area, then waited for a westbound streetcar. Checking his searches on his phone, he found most of the hip sneaker stores were in the west end, within a five-mile radius. He could easily walk to about half of them.

The first store was the top hit on his list. A three-story black building, it had a mural consisting of several Toronto Raptors players.

Inside, the white shelves and walls were a perfect backdrop for the sneakers that came in every color. The floor was an ingenious idea—skateboards were displayed beneath a thick plexiglass cover. *Look, but don't touch.*

In the middle of the space were floating glass displays of rare sneakers, caps and T-shirts from some of the most famous brands out there. A security guard stood at the front door, carefully watching everyone.

Mark headed toward the back, where a cashier was ringing through a purchase. As he waited, he checked out the prices on a couple of interesting pairs. "Holy hell," he whispered, and glanced at some of the others. The average price was five hundred dollars and up. It wasn't that he couldn't afford a pair, but he didn't think he'd wear them outside.

When the cashier had finished, he approached her. "Good

afternoon," he said, then showed her his badge. "Detective Mark Hawthorne with York Regional Police 4 District in Vaughan."

The woman, in her twenties, with thick black hair tied up in a bun and bright brown eyes, frowned. "I was told the theft from a couple of weeks ago had been resolved."

"No, this isn't about that." He pulled out the picture of the footprints from the crime scene. "Someone was assaulted, and I recognized these prints from a limited edition that got backlash because the symbol resembled a holy Arabic word."

"Yeah, I heard about that. It was before I started working here." She leaned forward. "You're looking for a guy who owns these?"

"Yes, and in particular, the person who bought a size 14 right foot and size 12 left."

"Wow, different foot sizes. I've heard of that, too, but it's rare. Give me a second."

He waited as she typed, but in a few minutes, she shook her head. "We don't have a sale like that in our records," she told him. "I'm not too surprised, either."

"Why is that?" Mark noticed a waiting customer out of the corner of his eye.

"With limited editions, we want to sell the matching pair, especially as they're collectible items." She tugged on her earlobe. "There are other stores in the area. Do you want me to find out anything for you?"

"No, thank you. I'm going to visit each one until I find my answer. Thanks for your help."

"Good luck."

Well, that was a strike. He crossed the store off his list. But the cashier made an interesting comment. Selling matched pairs of sneakers made sense if a collector hoped to eventually sell them to another interested buyer. What if there were *two* customers with different-sized feet? Was it possible one store might have sold a set to the suspect, knowing the second set would be bought by someone else? It was one hell of a long shot.

The next three stores on his list were within a two-block radius, and didn't give him any results. When Mark walked into the fifth one, however, he was impressed. It was larger, with more stock, and emitted a cozier, warmer atmosphere. He could see why this store was in his top five results when he had searched for cool sneaker shops. There were two security guards this time—one each at the front and back of the store—and it was even busier.

The young man behind the cash register was on the phone, and as Mark waited, he noticed something that offered promise—this particular store had four locations, and the pictures displayed behind the cashier were famous basketball, football and baseball players.

"Hey," the young man greeted him after he hung up the phone. "How can I help you today?"

Mark showed him his badge. "I'm looking for a customer who bought a pair of limited-edition sneakers from a few years ago, featuring a symbol that was offensive to a religious group." He mentioned the brand.

"Yeah, we had those." The cashier hit some keys on his computer. "I've got the list pulled up. There were only about fifteen sneaker stores that got these, all in the downtown core. Each store got fifteen pairs."

"The customer I'm looking for had different-sized feet. Right foot is a 14, the left a 12."

The man's gaze traveled down the computer screen. "Oh yeah, I know the dude. The only reason we offered to sell them that way is because we have a customer in Abu Dhabi who bought the other set."

Mark couldn't believe his luck. "Can you provide me his name, address and phone number?"

"Sure, let me print that out for you."

Several minutes later, he stood outside, looking at the sheet of paper. Henry Toussaint. His address wasn't far from Britt's bakery and Mr. Ferguson's building site.

The streetcar ride back to the parking lot took longer because of traffic and road construction, and he chafed at the delay. He finally got to his car and drove to Toussaint's address. Mark wanted to check out the house and neighborhood first before charging in with a team. He knew he had struck pay dirt finding the shoe owner so quickly, and he couldn't afford to mess it up by going in half-cocked.

About thirty minutes later, Mark cruised along Sierra Court. The houses were two-storied, with wide, deep lots and mature trees. Every house had at least two cars parked in the driveway. Nearby was a school and day care center, and as he continued driving, he noticed that the houses got bigger. The street ended in a cul-de-sac, and he turned around, continuing to mentally record the area while wondering how the hell he was going to arrest Toussaint without causing too much of a scene.

It made sense the suspect could afford those sneakers. This neighborhood was upper middle class, if not higher.

Henry Toussaint's house sat just south of Lomond Avenue, and Mark slowed his car down to get a good look. Deep driveway—it could easily hold eight cars. Large two-story home, big front yard, several trees and a nice landscaped area filled with flowers. He could just see the security cameras, one over the front door and another covering the double garage. He was sure the backyard would be even bigger.

Mark decided to drive around the neighborhood, as he'd never been up here before. It was large, with Cunningham Pond and a park and play area beside it. Traveling north, he discovered another park, a huge spot with an off-leash area, with dogs barking and running in all directions. Behind it, a kiddie splash pad and a large stage made up the center of the park. It was certainly family friendly. Maybe he'd bring Mom up here once she was out of the hospital, to give her a new place to check out.

At the precinct, Mark turned to the computer to see what information he could dig up on Toussaint. There wasn't much—former soccer player for the Toronto team but had to retire due to an injury. There was some noise about offering him an assistant coach position, but as Mark read through the sport articles, he couldn't find anything else. He added these findings to his ever-growing folder and sat back in his chair, thinking. If he could get his hands on Toussaint tomorrow, he felt sure he could wrap things up by Monday night. However, there was something about Mr. Ferguson that nagged at him. He just wasn't sure what it was. Maybe paying the CEO an unannounced visit tomorrow morning would catch him off guard.

Mark liked that idea. He scheduled the two items into his work phone, alongside a visit to his mom in the hospital.

Suddenly, his personal phone pinged with a text. When he retrieved it and read the message, he smiled—his Saturday night just got a whole lot better.

Hello, Mr. Detective, I wondered if you'd like to solve the case of finding a good meal? It has to be within a five-block radius of Konditori, fast and most important, tasty. Are you up for the challenge?-The Nordic Princess

P.S. I close up shop in forty minutes, just to give you added incentive.

BRITT SAT IN her office, sipping a cup of tea as she reviewed emails. Today's order for an afternoon party had been a hit with the guests, judging by the three very happy messages from her repeat customer. Jacques and Thomas had Sunday's order well underway, with Betty, her full-time weekday employee, coming in to help them. Jacques had mentioned Betty possessed the instincts of a natural baker and wanted to foster that, to which Britt agreed. She wanted her employees to be happy, with ambitions to do what she and Jacques had accomplished. Nurturing dreams had become a mantra for her.

Her cell phone pinged. When she glanced at the message, a little thrill of excitement zipped through her.

Evening, vakker, mystery solved. I'll report to you in fifteen minutes.-Mr. Detective

Wait a minute. Britt read the message again, focusing on one particular word. *Vakker?* That was the Norwegian word for *beautiful.* Did he really just call her that?

Oh, Detective Hawthorne was really stepping up his game.

She shut down her laptop, stuffed it into her tote and headed into the store. "I'm going to start closing up," she announced to a few remaining customers who stood in line, and her weekend staff, Jasmine and Oliver. "Oliver, can you stand at the front door to let the customers out? I'm going to get the lights." Britt had learned the hard way that leaving the lights on was like a beacon. It was fantastic being so popular, but it had its annoying moments, too.

With the last customer finally gone, she and her staff cleaned up, pulled down the blinds at the front window and got everything ready for tomorrow. "Thanks, you two," Britt told them. "I'll see you tomorrow at ten."

In the kitchen, Jacques and his team were working steadily. "Are you sure there's nothing I can help you with?" she asked, looking around. It seemed chaotic, but her head baker had a method to his madness.

"Don't worry, *chérie*, we'll be fine. Another hour, ninety minutes tops."

"All right." Jacques knew she worried about her staff. "I'm heading out the front door tonight. I'm meeting someone. I'll see you all tomorrow. And don't forget to set the security alarm."

Betty picked up a large piece of dough and moved as if to throw it at her. "Would you get going already?" she demanded, laughing.

As Britt walked back to her office, she noticed a figure standing at the door and went to see who it was. Detective Hawthorne was waiting. She unlocked the door. "Hours are ten to five on the weekends," she quipped.

He kept a serious expression. "I was told there was a damsel in distress at this address. Said she would die from starvation if I didn't save her."

Britt's laugh turned into an undignified snort. "Oh my God, look at what you made me do!" She hadn't laughed that hard in months.

His grin was wide. "Are you ready to go?"

"Let me get my purse." She let him inside, then ran back to the office to collect her stuff.

"Soo, what is tonight's mystery, detective?" she asked as she bolted the door behind her.

"About two blocks west and one street south. And the name's Mark. Only my mom loves calling me detective every chance she gets." He rolled his eyes.

"How sweet! I go by Britt, but I don't mind being called Nordic princess if the mood hits you." Man, that was a bold statement, even for her.

His smile looked sweet, almost shy. "Would you like to walk? If not, I brought my car..."

"No, walking's fine. It's nice to get outside."

They strolled toward the stoplight. "How was your day?" he asked.

Britt sighed. "Busy, as always."

"That's a good thing, right?"

"It is. I can't complain. And I have great staff, too. I wouldn't have gotten this far without them."

At the red light, Mark turned toward her. "It's rare to hear an owner compliment their staff like that. You have a kind heart."

This close, Britt noticed the dark stubble on his face and fought the urge to touch it. "Thank you."

People had started to cross when the light changed, but he held her gaze for a moment longer before following the crowd. She kept pace, her mind a whirlwind of untapped feelings.

The Korean restaurant Mark had chosen was small and brightly lit, with wide open doors letting in the evening's cool air. Several voices chattered loudly as Mark stepped aside to let her in first.

"Welcome!" a young man called out. "Please have a seat."

Britt stopped for a minute to look around. She'd never eaten Korean food before, but the smells were delicious.

He stood beside her and touched her back. "Let's sit near a window," he said into her ear.

She eased into a bright red wooden chair and plopped her tote on the table to one side. "I have no idea what to eat," she told him. "You've taken this mystery to a whole new level."

He inclined his head. "I aim to please."

That comment could be taken in so many ways, and she chided herself for going down a dirty-minded route. Although, looking at Mark, could she blame herself?

A waitress came over and handed them menus. Britt looked at the pictures and brief descriptions for each meal, unsure.

"Most of the food I've tried so far has a bit of a spicy kick to it." Mark leaned in close and pointed at a couple of items. "Since you haven't had Korean food before, let's stick with something less intense. Bibimbap is rice, mixed veggies, beef and an egg on top. They add chili paste for seasoning, but it's on the side. I like the *japchae*, that's glass noodles, vegetables and pork sautéed in soy sauce."

"That sounds great."

He placed the order, and she listened in wonder as he spoke a few words in Korean. "Do you know the language?"

He laughed. "No, just some words and a few simple phrases."

She was still impressed. "But you made an effort to learn, which says a lot." She wondered what else he could surprise her with. "How was your day at work?" Britt asked.

"Tiring… A lot of footwork today."

"Are you still trying to figure out what happened to Mr. Ferguson?" She bit her lip, nervous. "Sorry, I wasn't sure if that was classified…"

"It is, in a way. I can't discuss active investigations."

She nodded. "Gotcha. The mystery thickens."

He smiled at that. Britt noticed the dimple in his left cheek, which made his handsome face even more so.

Before she managed to say something embarrassing, their dinner arrived, along with a teapot and two small bowls. Britt admired her meal while Mark poured the tea. "This looks delicious," she murmured, then looked at his. "Those are noodles?" she asked, staring at them. "How are they so translucent?"

"I just know they're made from starch, like potatoes or beans."

"Oh, I see." Her cooking hat came on. "And probably mixed with water, then shaped into the noodles."

They ate in silence. Britt had used chopsticks when eating Japanese food, so she had no problem. Mark showed her how to mix the egg into the meal before taking her first bite. "Oh my God, this is so good," she exclaimed, talking around a mouthful of food. "How did you find this place?"

"During one of my investigations. There was an assault in the neighborhood. A respected elder got beaten up by a pair of teenagers who stole his money. Found them hiding in here, holding the owner as a hostage."

"Holy crap, they were armed?" This sounded like a thriller novel.

"No, but every kitchen utensil known to man was back there. I couldn't take a chance they'd use a knife."

"What did you do?"

He scooped some *japchae* into his mouth and chewed for a moment. "Basically, I told them don't make it worse. I had a neighbor translate my commands until they finally came out." He frowned. "The old man needed to go to the hospital for treatment. He didn't want to press charges, but I told him if you expect them to learn their lesson, they needed to go through the procedures." Mark's expression was sinister. "I had them locked up overnight and told them every possible thing that could happen. Next day, they were very apologetic. Last I heard from the waitress here, they were doing volunteer work for seniors and the homeless."

"So you had a positive influence on them. I like that."

All too soon, dinner was over, but Britt knew it would be another long, busy day tomorrow. "Thank you for dinner," she said as they made their way back.

"Thank you for inviting me. I loved your text."

She giggled. "Your mission, if you choose to accept it," she replied in a robotic voice, which had Mark laughing out loud.

He had parked his car close to Mighty Big Bakery. "Could I give you a ride home?" he asked quietly.

"Thank you." When she slipped into the passenger seat, Britt glanced up at the construction site, a stark building against the bright security lights. "Mark, I need to tell you something." Listening to him tonight, she knew she had to let him know about her first encounter with Mr. Ferguson.

He turned the car light on. "What is it?"

She felt foolish for not saying something during her interview, but her mind had been on Mark. "Mr. Ferguson tried to buy my bakery."

He nodded. "I'm not surprised. When I talked to the other store owners on your street, they said the same thing." He frowned. "Did he threaten you?"

The question stirred up ugly memories she'd rather forget. "My neighbors and I got a peace bond against him. He wasn't allowed to come within one hundred feet of our stores."

His expression hadn't changed. Britt felt sure Mark picked up on what she didn't say, but didn't push it. "Seriously? That's some accomplishment." He got the car started. "Where to?"

She gave him the address, then eased back into her seat, watching the city lights pass by in their multitude of colors. Tonight had been the first night in a long time that she'd gone on a date, but it felt different with Mark. They had immediately clicked, like two pieces of a puzzle that fit, and she bit the inside of her cheek, pondering that thought.

The drive was short, surrounded by a comfortable silence until he reached her condo. "I had a really good time tonight," he told her as they walked to the front door.

"So did I. Are you up for doing it again?"

"Definitely." His voice had grown deeper. "Just say the word."

Britt suddenly remembered. "I need to know something. In your text, you called me *vakker*. Do you know what that means?"

"Yes." He stepped close, and she could smell the cologne she hadn't noticed at all until now. "And it's so goddamn true."

His eyes reflected her own emotions—how a chance meeting evolved into the possibility of something they'd both been looking for.

He caressed her chin with a finger, and on a sigh, Britt touched her lips to his, tasting their texture and warmth.

Mark muttered under his breath, and she gasped as his arms wrapped around her. He tasted of hopes and promises, of a future that didn't feel so lonely anymore.

Chapter Four

Mark parked the car in front of Mackenzie Richmond Hill Hospital the next morning, knowing his mom was expecting him. He loved spending time with her, just not under these circumstances.

On the eighth floor, he turned left, then right, walking down a long hallway. He heard two voices laughing before reaching the nurses station.

"Mark!" Evelyn was a slim and fit woman in her forties. She'd been a nurse for close to twenty years. "How are you? How's your weekend been so far?"

He shrugged. "I'm on weekend shift and I have a case."

"Well, damn." She propped her hands on her hips. "I hope you get that solved soon. Come on, your mom just finished breakfast."

Evelyn sang a tune under her breath as she led the way, her voice enriched with a Barbados accent. Mark had immediately connected with her when they first met, and he was glad Evelyn had made herself the primary caregiver for his mother.

She swung open the door. "Ms. Hawthorne, I have a visitor for you."

Mom turned away from the television tuned to a talk show. "Mark! Sweetie, I'm so glad to see you."

"That makes two of us." He thanked Evelyn and grabbed a chair to sit beside his mother's bed. "How are you doing today?"

"A lot better. The doctor said I could go home in about a week."

Mark grasped her hand and squeezed it. "That's great. You've always been a strong woman. It's one of the things I admire about you."

She smiled. "I've got you to thank for that. I had to keep you out of trouble."

He laughed. "You know I wouldn't risk my ass by hanging out with the wrong crowd. I was more scared of you."

"Got that right." She smoothed her hand over the bedsheet. "I'm glad you came by," she said quietly. "I'd love to see you more often, but I know you have your own life to live. And the detective work must keep you on your toes."

"It does, actually." He sighed.

"Are you working on a case?"

Mom was a puzzle-solver. She loved mysteries and putting the pieces together. Occasionally, he'd tell her about one of his investigations—leaving out names and certain information—and she would give him ideas that he never would have thought of. Some of her suggestions had panned out in the five years he'd worked at the precinct. "A man got beaten up pretty badly on a construction site this past Friday."

"Edward Ferguson? It was on the news." She made a face. "Asshole."

"Mom?" He sat back, surprised. "Do you know him?"

"I know of him. Owns Mighty Big Bakery. Odd name for a business." She snickered. "Maybe it's big to compensate for his small…ahem. You know what I mean."

Mark sat in shock for all of two seconds before he lost

it in a fit of laughter. "Did you just say that?" he asked between gasps.

She shrugged. "It's an ego thing, isn't it? He's a bully, too, from what I've heard."

"A lot of people are saying that." It seemed to be the CEO's reputation.

"Do you remember that little pastry shop we used to go to on Sundays?" Mom asked. "The French one where you liked the owner's daughter, but she ran away every time she saw you?"

He shook his head. Mom remembered the weirdest things. "They made the best chocolate croissants."

"That store was in the family for generations. Suzie, the girl you liked? She took over and ran it for several years."

He frowned, suspecting where this was leading. "Mr. Ferguson bought her out?"

"Mr. Ferguson threatened her—I was there when he showed up." She shuddered. "It was awful. I found out from Suzie he had bought the two properties next door to her and wanted her building, too. She told him where to stick it, and in French, too.

"Next thing I knew, I heard on the news that her store had been broken into several times that month. They trashed her equipment, broke things, spray-painted awful words…" Mom stopped to compose herself. "Suzie had no choice but to sell. She and I always suspected Mr. Ferguson had set up the vandalism, but we couldn't prove it."

Mark nodded. He wouldn't put it past Ferguson to do something like that. "I hope Suzie got a lot of money out of it."

"She definitely did. Enough to decide to move back to France and take her parents with her. They're living in a lovely village called Amiens."

Mom also had a knack for getting along with people. *When you're nice to them, they're nice to you* was her motto, and it worked every single time. "I'm glad to hear she's well," he stated. He squeezed her hand again. "Speaking of chocolate croissants, do you want me to sneak one in for you?"

Her brown eyes widened in surprise. "Have you found a bakery that would pass even my scrutiny?"

"I have. An amazing little place called Konditori. It's a Norwegian bakery. Best Danish and coffee I've ever had."

"That's amazing. Will you bring me something tomorrow?" Mom paused. "Only if you have the time."

"I'll make it work, don't worry."

"Wonderful!" She clapped her hands. "Let's hope that Ferguson man never discovers this bakery."

It was too late for that, but Mark didn't want to spoil the visit by telling her.

He chatted with Mom for about another hour and let himself be smothered with her hugs and kisses before heading out. At the nurses station, he waited until Evelyn finished her phone call. "Has Mom had visitors?" he asked.

She shook her head. "The nurses know to call me as soon as someone asks about your mom. Your father's photo is front and center on the bulletin board over there." She pointed at a large corkboard, and he sucked in a breath, staring at Dad's scowling expression. "Everyone knows they're supposed to call Security. One of my nurses knows self-defense. I've seen her in action at one of her competitions and I would not want to meet her in a well-lit alley. I also suspect a couple of the ladies have something in their bags, but…" She stopped.

"Let's just hope it doesn't come to that. Thank you for looking after her."

As he drove home, he thought about how his mom had ended up in the hospital—a freak accident, she said. She'd fallen down the stairs at home, broken her right leg and fractured her hip. She had managed to drag herself to the phone and call him, and he had summoned every emergency vehicle as he raced to her house, praying she hadn't passed out because she wasn't answering his frantic shouts. When he'd arrived, the police and ambulance were already there, her front door busted open, and Mom carefully strapped to the stretcher.

"She'll be okay," an ambulance attendant had told him while he fought back his tears and silently prayed for her to open her eyes. "She's unconscious but breathing normally. We're headed to Mackenzie Richmond Hill Hospital and immediately into surgery."

He had nodded, too stunned to speak. As everyone started to pack up and leave, Mark had a disturbing thought. "You two," he called out to the remaining officers on the scene. "I want to run a standard check through the house, make sure everything's as it should be."

They had stood guard at the front door while Mark looked around for…something. Mom wasn't the kind of person to just fall down the stairs—she was usually so sure-footed. While nothing seemed out of place, he'd called the best forensics investigator to beg for her help.

Cynthia Cornwall had been there in record time, and less than two hours later had the fingerprints in her lab. What she'd told him was disturbing.

His father had been in Mom's house, and more than once, if the amount of fingerprints Cynthia had found was correct—and she was almost never wrong. But was he there because Mom had invited him? Or had he decided to ignore the restraining order and sneak in when she wasn't around?

Mark had a lot of questions. But so far, his father hadn't been found, and his subtle inquiries with Mom resulted in her adamant replies that she'd had an accident, end of story.

"WELL, CHÉRIE, YOUR NEW, esteemed customer was more than thrilled to see us today, I think."

Britt nodded, her excitement so strong she almost squealed with glee. She had been starstruck when they arrived at the rap artist's mansion in the Bridle Path. "Can you believe he saw the lineup at the bakery one morning and sent his housekeeper to investigate?" She laughed at the image in her head—a middle-aged woman snooping around the store, asking customers questions and sitting in a corner, taking in everything. She could have worn a trench coat and fedora, and Britt wouldn't have noticed. "I guess he gave us a thumbs-up."

"But of course he did!" Jacques drove the company van around the block to get to their parking spot behind the store. "Why would you think otherwise?"

He was right, of course. Britt had a bad habit of not giving herself credit. In fact, she was her own worst critic. "Thanks for coming with me to help set up."

"*Avec plaisir*, with pleasure. Sometimes, it is good to get out of the kitchen."

He parked the van, and Britt stepped out, her mind on what to grab out of the back.

"I'll take care of the bags, Britt. Go inside and see how everyone is doing."

"Thanks, Jacques." He knew her mind was constantly on the bakery—that was one of the many things she had learned on her journey to becoming an entrepreneur. Her business absorbed almost all her waking moments, and she was constantly planning ways to stay one step ahead of her competitors. Moments of pure luck, such as attracting the rap singer's attention, helped, but it was increasing her steady stream of regulars that brought the money in, paid her staff well and kept her reputation in good standing.

She entered the store through the back and made her way to her small office located opposite the display counter and cash register. As she walked through the kitchen door, Britt was surprised at how many customers were inside. Jasmine and Oliver seemed to be keeping things moving, but she'd get out there and help as soon as she checked a few things.

Their website had been busy, too—orders were coming in for the next few weeks. Summer was their busiest time, but Britt refused to extend the store hours. She couldn't afford another full-time person yet, and Jacques and Thomas could only do so much, even with Betty's help. She had to think of their well-being, and not allow her staff to overextend themselves.

Right, better get out there.

She was greeted by enthusiastic people who sang praises about her bakery, the food and her staff. She grew embarrassed from all the attention and soon hid behind the counter, helping with orders and ringing up sales. At one point, she headed back to the kitchen, where Jacques was moving almost too fast for the eye to follow. Thomas was at the sink, chugging back a large glass of water. "How's everything back here, Jacques?"

He turned and gave her the okay signal with thumb and forefinger. "Thomas did a fantastic job with the prepping. We'll have more pastries in thirty minutes."

"Thank you." She smiled at Thomas, who had hurried back to his station. "Both of you."

She couldn't be happier with her little team, and especially Jacques—she'd really lucked out when she hired him.

The head baker brought out a tray of cinnamon rolls while Thomas carried one filled with Danishes, and a cheer went up from the crowd. She stayed out of the way as the chefs slid the desserts into the display case with ease before hustling back to the kitchen.

That was when she spied Mark standing by the window. He had a small paper bag with handles in one hand and a large takeout cup of coffee in the other, which he saluted her with. Smiling, she wove her way through a sea of people until she got to his side and wasn't ready when he suddenly kissed her full on the lips. She raised her hand to her mouth, surprised.

"It's more fun than just saying hi." His mouth curled up in a shy smile.

Damn it, how could Mark be so…well, damn cute?

He looked around the store in awe. "Do you play linebacker every time this happens?" he asked.

Britt leaned against the wall beside him. It had only been a couple of hours since arriving at the store this morning. She knew it would be busy, but this… "Pretty much. Usually it's more organized than this. I suspect we had more new customers today walking in off the street. My regulars aren't this rowdy."

"All of you handle it like professionals." He moved close enough that Britt felt the warmth from his body. He was a dangerous distraction, and if she wasn't careful, Britt could easily fall under his spell.

That was a sobering thought.

She tilted her chin at the bag. "Did you get what you wanted?"

Mark nodded. "I waited until there was a bit of a lull, then dived in. My mom wants to try your chocolate croissants."

"Oh, I hope she likes them."

"I would have brought her, but…" His expression clouded over. "She's in the hospital."

"Damn, Mark, I'm sorry. Is she okay?"

"Her doctor said another week to ten days. She's getting better, though, thank you for asking."

"Of course." Britt knew the importance of family. Her parents and younger sister still lived in Norway, and she missed them. "Did you want any other pastries? I can get something else for her to try. A cinnamon bun, maybe?"

"I'm good." He shook his bag. "But thank you." He sipped his coffee, but Britt noticed his eyebrows drawn into a frown as he looked across the tide of customers. "Oh, I wanted to tell you." He leaned in close. "I heard some customers chatting among themselves. It seems that there's some kind of event on social media to boycott Mighty Big Bakery."

She frowned. One thing Britt kept abreast of was news on the competition. Britt had nothing against another bakery opening nearby. No two stores were exactly the same, and in her studies, she found that customers in smaller neighborhoods loved the variety. But as for Mr. Ferguson's behemoth of a bakery… "I hadn't heard about that."

"I get the feeling people are upset that a Mighty Big Bakery is opening almost across the street from you, and someone did take their anger out on Mr. Ferguson, so…" He shrugged.

"Seems almost inevitable, don't you think?" Britt didn't condone violence of any kind, but she did believe in karma. "He must have known that his…less-than-desirable business tactics would get him into trouble."

"Justifying the assault doesn't make it right, though."

Britt decided to tell Mark the story behind her peace bond. "When I decided to lease this property, there were no other bakeries in the area. It was a prime spot—lots of foot traffic, nearby neighborhoods, other stores. Mr. Ferguson's construction site was originally a fruit and vegetable store, a butcher shop, and a clothing store that also sold flowers." Her hands clenched in frustration. "Those stores had been here for close to forty years, and Ferguson bullied them into selling out."

"How did he do that?"

Britt closed her eyes. That incident had been nine months ago, but it felt like only yesterday. "I had arrived earlier than usual one day to get started on an order. Jacques was already waiting at the front door. He said he saw three teenagers come out of the butcher shop carrying baseball bats. The grocery store had already been vandalized the week before, but no one saw anything. He managed to get pictures of the kids and turned them in to the police."

He nodded slowly. "I think I remember that. It caught our attention because the boys confessed some rich man had paid them a lot of money to wreck those stores."

"It didn't matter, did it?" Britt felt the anger bloom within her body. "Those teenagers were only issued a fine and released to their parents. As for Mr. Ferguson, the police couldn't track the payment back to him.

"In the end, he got what he wanted. He paid the owners of those stores enough money for them to retire comfortably." Britt blew out a loud sigh. "A lot of the neighbors, including myself, hoped the owners wouldn't sell, but in the end, I couldn't blame them. They were older and their kids weren't interested in taking over. It just feels…" She stopped, thinking of her own situation.

"Like they gave up?"

She looked at Mark, his gaze observant. "It sounds harsh, doesn't it?"

"In the end, it was their choice."

She bit her lip. Mark's conclusion made sense, of course. Every businessperson that came into contact with Mr. Ferguson made their choices, whether they were bullied or not. She'd made hers. "I should tell you that he came after me, too."

Something changed in Mark's demeanor. Britt saw the tensed jawline and the frown that made her step back in concern. The air around her cooled considerably. "What?" he exclaimed.

"I couldn't prove it was Ferguson. I had to use the back door that morning, and I saw it had been forced open and the security camera smashed." That memory was still fresh in her mind. "I hid behind a dumpster and called the police and kept my phone out in case I got lucky enough to take pictures. The cops didn't find anyone, and some stuff got broken, but nothing else. I was lucky."

She blew out a breath. "The next morning, there was graffiti scrawled all over my storefront with the letters *MBB*. I couldn't prove anything. All I could do was repaint." Britt smiled. "The pink basically screams *screw you* at him."

"Hey." Mark stroked a finger across her cheek. "In the end, you did what you felt was right. Not everyone has a steel backbone like my Nordic princess."

Man, he had a way with words, but he made her feel special each and every time. "*Takk.* Thank you."

"Listen, I have to run, but maybe we can talk later?"

"I sure hope so." This time, Britt initiated the kiss, and muffled a squeal of indignation when he pinched her backside. "I'll get you for that," she seethed between clenched teeth.

His expression gave her goose bumps. "I sure hope so," he said, his voice deep. He brushed past her, so close that their bodies touched from chest to thigh, and was out the door before she managed to collect her wits.

Oh yes, he was a very dangerous distraction.

MARK'S SECOND VISIT with his mom was short, because he had to make more progress on his case before his meeting with Captain Fraust tomorrow.

"I see work is more important than your own mother," she sniffed.

His body tensed in annoyance. "That's not fair," he growled. "I was here this morning, and I'm visiting you again because I wanted to bring a chocolate croissant for you. But my work shouldn't come as a surprise anymore."

Mom arched a brow. "And you should know better. Did you really think I was serious?"

Mark backed off, surprised and confused.

"Hmph, you did. Shame on you. I know you have an important job."

He blew out a frustrated breath. "Sorry, that wasn't like me."

"You're right. You sounded like your father."

Mark held his breath as his stomach twisted into a painful knot. He'd promised himself and his mother that he'd never be like that man. To hear her say those words… "That hurts, Mom."

"I'm sorry, baby. But you did ask me to tell you if or when you acted like your dad."

Mark had worked so hard to burn his father's abusive tendencies out of his life. When he was growing up, it had never occurred to Mark that he'd been doing anything wrong. *Angry friends are weak friends*, Dad used to say.

High school had been his turning point. No one was afraid to tell him he acted like a jerk. Mom had never said anything, until he told her that he needed to change—and then she'd become almost a different person. Her encouragement and support helped him become a better version of himself.

"I'm sorry, too, Mom. I don't know why…" He stopped, racking his brain to figure out what caused his relapse.

"I think you're more stressed than you realize. How is your case progressing?"

"Slowly. I need to talk to a couple of witnesses today."

She looked at him, her brows raised. "What are your plans for the rest of the day? I hope you're going to relax. All this work…" She paused.

Mark wasn't going to tell her about his surprise visit to Mr. Ferguson then, that was for sure. Instead, he said, "I had a dinner date last night."

"What?" Her excitement filled the room. "Why didn't you start your conversation with this? Now I know why your visits are short. Another woman's taking my baby's attention away from me."

"Mom," he warned, but her mischievous smile stopped him. "My God, you're doing it again."

"You're going to have to get used to it. If not me, then someone else."

"I know." Mark remembered Timmins's jokes about Jenny the construction worker, but he hadn't been upset, more annoyed.

"May I ask a question?"

He looked at her serious expression. What was wrong now? "Go for it."

"I'm just curious. Do you act so stoic at work?"

What was Mom getting at? "I don't believe so."

"No one teases you on the job?"

He nodded. "They do, but I try not to react to it. I guess

I'm worried about…" He didn't look at her, suddenly realizing that his deliberate act of being unaware only masked the real problem. He shuddered. "I don't think I'm handling this the right way." He looked at her, hoping she'd see his concern. "Do you have any suggestions?"

She nodded, as if realizing something. "Maybe you should ease up a bit."

"With my case? Mom, that's not going to happen."

"That's not what I meant. I mean lighten up. Have fun but be humble, too. You say you want to be better than your dad, so I'm challenging you to open up a little. Who knows, maybe your date will be the one to stick that Cupid's arrow into your heart."

Ah, if you only knew. He smiled. "I didn't know you were a romantic."

"Always have been." She rubbed her leg, now out of its cast and secured with a metal brace. "Always will be."

Mark watched her expression, but she gave nothing away. He really hoped she wasn't talking about Dad. "I have to go. Enjoy your treats."

"Oh, I plan to. Thank you for bringing some for me." She patted the paper bag that sat beside her. "I'm going to have one now and save the others for tomorrow. I'll see you soon?"

"You bet." He smooched her cheek several times, gave her a tight hug and headed out.

Evelyn was at the nurses station and looked up when he approached. "Everything good?"

"Yeah, thanks. Mom's in a good mood." He hesitated, worried that Dad might have tried to see her.

"He hasn't been here. Don't worry, I've got it covered." She gave him an impish smile. "Christie's taught us some basic self-defense moves."

He grinned—when Evelyn said she'd be ready for anything, she wasn't joking. "You're something else."

"I do my best." She reached into a drawer, and her hand came back into view with an envelope. "This came for your mom."

He pursed his lips and took it from her. The envelope was empty. "What was in it?"

"A letter. Your dad's name wasn't on it, but then after I gave it to her, I wondered... Well, I thought, what if he faked his name, but your mom recognized the handwriting as his?"

Mark looked for that now, turning the envelope over in his hands. This wasn't Dad's writing. "Nothing to worry about," he said, tucking it into his jacket pocket. "But I'll have it scanned for fingerprints."

"What would you like me to do if another envelope comes in for her?"

He sighed. He had no right to hold back Mom's correspondence, but if there was a slight chance it *was* Dad... "Keep it in a plastic bag so it doesn't get touched by too many hands, then give me a call or send a text. I'll let you know."

Chapter Five

Edward Ferguson lived on High Point Road within the Bridle Path, a very ritzy and expensive neighborhood located in the north end of Toronto. Mansions were surrounded by wide lawns and high decorative concrete walls, and all were barred with thick metal security gates.

Mark turned right at the third driveway and stopped his car before a set of barred gates and beside an intercom embedded within a stone pillar. He opened the window and reached out to press a button. It took just over a minute before he heard an audible click, and then a woman's voice. "Yes? Who is it?"

"This is Detective Mark Hawthorne from York Regional Police 4 District," he announced. "I'm the lead investigator on Mr. Ferguson's case. I'd like to talk to him."

A short pause. "He's currently working in his home office. May I ask if you have an appointment with him?"

An appointment? On a Sunday? "No, I do not."

Another pause, and Mark wondered if the woman was discussing the situation with the CEO in the background. He drummed his fingers on the windowsill, refusing to let his impatience get the best of him.

"May I see your badge, Detective?"

"Of course." He dug it out of his pocket and held it up in front of the intercom.

"Thank you. I'd like to verify your identity. It'll take a few minutes."

"I'm not going anywhere."

Mark didn't understand why Ferguson didn't just let him in. It was obvious the intercom had a camera—the CEO could have looked out and told the woman it was okay to let him inside.

Oh well, it wasn't worth burning through brain cells to try and figure out what Ferguson was thinking.

A cool breeze scented with flowers wafted into his car, and Mark took a deep breath. He closed his eyes and listened to the sounds surrounding him—birdsong, the rustle of leaves, the buzzing noise of a lawnmower in the distance. Sometimes, he'd forget that a few minutes of quiet solitude was enough to ease his jostling thoughts. Work would always be there, but he also had to balance it with self-care. He felt his body relax, and he inhaled again, letting his breath out in a slow exhale.

The intercom clicked. "Thank you for waiting, Detective Hawthorne. Please come in."

The thick iron gates swung open, and Mark slowly drove along a curved driveway toward the front of the house. He parked the car and got out, letting his gaze scan over the manicured landscape. A large fountain with a Cupid statue at its center gurgled with water as it flowed from a stone pitcher into the basin. Hedges and tall trees planted in front of the surrounding walls bordering the property offered natural privacy and dampened any sounds from the main street. He imagined himself sitting out here reading a good book.

Mark approached the pair of huge dark-stained doors and pressed the doorbell, curious as to why no one was already here to greet him. He stuck his hands in his pockets and casually strolled the length of the porch, spying the four security cameras—one over the front entrance and three others over the stretch of windows on the ground floor. He wouldn't be surprised if more surrounded the house. There was also another intercom embedded in the brickwork beside the door.

He blew out a frustrated breath, wondering if the CEO was deliberately making him wait. Mark would bet his next cup of coffee that Ferguson was looking at him even now through the security camera.

Annoyance bubbled through him, but Mark wasn't going to let it boil over. Instead, he stepped off the porch and walked across the impeccable lawn, stopping occasionally to smell the beds of flowers surrounding it. The lavender bushes that bordered the property were tall and lush with flowers, and he pinched several to release their heady fragrance.

Mark didn't experience a lot of moments like these—he was either buried in work, playing hard sports with friends or at home, trying to restore his energy after dealing with cases that tore at his emotions. He had few minutes to slow down, and he enjoyed these precious scenarios whenever he could.

His thoughts drifted to the woman who had entered his life, the stunning Nordic princess who had completely ensnared him with her voice, her looks, her eyes. Those eyes—such a bright, clear, sparkling green. He could stare into Britt's eyes all day and not notice the time going by. How could Mark ignore such beauty? He knew he was damn lucky that his reaction to her seemed to be mutual.

"Detective Hawthorne," a voice called out.

He turned around. A woman dressed in a housekeeper's

uniform stood at the doorway, her hands clinging together. "I'm sorry for the wait."

He nodded, and walked across the lawn again towards her, noticing her anxious expression as she glanced down at his feet. Mark had deduced that Ferguson wouldn't like anyone touching his stuff unless they had permission. Stepping on his near-perfect lawn and manhandling his shrubbery would bother the CEO a lot. As soon as he placed a foot over Ferguson's imaginary boundary, Mark knew the man would get angry and put a stop to it.

The CEO should have just let him in, instead of testing Mark's patience.

As he climbed the stairs, the housekeeper, who looked to be in her late thirties, smiled. "I apologize. Ever since those robberies last year, Mr. Ferguson has insisted on extra precautions."

"Of course. I understand." Timmins and Solberg had worked on that case until they caught a woman impersonating a courier. For some reason, women often weren't suspected as criminals until it was too late. "Better to play it safe."

When he stepped inside, Mark let out a low whistle of appreciation. The foyer, covered in black and white tile, was almost the size of his condo. Marble statues were displayed in four niches, two on each side of the wide space. The walls were a pastel green, making the area feel bigger than it looked. A grand staircase led to the second-floor landing.

"If you'll come this way." The housekeeper turned right and opened a door that led into a large study. Books graced two walls, while a heavy mahogany desk dominated the room. A wide bank of windows looked out onto the front landscape.

She pointed to a pair of leather chairs in front of the desk.

"Please have a seat. Mr. Ferguson is just finishing up his business. He should be here in a few minutes."

More waiting, but there was no use in getting mad about it. Mark sat in the plush high-back chair and crossed his legs.

The housekeeper seemed so nervous that Mark was worried she'd faint. "Would you like anything? Coffee, tea, snacks?"

He almost said no, then changed his mind. If Ferguson was going to make him cool his heels, he might as well enjoy it. "Yes, thank you."

Mark had finished his first cup of coffee and had popped a mini quiche into his mouth when he heard Mr. Ferguson's voice. Moments later, the bakery CEO strode in. "Sorry about that," he apologized. "If you'd let me know you were coming in advance, I would have made sure I had cleared my calendar."

"This is an impromptu visit." Mark stood and shook hands. "Everything good?"

The CEO looked surprised at the question. "Yes, yes, of course."

Mark watched as Mr. Ferguson settled in, grabbed a cup of coffee and a snack for himself, then sat down behind his desk. "So, Officer, how can I help out today? I would have thought you'd have Sundays off."

Mark hid his expression behind the coffee cup until he was sure he could keep a neutral face. "The law doesn't sleep, Mr. Ferguson, and my colleagues do rotations so that each of us can have a decent weekend off. It's called teamwork."

Mr. Ferguson pursed his lips but didn't reply.

"How are you feeling, by the way?"

"I saw the doctor yesterday and he gave me the all clear." He leaned back in his chair. "Thankfully, no concussion, broken bones or internal bleeding. Just a lot of bruises that'll take some time to go away. The swelling in my lip is already gone." He unbuttoned his shirt cuff and rolled up the sleeve to expose a large piece of gauze. "I don't remember it happening, but I got cut by something sharp. I had to get stitches." He rolled the sleeve back down and shot Mark a sharp look. "Any news on the scumbag who attacked me?"

"I have a couple of promising leads I'm looking into." He brought out his work phone, hit Record and placed it on the desk between them. "I wanted to ask some additional questions."

"Sure, that's why you're here."

Mark put his cup back on the serving tray and mirrored Ferguson's reclining posture. He wanted to observe the man's reactions without being distracted. "How long have you owned the Mighty Big Bakery?"

"Let's see." The CEO tilted his head back. "About thirty-five years. Well, I've been owner and CEO since that time. My father started it back in the 1950s."

"Was it called MBB back then?"

"No." He shook his head for extra emphasis. "Just Ferguson's. The original neighborhood loved the store—it offered a bit of everything."

Mark noticed the nostalgic expression on the CEO's face. "Why the name change?"

"The chain needed something more distinct, more powerful. I had plans for what I wanted to do—grow the business until everyone heard about it, bake the best of everything, beat out the competition."

"I've heard you had some problems considering that last statement." Mark decided to jump on that first, since he had an opening. "It seems that there are some people who aren't thrilled with your way of doing things."

Mr. Ferguson snorted. "What do you want me to do, huh? I'm running a business. My goal is to have a Mighty Big Bakery in every city and town of Ontario." He shrugged. "After that, I'll move on to bigger things. That's how business works, son."

"I get it, but you're steamrolling over small businesses using tactics that aren't, shall we say, ethical."

The CEO stared at him. "Are you pulling the bleeding-heart sob story on me?" He laughed. "Give me a break."

Mark linked his fingers together and rested them on his lap because he didn't want Ferguson to see the clenched fists he really wanted to show. This man sounded a little too much like his father. "Just saying what I've heard from others."

Mr. Ferguson sat up in his chair and leaned across the desk. "I offered the best deals when I bought out those businesses. If the owners turned it down, that was their choice."

"It wasn't their choice to be bullied when they stood up to you."

He sat back and blinked. "I don't know anything about that."

"Oh, I think you do, but you're too smart a man to admit to it." Damn it, Mark had to stop mouthing off before he got in trouble with the captain.

Mr. Ferguson frowned. "Are you accusing me of something, young man?"

"No, sir." Mark stood, knowing he wouldn't get any kind of confession out of the guy. He grabbed his phone from the desk and stuck it in his pocket. "Thanks for seeing me today."

"Of course." Mr. Ferguson followed him to the front door. "I'll help in any way I can. Maybe I'll put in a call to

Captain Fraust, let her know how cooperative and efficient you've been."

Mark hoped the surprise didn't show on his face. "Thank you. Enjoy the rest of your Sunday."

Outside, Mark gulped mouthfuls of fresh air as he walked slowly to his car. His plan to catch the CEO off guard hadn't worked. If Ferguson was hiding something, he was doing a damn good job of it. Also, the man's discreet threat that he knew the captain threw Mark for a loop—he hadn't expected that. He knew he needed to finish up any leftover work on his case today before updating Captain Fraust tomorrow morning with his findings.

Mark hoped the second item on his list—bringing in the suspect with the different-sized feet—would go off without a hitch and make up for his lack of progress with Ferguson.

WHEN MARK AND Timmins pulled their car into Henry Toussaint's driveway, the older detective hooked a thumb towards his window. "I just noticed the curtains moving."

"Good, that means someone's home." Mark hopped out of the car and strode toward the front door. Similar to Ferguson's house, there was a security camera above the entrance.

Mark pressed the doorbell then stepped back, giving the homeowner a clear view of him. "Mr. Toussaint, I'm Detective Mark Hawthorne with York Regional Police 4 District. We'd like to talk to you."

He heard a steady clicking as someone approached the front door. As it opened, a security chain blocked any entry, only allowing about three inches of free space to speak through. On the other side, a silver-haired woman almost as tall as him looked defiant. "What do you want?" she demanded.

It wasn't a greeting Mark expected, and it instantly put

him on alert. "Good afternoon." He pulled out his badge, and Timmins did the same. "I wanted to ask if Henry Toussaint was at home?"

"I don't know where Henry is right now." It didn't seem like she was going to be cooperative.

"Does he have a day job?" Mark kept his voice pleasant-sounding. He hated going into situations like this when people immediately got their hackles up and became combative.

"What has he done?"

"We'd like to ask him some questions about an assault last Friday evening."

"He doesn't work." Her frustrated expression gave Mark a clue that she wasn't happy about Henry's lack of employment.

Mark pulled out a notepad and a pen. "And you have no idea where he might be today?"

"Henry's an adult. He does whatever the hell he wants. I'm not his secretary."

"I understand. We'll come back later on today to see if he's returned."

The woman frowned. "You can't come into my home unless you have a search warrant."

Interesting—was she hiding something? "We only want to talk to Henry—I don't need a search warrant for that." Mark glanced at Timmins, who gave a slight nod—time to take it up a notch. "However, I can get one within a couple of hours. The next time I'm here, I'm allowed to come in, and you won't be able to say anything about it."

The woman looked surprised at that, but she didn't back down. "Fine," she sniffed. "Bring your search warrant. You won't find Henry here, and he's done nothing wrong."

"Fair enough. Have a good day." He turned on his heel and walked casually back to the car, but inside, he trembled with adrenaline. He felt certain Henry Toussaint lay hidden within the house.

He and Timmins would wait him out.

They drove onto Cunningham Drive, made a U-turn and parked one block from the entrance to Sierra Court. "I'm sure he's hiding in the house," Timmins stated.

Mark nodded. He didn't think Henry Toussaint would be hiding unless he had done something. "I have no idea how desperate this guy is," he murmured.

"We should call for backup just in case."

"Good idea." He listened as Timmins made the request, telling the dispatcher to inform the officers to stay at a distance so that the suspect couldn't see them until it was too late.

Unfortunately, the waiting game gave Mark too much time to think. Everyone he had talked to, including Britt, suspected the Mighty Big Bakery CEO of illegal activities that should have gotten him arrested. The fact that Ferguson still bullied victims to this day meant he'd never been caught or received more than a slap on the wrist. Was someone protecting his interests? Or did he just have a team of shrewd lawyers that got the CEO out of any tainted situation he found himself in?

Mark wouldn't be surprised at all. The man was like an eel, slipping out of any dirty kind of muck that surrounded him. If he could find any kind of evidence that would stick...

The police radio crackled. "Detective Hawthorne, we're in position."

Mark glanced over his shoulder. A squad car was parked about half a block behind him.

"And not a moment too soon. There's someone coming," Timmins said.

Mark stared at a man who came to a halt on the sidewalk across the street. He was tall, taller than him, and very fit. He wore a red-and-white soccer jersey with Toronto's team logo emblazoned on the front, black track pants, and smart-looking red, white and black hi-top sneakers. He stood at the corner of Sierra Court and Cunningham Drive and looked around. His gaze lingered on the police car a bit longer than necessary, making Mark twitch with excitement.

After a few minutes, the man turned and walked in the opposite direction.

"I'll follow him." Mark was halfway out the car.

Timmins scooted into the driver's seat. "Don't do anything heroic."

Mark jogged across the street and walked at a fast pace until he was about half a block behind the man. There were few cars and fewer pedestrians at this time of day, so he knew if the guy kept an eye on him, Mark would lose the chance to take him by surprise.

They walked for a few minutes, Mark matching his pace to the man's. Suddenly, the guy made a left-hand turn into a field of tall grass. His pace had quickened.

"Damn it." Mark managed to keep the same distance between them. He didn't dare glance over his shoulder to see where Timmins was, but he was certain his partner was close. He spied the wide half-hidden path and got on it, spotting his target in the distance. Timmins and the others would have to follow him on foot.

He was sure this was Henry Toussaint.

Mark's cell phone rang, and he answered it.

"Where the hell is this guy going?" Timmins demanded.

"Don't know. Just the fact that he came this way where I can barely see him is already suspicious. There's a large pond to the right behind all this grass, and up ahead is a huge park."

"He's going to try and lose us at one of those spots." Timmins swore over the phone. "I'll follow you, but I'm sending the officers parallel to the pond, see if they can get ahead and cut him off."

Mark craned his head. The guy managed to get farther away—shit, he was fast. "Tell them to move like Olympic sprinters or we'll lose him."

There were more people here—mothers with children, joggers, seniors out for a stroll. Mark remembered the children's play areas. He wanted to take the guy down before they got too close to people. If the suspect became desperate…

He caught a flash of white to his right—the officers had just passed him, moving quickly through the foliage. Mark hurried as well, his quickened steps turning into a sprint as he heard one of the officers shout out a command to stop.

When he came around a curve in the path, both officers had the man restrained. "What the hell is going on?" the suspect shouted. He didn't fight back and allowed the handcuffs to be snapped around his wrists. "Hey, I asked you a question!"

"Detective Mark Hawthorne with York Regional Police 4 District." He showed his badge. "What's your name?"

"I don't have to tell you shit!"

"Pat him down." Mark waited as the officers quickly checked the man over. Timmins had caught up, and was directing traffic, telling people to move on. A couple stood several feet away, recording the arrest on their phone—great, just what he didn't need.

"Here's his wallet, sir." One of the officers tossed it to him.

Mark caught it in one hand and opened it. Sure enough, it was their man—Henry Toussaint. Mark advised the man of his rights. "I need you to come with us to the precinct to answer some questions."

"And if I refuse?"

He had every right to do so and request a lawyer. Mark shrugged. "I'll talk to you one way or another. But it might seem like you saying no means you have something to hide."

"You've got nothing on me," Toussaint sneered. "I'll go with you, just to prove you're wrong."

Mark loved nothing more than a challenge. "Okay then. Prepare to be mistaken."

Mark, Toussaint and an officer waited while Timmins and the second officer brought their vehicles. The suspect was seated in the back of the squad car while Mark hopped in beside Timmins. Despite driving as fast as possible back to the precinct, Mark was impatient. "I can't wait to hear what this asshole has to say for himself."

"I get it, but don't get too cocky, either," Timmins warned. "The suspect could pull a fast one on you and you'd have no way to dig yourself out of that hole."

"I know, I know." At a stoplight, Mark cracked his knuckles. "Did you see his feet? One is definitely bigger than the other."

"And if his fingerprints match those found at the crime scene, we've got him."

At the precinct, Toussaint was taken down to interrogation. Mark had called Myrna along the way, and she was waiting for him in front of his office. "Here's his wallet," he told her, providing the evidence nestled within a plastic baggie. "See if you can lift a viable fingerprint from any of his cards in there. Pray that we get a match to those at the crime scene."

"Gotcha." She ran off.

When Mark arrived downstairs, Constable Turnbull was sitting in the recording room. "Sir, all set when you are."

He nodded and watched as Toussaint was seated at the metal table, his wrists unbound. He decided not to hand-cuff the suspect to the table, on the very slim chance he wasn't their guy. If he was, however, Timmins would be in the room with Mark, and the two officers who had arrested him would be standing just outside the door.

He remembered Timmins's warning as he walked in and sat down. "Mr. Toussaint, I'm Detective Mark Hawthorne. Detective Walter Timmins is here as well to listen to your statement. As I said, I have a few questions for you."

"What's this about?" Toussaint wasn't quite belligerent, but his slouched stance in the chair said otherwise.

It did give Mark a chance to study the man's feet. "Your right shoe is bigger than your left."

"Yeah. What about it?"

"Just noticing. I haven't seen that before."

Toussaint shrugged. "An anomaly among many in this world. What's that got to do with why I'm here?"

"If I'm lucky, a lot." Mark had brought his notes with him and started shuffling through pages until he found the picture with the shoe prints. "Do you remember the story about the high-priced sneakers that got recalled because its symbol on the sole of the shoe resembled a holy Arabic word?"

"Man, I got the sneakers before they got pulled." Toussaint sat up. "I put them up on a sellers' website just to see how much I could get for them. The price got up to over ten thousand dollars. No one cared they were different sizes."

"That's a nice chunk of change for a pair of kicks. How did you manage to get different sizes? Most stores wouldn't sell shoes like that."

"I got lucky." He picked up a foot and brushed his fingers against his sneaker, as if to wipe away something. "Some guy in the Middle East has the same problem as me, but the opposite feet. Worked out perfectly for us."

It worked out perfectly for Mark, too. "That's some story."

"Sure is. The ladies get a kick out of it." He grinned. "Pun intended."

Mark laughed, but not at the bad joke. "Then you'll be fascinated with what I have to show you." Mark slid the picture across. "Imagine the coincidence of finding the same shoe prints at a crime scene. Oh, and the right foot is bigger than the left. And the print matches that infamous symbol."

Mark watched Toussaint's face become slack-jawed and tried not to grin in triumph. "How about telling us why you were trespassing at a construction site, and waiting for Mr. Edward Ferguson, CEO of Mighty Big Bakery, so you could beat the crap out of him?"

Toussaint licked his lips and looked around. His eyes, wide and dark, flickered from Timmins to the door and back again. Mark sincerely hoped the young man wasn't thinking of fighting his way out. "What makes you think it was me?"

"Please." Mark tapped the photo. "Like you said, an anomaly. Plus, some old-fashioned detective work."

"Excuse me, Detective Hawthorne." Turnbull's voice came over the speaker. "Walsh is here. She says the fingerprints found in the suspect's wallet are a match for those found on the piece of wood used to beat the victim. The same fingerprints also match those found on the gas canister at the construction site."

Mark smiled. "Another coincidence. Your prints match those at the crime scene."

Toussaint wiped his hands over his face—he knew he

was cornered. "Look, it's not what you're thinking," he said quietly.

Mark eased forward in the chair, his body tense with anticipation. "Then how about explaining what happened that night?"

"If I do, will I go free?"

"Maybe you should think about whether to do the right thing and tell us why you were there."

Toussaint's attitude had completely changed. He looked defeated.

"Help me understand why you would take your anger out on Mr. Ferguson. And bring a gas canister to the site. You were going to burn the building down."

"Not with people still inside!" Toussaint got up and paced a tight path between the table and Timmins. "Look, I know it's going to sound outrageous, but here's the truth, I swear."

He came back and sat down. "You know who Mr. Ferguson is. Big-name CEO of those bakeries. He hurt a lot of people when he bought out the small businesses. A real scumbag."

Jeez, Ferguson had really made a bad reputation for himself. "I've heard the stories," Mark said.

"A friend of mine told me about someone who was holding rallies to speak out against Ferguson's tactics. The first one I went to was about two weeks ago."

"A rally? Isn't that unusual?" And why hadn't Mark heard of it? Rallies were usually logged so that they could obtain police security. Unless… "Or do you mean a protest?"

"Does it matter? It was undercover, though. My friend picked me up, and we had to follow these weird instructions to get to the place."

"So that you couldn't report them to the police when the time came," Timmins chimed in.

Toussaint nodded. "All I know is that it was near the rail yard."

Mark frowned. "How do you know that?"

"I could hear the trains stopping and starting. You know, when they make those big clanging noises."

"Sounds like train cars being hooked together."

Toussaint nodded. "Yeah, like that. We went to a small building. The inside smelled of grease and metal, but I could barely see anything. There was a guy standing on a box, dissing Ferguson and saying that we should stop him."

"How many people were there?"

Toussaint shrugged. "Maybe a dozen? I don't know. But listening to the guy talk, he had a way of getting us riled up, to do something against Ferguson, you know?"

There was nothing more dangerous than a leader with charm and incentive. Under the right circumstances, that leader could send a frenzied mob to do whatever he asked. "Did this leader provide instructions on what to do?"

"A few. A popular one was graffiti on the Mighty Big Bakeries, but someone yelled that spray-painting the stores wasn't enough. I heard another person saying something about torching the bakeries. Then some other guy shouted that we should beat up the employees." Toussaint shook his head. "It was getting out of control, but somehow the leader managed to calm everyone down."

"Could you see his face?"

"No, man, he wore a mask that covered the bottom of his face and a baseball cap."

Mark jotted some notes down. "So you decided to burn down the new Mighty Big Bakery store that's going up nearby?"

"No, that was my friend's idea. She was more excited

than I was. She said she could get me onto the construction site with no problem."

A coil of anger wove up Mark's back until it hit him square in the face. If it was her... "How did she manage to do that?" he said through gritted teeth.

Toussaint gave him a weird look. "How else? She's a construction worker. Jenny was all for taking that bakery down. Now I want to talk to my lawyer."

Chapter Six

Britt read Mark's text and wondered what the hell had happened to him.

Have you ever wondered how it would feel to just stay home all day and IGNORE EVERYONE? Cuz I wish I had done that today.

Instead of texting back, she called. "Hey, Mr. Detective."

"Hi, Britt."

Okay, that did *not* sound like him. Work must have been especially stressful today. "Is everything all right? What's going on?"

A sigh. "Too much, but I think I have a handle on it now."

She didn't think looking for Mr. Ferguson's attacker would take that much effort, but what did she know about police investigations? "Excellent. That means we can have dinner together."

He was silent on the other end, and Britt mentally smacked herself. Mark must be exhausted. "I'm sorry," she started. "I shouldn't have presumed…"

"Are you kidding? Spending time with my Nordic princess is the perfect ending to a day like this."

"Mr. Detective, flattery will get you everywhere. Where would you like to go?"

"How about you make the choice? I'll be at your place to pick you up in about half an hour?"

"It's a date."

It was going to be a warm night. Britt chose her blue maxi dress, as she loved how it flowed around her legs. A small purse and comfortable sandals finished the outfit. She thought about leaving her hair down, but hated how it got easily tangled around things, so she swept it up into her usual ponytail. A bit of lipstick, and she was ready to go.

As she waited in the lobby downstairs, Britt thought of what she'd normally be doing right now, which would have been making dinner and watching another repeat show on television. Or work. She noticed she had picked up the bad habit of checking her laptop for customer emails during her downtime. Once, she had told herself it was necessary to stay one step ahead, but now she knew it was to fill in the long evenings until the next day arrived.

She had to be honest. Work had started to take up too much of her time. Oh, Britt loved it and wouldn't give it up, but she knew there was more to life than that. She had no problem being alone, but being lonely? That sucked.

Several times, she had thought about moving back to Norway. Her family would have been thrilled, and she could return to a familiar routine with no problem. Britt wouldn't be alone, but that was not what she needed. Independence was a critical part of her existence, supported by family, friends and work. She had all of that, but she'd realized something was still missing—a person to fill the remaining void in her heart.

Britt had been so busy building a life for herself, she'd forgotten about everything else. But she'd needed to do something—anything—to get her mind off the pain and humiliation she'd suffered before creating Konditori. She had built her dream from scratch—learning, failing and learning again had been the catalyst she needed to realize that she was capable of anything, and no one could tell her different.

However, Britt also believed in the Nordic Fates, that everyone's life was woven to follow one particular destiny. Was Mark one of the threads to be woven into her life's journey? Britt didn't know yet, since they'd only met a couple of days ago. However, their instant connection was something she'd never experienced before. It had been solid, never wavered, and if the gods were smiling down on her, it would last.

A horn beeped twice, and she mentally shook herself out of the past and into an exciting present. Mark was already out of the car and holding the passenger door open for her. "How are you, *vakker*?" he asked in a deep tone before managing to sneak a kiss on her cheek.

God, his voice... She smiled. "Starving. Oh, and happy to see you, too."

He raised a brow at that. "I'm not sure I'm convinced."

Oh, he needed convincing, huh? Britt grabbed his face and pulled him down so she could mold her mouth to his. Damn, he tasted good, like something rich and delectable. She backed away before she got too mesmerized. "I hope that helped."

His expression made her insides tie up in knots. "What's that look for?" she demanded.

His gaze traveled slowly down to her feet, then back up. Britt's nerves were lighting up and tingling. "Are you sure you want dinner? Or are you hungry for something else?"

She swallowed the lump that formed in her throat, knowing exactly what he meant and fighting to keep herself in check. "You are a very naughty boy," she whispered, "making suggestions like that."

"You don't seem shocked."

He noticed that? Damn it, Britt, of course he did—he's a detective. "You're very observant."

"With you? Yes, I can't help myself."

She didn't have a comeback. Instead, with a shaky smile, Britt slid into the car.

"Where would you like to go?" he asked.

"Do you like sushi?"

"Love it."

"I was hoping you'd say that. I found a great place on Yonge Street, just north of Highway 401."

They parked at a corner close to the restaurant. After Mark helped her out of the car, he didn't release her hand. With his fingers closed over hers, that strange feeling of belonging hit her again, along with something else—she was relaxed and content. And damn if that didn't feel wonderful.

The restaurant wasn't busy yet, and the hostess and staff greeted them in Japanese before taking them to a booth that offered a view of the sunset and the gradual uptick of nightlife.

"This is a nice place," Mark said. "I haven't been here yet."

Dark paneled wood covered the walls, which were decorated with bright prints of Japanese figures. The sushi kitchen was at the other end of the spacious room, with the chefs hurrying around each other as they made the meals. Soothing Japanese music played in the background. "Oh? Were you planning on trying it out?"

"Eventually. I worked a burglary case in the area a few months ago." He stopped as a waitress brought green tea and two cups, then poured for them. "I came in here to ask

questions, and the hostess at the time had valuable information that led to the perp's arrest. She was very observant."

"That's amazing." They clinked their cups, and she took
a sip. The tea was hot and refreshing. "So, how was your
day? You sounded pretty stressed over the phone."

"Busy. But I'll have a final report for my captain tomorrow."

The only police procedures Britt knew were from the re-
ality shows on television. They were real but didn't have the
same impact as actually talking to a live person. "I don't
want to sound nosy, and you can stop me whenever you
want. Did you find Mr. Ferguson's attacker?"

"Yeah."

Short and to the point. "And the person will be charged?"

"There are a few steps in between, but yes, he'll be formally charged with assault."

Britt didn't think she could do Mark's job. It seemed like
there was too much emotional back-and-forth. "I guess Mr.
Ferguson could sue the attacker, too."

"If he wanted. I'd rather he backed off, but..." Mark didn't
say anything.

Damn it, Britt, think of something else! "How's your
mother doing?"

"Much better, thank you. She'll have months of physical rehab, though." His expression grew clouded. "I hope
she's up for it."

"Why wouldn't she be? I'm sure your mom will have excellent help from the nurses." On an impulse, Britt rested
her hand over his. "Maybe you can go to her follow-up appointments and encourage her."

He turned his hand over and laced his fingers with hers.
"Thank you, I needed to hear that." He grinned. "She loves
your pastries by the way, and it takes a lot to impress her."

She smiled back. Britt sensed that Mark loved his mother very much.

The waitress had returned, and they placed their order.

Britt kept their conversation light and away from work as much as possible. "Do you watch cartoons?" she asked.

He gave her a weird look.

"You're kidding, right?" she demanded. "Everyone should watch cartoons. There's too much serious shit going on in the world, and I don't think that's going to change. I find watching cartoons makes me remember how funny life can be sometimes."

"Which ones do you watch? And if you say the coyote and weird-looking bird with the long legs, I might walk out."

She burst out laughing. "It's one of my favorites!"

Mark made a move as if to get up, but she grabbed his arm. "Hear me out," she demanded. "Since you know the cartoon, tell me—have you ever seen a more motivated individual? He goes after what he wants and nothing gets in his way."

Mark cocked a brow, which put her on the defensive.

"You know it's true," she insisted. "Okay, how about the two mice? The really smart one that wants to take over the world? That's what I call dedication."

Mark shook his head. "You sure are something else."

"And what's that supposed to mean?"

"I mean you're different. Your bakery is your job, but I sense it's a lot more than that."

Britt sat back, watching him. "It's my passion. I love what I do. And I think that's allowed me to look at life a little differently, too. Life's too short to, I don't know, worry about mortgages or what people think of me. If I enjoy it, that's what counts."

He nodded slowly, as if thinking.

Their dinner arrived—miso soup, salad, two different kinds of sushi rolls and tempura vegetables. "This looks delicious," she said in a singsong voice, moving several pieces onto her plate. She grabbed a piece of spicy tuna sushi and popped it into her mouth. "So good!" she groaned, as she chewed. "I never would have thought I'd love sushi until a friend introduced me to it."

"Have you tried a lot of different things?"

"Before I became an entrepreneur, yes." She started ticking items off her fingers. "I wanted to be a ballet dancer, but I hated the training and the eating lifestyle. I couldn't eat sushi if I kept it up. And I was in the army."

"Seriously?" Mark's brown gaze widened in awe. "How old were you?"

"Nineteen. All Norwegians are mustered at that age. Then I took the military's compulsory training. That was nineteen months of hard work."

"So, wait a minute. If there's a war, are you called back?"

She shook her head. "I don't know... I think it's possible."

"Shit." He looked upset.

"Hey, let's hope it doesn't happen. Trust me, if it did, I'd look for an administrative job." Damn it, she hadn't meant for the conversation to head in this direction. Maybe it had been her conscience telling her to warn him of the possibility? *Yeah, thanks, brain.* "Then I decided on politics. That didn't go so well." Just thinking about it made her a little sick to her stomach.

"What happened?"

Britt knew Mark would ask the question, but she wasn't ready to tell him. "A lot of crap that could have been avoided." She started eating again to keep her mouth busy— she didn't want to get into it. Except... "Now you see why I love cartoons. Oh! And anime. Japanese anime movies are just so beautiful."

He remained quiet but watched her while he ate, which made her squirm in her seat.

The restaurant started to fill with more customers, and the noise from their conversations got too loud. As the waitress returned, Britt had an idea. "Did you want to stay? Or maybe we could go for a walk?"

"Yeah, I'd like that."

THE SIDEWALKS WERE filled with people. It was a warm evening, and it seemed everyone wanted to take advantage of it.

Mark saw Britt glance back at the restaurant, as if she missed its atmosphere. "Come on, I know just the place." He grasped her hand and tucked it beneath his arm. At the next block, he turned right and entered the neighborhood just beyond the busy atmosphere of Yonge Street. He breathed in the scented air and felt himself relax as the quiet settled around them.

"I never knew about this," she murmured. As they crossed another street, a large park appeared between the stand of tall trees bordering it. The security lights came on as the sky grew darker, illuminating a group of kids playing soccer. Town houses and large older homes stood side by side and stretched out into the distance.

"You need to explore the city more often. I came through here because—what else? Another case." It felt like Mark only found out about hidden areas of the city when he was working. He led them into the park and walked to its edge, then stopped and offered her a bow. "Shall we take a turn, my lady?"

Britt giggled and curtsied. "You are too kind, milord."

Unlike on Yonge Street, the only other sounds here

were songbirds and the children's laughter. They walked the length of the park in comfortable silence, not hurrying, and Mark suddenly realized this was what he needed—time to himself, not rushing headlong to his next case.

The thrill and excitement of his job was great—he had no complaints. He loved the adrenaline rush, hanging out with the guys during their downtime, or collaborating and throwing out theories over a complex investigation. But his colleagues had something else that, if he was honest, made him jealous. Solberg and Cynthia were dating now, and Timmins was married. Occasionally, the guys would talk about their significant others, their plans, their futures. Mark wanted that for himself.

He had no problem meeting women and had been on plenty of dates. However, there was always something missing. He couldn't explain it, but he felt it. Mom once told him he'd know when a woman was "the one." He had scoffed at the idea, but now...

He looked at Britt while she talked and pointed out things that interested her. Her body was warm against his, and Mark felt that same sizzle of awareness as when he'd seen her the first time. He knew it was too early to decide if she would be the woman in his life, but she'd certainly made one hell of an impression on him.

So far, so good.

They had almost reached the other end of the park. A soccer ball rolled toward them, but one of the boys intercepted it and kicked it back to his friends.

"Mark, could I ask you something?"

He looked down into her ocean-green gaze, those sparkling eyes that filled him with an emotion that ached in his chest. "Only if you let me kiss you first."

"Ah, you're not above bribery then." She tilted her face up

to his, her full lips puckered and making smooching noises that had him snorting with laughter.

"Will you stop that?" he told her.

"Make me."

That was a challenge he would not pass up. He molded his mouth to hers, trying to get past the humor of her kiss until she suddenly relaxed against him. Her lips parted, and he gently delved his tongue into her warmth, exploring every bit until she groaned softly. The sound almost had him begging for more.

He reluctantly backed away, and that's when he heard the kids whistling, hooting and howling wolf calls.

Britt blushed a deep shade of pink. "Mind your own business! I thought you were playing soccer!"

"This is a family park, lady!" a tall boy yelled out. "Go find a room!"

Amid the jeering, Mark finally settled on her question. "What did you want to know, Britt?"

They reached the second corner and turned right. Their stroll took them past a small playground. Moms helped their kids onto the swings, caught them as they reached the bottom of the slide and called out when one got too ambitious on the monkey bars.

"How did you become a police detective?"

He expected the question. He just wasn't sure how much to say. "My family used to live in British Columbia," he started as they walked back. "Mom and I loved it there, but Dad was too much of a nomad. He'd travel for work and leave Mom and me a lot."

That wasn't exactly how he wanted to start the conversation. "I got into a lot of trouble as a kid. Getting into fights, picking on the smaller kids. Mom tried her best and finally got me to settle down, but I didn't want to do anything. I didn't have an interest in school."

Mark remembered those days and wished he could take them back. "When I got to high school, I had a difficult time with my courses, and nothing grabbed my attention. I knew Mom was worried, and I tried to apply myself, but nothing worked."

He bit his lip against the pain and anguish swelling within him. He remembered hearing Mom crying one night in her room after a heated argument they'd had, and him storming out of the house. He had never meant to hurt her, but Mark had been too angry at himself to notice until that night.

"What did you do?" Britt asked quietly. They had reached the end of their walk and stood beneath the trees.

"Someone came to my rescue. My phys ed coach. He must have found out about my failing grades from one of my teachers. Gave me a swift kick in the ass first, then mentored me through high school. He was exactly what I needed."

Stanley Tucker had saved him from a life of regrets. "Next thing I knew, I got high grades and earned a scholarship. I studied law enforcement because I wanted to do what Stanley did for me, helping others." He looked at her. "Mom was proud of me, but I needed to be proud of myself or I was going nowhere."

"That's an amazing story, Mr. Detective. You've really impressed me."

Suddenly a voice yelled out. Mark approached the soccer ball bouncing in their direction and his competitive streak kicked in. He juggled it with his feet to the delight of the young boys, before kicking it out toward them.

"I see you like sports as well."

"It helps me release a lot of pent-up energy."

"Are you on any sports teams?"

He shook his head, looking out at the boys as they raced across the field. "Just too busy."

Britt moved up to him until their bodies touched. Jesus, he wanted to explore the woman beneath the clothing, discover her secrets and desires. Her flirtations were making it hard for him to concentrate on her as a person. "I think I did say that life was too short to not enjoy what you love." She caressed his cheek with her hand. "You should consider it."

He turned his head slightly and pressed his lips to her palm. "I will, *vakker.*"

"God, I love how you say that. It almost makes me want to do anything."

He stared at her, thinking of the delicious things he'd love to do with her. "Really?"

"Mmm-hmm."

It felt like the air around them had stilled, as if holding its breath. His finger touched her chin, but he didn't move—he waited. He wanted Britt to be sure that this was a moment of no looking back, to know that he wasn't going anywhere, that he wanted her with every fiber of his being.

Her lips parted in a slight gasp. He wondered if she was thinking the same thoughts, but then his brain shut down when she leaned in and brushed her mouth across his.

He uttered an unintelligible sound and wrapped his arms around her, dying to caress her body with his eager hands and fighting against the urge. Standing in a park with kids watching was not the ideal spot. But when her arms came around his neck and he felt her fingers grab his hair, he almost lost it. He gently grasped her bottom lip with his teeth and was rewarded with her soft sound of desire.

This moment felt right. He had no other way to explain

it. His Nordic princess wanted him just as much, and when the time was right, he would lavish all his attention upon her like the true goddess she was.

Chapter Seven

Sunlight was pouring through the window when Britt woke up, yawning and feeling refreshed. She'd slept through the night.

She stayed in bed, hugging the pillow to her chest as she reminisced about her dinner date with Mark. She imagined herself in one of those romantic movies, where the couple strolled around a city at night, looking at the bright lights and staring into each other's eyes. She wasn't one for clichéd plotlines, but now that she had experienced it for herself...

Britt stared at the ceiling. She hadn't wanted last night to end, and if she read Mark's actions correctly, he hadn't wanted to stop, either. But she wasn't quite ready to take the next step. Things were moving pretty quickly, and despite the swirl of euphoria that still rushed through her, she wanted to take things just a little easy.

Mark had more or less indicated the same thing, although while he was driving her home, his hand couldn't stop touching her arm and thigh. Which sure as hell didn't help. By the time they got to her place, she was ready to drag him upstairs, but she'd convinced her lust to calm down.

Maybe next time.

Giggling, she went to the bathroom to get a shower. Today was a new day. Mark had warned her about his busy work schedule, so Britt would have to daydream about last night until she could see him again.

But man, to have him kiss her like that…

She turned the tap to Cold to allow the water to wake her up and hopefully cool off the very sexy thoughts roiling around in her head. She had a business to run.

The bus ride gave her time to check her emails. She had received a couple more party requests for her pastries for this coming weekend. If this kept up, she'd need to consider hiring extra help. She hadn't wanted the bakery to grow too fast—she wanted to keep the small-business charm intact. It was something she'd need to discuss with her staff, especially Jacques and Thomas. She refused to overwork them.

When Britt arrived at her stop, other people were also hurrying to work. It was almost nine, but the bakery opened at eight during the workweek to take advantage of the early-morning crowd. As she approached the store, she noticed a couple of customers peering in through the window, and as she reached the door, Britt was shocked to discover how busy it was inside.

"Helvete." Hell. What was going on?

She hurried around the side of the store, intent on using the back entrance so that she could get inside and help out. However, as she turned the corner, she almost bumped into someone who looked like…

"Ms. Gronlund." Mr. Ferguson was almost unrecognizable, wearing blue jeans and a white shirt instead of his usual two-piece business suit. But it was his expression that made her take a step back—he was furious. "I couldn't get into your bakery this morning. You certainly have loyal customers and staff."

"What are you doing here? Have you forgotten about the

peace bond and what it means?" He was the last person she expected to see. "It means stay away from my shop."

Britt glanced over her shoulder—she was about six feet from the sidewalk. The odd person glanced in her direction and kept going, not seeing anything wrong. But if she decided to scream...

Suddenly, his hand clamped over her wrist. "I can see what you're thinking," he growled. "I just want to talk."

"We've talked enough." Britt tried to wrench her arm free, but no luck. "Get your hand off me."

"Why didn't you sell your business? I offered top dollar. Do you want more? I'm sure we can come to an agreement."

"And I already told you where you could stick your offer." Mr. Ferguson was stronger than Britt expected, but she wasn't a lightweight, either.

"Name your price."

"Why?" She waved her other hand at the construction site across the street. "You got what you wanted. Leave me alone."

"No, I didn't. I've never had anyone refuse my offers. Tell me your price." He actually bared his teeth in a snarl.

"How about this?" She set her stance, then swung one leg up, aiming her foot at his crotch.

Mr. Ferguson howled in pain and let go of her hand to clutch his manhood with both of his.

"Stay away from me and my bakery!" She took off down the short alleyway. At the back, she scrabbled for the key that opened the back door, and after what felt like agonizing minutes, managed to grasp it between her shaking fingers. Moments later, she was inside, the thick metal door between her and that creep. She fought to slow her rapid breathing, but it was hard. The adrenaline had kicked in, and it would take some time before it wore off.

How dare he? Mr. Ferguson had some nerve, coming to her business like that. Competition she understood, but this—this smelled of desperation. She wondered about the CEO's comment of being refused entry into the bakery. Did he finally understand that trust and loyalty were the two things necessary to run a successful business?

"Nah," she told herself. He just resented it when a competitor was doing better than him.

As she walked through the large kitchen, she saw Jacques and Thomas moving quickly through the space like two synchronized partners. As she watched, Britt wondered with a bit of awe how they never bumped into each other.

"Ah, Britt, *bon matin*, good morning!" Jacques called out. He said something to his assistant, then hurried over to her, wiping his hands on his apron. "Our pastries are selling faster than we can bake them today! What has happened?"

"Konditori becoming popular is what happened. I couldn't get in through the front door. I had to come in the back way."

"*Mince!* Damn." Jacques wiped his sweaty brow with a dishcloth, then threw it into the laundry basket behind him. "This frenzied pace, *chérie*. I love the excitement, but…"

She grasped his arm. "I know. We'll need to have a meeting. I have a couple of ideas, but I want to hear from all of you, too." She'd also have to tell them about Mr. Ferguson threatening her in the alleyway. Her staff was going to be infuriated.

Britt joined Betty and Kevin in serving the customers, and about an hour later, it finally slowed down.

"Britt, you gotta stop with the billboard advertising," Betty said with a laugh.

This time, her fast breathing came from excitement. "Seriously, I haven't done anything different."

"It's word of mouth," Kevin said. "And those party pastry trays we set up. We hear what the customers are saying— they love this place. And it's getting around."

She nodded slowly, knowing Kevin was right, but she'd never expected this kind of popularity so soon. She'd have to decide on that fine line between expanding and keeping the coziness of the bakery.

Thankfully, the rest of the day was manageable. Britt finally had a chance to sit down in her office and let her body go limp. As she let her brain process the day, she realized she hadn't told her staff about her encounter with Mr. Ferguson. It was probably better this way.

"WHAT HAVE YOU got for me, Hawthorne?"

"Captain." Mark hadn't been able to get a read on Captain Michelle Fraust since she took over two months ago. Late forties, no-nonsense, and with a list of awards for her leadership and competency, she was one of the youngest officers to make the captain's list.

There had been speculation—and gossip—about her in the precinct. It was expected. But, Mark surmised, unless Fraust decided to suddenly open up about her personal life, all they had were guesses and theories.

He pulled out his notes from the thick folder he had brought with him. "After confirming that Mr. Ferguson was okay, Forensic Investigator Walsh and I collected evidence at the crime scene. Initially, the suspect's fingerprints were found and processed, but the database hadn't provided any positive hits. However, we found distinctive shoe prints in the area that helped to considerably narrow down our search."

"How so?" She sat on the other side of the meeting table, back straight in the chair, with no sign of emotion on her face. It was like talking to a statue, which creeped him out a little.

Mark summarized for the captain the work involved in locating the suspect who owned the limited-edition sneakers.

"And how did you find the right suspect? Shoe size?"

"Not just shoe size." Mark pointed at the left and right footprint. "Do you see the distinction?"

She frowned for only a moment before her blue eyes widened in surprise. "Different-sized feet?"

"Yes, ma'am. On Saturday I went to several stores until I got a hit. I found Henry Toussaint Sunday afternoon and brought him in for questioning. He didn't admit to the assault despite the evidence pointing to him. However, he told me that someone else came up with the plan to commit the arson." Mark still wanted to kick himself for missing that. "Jenny, the construction worker who first reported the incident."

Her ice-blue gaze riveted him in his seat. "Has Mr. Toussaint been charged?"

"No, ma'am." Mark thought carefully on how to phrase his next words. "I think Toussaint has been getting directions from Jenny. I also think Jenny knows pertinent information about these anti-Ferguson protests. If she's in hiding, I'll never find her. But with Toussaint out there…"

"He should lead you to her. A little unorthodox, but I understand your reasoning." She paused. "Mr. Ferguson may want to press charges against Toussaint and Jenny once they're arrested, but we'll wait and see if that happens. Was there anything else?"

Mark kept his expression neutral—he knew what she meant, but he was going to take a risk and feign ignorance. "No, Captain."

Fraust rose and slowly paced the room. "I received a call

from Mr. Ferguson first thing this morning," she started. The captain looked over her shoulder. "He complimented you on being thorough with the investigation."

"I'm glad to hear it, ma'am." He was waiting for the other shoe to drop.

"However, you paid him an unexpected visit at his home Sunday morning." She came back to the table but remained standing. "Was there a reason for that?"

"More a gut feeling. I didn't feel that Mr. Ferguson had told me everything that had happened."

"I see." She sat down again. "What was the result of your surprise interview?"

"Not a damn thing." He should have known better than to think a shrewd businessman like Ferguson would accidentally disclose information about his business tactics.

"You should know that Mr. Ferguson is not a man to be taken lightly."

Surprised, Mark looked at his boss. "I understand, Captain."

"Do you?" Her smile was dangerous. "He didn't climb his corporate ladder with just grit and determination. He did so with a ruthless ambition that would scare off CEOs running the best-known global conglomerates."

Captain Fraust was giving him a hint, and Mark got it— if he was going to accuse Mr. Ferguson of his unethical business dealings with small-business owners, he'd better be damn sure he had everything lined up.

"I'm going to provide an update to the media, but you don't need to be there. My statement will be short, with some diplomatic phrasing that we're still investigating."

"Thank you, Captain."

"Good work so far, Hawthorne, both you and Walsh. Keep me updated. Dismissed."

Mark got on the elevator and hit the button for his floor. That had gone a lot smoother than he'd anticipated. He had felt sure Captain Fraust would browbeat him for suspecting a crime victim, especially a high-level CEO.

Maybe she knew something about Mr. Ferguson that shouldn't be known.

"Huh." Maybe, if he had time, he might poke around to see what he could find. There was no way Ferguson could threaten people and destroy property without suffering some of the consequences.

His personal phone pinged with a text, and Mark glanced at the short, humorous note from Britt.

Hey, how's it going? How was your meeting with the dreaded captain?

Mark couldn't get over Britt's choice of words. He texted her back.

I'm not walking the plank.

Chapter Eight

Britt sipped her tea. "I'm telling you, Joyce, seeing Mr. Ferguson in the alley like that freaked me out."

Before the bakery had closed, her friend Joyce came in to say hi. Britt felt guilty for not keeping in touch with her, but between the CEO's threats, a busy bakery and Mark's sudden appearance in her life, she felt like she'd been stretched in too many different directions.

"Did you report it?" Joyce Mathurin had been hired to do the interior design of the bakery. In her thirties, she was a beautiful dark-skinned Torontonian with roots in Saint Lucia, and the two of them had hit it off almost immediately. Because of their busy schedules, getting together to socialize had been hard, so they made the most of each personal visit.

They were sitting in Britt's office. The bakery had now closed for the day, but she told Joyce to wait in the office while she and the staff cleaned up. The store sat in darkness except for the one lamp in the room, and the security lights located at the front and back of the building.

"No. I know I should, but it feels like I'm not getting anywhere with the police. I took it upon myself to let the man know how much I didn't like him."

Joyce's eyes widened with curiosity.

"I kicked him in the nuts."

Tea spewed from her friend's mouth as her laughter rang through the small office. Britt calmly handed her a napkin. "Are you kidding? Oh gosh, I wish I'd seen that!"

"I think it was more instinct than anything else. I just reacted."

"Hey," Joyce said suddenly, pointing at her. "Where's your bracelet?"

Confused, Britt looked at her left wrist. It wasn't there. "I'm sure I had it on today."

"I only noticed when you handed me the napkin. Maybe you forgot to put it on this morning?"

"Maybe." The rune bracelet had been a birthday present from her family—she rarely left home without it. "I've been distracted lately."

Joyce nodded and bit into a mini cinnamon roll. "I remember you saying you had a lot on your mind, and now this Ferguson guy is ignoring your peace bond. It's too bad you didn't have him in your security footage. I'll bet the police would have done something more."

Britt sat up. "You know what? I just might." Mr. Ferguson had told her he tried to get in the store, but the customers had blocked his way. Her laptop was still on, so she clicked on the security app and used the arrows to slide back to the time just before she arrived.

The scene she watched was chaotic. Several customers jostled in the tight space in front of the door, and in the middle, Mr. Ferguson was using his arms to protect himself from the shoving. Someone landed a punch on his chest.

"The bastard lied. He was actually inside my store," Britt whispered, her voice trembling with anger.

"Holy crap," Joyce breathed. "I can't believe that guy had the balls to walk in here."

"I admit to being more nervous that Mr. Ferguson might charge me with assault."

"You? But you didn't do anything—you were defending yourself!"

"It happened on store property." Britt sighed. "But, with the peace bond still in force, he shouldn't stand a chance if he tried to charge me."

They continued watching until Mr. Ferguson was forcefully shoved out of the store. He shook his fist and yelled something, then straightened his clothing. At that moment, a bus arrived at the nearby stop.

"I'm sure that's the bus I was on," Britt murmured.

The CEO looked over his shoulder, then hurried away and out of the camera's view. A minute later, Britt appeared on screen, opened the front door, looked inside, then left.

"That's when I realized I couldn't get in." She closed the app and shut the laptop.

"So it was coincidence when the two of you saw each other." Joyce wiped her hands on a paper napkin.

"A coincidence that I don't want repeated. How the hell am I supposed to keep this guy away from me and my staff if he deliberately ignores the peace bond?"

Joyce shook her head. "I honestly don't know. If you report it and provide this footage, the police should charge him with a criminal offense."

Britt snorted with disdain. "As if. With his slimy lawyers, Ferguson will only get another slap on the wrist."

"You've done the right things, Britt. The only other idea I have is moving your location."

"Like hell I will." Britt refused to be scared off.

Joyce laughed. "That's what I wanted to hear." She leaned forward in her chair. "So," she said, dragging out the word. "Anything else going on in your life?"

Britt looked at her friend's inquisitive expression and tried not to smile. "Just me and work."

"Mmm-hmm." Joyce picked up her mug. "Work must be more fascinating than usual. Other than dealing with Edward Ferguson of Mighty Big Bastard."

"Oh my God, did you just say that? That phrase is going to be stuck in my mind now." She laughed, enjoying the sound and how it made her feel. She could always depend on Joyce to find the humor in everything.

"So, tell me—what has made you look so glowy?"

"What?" Britt tried to act naive, but by the look on Joyce's face, that wasn't going to work anymore. "All right, you found me out. I met a guy last Friday."

"Oooh, good for you! Who is he? Give me all the deets."

"Well, he's a detective with York Regional Police."

"He's in law enforcement? How intriguing." Joyce propped her chin on her hands. "How did you meet him?"

"Would you believe me if I said our eyes locked on each other from across the street?"

Joyce frowned. "Sounds like something from a movie."

"Right? But that's what happened. I saw him as he was going to his car, and my eyes just went *boing*! You know, like how it happens in the cartoons when their eyes bug out?"

Her friend chuckled. "You and the cartoons...but I know exactly what you mean. Have you been on a date?"

"A couple, actually."

"Girl, you're not wasting any time—I love it! What kind of a kisser is he?"

Britt felt her cheeks heat up in a blush. "A thorough one."

"I'm liking this more and more." Joyce waggled her brows.

"That's as far as we got. I..." She realized that she didn't want to mess this up. Not because she hadn't been on a date in a long time, but because Mark meant much more than that to her. "I don't want to rush things."

"Totally get that. You're being smart. What does he look like?"

"Over six feet. Thick, beautiful hair—it's so soft. Brown eyes with these gold flecks I can see when I'm close enough. I'm pretty sure he's built, but I haven't had the chance to check out under the hood, so to speak."

Joyce laughed and clapped her hands. "Don't worry, you will. I'm so happy for you! I know the store has been your focus, but you need to live your life, too."

Britt couldn't have put it better herself.

"We should get going." Joyce looked at her watch. "Time flies when you're—"

The sudden noise of shattering glass reverberated through the office. "What the hell...?" Britt started to say.

"Someone's breaking in!" Joyce sprang to her feet and peeked out while Britt grabbed her laptop and stuffed it into her purse. Her friend shut and locked the door. "There's three guys, all with baseball bats," Joyce whispered urgently. "We need to hide."

"Joyce, they're going to destroy my bakery!"

"Better that than hurting you. Come on, where can we hide?"

Britt thought furiously. "Not in here, especially if they break the door down." She turned, trying not to panic as several loud voices traveled through the air toward them. "The window. It's our only chance. Hurry!"

Britt slid it open. Although she had installed security lights in the alley, she worried that one wrong move could spell injury for her and Joyce, or alert the intruders.

Joyce climbed out first, displaying her strength as she slid over the windowsill with ease. "Give me your stuff," she said, while holding her hands through the window.

Britt gave her the purse, then proceeded to perch her butt on the sill. Another loud crash, closer this time, caught her attention—they were destroying the display counter.

"Come on!" Joyce called.

She swung her legs over the sill and, grasping her friend's hands, eased down into the narrow alley. "If they get in the office and see the open window, they'll know I was here," Britt said, her voice trembling.

"I'll give you a boost up." Joyce linked her fingers together to form a makeshift step. Britt took her shoe off and stepped into her friend's hands, and held onto the sill while she was slowly lifted upward. Whatever Joyce was doing to stay in shape, Britt needed some of that.

She reached the edge of the window and pulled it down. She couldn't lock it from this side, but she wouldn't worry about that—she was going to call the police as soon as she and Joyce put some distance behind them and the intruders. Britt got her shoe back on. "We have to get out of here." She hurried toward the main street.

"Not that way." Joyce grabbed her arm. "They might have a lookout. Stay close to me."

They hurried down the walkway. At the back of the bakery, Joyce peered around the corner.

"Come on," Joyce whispered, taking the lead. Britt was right behind her, trying not to imagine what those thugs were doing to her bakery.

They had to be careful in the rear alley. While several streetlights helped them to navigate the uneven surface, there were still pools of darkness to walk through. Add the broken, chipped concrete, and it made for a treacherous path. At one point, Britt cried out as she stumbled and fell to her knees on the hard surface.

"Shit, are you okay?" Joyce wrapped an arm beneath her shoulders and got her to her feet. "Give me your bag. We're almost there."

Britt leaned heavily on her friend, her knees burning with pain. Her feet dragged like lead weights, and she used all her energy to move one foot in front of the other. Her hands throbbed painfully from certain cuts. "Joyce, I don't know—" She gasped.

"Yes, you can. Just a few more steps. We're almost on Melville Avenue. We'll call the police then."

It felt like hours later before they finally sat on a sidewalk bench. Joyce had wanted to have at least a block between them and the burglars before stopping. "Hang on, I'll call them," Joyce told her.

"Wait." Britt was fighting to catch her breath. "Ask for Detective Mark Hawthorne if he's still at work. He'll bring the troops."

"The man who makes you go *boing*? Gotcha." Joyce hit a button on her cell, then started talking.

Beneath the streetlight, Britt assessed the damage. The skin on her knees was torn, and blood dripped down her legs. She tried to pick the debris out of her wounds, but it wasn't easy. Her palms were in better shape, just scraped a little, but they hurt like hell. She'd have to go to the hospital.

"They're on their way." Joyce sat beside her, then looked around. "Less than five minutes."

True to their word, three police cars sped toward them, their sirens off. Two vehicles raced by and turned the corner at full speed, while the third screeched to a stop in front of them. Mark literally jumped out of the car. "Britt!" he yelled, running toward her. "*Vakker*, are you all right?"

"Yeah," she said quietly, then hissed when the pain in her knees started to pulse up into her thighs. "I think so."

"Damn it. Hey, get me the first aid kit!" he yelled at the officer who was with him. "What the hell happened?" he demanded.

"Tried to run in heels down a dark alleyway." She smiled at Joyce. "But my friend got us out safely. That's what matters. Sorry," she apologized. "Mark, this is Joyce. She did the interior design for Konditori."

"Pleased to meet you." Mark shook hands. "And I'm glad the both of you are okay."

"That makes two of us," Joyce replied dryly.

Suddenly, a loud static noise came from a walkie-talkie on the officer's belt. "We're at the store," a voice called out. "No one's here. Repeat, the place is empty."

"Son of a bitch!" Britt's anger made her temporarily forget the pain. "They were just there!"

Mark looked at the officer waiting with him. "Tell them to make a sweep of the area, see if anyone's hanging around." He turned to Joyce. "Any idea what they look like?" he asked.

Joyce shook her head. "I managed a peek out the office door but didn't waste any time trying to see their faces. I locked it and got us out the window."

"Smart move." He broke open the kit and pulled out a tube and some gauze. "I'm taking you to the hospital," he mentioned. "But I want to at least get some of this on you and bandage it up." He popped the top off the tube. "I'm going to put this antibacterial ointment directly on your wounds. It's going to sting. You ready?"

Britt nodded, then bit her tongue as the cream burned her skin. "Holy crap, that hurts!"

"Sorry." His hands were comforting and gentle as he

carefully taped gauze over both of her knees while the other officer held a powerful flashlight over them. He used the ointment on her hands as well, and after careful inspection, taped gauze over them as well.

Joyce insisted on riding in the front seat, giving Britt a coy wink as she slid into the police vehicle. Mark helped her inside, then sat beside her. "Check in with the others," he said, his voice demanding. "See if they found anyone."

As Britt listened to the officer's conversation over the radio, Mark shifted until he was up close and personal. "You're sure you're okay?" he asked quietly. Under the car's interior light, his worried expression made her heart thump hard in her chest.

She nodded. There was no way Joyce or the other officer could miss the intimate tête-à-tête going on behind them. "Yeah, I'm good. Just really mad that Ferguson sent more assholes to bust up my shop."

He raised a brow. "What makes you think Ferguson is responsible?"

"You mean besides the other time my bakery got vandalized?" She hadn't meant to sound sarcastic, but it was obvious to her the CEO was involved. But Mark also didn't know about her other unpleasant visit. "He was here this morning, trying to get into the store, but the customers kicked him out. I had the misfortune of running into him when I arrived."

She told him what had happened as the police car sped toward the hospital. "He's really pushing the boundaries," Mark growled. "Until we can prove Ferguson's responsible for the breaking and entering, the police can't do much."

"He's violated the peace bond Britt put on him. And Britt's customers are doing more than you guys," Joyce called out from the front seat. "If that Ferguson guy shows up again, something worse could happen. Shouldn't you all put a stop to it?"

"Trust me, I agree with you. But without hard evidence, I can't do anything."

"Mr. Ferguson is recorded on my security footage from this morning," Britt told him. "That should be enough?"

He nodded. "Yeah, that would do. But let's look after you first."

They arrived at the hospital within minutes, and Mark carried her into the emergency room. "I can walk," Britt complained, wiggling in his tight grasp. "You don't have to do this."

"What? Caring for you? What if I told you I want to?"

That shut her up. Mark had come charging in like a knight in shining armor and taken over. In the back of her mind, Britt quickly realized she didn't mind at all. She'd spent so much time doing everything herself that having someone else look after her made her feel comfortable, protected. And with Mark, she liked it—a lot.

An hour later, her knees and hands were thoroughly cleaned and bandaged. "I need to get to the bakery," she said as she slowly limped beside him and Joyce. The crutches felt alien in her hands. "I have to see what damage they've caused."

"I'll do that, Britt. It's a crime scene now. If you have the security footage on Ferguson and the B and E, it would certainly help."

"I'll email that to you tonight. And I'll text my staff and tell them to stay home tomorrow." It was a serious blow, to both her business and her pride. If there was any shred of proof that Mr. Ferguson was responsible for the destruction of her store, she'd make sure he suffered for it.

"Britt, call me when you get in and settled, so I know you're all right." Joyce sent a meaningful glance in Mark's direction.

She almost laughed at her friend's expression. "I will. And thanks again for saving my butt."

"What are friends for? I'll call tomorrow to see how you're doing." She shook Mark's hand. "Thanks for getting us out of there so fast. Look after her." Joyce hurried to a nearby taxi parked at the curb.

It was just the two of them, and the tension built up in the air.

"Are you sure you're okay?" Mark asked her quietly.

His voice was a beautiful deep rumble, full of emotion. Britt couldn't help herself and turned to face him. "Yeah, thank you." She shook her head. "I can't believe I fell and skinned my knees, though. I know how to walk in my heels."

"You certainly do."

She knew her eyebrows went up at that. "What do you mean?"

"I've seen you walking in them." He leaned close and whispered in her ear. "And it's sexy as hell."

So, he'd been observing her from behind? Britt smiled. "I'm glad you noticed."

"I'd better get you home." He helped her to the police car and held out his arm as a brace while she hung on and lowered herself into the seat. This time, he rode in the front, talking to the officer and getting updates from the others still at the bakery. A jolt of disappointment hit her, but Britt understood the importance of Mark displaying leadership to his colleagues.

He did take her up to her apartment. "I'm sorry, I have to run."

"Mark, it's fine. You did so much more than I expected." She leaned the crutches against the wall and hobbled close to him, then grabbed his shirt collar to keep herself from falling flat on her face.

He prevented that easily enough, wrapping his arms tight around her. He rested his head against her shoulder. "I'm just relieved you're all right."

Britt relaxed against his warmth and inhaled the scent that was uniquely him. To be in his arms… It was so comforting, like sitting in a favorite chair with a wonderful book and a cup of hot tea. She didn't want it to end.

But Mark finally released her, slowly, and his hands rested on her hips. "I'll call you tomorrow and let you know what's going on," he said, his gaze intent as he stared at her. "And if you need anything—anything—call me."

"Sure." Britt caressed his face, feeling the slight stubble from a day's growth of beard. She leaned in and kissed him, her lips just touching his, hoping he sensed how grateful she was for his help.

He angled his head and molded his mouth to hers. Damn, he tasted good, and when his arms went around her again and tightened, she couldn't help herself. Her own arms encircled his neck as she melted into his embrace, her emotions weaving a spell around her that she didn't want to break. All this still felt like a dream.

Hmm… She reached down and pinched Mark's butt.

He backed away quickly, uttering a loud yelp of surprise. "What the heck?"

"Sorry. Well, not really. That was payback."

And confirmation that Mark was definitely real.

BRITT DIDN'T CALL Joyce right away because she needed to email her staff the bad news. As soon as she sat on her bed, she lay down and slept right through the night—she'd been that tired.

The next morning, she sent Mark a file of the security footage from the day before. Britt still didn't think Mr. Ferguson would be charged despite breaking the peace bond. As for the burglars, she saw they had worn masks—fat chance being able to identify them.

Finally, Britt called her friend after settling on her couch with a mug of tea.

"So, any news about the break and enter?" Joyce asked over the phone.

"Nothing yet, and I don't want to bother Mark, either. My staff wasn't happy about it when I emailed them last night."

"How are you feeling?"

"Much better. A little stiff in the legs, but I'll walk around to loosen them up."

"Awesome. So…that was the detective, huh?"

She laughed. "Yes."

"Very handsome. And attentive. I know it's none of my business, but what do you think?"

Britt knew what Joyce meant. "I want to be sure, so I'm taking things slow right now."

"Best decision to make. But I saw the way he looked at you. That detective gives me the impression he'll hang around if you give him half a chance."

Britt swallowed the sudden lump that lodged in her throat. "I thought that, too," she said quietly.

"I don't have to go into work until eleven, so if you want, I can come over and…" Joyce's voice trailed off into silence.

"Joyce? You there?" Nothing. "Joyce!"

"Yeah, sorry." A pause. "You'd better turn on the television."

"Why? What's going on?" She grabbed the remote and clicked the television to life. "What am I looking for?"

"Any national station. I'm sure all of them are covering the story."

"Joyce, you can be such a mysterious drama queen..." Britt's own voice stuttered to a stop as she watched the breaking news.

Edward Ferguson, Mighty Big Bakery's CEO, had been found dead in his backyard early that morning.

Chapter Nine

Talk about being up shit creek without a paddle.

Mark stood on an expansive back porch made of fragrant cedar. Off to one side, furniture and a large BBQ dominated the space, while the other side was bare except for flowers that decorated the railing and roof beams. Directly in front of him, a set of stairs led down to a wide stone patio, and beyond, an in-ground swimming pool was surrounded by a spacious green lawn. More flowers and mature shrubbery bordered the high stone wall that he could just see between the slim gaps created by the tall hedge that offered additional privacy.

Edward Ferguson lay sprawled at the back entrance to the three-car garage, to the left of the porch. He was face down, his head resting against the flagstone. The back of his head showed blunt-force trauma. He'd been hit so hard that a trail of blood had oozed several feet toward the fence.

Mark couldn't say that he was surprised by what happened, but it still bothered him. The bakery CEO seemed to have made a lot of enemies, judging by what Mark had discovered during this investigation. He had hinted at something similar to Captain Fraust during his last update. Somehow, the media had gotten their greedy hands on the story before he arrived, and it had already been broadcast on the morning news.

Myrna was prowling the backyard looking for clues. Several officers were posted around the house to provide security.

He glanced over his shoulder. Ferguson's wife and the housekeeper were in the kitchen, and he could hear their grief echoing through the room.

This wouldn't be easy.

"Keep an eye out for nosy neighbors," he told the two officers that stood beside him. "The coroner should be here within the hour."

Mark had kept his arrival as low-key as possible. Along with his car, which he and Myrna had driven in, two police vehicles were parked on the curb about a half block away. It was possible that someone had spotted them going up to Mr. Ferguson's door, but he hoped that everyone would keep to themselves and not grow curious. As for the coroner van, Mark had asked that they drive straight in, and an officer would direct them to the back. He suspected the media would make another appearance and made sure the other four officers who arrived with him were advised to keep the gates closed and the area clear. It was the best he could do.

He approached Myrna, who was kneeling to one side of Ferguson's body. "Need any help?" he asked.

"I did a sweep of the backyard, but I'm pretty sure the attack happened around here." She lowered herself until she was almost at the level of the body. "I can see strangulation marks around his neck," she stated. "I can't tell if there are any fingerprints, but I'll check in with the coroner after he's finished examining the body."

Mark nodded. Mr. Ferguson was dressed in his usual business suit, which could mean he'd been heading to work.

One of the garage doors was open, revealing a dark green luxury sports car. Mark walked inside in a wide arc so as not to disturb anything, even though he had plastic booties on. Turning on his flashlight, he ran it over the car's gleaming surface. He saw some smudging, but nothing that looked like a print—still, he'd let Myrna know.

The other side had something interesting—a long scratch down the driver's side of the car. "I've got something here," he called out.

She looked up. "I saw that. Got pictures, too, but I can't find the keys."

Although he trusted his forensic investigator to be thorough, Mark knew he'd feel better if he reviewed the lay of the land so that it was clear in his mind. He did a slow walk around the perimeter of the backyard, stopping each time he thought he noticed something, then moving on. It wasn't until he almost reached Myrna on the other side that he noticed something between a pair of thick hedges. "Did you see the footprints?" he called out.

"What?" She jumped to her feet and hurried over. "Where?"

"They're actually behind that row of hydrangea." He only spotted them because he was particularly searching for footprints. "You have your kit with you?"

"Yep. Can't believe I missed that," she grumbled as she pulled out her tools, took photographs of the evidence in question and made a cast of the impressions. "How did you find them?"

"I was looking for them. I'm hoping they belong to Toussaint."

"With the different-sized feet? It would make our lives easier."

The cast had already dried, and Myrna carefully lifted

it out. "Great," she said, placing it on top of a plastic bag. "And not so great."

"What happened? Did it crack?" Mark looked over her shoulder and swore in disbelief. "Those footprints don't belong to Toussaint. They're actually smaller…" He paused, his brain firing off a possible answer that made him want to throw something. "Son of a bitch!"

Myrna watched him, a quizzical expression on her face. "Care to clue me in?"

"Jenny."

She frowned. "The construction worker?"

He nodded. "She's been playing me from the beginning. Not anymore."

"MRS. FERGUSON."

The woman looked up from her pile of tissues. She was in her early fifties, with black hair and green eyes. She wore a silk pajama set beneath a thick, plush white robe.

"Do you think you can talk to me now?"

She nodded and blew her nose.

Mark sat down opposite her. She'd been crying—her eyes were red and swollen, and her mouth compressed into a thin line. He could tell she was trying hard to remain composed, but her trembling body spoke otherwise. "Can you tell me what happened?"

"Normally, I'd wake up before Edward around seven. But when the alarm rang, I didn't see him." She shrugged. "I thought he'd gotten up early to go to a meeting."

"Does he tell you his daily schedule?"

She nodded. "Or he'd have it written on a calendar in the kitchen." She frowned.

"Is that the calendar over there?" Mark pointed. She looked over her shoulder. "I don't see anything written down for today."

"And he didn't mention anything to me or Gloria, our housekeeper. But he had his business suit on. The good one."

"What does that mean?"

"Oh." She waved a hand. "Edward wears the really good suits when he's taking over a business."

Mrs. Ferguson said that nonchalantly, but Mark could feel his temper starting to rise. He fought to control it. "He dresses up to take over someone else's company?"

"A weird habit, I know. It shouldn't matter what he wears. The ending is still the same."

Shit, she sounded just like her husband. "What did you do next?"

"I came downstairs. My housekeeper had already come in."

"Does she have a house key?"

"Yes, and she knows the security code."

He nodded to encourage her to continue.

"Gloria—my housekeeper—and I talked for a bit in the front hall while she put away her things, then we both headed for the kitchen. I turned on the television while she tidied up and made coffee."

"And Mr. Ferguson wasn't in the house."

"No."

His next question was critical. "How did you find him?"

Her hands scrunched the tissues, but that was the only movement he saw. "Gloria opened the kitchen blinds, then stepped out to look at the plants. She noticed the garage door was open, which was odd, and when she stepped down to the patio, she saw Edward lying on the ground." She shuddered. "Her screams were so loud they echoed into the kitchen. When I got outside and saw him…" She paused and dabbed at her eyes. "I pushed Gloria back into the house and told her to call 911. I tried to turn him over, but he was too heavy, and I—I couldn't…"

"It's okay. You did your best." Finding a critically ill or deceased loved one so unexpectedly was a fear Mark had lived with for too long. When Dad's abuse became more violent, he was scared that he'd find Mom on the ground every time he came home from school. Their divorce gave him peace of mind until that day when he'd found her at the bottom of the stairs with the broken leg and hip. "You can't blame yourself." But he knew she did—just like how he felt guilty every time he left Mom alone with that devil. "Did you notice anything odd about him? Or anything on the property?"

"No. I thought someone was trying to steal one of the cars since the garage door was open."

Made sense. "I'm going to talk to the housekeeper. If you need anything, let one of the officers know."

He found Gloria sitting on an ornate wooden bench in the hallway. Compared to Mrs. Ferguson, the housekeeper's grief seemed more palpable. He sat down beside her. "How are you holding up?" he asked gently.

In answer, her face twisted in pain, and a loud sob broke free. He gave her a few minutes to calm down before trying again. "What happened, Gloria?"

She blew her nose, then shook her head. "I don't know. Nothing seemed out of place."

"Tell me what you remember from this morning."

The housekeeper gave the same information as Mrs. Ferguson, except... "His briefcase was missing."

"Missing?" Mark pictured the area around the garage in his mind. She was right. "Did you look for it?"

"No. I was..." She waved a hand helplessly.

"Maybe it's in his car. We'll look for it. What does it look like?"

She blew her nose. "It's a metal briefcase. I think it's the fancy one that can withstand a lot of heat."

Damn, if it's the case Mark thought it was, it could do a lot of damage to a person's skull. On a hunch, he asked, "Any idea what might be in it?"

Something—a flicker of recognition—skimmed across her face. "Not at all."

He sensed a lie. "Are you sure?" he pressed. "It's possible whoever murdered Mr. Ferguson was after whatever was inside this briefcase."

"I don't know what you're talking about." The housekeeper rose. "If you'll excuse me, I'd like to tend to Mrs. Ferguson."

Mark got up as well. "Of course." As he watched her hurry toward the kitchen, he knew there was more going on than what the housekeeper was admitting to. He would need to question the ladies further anyway, and then he would sniff out the secrets Gloria was obviously hiding.

Back outside, the coroner had arrived. Mark mentioned the missing item to Myrna. "His briefcase?" She frowned. "I haven't seen anything lying around. Maybe it's in his car?"

"We'll need to see if the keys are in his pockets."

"Let me ask. I didn't want to turn the body over until they got here to supervise." She approached the coroner and after a moment, he and his assistant had deftly flipped Mr. Ferguson onto his back.

Mark grimaced. The CEO's face had turned an ugly shade of purple and blue and was horribly swollen. Which made him wonder… "How long do you think his body has been lying there?" he called out.

Both Myrna and the coroner looked up. "Judging by the body's state of rigor mortis," the coroner answered in a dull voice, "the male victim has been dead since very early this morning. Say, between one and five in the morning."

So, Mr. Ferguson would have gotten out of bed while his wife was sound asleep. The housekeeper wasn't a live-in, so he could sneak out and be back before Mrs. Ferguson knew. But what would prompt the CEO to go out at that time of night?

Mrs. Ferguson did say the suit her husband had on was only worn when he was about to conquer a business. What kind of business deal was so critical that he had to sneak out to complete it?

"Mark, here are his car keys." Myrna held them up with a gloved hand.

They opened the car door, but after searching the interior, didn't find the briefcase. Mark had just climbed out when he noticed a soft glint of something sitting on the dash. When he took a closer look, the blood chilled in his veins. It couldn't be…

Britt's bracelet.

"Myrna, can you collect that?" He pointed at the piece of unique jewelry, watching his hand shake. Confused, angry, hurt—he wasn't sure how he felt at the moment.

"It's pretty." She held it up and looked at it closely. "Huh. They're small Nordic runes, and it looks like they spell out a name. B, R, I…"

"Britt."

She squinted. "Yeah, you're right." Myrna looked at him with wide eyes. "And you know this because…?"

He chewed the inside of his cheek. "It belongs to someone I know."

Captain Fraust had her back turned to him as Mark updated her on his findings at the murder scene. "So you don't believe this Toussaint had anything to do with Mr. Ferguson's death." It was a statement, not a question.

"No, ma'am. The evidence at Ferguson's house doesn't support it."

"And this Jenny, the construction worker? Why did you bring her up?"

Mark tried not to bite his tongue in frustration. "Toussaint said she thought of the arson idea. I don't know if she's capable of murder, but the footprints we found were about her size, and the brand name stamped on the soles of the boots belongs to a well-known clothing company that specializes in construction gear."

She turned around, her brows raised. "You understand that you can't make that kind of assumption without additional hard evidence?"

"I know, ma'am, but it's one plausible answer. I'm going to bring her in on the premise that I have further questions. If Jenny gives any hint that she's responsible for the arson attempt or knows the identity of the murderer, I'll have her charged. Maybe sitting in a jail cell will get her to talk. I know it smells of desperation, but I think she'll provide the information I need."

Fraust cocked a brow. "This is highly unusual of you, Hawthorne."

"Yes, ma'am. But the two viable suspects I found are not talking." Mark paused, feeling unsure of himself. "I'm also afraid that if I let Jenny go after questioning her, she'll dig a hole so deep we'll never find her again."

The captain nodded. "Normally, I wouldn't endorse this kind of thing, and would recite all the reasons why it's wrong. But after listening to your theories, I'm going to let you go ahead. However," she warned. "Remember her rights."

"Yes, ma'am." Mark's gamble had paid off.

"What have you found out at the house?"

Mark felt like he was back in school, with the teacher singling him out to answer a particularly difficult question. "I believe the housekeeper knows more than she's letting on. I found out from Myrna—Investigator Walsh—that the coroner told her the method of death. The murderer strangled Ferguson first, then hit him in the back of the head several times. Approximate time of death was between the hours of one and five in the morning. We also can't find his briefcase."

She nodded. "The only way the murderer could even get close to Mr. Ferguson at that time…" Fraust let her voice trail off.

But Mark got the hint, and as he came to the most logical conclusion, he smacked the table, causing the papers to flutter. "Son of a bitch, the suspect arranged it. Must have called Ferguson and told him a lie so big that it made the CEO put on his best suit in the middle of the night to meet him."

"Agreed. We'll need to find out what business deal Mr. Ferguson had arranged that would make him go off schedule." She paused. "Anything else?"

Britt's jewelry burned a hole in his mind. For God's sake, why the hell was it even in the CEO's car? "We haven't located the suspects who pulled that B and E on the Konditori bakery," he said instead. "We received security footage, but the burglars were wearing masks. However, I believe they were hired by Ferguson to destroy it."

"It seems a moot point now. However, we can't let destruction like this go unpunished. Someone in Mr. Ferguson's small circle must know something. I want them flushed out."

"Yes, ma'am." Mark gathered his things and headed to

his office. He should have thought of the suspect getting in touch with Mr. Ferguson. Honestly, he couldn't stop thinking of Britt's possible involvement. Her bracelet was a damning piece of evidence in the middle of this murder investigation.

Timmins was in the office when Mark walked in. "Hawthorne, you haven't told me what happened at the murder scene. How did the search go?"

He gave the older detective a rundown of his findings.

"Shit. An attack like that would need strong upper body strength."

And it was probable Jenny possessed that kind of power to cause lethal damage.

Mark couldn't stall any longer. Both women had a lot of explaining to do.

Mark just hoped Britt had nothing to do with the bakery CEO's death.

Chapter Ten

Britt climbed out of the taxi, her injuries almost healed, though her knees were still stiff from not moving much yesterday. She walked the few steps to Konditori, her gaze scanning over the building. Her insurance company had been here since this morning, evaluating the property damage alongside the police, and they had called an hour ago to tell her they would help pay for the renovations. It wasn't as bad as it looked. Someone would be at the store tomorrow morning to give her the key to the padlock, and she could start cleaning up the pieces of her bakery.

The large picture window was completely smashed. Wooden boards had replaced it to keep the curious and the thieves at bay. The front door was sealed tight with a large padlock and covered in a crisscross of bright yellow tape with the words DO NOT CROSS.

The letters *MBB* were sprayed across the storefront multiple times with black paint, leaving only small glimpses of pink through the mess.

She hated to think what she might find inside and began to doubt her insurance company's reassurances.

She walked down the alley, remembering Mr. Ferguson's skulking form half-hidden in the shadows. His anger at her refusal to sell couldn't match the fury Britt felt deep in her stomach. That pretentious dickhead hadn't cared who he hurt—he had steamrolled over small businesses, families and innocent people to get what he wanted.

He wouldn't be doing that anymore.

Britt peeked around the corner before walking toward the rear exit—she didn't know if those jerks might still be around. There was no damage to the steel door or the windows here. It seemed that the police had arrived before the thugs could do anything else.

She completed her circuit, her emotions jumbled, but her anxiety was sitting pretty high. She would need to find additional money to make repairs. Even though her insurance said they would cover most of it, until she got inside, Britt didn't know what would need to be replaced. If the expensive kitchen equipment had been damaged...

She sighed. There wasn't much she could do.

Her cell phone pinged with a text. It was an officer from York Regional Police 4 District, advising her that their investigation was complete, and she could go into her store. Thank God for that.

Britt looked across the street to where Mr. Ferguson's latest bakery sat partially finished. Despite the CEO's death, she was sure his company would continue building, while she would scramble to make ends meet.

Her one consolation was the loyalty of her staff and customers. She had received emails that offered their condolences, reassuring her that they would return as soon as she got back on her feet. She had almost cried while reading those comforting notes, never realizing how she made an impact on strangers. Joyce had already insisted on helping her get Konditori back on its feet, and Britt could pay her back when she had the funds.

Britt sighed. Mark. She hadn't talked to him at all today—

he had to be busy working on Mr. Ferguson's murder investigation. She pulled out her phone, focused on calling to find out how he was.

He picked up on the second ring. "Britt, how are you?"

His voice sounded different—a bit strained, tired. "I'm fine. I managed to see my doctor this morning. My knees look good, just a bit raw and achy. How are you?"

"Okay. It's been a long day."

He didn't sound all right, though. In fact, he sounded like a stranger, not the warm, attentive man she had gotten to know over the last few days. "You don't sound okay," she said gently, hoping everything was fine. Did his mom take a turn for the worse? "Maybe you'd like to come over later? I could make us dinner." Those words came out of nowhere, but to her, they felt right. Mark had begun to bring out a portion of herself she hadn't seen in a long time.

"I'd like that, but…" He stopped.

This wasn't like him. In fact, this whole conversation felt wrong. "Mark, what is it? Talk to me."

"Are you home?"

She was sitting on a sidewalk bench near the store. Her knees weren't bothering her—Mark's strange attitude was. "I got restless. I'm at my bakery, assessing the damage from the outside."

"You are?" A moment passed. "You're not trying to sneak in to take a look, I hope."

"I did get the go-ahead from both the insurance company and the police. An officer just texted me with clearance, so I can finally get organized." Knowing this offered some closure. It meant she could move forward with plans, get her staff back up and running. They'd been anxious, worried they'd have to find other jobs to make ends meet. She'd also toyed with the idea of renting out another, smaller space nearby to get Konditori back on its feet while repairs were being made to the original bakery. In fact, she might have to look into that, depending on what she found inside...

"I...need to ask you something, Britt."

All her senses were instantly on alert. Mark's voice sounded professional, almost distant. "Yes?"

"I have to ask you to come to the station."

Was that all? Did he want to give her a tour of his workplace, maybe introduce her to his colleagues? She rubbed her chin—Mark was taking their relationship a little too fast. "Mark, it's sweet that you want me to meet your fellow officers, but I don't think that's—"

"No, that's not what I meant." His voice had gotten quieter, and now he sighed. "I need you to come down to the station in order to ask you some questions about Mr. Ferguson."

Did she hear him correctly? "Mark, what are you talking about?"

She heard a car door slam. "Stay at the bakery. I'm coming now to pick you up."

"Mark, you'd better explain what you mean by that." She rubbed her stomach at the ache that flared inside. Something was horribly wrong, and Mark wasn't giving her any answers. "What's going on?"

"I'm almost there. Give me a minute."

The urge to run off and hide had Britt on her feet, even though she knew she hadn't done anything wrong. She could easily meld into the early-evening rush-hour crowd and lose him until she got home. Or maybe stay with Joyce until she could figure out why he needed to question her about a dead man who had threatened her hard-won business.

Too late. Mark pulled up in front of her. As he got out of the car, Britt moved to keep the bench between them.

"What's this about?" she demanded, drawing stares from nearby pedestrians.

He stopped, his expression a mix of confusion and hurt, touched with a bit of anger. "Maybe you'd like to explain this to me."

He held up a plastic bag, and as she peered at its contents, her breath caught in her throat. It was her runic bracelet, a birthday present from her parents. "Where did you get that?" she asked, automatically rubbing her left wrist.

"Would you like to get in the car and I can tell you privately, or shall I announce it for everyone around us to hear?"

His anger sent a shock wave of trepidation coursing through every part of her limbs. She should have escaped when she had the chance.

Refusing to cause a scene, Britt came around the bench and quickly got into the car, slamming the door hard so that he got the hint she was frustrated with him. He climbed in, tossed the bracelet on the dashboard and gunned the motor. He waited until she got her seat belt on before driving off and merging with the busy evening traffic. Britt saw how tense his body was, from the white knuckles gripping the steering wheel to his clenched jaw. "Mark, talk to me. What's bothering you?" she asked.

His gaze hovered over her bracelet before he returned his attention to driving.

"My bracelet?" How did Mark find it anyway? She reached for the baggie.

"Please don't touch it, Britt."

Her hand froze in midair from the shock of his words. "Why not?" she whispered. "What does my bracelet have to do with Mr. Ferguson?"

She watched his expression, unsure what he was feeling. "Your bracelet was found in Mr. Ferguson's car."

There was a moment of pure disbelief before she burst out laughing. "Jeez, Mark, for a moment there you terrified me."

He frowned. "I found it in his car, Britt. I'll show you the evidence when we get to the precinct."

No hint of a smile or anything to portray that he was joking. And she suddenly realized he wasn't.

When they reached the precinct, Britt immediately got out of the car and walked to the front doors. Inside, she had to take Mark's lead and followed him onto an elevator at the back of the building. He hit a button two floors down, then turned to her. "Look, I'm sorry to do this to you…"

"No, you're not." During the ride to the police station, she had time to think about Mark's allegation. "You're doing your job—I get that. What I don't understand is how my bracelet ended up in Mr. Ferguson's car—it's not like I gave it to him. And in case you haven't noticed, you're making me nervous."

The elevator pinged. When the doors opened, they were in a brightly lit hallway, and stretching to either side were square rooms. She saw an officer open one of the doors and step inside. "Where are we?" she asked.

"These are the interrogation rooms." He guided her to the same room the officer stepped into. When she hesitated on the threshold, Mark said, "Step inside, please."

He indicated a chair. Jeez, he wasn't even going to be a gentleman and pull it out for her as he usually did. With a huff of disdain, she dropped her butt onto the hard seat.

Mark looked at her for a moment, and she stared back, hoping he'd see her furious expression. He bit his lip, then turned back to the door. An older officer had come in and sat in a chair behind her.

Britt glanced over her shoulder, then looked back at Mark, willing herself to relax. She told herself again that she'd done nothing wrong, and this was just a simple Q&A Mark had to do as part of his job. She would wait until he started talking.

"Britt Gronlund, I'm Detective Mark Hawthorne with York Regional Police 4 District." His introduction was cold, unfeeling. "Behind you is Detective Walter Timmins, who is my backup."

She nodded and wrapped her arms around herself.

"I'm investigating the murder of Mr. Edward Ferguson, CEO of Mighty Big Bakery." He had a small pile of documents in front of him, and he shuffled through them until he pulled out a picture. When he slid it over, Britt looked at it and frowned. That was her bracelet, sitting on someone's car dashboard.

He then reached for the piece of jewelry, still in its plastic bag. "Does this item belong to you?"

She almost snapped at him. Of course Mark knew the bracelet belonged to her. However, she held back, and after taking a deep breath, she settled her emotions into a kind of calm detachment. "Yes."

He placed it to one side and wrote something down. "I need to advise you that during my investigation at Mr. Ferguson's home, your bracelet was found in his car."

She blinked, still not believing what she'd heard, but remained silent, waiting to see if Mark would add any further context.

He looked at her, his brow raised. "Can you explain how your bracelet got into Mr. Ferguson's car?"

Mark wasn't seriously thinking… "I have no idea how my jewelry got into that jerk's car."

A small smile ghosted his lips before it disappeared.

"Are you saying you weren't in Mr. Ferguson's car at all, Ms. Gronlund?"

She turned to stare at the older man who had asked the question. "Not at all."

He gave her a look that had *I don't believe you* written all over it.

"Can you explain how it might have gotten into Mr. Ferguson's car?" Mark asked.

Britt kept her gaze on Mark. "On Monday morning, I arrived at my bakery, but it was filled with customers—I couldn't get in. I went around to the alley to go through the back door, and Mr. Ferguson was there." The angry look on the man's face still gave her the creeps. "He told me the customers threw him out when he tried to come in, and for some reason, he hung around until I showed up.

"He went through his usual spiel of trying to buy my business. I told him it wasn't for sale. He got angry and grabbed me."

A dark shadow crossed Mark's face. She hadn't told him that part because she knew she could handle the CEO. Besides, there were plenty of pedestrians at the time—a few high-pitched screams would have brought someone running to help her.

"What happened next?"

"I kicked him in the balls and left him there. I had a business to run."

This time, a full smile lit up Mark's features. "Very proactive of you."

Britt kept her professional stance up, despite the warm feeling seeping through her at Mark's grin. "I can only think that Mr. Ferguson pulled my bracelet off when he grabbed me. It makes the most sense."

"Do you think he planned on returning it to you?"

"I hope so. Although I wouldn't put it past him if he tried to bribe me with it. The bracelet has a lot of sentimental value."

"Can you tell us the rest of your day?"

Britt explained in detail up until Joyce had called the police. "The rest you already know, Detective Hawthorne. Thank you for assisting my friend and I last night." Being detached and polite worked both ways.

"We'll need to hang on to your bracelet for the duration of our investigation." Mark slid the picture back into his stack of documentation and placed her bracelet on top, then stood. "Thank you for your cooperation. We may need to call you in for further questioning."

She nodded, biting the inside of her cheek, only because she wondered what Mark was playing at.

He glanced over her shoulder. "I'd like to escort Ms. Gronlund outside, Timmins. Would you mind taking my notes to the office?"

Glancing at the other detective, who had grabbed Mark's stuff and was heading out, she finally surmised he probably had to be professional when questioning her. Still, he could have warned her.

When they got outside, he took her elbow and led her to his car, remaining quiet until they got in. He breathed a loud sigh of relief. "*Vakker*, I can't tell you how sorry I am for putting you through that."

Britt twisted her hands in her lap. "You're a real jerk, Mark Hawthorne."

He jumped in his seat, his eyes wide with surprise. "Britt, I mean it…"

"I get it. You were playing detective—can't get too close to the witness. Gotta keep it professional."

"Britt, that's not fair." He got the car started.

"No? Was treating me like a criminal fair?"

"I didn't do…" He stopped, his breath loud and harsh within the car interior. "We found your bracelet in Ferguson's car. How else did you expect me to treat it? And you?"

"You could have simply asked, instead of dragging me through a police interrogation and embarrassing me."

"No, Britt, I couldn't. Your jewelry was found at a murder scene. Think on that. If I treated you any differently to the other witnesses I'd brought in, Detective Timmins and the officers outside that room would have questioned my motives. I can't play favorites in this job." He drove out into the busy traffic. "If I'd given you any hint about what was going on, you wouldn't have been surprised or upset. That would have tipped off Timmins for sure. He's an old pro at this. He would have given me a world of grief."

Britt listened as Mark explained his actions. She understood the intent, but it didn't quite make her feel better. "Did you really think I killed Mr. Ferguson?"

"No!" His voice was firm, assuring. "You would beat him up, but not kill him. I knew you would think Ferguson wasn't worth going to jail for."

"You got that right." At least they were on the same page with that. She started to calm down, thinking through everything Mark had said, and coming to the conclusion that, yes, he was doing his job. She knew she was innocent and had nothing to worry about.

"Why didn't you tell me about Ferguson grabbing you in the alley?" he asked.

"Because I knew how you would react. Besides, he didn't expect me to know self-defense maneuvers."

"Wish I'd seen that." His smile was his own, filled with humor. "And how are your knees?" He rested a hand on one. "I noticed you didn't have trouble walking."

Britt had worried she'd flinch, considering what he'd put her through. But her anger had almost melted away, and the warmth from his touch felt good. "A lot better, thank you." She thought of something. "Have you found out anything about those jackasses that broke into my store?"

"No. Thanks for the security footage, by the way. Unfortunately, it doesn't help since the thugs were disguised. Myrna, my forensics investigator, did find some fingerprints, but she didn't get any hits."

"I wonder what they'll do now that Mr. Ferguson's dead."

"Best scenario? Stop trashing people's businesses."

For some unexplained reason, she didn't think that would happen. "Do you honestly believe that?"

Another sigh, but he sounded tired. "I don't know. Until I can collect more information, I can't do anything."

Britt noticed he was taking her back to her place. "Listen, do you want to grab a bite to eat? I'm starving."

"Great idea. So am I."

They found a well-known sandwich shop. It was empty, which Britt was glad for. In her gut, she felt that they needed to discuss some things—not just what had happened with Mr. Ferguson, but themselves, especially her. She hadn't opened up about her past because she hadn't been ready to revisit the pain and humiliation. Britt knew that if she didn't get it out of her system, it would continue to fester like an untreated wound, and she couldn't move forward with her life. It seemed the best time to talk to Mark about it.

They sat at a table near the front window. Despite the noise of traffic, it was unusually quiet in the shop. "Other than interrogating me," she started, "how was your day?"

Mark frowned and twisted his mouth. "Frustrating."

"Can you talk about any of it? Or is it confidential? Maybe I can help."

His look was curious. "You have enough going on with the bakery. I don't want to add to that. Besides, it's part of my job to be pissed off when the clues don't come together."

"But you must discuss investigations with your colleagues, right? Just think of me as one of them." She imitated Detective Timmins's stance, crossing her arms and attempting to make a stern face. "Come on, Hawthorne," she growled in a deep voice. "Let's hear what you've got."

His widening grin burst into a loud snort of laughter. "That was almost perfect. Thank you for that."

Their meals arrived, and Britt stared at the smoked salmon and cream cheese specialty she had ordered—the sandwich was big, and it came with a salad and a chocolate-almond croissant for dessert. She could take half of it home to have for lunch tomorrow. She glanced at Mark's, inhaling the scent of steak, cheese and onions. "Oh my God, that smells delicious."

"I'll give you a piece." He used a fork and knife to deftly cut off a corner and put it on her plate. *"Bon appétit."*

They spent a few minutes enjoying their meal. By the time Britt came up for air, she'd finished her sandwich and half of her salad. "Crap," she mumbled, wiping her mouth with a napkin. "I didn't realize how hungry I was."

"I've heard that stress can increase one's appetite," he murmured.

"Oh, great." She eyed the croissant with disdain. Ah, what the hell. She took a bite of the sweet, flaky pastry. "Mmm, this is good. Maybe I should ask Jacques to come up with a similar recipe, Norwegian style."

Mark stirred his cappuccino. "How did you two meet each other?"

His question meant talking about her past, and it was as good a time as any. "I had Konditori all planned out. I found the perfect spot for it and hired Joyce to do the interior design. I started looking for staff, and Jacques answered me the day I posted the job, and I was honestly shocked at his experience. He worked at a Michelin-starred restaurant while living in France, before moving to Toronto."

His brows rose. "Why would he move from France?"

"He said better opportunities. He never talked about it, but my hunch is, he wants to open his own business someday."

Mark nodded. "You might lose a great baker."

"I know. But I'm not going to begrudge his ambitions. He'll do what's right for him." She paused, thinking of herself.

"How did you become a bakery owner, Britt? I don't think I asked you that."

Britt took a breath as her muscles wove into tense, painful knots. Here it was, her opportunity to clear out her past.

He grabbed her hand and squeezed it. "Hey, if you don't want to talk about it…"

"I have to." The words rushed out of her. "Because if I don't, I'll feel like I'm keeping secrets from you, which isn't fair to either of us."

His eyes widened, sparkling beneath the lights in the shop.

"When I was in university, I majored in economics with the goal of becoming a parliamentary secretary. My ultimate dream was to become a member of Parliament. I wanted to try to change some of the things going on in the country."

"A lofty goal."

"But achievable. I graduated with honors and was determined to find a position within a year." Back then, her ambitions were laser-focused. "I had my pick of various jobs everywhere from Fisheries and Oceans Canada to the federal security agency.

"I finally decided on working with the minister of international trade. That was five years ago. I loved it. I learned so much from Minister Frank Strathmore. But I started hearing strange rumors about the minister's mannerisms, especially toward women."

Mark's face darkened with anger, which she expected. "I found out the world of politics was still a man's domain, and of course, they like to do things their way. Minister Strathmore was no different. When he became a little too friendly, I accused him of assault. He just laughed in my face."

The awful, familiar feelings of humiliation and embarrassment reared their ugly heads, demanding that she acknowledge them. This time, Britt did, but chose not to let those emotions make her feel bad or ashamed. She fought them back, showing that she was in control, that she was sick and tired of feeling guilty for standing up for herself. "I learned quickly that every man and woman had to fend for themselves. After I reported the minister's actions, nothing was done. In fact, I was told to suck it up and be proud that Minister Strathmore was giving me 'personal support,' as Human Resources called it."

"Jesus," Mark breathed. He squeezed her hand. "One of my female colleagues at work talked about that. She had to prove her worth almost twice as much as the men. I used to think of her as aggressive, but when she told us what she went through…" He stopped. "Did you quit the job?"

"I thought about it—many times. But I wanted to put Minister Strathmore's head on a platter first.

"I collected evidence over a six-month period. Photos, calls, video, text messages, to support myself and the other women he'd been harassing. I called HR out on their crap, and next thing I knew, I was being summoned to defend my actions." She sighed. "Those were the worst five weeks of my life." Britt could see the scenes in her mind—the courtroom, the minister and his friends giving her the evil eye, the women who said they would support her instead looking at their hands while she testified.

"I had enough physical evidence to get him fired from his position, that's all. And the next time I heard his name, Minister Strathmore had somehow become an independent member in the Parliament of Canada." She chewed the inside of her cheek. "Just goes to show you what a person can do with enough clout."

Mark hadn't moved or said anything while she talked, but his being there helped to keep the demons away. "My ability to trust took a serious nosedive," she concluded. "I became introverted, closed myself off after the trial. Thank God I was too stubborn to stay that way. So I pivoted and worked on my next dream job, which was owning my own bakery. Now here I am, making Nordic pastries and comparison shopping for supplies."

"But you love it. That's what counts."

"Sure do. And getting the all-clear from the insurance company to rebuild has taken a weight off my shoulders. My staff and I can start cleaning up tomorrow."

"That's great news, Britt." He finished his cappuccino. "Maybe I'll swing by to visit."

His cell phone pinged with a text. As he read it, she noticed his worried look. "Is everything all right?" she asked.

"Yeah." He raised his hand to get the waiter's attention. "It's my mom. She wants me to come to the hospital to visit."

"I hope she's doing well." They headed for the car.

Mark grasped her hand in his as they strolled down the sidewalk, and Britt could easily get used to this. To not just have a man in her life, but someone who was also in her corner, to provide support and encouragement. She'd love to return the favor. However, his line of work may not offer a chance to provide ideas or theories that could help in his cases. She could certainly ask. "You know, if you need a sounding board during your investigations, you can let me know. I won't tell anyone anything."

He raised her hand to his lips. "Thank you, *vakker*. That means a lot."

At the door to her condo, she wrapped her arms around his neck. "I'm not sure if I should even kiss you," she whispered, a breath away from his lips. "You thought I was a criminal."

He cocked a brow. "No. I thought you were up to something with that bastard."

"Ewww." She pulled at his ear. "I can't believe you'd think that!"

"No, I didn't mean it that way. I meant..." He paused. "I was worried you had changed your mind about selling your bakery."

"If there's one thing you should remember, Mr. Detective, it's that I'm stubborn. I get what I want, but not by hurting others."

"Yup, that's my Nordic princess." His kiss was thorough, lingering. She didn't want it to end.

Another ping from his phone. He groaned as he slowly released her. "I'd better get going before Mom sends a hunting party out looking for me."

She grinned. "Your mom sounds like fun."

"Great sense of humor. I think you two would like each other." With a wink and another kiss, he disappeared down the hallway.

Britt had plans of her own to organize. She emailed her

staff with the good news and told them to wait for her by the rear door so she could let them in. Then she called Joyce, who screamed with delight, and said she'd be there by ten o'clock tomorrow morning to assess what needed to be done.

All in all, a good day despite the vandalism hanging over her head. Britt was taking baby steps to move her life forward again, this time with Mark at her side.

Chapter Eleven

Mark had never felt so scared. He could handle mouthy dickheads with ease as he dragged their sorry asses to jail. No problem at all.

Britt, on the other hand… The drive to the precinct yesterday to interrogate her about her bracelet had him on pins and needles. He had no way to know how questioning her would turn out.

What hurt the most was remaining silent. She may not have noticed, but he heard the increasing note of panic in her voice as she demanded answers. Answers he couldn't provide until he got back to the police station.

Perhaps there was a better way of handling the situation. Mark certainly hadn't been thinking straight when he'd found her bracelet in Ferguson's car. Considering all that had happened these past few days, how else could he have viewed that damning piece of evidence?

But his instinct had told him how wrong he was. And while instinct was a great indicator, it was hard to ignore what was in front of him—Britt's bracelet, in the car of Mighty Big Bakery's dead CEO.

He remembered how the weight lifted off his shoulders when the interrogation was over, although he still had an angry Nordic princess chewing him out when they'd left the precinct.

Mark sat at his desk, piecing clues together, thinking on theories. The footprints at Mr. Ferguson's home and the fingerprints found on the CEO's body didn't match Henry Toussaint's as he'd first hoped, but he had to be sure. As for Jenny the construction worker, she had already lied to him once, so he'd have to be ready for any tricks, including that flirtatious manner of hers. If she was the killer, she would do everything possible not to get caught.

Mark still believed he hadn't received all the truth from Toussaint, either. He thought the young man might know who the protest leader was, but scratched that idea. Since it was Jenny who drove them to the secret protest site, Mark might have a better chance of obtaining that information from her.

Now all he had to do was locate her.

As for the housekeeper and Mrs. Ferguson… Well, something definitely smelled fishy about Gloria. He would explore that after talking to the construction worker.

His first visit, to the partially built Mighty Big Bakery, yielded no results. Mr. Smith, the supervisor who was still in charge of the site, told him that Jenny got called to another location. "Damn pain in my ass," he grumbled. "How the hell am I supposed to stay on schedule when I'm down a person?"

"Is that normal?" Mark asked.

"No, it's not. And with Mr. Ferguson dead, I don't know who's taking over this project."

The comment made Mark's ears perk up. That was right—there should be a succession plan in case the owner couldn't direct anymore. He'd have to pay a visit to the MBB head office. "No one called?"

"Not a peep. I'll keep going until I hear otherwise."

"Thanks." He headed back to his car, thinking. Toussaint no doubt told Jenny about his interrogation with the police, and she was probably in hiding. He had her address, which wasn't far from the sushi restaurant he and Britt had gone to.

It was an old duplex apartment, which blended in with the large houses on the street. He hit the buzzer twice, and when he didn't get an answer, tried calling her cell phone. It went immediately to voice mail. He left a message, asking her to call as soon as possible, then slowly went down the stairs. He turned around to look up at the apartment. The blinds were shut—maybe she was sleeping in and had turned her phone off.

Maybe…

Mark hopped back up the stairs and hit the buzzer for the other apartment. This time, a dog barked furiously but went quiet when a stern voice hushed it. The inner door opened to reveal a man in his late fifties. "Yes? You looking for someone?"

"Good morning." He showed his badge. "I wanted to ask if you'd seen Jenny recently."

"The young lady lives here, but I haven't seen her today. Might be with that boyfriend of hers."

Mark felt like a first-class douchebag—why hadn't he put two and two together? "Don't tell me, Henry?"

He nodded. "Yeah, that's the name. He came by around five or so yesterday. Jenny gets home about that time. Did the horizontal mambo for a couple of hours before taking off. I don't know where."

Mark had his suspicions. "Thank you, sir."

THIS TIME, NO more Mr. Nice Guy.

With a search warrant in his pocket, Mark pounded on

Henry Toussaint's door. "Open up! York Regional Police 4 District! I know Henry Toussaint's in there!"

Timmins, his hand resting on a stun gun, glanced at him. "What do you think?"

"I think they'll make a run for it. Ergo, officers watching the back door and windows."

The front door finally opened, and the woman he had met a few days ago appeared. "Oh, it's you again," she sneered. "Henry's not here."

"Now you're just bullshitting me." Mark's temper was getting hot, but he wasn't going to lose it.

The woman's surprised expression morphed into anger. "How dare you talk—"

"Where's Henry?" He pushed against the door, but the woman held her ground. "Look, Mrs. Toussaint, I have a warrant to search the premises and bring Henry and his girlfriend in for further questioning."

"Henry doesn't have a girlfriend," she spat.

"Well, you're in for a surprise." The woman was strong, but not enough to keep him and Timmins out. "Unless you want my partner and me to thoroughly search through the house for your son," he warned, "I suggest you tell him to make an appearance." He took the warrant out and waved it in the air. "Your call."

The expression on her face would have scared off a grizzly bear. "Henry!" she yelled out. Damn, she had a powerful voice. "Henry! Get down here, now!"

No answer. She frowned, then turned back to him. "He's not home. What's this about anyway?"

Mark knew his brow went up at that. "He hasn't told you?" He glanced at Timmins, and at his nod, barged in and raced for the stairs.

"Hey! What are you doing?"

Mark got on his walkie-talkie. "This is Hawthorne. Anyone show up?"

"No, sir, the windows are clear."

"One of you get to the garage. Bust the back door down if you have to."

With the older detective at his back, they checked each of the rooms on the second floor but couldn't locate Henry or Jenny. "Team, tell me you have them!" he said into the walkie-talkie, running back downstairs.

"Negative, sir. No one's out here."

He and Timmins checked the rooms on the main floor before Mark stepped up to Mrs. Toussaint. "If you don't tell me where Henry is, I'll arrest you for obstruction," he growled out.

"As if. Henry hasn't done anything wrong."

"Your precious Henry beat up the CEO of Mighty Big Bakery," Timmins chimed in. "And now the man is dead."

Whoa, Mark hadn't expected Timmins to be so blunt. But maybe it would get Mrs. Toussaint to open her eyes and help them find her son and Jenny.

She grasped the front of her blouse, and Mark watched with growing concern as her face turned a ghastly shade of white. Her mouth trembled, but nothing came out.

"Mrs. Toussaint," he said gently. "We need to find your son and take him and Jenny in for questioning. We believe they haven't given us their full story."

Every minute the woman remained quiet was another minute that Henry and Jenny could escape. Mark snapped his fingers in front of her face, concerned that she'd gone into shock. "Mrs. Toussaint."

She blinked slowly, as if waking up from a dream. But then her face screwed up in anger, and he was now worried she wouldn't help at all.

"Follow me." She headed toward the back of the house.

He eyed Timmins, who shrugged, then hurried to catch up to Mrs. Toussaint. "This is Hawthorne," he called over the walkie-talkie. "Maintain position. Repeat, maintain your posts."

They followed her into a spacious kitchen. Wide, ceiling-high windows let in plenty of sunshine and offered an amazing view of the expansive backyard, with a swimming pool and BBQ patio. She veered to the left, then stopped in front of a door. "This leads to the family room in the basement," she told them. "He's down there."

"Is there any way for him to escape?" Mark asked, eyeing the entrance.

"There's a door that leads into the backyard. I guess if he was desperate, he could crawl through a window that faces the front."

"Would you mind calling him out, Mrs. Toussaint? I'd like to conduct this with the least resistance."

"If you need to knock him about the head, I don't mind."

Mark kept his surprise in check as she indicated to him and Timmins to stand around the corner. Mrs. Toussaint opened the door. "Henry! Get your ass up here!"

Timmins gripped his stun gun in one hand. Mark had debated taking out his weapon but held back—this could get ugly really quick. "Stand by," he whispered into the walkie-talkie. He noticed two officers at the back door and hurried over to quietly slide it open. "Stand with Timmins," he told them. "Suspect's coming upstairs from the basement."

They remained silent, the tension building.

"I'm busy, Mom," Henry called out.

"I don't give a shit. Just get up here. I need you for something."

Mark indicated to the officers to have their stun guns ready.

"I told you I didn't want to be bothered," Henry told her. His voice held a hint of frustration. "Come back later."

Wow. He saw Timmins rolling his eyes.

When Mrs. Toussaint glanced at him, Mark nodded in encouragement.

"Henry, we've talked about you living here, remember? If you don't pay rent, you have to help around the house, that was the deal. Now I need your help with something."

Mark backed away and radioed the rest of his team. "Keep an eye on the garage and backyard for the female," he whispered.

Footsteps stomped on the stairs. Mark motioned for Mrs. Toussaint to stand away from the door so that she didn't get caught in the middle. "You had to bring that up, huh? I've been trying to find a job for weeks."

"Which tells me how much effort you're putting into it," she retorted. She appeared at the corner and continued backing up, keeping her gaze on Henry.

As soon as he stepped into view, the two officers jumped him. Henry yelled out in surprise and fought, kicking out and landing a bare foot against an officer's knee. The officer's grip loosened, and Henry pushed him away, before turning his attention to the second cop, throwing punches into his face.

"Henry!" Mark shouted. He managed to grab and pin the man's arm and held on tight as the first officer cuffed him. Damn, this guy was strong. Mark kept his legs together as Henry tried to kick him in the balls. "Hey, calm down!"

The young man continued to struggle. "Get your hands off me!" he yelled.

It wasn't working. "Henry, if you don't calm down you'll leave me no choice but to stun you," Mark warned. "Do you want me to Tase you in front of your mother?"

That seemed to do the trick. Henry finally stopped thrashing around. "Get him in the car," Mark demanded. "And read him his rights."

He moved to stand at the top of the basement stairs. "Jenny, I know you're down there," he called out. "We've got Henry. Don't make this hard on yourself."

A couple of minutes went by. "Detective Hawthorne, I didn't see anyone come in with Henry," Mrs. Toussaint said.

"He might have sneaked her in through that back door you told me about." He tried again. "I'd better not have to come down there to flush you out. The house is surrounded. You won't get away."

He tensed at the sound of a door. He was about to call in to the officers when a person appeared at the bottom of the stairs—Jenny, with her hands raised in the air.

"Get up here," he shouted, and backed away as she reached the top. "Turn around."

She complied, and an officer slipped the cuffs on her. "Aren't you going to read me my rights?" she asked, sounding cheerful, for the love of God.

"The officer taking you to the police car will do that." Mark was still trembling with adrenaline after the scuffle with Henry.

As the construction worker was led out of the house, he turned to Henry's mother. "Mrs. Toussaint, I need to find Henry's sneakers."

"He keeps them lined up downstairs in the closet. Second door to your left."

When Mark opened the door, he couldn't believe his eyes. There were eight pairs of limited-edition sneakers, as clean as if they'd come out of the box. He pulled on a pair of gloves and grabbed the ones he needed, noticing smudges of dirt in the creases and more stuck to the sole. He dropped them into an evidence bag and headed back upstairs.

He and Timmins were the last to leave. "I'm sorry, Mrs. Toussaint," he apologized. "I had a feeling Henry might have resisted the arrest, but I didn't think he'd actually start fighting. Are you okay?"

She nodded, her expression sad. "Henry never said anything to me about this. It happened last Friday night?"

"Yes." How did she know?

"When he came home, there was mud on his clothes and his best sneakers." She frowned. "He treated those shoes like they were his pets. When I asked him what happened, he ignored me and hid in the family room for most of the weekend until you showed up on Sunday." She shook her head. "I don't know what's gotten into him recently."

"That's what we hope to find out. An officer will call with an update." Mark didn't know what else to say, so he nodded at her before leaving.

At the precinct, Mark was all business. "Henry and Jenny in their own interrogation rooms," Mark demanded. "I'm getting tired of the bullshit."

A CHEER WENT up when Britt turned the corner. All her staff were waiting at the rear entrance. "Good morning, everyone."

"Chérie." Jacques grasped her shoulders and kissed both cheeks. "We heard what happened to you. Are you all right?"

"Yes, thanks to Joyce." His worried expression tugged at her heart, and she placed her hand on his cheek. "I'm fine, Jacques. See? The scrapes have almost healed. My calf muscles are just a little stiff, that's all." She moved past the rest of her employees. Betty gave her an impromptu hug, while

Kevin, Jasmine and Oliver gave her big smiles. Thomas, Jacques's assistant, tilted his head in a nod—he'd always been shy and quiet around her.

Inside, everyone was silent as Britt led them to the kitchen. As she went through the swing doors and took one look at the room, she breathed a sigh of relief.

Everything looked to be in place. The door leading to the front had been knocked off its hinges, but as they moved farther in, she didn't see anything out of place or smashed on the floor. "Thank God they didn't get in here before the police arrived," she breathed. "Jacques, can you and Thomas go through everything carefully and let me know?"

"*Bien sûr*, of course." He took off his jacket and talked to Thomas about how to inspect the kitchen properly.

The front of the bakery was where the most damage had occurred. The display cases were destroyed, tables and chairs thrown about, the bookshelf shattered on the floor. Some of the books had been torn to shreds and the pages strewed everywhere. The office door had been kicked but had held in place.

It had been a scary night—Britt was so glad Joyce had been with her. Without her friend's support, she might have done something unthinkable, like confront the jerks.

"I honestly thought it was going to be a lot worse than this." Britt turned in a slow circle, glass crunching under her feet. "Let's get this cleaned up," she announced. She got her key in the lock to the office, but it took a bit of persuading before it opened. The room was undamaged.

She put her things in the desk drawer and got her laptop fired up to check for messages. Other than Joyce reconfirming her arrival, her new emails were from customers, reiterating their support and good wishes.

Britt wanted to cry she was so happy. This was what she

loved the most—the loyalty and trust from almost perfect strangers. Many of them stated they would wait until Konditori reopened, as they didn't want to spend their money anywhere else.

She called everyone into the office and read some of the emails out loud. "Wow, now that is something," Betty exclaimed. "I hadn't realized how much our customers loved the bakery."

"And the staff," Kevin added. "Without Britt, I think we'd just be another bakery like MBB."

"Bite your tongue, young man." Jacques trembled. "That will never happen."

"How does the kitchen look, Jacques?" Britt asked, worried there might have been damage that she'd missed.

He kissed his fingers. "The criminals didn't have a chance to destroy the appliances, but everything is covered in dust and debris. The power had been turned off, no doubt during the police investigation, but *merde*, they could have turned it back on when they were finished. Everything is spoiled in the fridge and freezer."

"The food is the least of my worries, and honestly, I'm glad everything was turned off. Heaven help me if a fire started in here."

They got to work. Britt grabbed a large broom and carefully swept the glass to one corner while Kevin and Oliver stacked the broken pieces of the bookshelf in another. Betty managed to stack the chairs, then Britt, Oliver and Kevin helped manhandle the tables until they, too, were stacked on top of each other.

Suddenly, there was a loud knock on the door, followed by the sound of the padlock being opened. The makeshift door swung open. "Good morning. Is Britt Gronlund here?"

That must be the insurance representative. "Hi, that's me."

The representative stepped inside carefully and put the padlock down on the windowsill. "I've brought an extra key for you," she said, holding it out and giving it to her. "I'm glad my insurance company was able to help you."

"So am I. The payment will cover everything that needs to be replaced."

"Oh, speaking of which." The woman opened her purse and pulled out an envelope. "You'll receive two insurance payments instead of four. You're a longtime client, and we want to help get you back on your feet as soon as possible."

Frowning, Britt opened the envelope and stared at the number on the check. "Seriously?"

"Uh-huh." The rep smiled. "I'll have to come down one day and try your pastries. I've heard a lot of wonderful things about the bakery. The second payment should arrive in the next two to three weeks."

Britt squeezed her eyes shut to keep the tears from flowing. "Thank you," she whispered.

"You're most welcome. Good luck." And just like that, the rep was gone.

Joyce arrived about a half hour later. "Shit, the storefront looks like it got hit with a bomb."

"I'm glad those assholes didn't come up with that kind of plan." Britt swept her arm around the room. "The kitchen is in one piece—I have the Fates to thank for that. Jacques and Thomas are cleaning it up now. As for here, well, you see what we're dealing with."

Joyce swept her gaze around the room. "Honestly, sweetie, this won't take long to fix up. I'm glad it's just this space. Replacing the kitchen would have cost you a pretty penny."

"Tell me about it." She showed her friend the check.

"Whoa, I didn't expect that much."

"The insurance company decided on giving us two payments within a month. I can get the bakery up and running in that time."

"Then we should go shopping. I brought my laptop, so I'll show you the latest styles I have in furniture, paint and fabrics." She looked at the walls. "Do you still want to keep the same colors?"

"Absolutely."

For the next hour, they worked out a plan for rejuvenating Konditori. "I can have a team here in a couple of hours. We can start work on replacing the display cabinets and front door, getting glass for the windows and giving the walls a power wash and a fresh coat of paint. I still have all the original measurements, so it won't take as long."

Britt nodded—she couldn't speak she was so grateful.

As Joyce made her calls, Britt went into the kitchen to see if Jacques needed any help, but her staff was already there, working under Jacques's exacting demands. The back door was open to let in fresh air, and it looked like everything was under control.

Britt returned to her office and dropped into her chair, mentally exhausted. Things were moving faster than she had anticipated, all because of a few people who cared about her bakery. She wanted to call Mark to give him the good news. Instead, she grabbed her phone and sent a text, knowing he was probably busy with Mr. Ferguson's murder.

Goose bumps prickled her arms as she thought about her reaction when Mark had held up her bracelet. Joyce had noticed it was missing, and for the life of her, Britt hadn't remembered whether she'd put it on or not that morning. The simple move of clasping it over her wrist was so automatic, she never thought about it. She had never noticed it coming off during her scuffle with Mr. Ferguson, and because she'd been so upset with everything else, she'd completely forgotten about it until she got home and started looking for it. She was only glad that it had been found—it was a custom-made birthday gift from her parents.

There was another loud knock at the front door to the bakery. She rose and watched as Kevin scooted across the space and opened it. "Yes?"

"Hi there." It was a woman in her fifties, and Britt recognized her as a regular customer. "Will Konditori be open again soon?"

"We're hoping in the next few days."

"Thank God!" She waved at someone. "I told you I saw someone coming in here!"

Britt watched in fascination as several people crowded around on the sidewalk. "What's everyone doing here?" she asked.

"We hadn't heard anything about the bakery since that horrible break-in," the woman told her. "And we were worried that Mighty Big Bakery had bought you out."

"No, that won't happen." It felt good to say that with certainty, although horrifying that Mr. Ferguson had to pay with his life. She shook her head at the senseless loss, wondering if he had a wife, family, friends.

"We're glad you're reopening," a young man called out from the crowd. "I miss my morning Danish!"

Everyone laughed, and at a gentle push from Kevin, Britt stepped into the animated crowd, shaking hands and answering questions. As she turned, Mighty Big Bakery's construction site across the street came into view, but now, she wasn't worried. With an incredible staff, wonderful friends and customers who stood by her, Britt believed she had turned a page in her life. The next chapter held new opportunities, including a man who had literally swept her off her feet, and the future looked glorious.

Chapter Twelve

Mark had left Henry and Jenny to cool their heels in separate interrogation rooms while he sat at his desk, thinking. Some of the clues he had found didn't make sense, such as the footprints behind the shrubbery in Ferguson's backyard, the missing briefcase, and the fingerprints that didn't match Henry's or Jenny's. Evidence that had been found at the construction site only led to Henry, despite the young man's admission that Jenny was the mastermind behind the attempted arson.

"You okay, Hawthorne?"

He glanced at Timmins, who was leaning back in his chair, hands clasped behind his head. He knew the older detective would help him if asked, but sometimes, Mark's stubborn streak got in the way. "Just trying to sort everything out."

"Let's hear it. I know you're eager to get at those two downstairs. But go over what you've got out loud, and I'll chime in if necessary."

Mark rehashed everything from the beginning, starting with Mr. Ferguson's assault. "The one thing that has remained consistent is everyone's hatred for the CEO, and someone took it far enough to kill him." He looked at his list of potential suspects. "That could be anyone listed here."

"Who stands to gain the most from this?"

"Mrs. Ferguson, definitely. But she already has everything. Of course, if his business personality was the same as his personality at home…" Mark knew he had to get back out there to question her and the housekeeper.

"What else?"

Mark was glad to have Timmins hit him with questions—his mind had been a jumbled mess even with his notes all neatly organized in front of him. Too many pieces were not fitting together. "The housekeeper gave off a weird vibe when I asked about Ferguson's missing briefcase."

"Then you can ask the ladies to come in later today. As for those two downstairs, do you think they're capable of murdering Ferguson?"

He shook his head, more out of confusion. "I think Henry's capable of it, but not on his own."

"Agreed. What about Jenny?"

"I don't get the impression she'd get her hands dirty, but I can totally see her guiding someone into doing it. I'm not sensing that here, though."

Mark closed his eyes, a trick he used to block out everything around him and concentrate on one item. Henry and Jenny were his immediate focus. They had lied to him to cover their butts, that was now obvious. But why? To avoid being tied to Ferguson's murder or just avoid jail time for the beating and attempted arson? He believed it was the latter, but he would ask Myrna to reconfirm that the fingerprints found at the murder scene did not match either Henry's or Jenny's.

Mrs. Ferguson and the housekeeper were on a different level, being much closer to Mr. Ferguson. He couldn't see them attempting anything as risky as murder, but he couldn't rule them out either. Mark was sensitive to the fact that Mrs. Ferguson would be mourning, and bringing her to the precinct for questioning felt wrong. A visit to her home would be more sympathetic, and might yield better results.

It only took a couple of minutes. When Mark opened his eyes, he felt clearheaded and had a direction. He hit a button on his office phone. "Myrna, sorry to bother you. Can I ask you to compare our two suspects' fingerprints again with those at the murder scene? Yes, I do trust your results, just humor me, okay? Thanks. I'll be in the interrogation room with Jenny."

Five minutes later, he sat across from the construction worker with Timmins in the background. "You've already questioned me," she snapped, leaning forward in the metal chair. "What the hell am I here for now?"

So, she was going to be like that? "I'm waiting on confirmation that fingerprints found at Mr. Ferguson's murder scene match yours. My forensics investigator got clear fingerprints from your purse."

Yep, that got a terrified look out of her—even Timmins's jaw dropped. "No, no! There's no way. I didn't kill him!"

"Guess we'll wait and see." He kept his tone and stance professional, refusing to let her try to bait him into anger. "In the meantime, let's talk. You never mentioned that you and Henry were an item."

"More like friends with benefits." Her smile was crafty. "I was more into you."

He let that comment slide. "You're already implicated, in case Henry hasn't told you. Why did you want to burn down the new Mighty Big Bakery location?"

"I'm sure you already know the answer to that," she spat out.

"Humor me."

She sat back in her chair. "You saw what Mr. Ferguson

was like. Arrogant, a bully, a first-class asshole. If he didn't get his way, he'd threaten, cheat and steal to get what he wanted. I never understood why the *police*—" she emphasized the word "—never arrested him."

"I don't know about the other precincts. As for us, we never had enough evidence to charge him."

"That's horseshit!"

Mark let that one go, too. "You haven't answered my question."

Jenny blew out a loud breath. "My friend and her family got caught in Ferguson's vicious net. That jerk sent his goons after them and trashed their store. When that didn't work, they upped their game and burned the business to the ground." She shook her head, upset. "I'm sure you've had your share of grieving witnesses. It was tough on them."

Mark knew exactly where Jenny was coming from, since he had seen what had happened to Britt and her bakery. His fury almost had him hunting down Ferguson, except that Britt's needs came first. "I know how you feel."

Her eyes blazed with rekindled anger. "Then you know why I did what I had to do. Get revenge. An eye for an eye. Why should my friend and others suffer the loss of their life's work, while that dickhead acted like he'd done nothing wrong?"

"If Mr. Ferguson had any involvement with the arson and B and Es, we haven't found any proof. We need facts, Jenny, not theories."

She shrugged. "Guess it doesn't matter anymore. He's dead, and good riddance."

Jenny explained how she got Henry inside the construction site by leaving the gate unlocked. She had provided him with a hard hat and a high-visibility safety jacket so that he'd blend in. The idea was to hide the container until everyone had left, then go back, spread the gasoline around and light it up. Unfortunately, when Henry saw Mr. Ferguson, he let his anger do the talking and gave the CEO a thorough beating.

Mark digested her story as he wrote his notes. "What about the leader of these anti-Ferguson protests? Do you know who he is?"

"Like I'd tell you if I knew. You'd just arrest him and do nothing about Mighty Big Bakery's abusive takeovers."

"Not true, but I know you don't believe me. For now, I'm charging you with attempted arson."

Jenny jumped up so fast, the chair went flying. "Are you shitting me?"

"Nope. If you want a lawyer, I'll arrange your phone call. You already know your rights." He stood up. "Be glad it's not worse. If I find out you had anything to do with Mr. Ferguson's murder, I'll make sure you won't get out."

The young woman screamed a litany of curses as he and Timmins left the room. Two officers who had been guarding the room hurried past them to subdue Jenny and take her to a cell.

"Well, Hawthorne," Timmins said as they approached the second interrogation room where Henry waited, "I didn't quite expect that."

"It got results. That's all I wanted."

Their talk with Henry didn't reveal anything new, other than his relationship with Jenny. He did blame her for coming up with the arson idea. "I had nothing to do with that," he complained.

"You went with her to a secret protest to find out how to piss off Mr. Ferguson," Mark told him. He jabbed a finger onto the table. "You impersonated a construction worker and carried a gasoline container onto the site. You deliberately hid it with the intent of burning down the building. But when you saw the CEO, you also beat him up because hey, why not." Mark wasn't going to waste any more time with the young man and rose. "You'll be charged with attempted arson, as well as assault."

"How can you charge me with assault if the man's dead?" Henry yelled.

"You'd better hope I don't find out you had anything to do with Mr. Ferguson's murder as well."

This time, Mark was ready. When Henry jumped out of his chair and dived over the table, Mark grabbed the young man's arm and put a knee into his back.

Henry yowled in pain. "Get off me!"

Timmins had let the officers inside, and they deftly took over, cuffing Henry and getting him on his feet.

"If you had hit me, that would have been a charge of assault on an officer," Mark told him in a flat voice. "Get him out of here."

So far, Mark had solved a part of the puzzle, but he worried it wouldn't be enough for Captain Fraust. He knew the captain wanted a murder suspect captured as soon as possible—hell, so did he. He dropped into his office chair and blew out a frustrated breath.

A knock on the door, followed by Myrna. "Hey," she called out. "Sorry to say, but my analysis still stands."

He scrubbed his face with a hand. "Thanks, Myrna. It was a long shot, but I was hoping. I hadn't meant to insult your work. Sorry."

She shrugged. "There's nothing wrong with double-checking."

"What's next?" Timmins asked.

"I need your help," Mark said. "Can you go to Ferguson's head office and find out who's next in line to take over?"

"Any reason why?"

Mark knew Timmins was testing his methods, and he appreciated it—it kept him on his toes. "It's possible the head office didn't like Ferguson's methods. Maybe someone there wanted to get rid of him?"

"Now you're thinking." Timmins rose and grabbed his satchel. "No time like the present. It'll throw them off if I suddenly show up."

Mark smiled. "Good idea."

His phone pinged. As he read the message from Britt, his body tingled with pleasure. She mentioned that she and her staff were inside the bakery, cleaning up. She then sent a second text.

If you'd like something sweet, why don't you come over and see me.

How could he ignore that invitation?

"What's got you smiling so big?" Myrna asked.

Startled, he put the phone back in his pocket. "Good news from a friend."

"You mean the blonde beauty you rescued a couple of nights ago?" Timmins chimed in with a wink.

"'Blonde beauty'?" Myrna demanded. "Who? What did I miss?"

"She's just someone I met last week." It was bound to happen that one of the guys would pick up on something, but Mark had hoped for a bit more time.

"I'll bet she is. Don't get distracted, Casanova. Let's get this case solved first."

Mark couldn't help himself, though. As soon as he got in

his car, he drove straight to the bakery. He wanted to spend a few minutes with Britt to show his support before driving over to talk with Mrs. Ferguson and the housekeeper.

He parked a block away and walked quickly to the front door, which stood open. Inside, it was a chaotic blend of work, chatter and laughter as debris was cleaned up and furniture moved to one side. A couple of employees swept the floor.

One of the staff noticed him. "Hey, aren't you the guy that asked for Britt last weekend?"

Mark stuck out his hand. "Good eye. Yeah, I am. Is she around?"

"I'll grab her. Just be careful. There's glass everywhere."

Mark took a good look around. Anything that wasn't nailed down had been smashed to bits. Even the display case had a couple of holes where someone had kicked it in. The bookshelf was nothing but a pile of firewood, and even the books hadn't survived—they were torn to shreds. The letters *MBB* were scrawled on the bright storefront. It almost felt like…this was personal. The vandals had managed a lot of damage in the short amount of time they had.

"Hi, Mr. Detective."

He turned and smiled as Britt approached, wearing jeans and a white T-shirt. "Hey. I see you've already started getting things back together."

She nodded and looked around. "I was lucky. No one got into the kitchen. That's where the most expensive stuff is."

"Did your insurance pull through?"

"With flying colors."

She told him how much she received, and he whistled. "That's a healthy chunk of change."

"It'll go toward buying foodstuffs and replacing the

glass in the windows and a new door." She looked around. "And giving the inside a good makeover. We'll hang on to the salvageable furniture until we receive the second payment."

"Sounds like you have everything in order, *vakker*." He stepped closer but watched her carefully. He was suspicious that Britt might not want to get too intimate in front of her staff, but he couldn't resist teasing. "How about a kiss before I go?"

Her eyes widened in surprise, but their color darkened as well, a deep emerald. He kept his gaze on her, waiting, because she hadn't said yes—or no.

"Damn you." She licked her bottom lip, and he drew in a sharp breath. How could he back away now? "I want to, I think a little too much, but…" She glanced over her shoulder and gasped.

He looked up and saw her friend Joyce standing at the doorway to the office, arms crossed and the biggest smirk on her face. "Hello, Detective Hawthorne." She came over. "I want to thank you again for saving us."

"Don't mention it." He glanced at Britt until her cheeks flushed a light pink—damn, she looked adorable. "And I have to commend you on your fast thinking. To go out the office window and through a dark alley? That's gutsy."

"No, that's desperation. I wasn't going to let us sit in the office and wait for those shitheads to break down the door." She paused, and Mark noticed her clenched hands. "Any news?"

"I haven't heard anything, but I'm not on the case. I'll follow up and let you know what I find out."

"Thanks, Mark." Britt raised her hand as if to clasp his, then let it fall.

Joyce made a noise. "Could you two go outside and, you know, make out? I'll hold the fort."

Britt led the way—she hadn't hesitated at all. Feeling encouraged, he was right behind her until they stood at the entrance to the alley. "Joyce knows you well."

She laughed, a joyous sound that rang free and happy. Britt seemed more at ease. "I didn't have to tell her anything. She figured it out before you came to rescue us."

He reached for her hand, and her fingers wrapped around his. "I might have been too protective that night," he whispered, kissing her hand.

Her smile was bright. "I loved every moment, even when you cleaned my knees."

He laughed. "Jeez, I felt like a guy trying to hold on to a condom, my hands were shaking so bad." He sobered. "Are you still mad at me about bringing you to the police station for questioning?"

"No. But you really caught me by surprise."

"That makes two of us. I'm sorry, Britt, but I had to be an officer. I didn't know what to expect."

"I get it. I'm just ticked that Mr. Ferguson had my bracelet, instead of me finding it in the alley or at home. Will I be able to get it back?"

"As soon as everything's over. Speaking of which, I have to go." Although he didn't want to—he wanted to drag Britt away and spend the night with her. "Duty calls."

"I understand." She came up to him and wrapped her arms around his neck. "Maybe you and I can do something fun when duty finally stops calling?"

"Oh, you mean I can have that sweet treat you teased me about?"

Her surprise lasted only for a moment. "Haven't you heard? Norwegian treats are the best."

He crushed his mouth to hers, trusting that his intent was clear. *I'm here for you,* vakker, *no matter what.*

Chapter Thirteen

Mark hit the buzzer beside the main gate. At the same time, he got a text from Timmins.

Call me as soon as you're finished.

Intriguing.

"Yes. Who is it?" The housekeeper's voice echoed through the intercom.

"Detective Hawthorne." He held up his badge to the security camera. "I'd like to talk to Mrs. Ferguson."

"Well… Mrs. Ferguson has had a long day preparing for her husband's funeral."

"I'm really sorry, but I wouldn't be here unless it was urgent."

It remained silent for so long that he thought the housekeeper had hung up on him. Then she said, "Please enter through the small gate to your right."

He heard a faint buzz, then walked through and shut it behind him. It locked with a loud click.

The housekeeper was waiting at the door when he reached the front steps. "Detective, good evening." They shook hands. "Please come in. Mrs. Ferguson is waiting for you in the library."

"Thank you. Oh, and I'd like you to join us as well."

That got a reaction. "Oh? Well, I'm trying to get last-minute preparations ready for tomorrow."

"I won't be long, I promise." He indicated to her to lead the way.

She clearly wasn't happy about it but walked down the hallway and stopped at a door to their left. She knocked twice, then entered. "Detective Hawthorne is here, Mrs. Ferguson."

The widow sat in a plush high-backed chair. She wore a long-sleeved black dress and black slippers. Her hair was tied back into a fashionable bun. She seemed calm, poised, but on a closer look, Mark noticed the swollen red eyes and a faint trail of black smudge down one cheek. She'd recently been crying.

"Mrs. Ferguson, I'm so sorry for your loss."

She remained silent, but waved her hand at the seat opposite her.

"Actually, I've asked your housekeeper—Gloria, is that right?—to join us. Please." He pointed at the other chair.

Both women glanced at each other before the housekeeper sat down, back ramrod straight, clenched hands on her knees. She seemed nervous.

Mark had thought about what to say to the ladies, and finally decided he'd be blunt in explaining what he was looking for. "I want to thank you for seeing me unannounced. We've cataloged everything from the scene—" he wanted to be careful in his choice of words for Mrs. Ferguson's sake "—and we're working on some leads. There are two things I'm curious about." He paused, watching their faces.

The housekeeper refused to look at him. Mrs. Ferguson glanced up. "What is it?"

He slowly paced across the width of the room. "Mrs. Ferguson, do you know who will inherit Mighty Big Bakery with your husband's death?"

"I do. I would have thought that was obvious."

He glanced at her. "I thought perhaps you had children, a son maybe, to run Mr. Ferguson's business."

"Oh." She paused. "No. We don't have children."

"So, as heiress, you'll take over?"

"I'll have Edward's leadership team continue with the day-to-day business operations, of course. I don't plan on changing any of that."

"And they'll hire a new CEO as well?"

"Yes. I'll need a crash course on understanding how to elect, but I'll be a part of that process with them as well."

"Thank you." Mark stopped in between the women. "My second concern is your husband's missing briefcase. Would you know if he had any important documents in it?"

Mrs. Ferguson shook her head. "Leaving the house at that time of night in one of his best suits, I think it might have been contracts to sign over whatever business he planned to buy. That's the only thing I can think of."

"I see. And what about you, Gloria?"

When she faced him, her frightened expression raised a red flag. "What about me?"

"Well, you were the one who told us about the missing briefcase. Did you look for it? It's possible he didn't take one with him. Maybe it's in his study or in the bedroom?"

"I—I don't know. I didn't search for it."

"You didn't?" Mark stared at her, another red flag waving in his face. "Why not?"

She shrugged. "It didn't seem important at the time."

"So here I am, under the impression that the briefcase was stolen, when in fact, it might be here? It's a crucial piece of evidence, Gloria. Now I'll have to bring the police in to look for it."

"Gloria, you told me Edward's briefcase wasn't in the house." Mrs. Ferguson's hands were wrapped around the armrests. She was shaking and angry.

Gloria glanced from her employer to him, then back again. "I'm sorry, Mrs. Ferguson. I didn't want you to worry about it."

"You're not in a position to tell me what to worry and not worry about! Because of you, Detective Hawthorne will be bringing in officers to search my home! While I'm grieving! And everyone in the neighborhood will see this! All because of your incompetence!" She started crying, loud sobs that filled the room and tore at Mark's feelings. Mrs. Ferguson no doubt had kept her emotions in check, but Gloria's admission broke it. "How can I trust you now?"

"Mrs. Ferguson, I'm sure Gloria meant well." He knelt by her chair and rested his hand on hers. "I'm probably breaking protocol, but how about I wait until after the funeral? And I'll only bring in about five officers. I'm sure with Gloria's help, we can get this done in about a couple of hours. And we'll be discreet—no police cars, no flashing lights, I promise."

She held a handful of tissues to her face as she struggled to calm down. It took a few minutes before she looked up. "Thank you, Detective. That means a lot to me."

"Of course." He glanced at Gloria. Her expression betrayed the guilt she felt, which was part of the plan. He wanted her to confess what she knew, but the housekeeper wouldn't do it in front of Mrs. Ferguson. He got to his feet. "I'll leave you alone, and I apologize again for coming at this difficult time. I'll call in a couple of days, and we can arrange a suitable time."

Gloria led him out, leaving Mrs. Ferguson crying quietly in the library. As they reached the front door, the housekeeper turned on him. "How dare you pull a heartless stunt like that!" she seethed through a clenched jaw.

Mark feigned surprise. "Heartless? You're the one who lied."

"So that Mrs. Ferguson wouldn't worry!" She placed her hand to her forehead. "And now she doesn't trust me."

"She will if you find the briefcase. Where is it?"

Her innocent wide-eyed expression had him on alert. "I don't know."

"I think you do. You either hid it in the house, or maybe…" The thought struck him. "Maybe you know the murderer and let him take it."

"That's preposterous!" she yelled, then quickly lowered her voice. "I had nothing to do with Mr. Ferguson's murder."

"Then prove it to me. Where's the briefcase and what's in it? You know something, Gloria. Talk to me, or I'll have to bring you in for questioning and still search the house."

"No, not that, please. It'll tear Mrs. Ferguson apart."

Mark waited and watched while the housekeeper seemed to struggle with a decision. "I know where the briefcase is," she said quietly.

"Why didn't you say something when my team and I were here?"

She tangled her hands together and looked over her shoulder where they left Mrs. Ferguson. "Because of what's inside it."

Silence. He waited while she fidgeted, but she didn't say anything more. "Gloria…" he warned.

"I can't get the briefcase now. If Mrs. Ferguson saw…" She stopped and took a deep breath. "Can you come back tomorrow morning, around eleven? I'll give you the brief-case then."

He frowned. "Isn't the funeral tomorrow?"

"Yes, but I'll get out of it. Mrs. Ferguson will have her two sisters and brother with her." Gloria pinched her lips together. "Besides, she doesn't trust me right now."

THAT HAD BEEN a productive, though emotional, evening. His unexpected visit with Mrs. Ferguson filled him with mixed feelings of guilt and accomplishment. The only other good thing that came out of this was that he wouldn't need to bombard the woman's home with officers turning every-thing upside down to find that briefcase.

In the car, he checked his text messages. Timmins had obviously found something out, but that could wait a few minutes. He texted Britt, letting her know he was finished for the night and asking if her offer still stood. As he waited for her to reply, he called his partner. "Hey, it's me. Before you start, just letting you know the housekeeper had the briefcase all this time."

"Say what?" Timmins yelled into the phone. "You're kid-ding me."

"Nope. She was acting strange, so I was expecting some-thing. Threw me for a loop. The housekeeper deliberately said to Mrs. Ferguson and me that she hadn't searched for the briefcase. When I told the ladies I would have to come back with officers to look for it, Mrs. Ferguson lost her cool and chewed out Gloria.

"The housekeeper and I had a private chat. Gloria fi-nally admitted to hiding the briefcase and said to come back Thursday morning to grab it, as she won't be going to Fer-guson's funeral. I hope Myrna can lift some viable prints from it." Mark paused, reabsorbing the unexpected turn of events. "What did you find out?"

"Edward Ferguson's head office is a well-oiled engine," Timmins began. "His board of directors had instructions that in the event of his death, they would hold a vote among themselves, their shareholders and Mrs. Ferguson to see who would become the new CEO. That's ongoing, and they know Mrs. Ferguson will inherit the business. No surprises there.

"What caught me off guard was a couple of security guys. My guess is they were hired after Mr. Ferguson was assaulted. As I was leaving, one of them asked about the investigation. I told him it's moving along. Then he had the nerve to say that if we were doing our job, Mr. Ferguson would still be alive."

"I'll bet you weren't expecting that," Mark told him.

"Nope, but I took a page out of your book and kept quiet. But what concerned me was that these two had the smell of *bad guy* on them."

That caught Mark's attention. Timmins had been doing this job for years, and his instinct was never wrong. "What are you thinking?"

"Possible mercenary."

Whoa—that was taking it to a whole new level.

"The guy also had a strong accent. I couldn't place it. Then he says if he was looking for the killer, he would do whatever it took to find the bastard. When I got back to the precinct, I asked Myrna to run all the fingerprints from your love interest's bakery and the murder scene through Interpol's Automatic Fingerprint Identification System database. It's just a hunch, especially after listening to that muscle-head jerk, but—"

"No, that's a good call, spread the net wide. Thanks for checking it out, Timmins."

"You bet, but my day got even weirder. Found out that Jenny wants to cut a deal."

"What?" How many strange things could happen in one day? In this case, a lot. "Tell me."

"She said she could get you into one of those secret protest meetings she'd talked about. Get you close to the leader."

"What's the point of that? Ferguson's dead—that should be the end of it."

"Not in this leader's eyes. Mighty Big Bakery is still here, and as long as they continue to run over the little business, Jenny said her leader won't back down."

"Goddamn it." For every answer Mark found, two more questions popped up. He'd have to find a chance to sit down and get all of his shit together and rethink probabilities. Captain Fraust would be asking for an update, too, and he'd need to be ready for that. "All right, thanks, Timmins. I'll see you tomorrow."

When he checked his phone, Britt had sent a text.

You'd better show up or I'll hunt you down, but you might already know that.

He coughed out a laugh and replied.

There's that Nordic warrior coming out of you. I'll bring dinner as tribute.

Her reply was short and promising.

Just bring yourself.

"Thank you for bringing takeout," Britt said, licking her fingers. "That was delicious."

Mark had an odd look on his face. "My pleasure." His voice was deep, almost rough.

Nervous, she grabbed the dishes and headed for the kitchen. Britt knew what to expect—she had invited him over for goodness' sake—but the anticipation and awkwardness made her feel like a teenager.

A very excited teenager.

She rinsed the dishes and placed them in the dishwasher. "Mark, would you like anything to drink?" She turned around and squawked in surprise. He stood inches away, hands in his pockets, his dark gaze traveling slowly over her. "You startled me."

"Sorry." He reached out his hand.

She could almost see the wheels turning in his head. Honestly, she wondered if her thoughts matched his. Britt grasped his fingers and watched in wonder as he raised her hand to his lips. The touch was warm, but her whole body burned inside.

When he looked at her, his brown eyes held a light of their own. "What are you thinking, *vakker*?"

His question, though innocent, wrapped itself around her, a force she couldn't fight against. She knew exactly what she thought, what she wanted, and was sure Mark picked up on it.

The past four years after the debacle with Minister Strathmore had been difficult and lonely, despite building a new life around her bakery. But finding Mark… She closed her eyes, because staring at him made her heart ache.

Movement, and then the warmth of his body against hers. "Britt."

She opened her eyes and looked into the depths of his own. "I was thinking that I shouldn't have been such a chicken Friday night."

He touched her cheek, a soft caress. "I figured you had your reasons."

She nodded, trying to form her next words. "I was scared, I think. I was sure you were married or in a relationship or something."

"Nope. You have me all to yourself." He leaned in, his mouth barely brushing against hers.

She trembled, the force of this moment intense and electrifying. Without thinking—Britt didn't want to think, just go for it—she wrapped her arms around his neck, pressing her breasts against his hard chest. She was tired of tiptoeing around her uncertainty.

Mark's grip was so tight she could barely breathe. He picked her up and managed to get them into her bedroom. He let her go and grabbed her hands. "Are you sure?"

"Just shut up and kiss me."

Mark didn't hesitate, kissing her so thoroughly Britt thought she would pass out. His hands slipped beneath her T-shirt and massaged her breasts until she groaned into his mouth.

"Damn it, *vakker*, you're driving me crazy. Lift your arms."

She did so, and Mark had her top and bra off in moments. His hands rested lightly on her skin, skimming over her nipples until they hardened with a will of their own. "Absolutely gorgeous," he whispered in a hoarse voice.

Undaunted, Britt reached for his shirt, her fingers shaking as she unbuttoned it. She pushed the material off his shoulders, letting her hands travel over firm muscle. His upper body was wide and defined, and Britt trailed her fingers across his chest and down his abs.

He hissed. "If you keep this up, I don't know how much longer I can hold still."

Mark was fighting to keep his desire in check, and hearing that made her feel mischievous. "You mean I can't tease you?"

He arched a brow. "There could be consequences."

She bit her lower lip, and his gaze focused on the movement. She didn't want to tease—she just wanted him.

Britt reached for his belt, unhooking it while keeping her eyes on him. He glanced down at her busy hands but slowly raised his head, his gaze dark and focused as he studied her body. He rested his hands over hers as he pushed his clothing down to his ankles before kicking his pants and underwear off with a swift movement.

Britt held her breath. Now that Mark was completely naked, she could ogle to her heart's delight. His body was covered in thick, dense muscle courtesy of the sports he enjoyed playing. She ran her hands over his arms again.

He moved close enough to let her feel his manhood against her stomach. "Let's get you out of those leggings, shall we?"

He kneeled in front of her and grabbed the waistband, pulling both tights and panties down in a slow, torturous movement. Britt couldn't look, but she felt his warm breath on a spot just below her belly button. She lifted her feet to remove the clothing, but Mark hadn't gotten up yet. The tension built up within her as she realized he wasn't in any hurry. "Mark…"

"Shh."

His hands caressed her legs, moving up until he grabbed her backside in a firm grip that made her bite her tongue. She held her breath, wondering what he would do. "I think you're teasing now," she managed to say.

Silence, but then she inhaled sharply when his lips kissed

just below her belly button. Without thinking, her hands grasped handfuls of his hair to steady her shaky legs.

He rose, and in one movement, swept her into his arms and laid her on the bed. He hovered over her, his mouth trailing hot kisses across her body until she squirmed, desire flushing her skin with heat.

He reached the delicate skin between her legs, and her body tensed, emotions conflicting with each other. He massaged her with firm, slow movements that finally allowed her body to relax. When his tongue touched her sensitive folds, Britt arched off the bed, crying out in surprise at the strong reaction. Heat pooled in her lower body, and fast breathing turned to quiet cries as Mark relentlessly probed at her. He touched a spot that sent her over the edge, and Britt gave in to her orgasm until she fell limp against the pillow.

He propped himself above her and kissed her face. "How are you, *vakker*?"

"Mmm, I'm not sure yet." She flicked her tongue along his mouth.

"Hold that thought." He scrambled off the bed and reached for something in his pants pocket—a condom.

"I might need to keep a few of those handy around here," she quipped as he rolled it on.

He gave her a heated look as he crawled into bed beside her. "That sounds like a hint."

It did, didn't it? Britt didn't want to dwell on that, not now. "Come over here," she whispered, reaching for him.

Mark held his body above hers, and she didn't need any prompting, wrapping her legs around his waist as he pushed slowly into her. She hadn't realized she had held her breath until he looked at her, his expression concerned. "Are you all right?"

"Yes." Without thinking, her body rocked to its own beat,

pushing away all thoughts until she only saw him, smelled his scent and tasted his sweat. Her soft whimpers in Mark's ear encouraged him, his own pace increasing until with a loud drawn-out cry, her body spasmed, leaving her no choice but to ride the waves of desire that overtook her.

Mark wasn't far behind. His grip around her tightened as he shook from the force of his own orgasm, his deep groan loud in her ear.

He rolled onto his side and kissed her so hard she thought she saw stars. His hand gently caressed her as he stared into her face, remaining quiet.

Britt wondered what he was thinking but didn't ask. "I've heard that the first time is always the best."

He frowned and propped himself up on an elbow. "And?"

"It doesn't make sense if you have the right person in your life."

He stroked her hair, damp from their lovemaking. "Is that what you believe, *vakker*?"

"Yeah," she whispered, her chest swelling with unknown emotions. "Yeah, I do."

Chapter Fourteen

When Britt woke up, sunlight had eased into her bedroom, a gentle warmth against her bare skin. She yawned and reached over, ready to caress Mark's body. But he wasn't there.

Alert, she turned onto her side. An empty, wrinkled spot on the bed was all she saw.

For a moment, a sharp pang of bitter disappointment hit her chest. He'd already left, probably going back to his place to shower and change before work. Logically, it made sense, and yet…

A toilet flushed, and a minute later, Mark appeared, dressed only in his boxers. "Morning, *vakker*," he called out.

"Good morning." Glancing around her bedroom, she finally spied Mark's clothing neatly arranged on a chair, and felt a little embarrassed at thinking that Mark had taken off during the night.

"What's wrong?" He sat on the bed beside her.

She shook her head, not wanting to admit her rash thought.

He frowned, his brown eyes not leaving her face. "You didn't think I'd leave, did you?"

Britt shrugged, refusing to meet his gaze.

His finger touched her chin and gently tilted her face so that she was forced to look at him. "I was kicking myself when I didn't follow you that night. You think I'm going to screw up now?"

She swallowed the lump in her throat. Mark had a way with words that made her insides tie up in knots.

His smile was devilish. "Besides, how can I resist this hot body of yours?" He whipped the bedsheet aside before she could hang on to it.

"Mark!" She covered her breasts with her hands.

"Oh, no, none of that." He kissed every bit of skin he could reach until he stretched his body over hers. She giggled at a ticklish spot above her navel, and he hovered around it, taking advantage until she gasped from laughter and tried to fight him off.

"Stop, please!"

When he raised his head, his brow was cocked up at a high angle. "I hope you won't doubt my intentions again."

Her throat constricted so much she could hardly breathe. "I'm sorry," Britt whispered, fighting to hold back a sob. "It's just…well…"

"Hey." He kissed her nose, her forehead, then her lips. His gentleness pulled at her heart until she thought it would shatter into a million pieces. "I plan on hanging around. You won't get rid of me that easily."

Their lovemaking this time was slow, filled with whispered endearments and gentle caresses. Mark's gaze never left hers as he explored her body again, his hands smoothing over her skin until the heat built up inside and her body trembled with excitement. His encouragement and urgent desire mirrored her own and then, with a shudder, Britt's orgasm burned through her body until she felt turned inside out.

A peaceful bliss settled over her. She was relaxed, her skin still warm. She yawned and stretched her arms over her head, thinking she'd like to stay in bed with him all day.

But it wasn't meant to be. A cell phone rang, and with a muttered curse, Mark jumped out of bed and dug it out of his pants pocket. He talked quietly for several minutes, and Britt heard the word *case* a couple of times—it was work. She gathered the bedsheet around her and headed for the bathroom while Mark watched her. Just as she passed him, he reached out and wrapped his arm around her waist. "It's seven now," he said into the phone. "I'll be at the station in about an hour."

He hung up, then kissed her on the cheek. "Sorry— work," he apologized.

"That's okay." Smiling, she returned the gesture but kissed him full on the lips.

"Damn, I wish I could stay with you." He wrapped his arms around her waist and grabbed her ass. "I'd like nothing more than to ignore work and love you all morning."

Her heart smacked against her chest. Hearing Mark say that he'd rather be with her than doing his job… She swallowed, but didn't say anything.

He released her and got dressed, putting his keys, phone and wallet into various pockets. She followed him out of the room and to the front door. "Talk to you later?" he said.

Britt smiled. "You bet."

He gave her a lingering kiss, his lips warm, gentle. With a squeeze of his hand, he was gone.

She locked the door, then turned and leaned against it. If she had told herself two weeks ago that she would meet the man of her dreams on a busy street, she would have laughed so hard she'd scare her staff.

MARK FOUND IT hard to focus on work with Britt constantly on his mind.

He'd gone home to shower and change, and arrived at the precinct just after eight to add yesterday's surprising revelation to his notes. The captain would want another update for sure.

He wanted to think about Britt, spend time dreaming of what they could possibly have together, but right now, the job called out to him to defend the less fortunate, including a man like Ferguson. Work was his balm, his comfort. Mark wanted to excel—he loved solving his investigations and bringing closure. He knew he was good at his job. Dad was finally out of the picture, and his and Mom's relationship had become tighter. Mark had a good life, and when he was ready, he'd hoped to find a woman he could love unconditionally.

To say that karma had blessed him when he saw Britt at Konditori was an understatement. The chances of ever finding someone like his Nordic princess seemed slim to none. If she hadn't stopped to check him out, he never would have recognized her at the bakery.

He blinked, refocusing his thoughts. Britt was here, he had spent a passion-filled night with her and she hadn't pushed him away or told him it couldn't work. This was real—*she* was real, and Mark wanted to find out how far they could take their journey.

He sat at his desk, coffee mug in hand, and pulled out everything from his work bag. As he waited for the computer to boot up, he read through his notes again, looking for areas he could link together. They hadn't found the weapon used to kill Mr. Ferguson. It was possible the briefcase was used to hit the CEO over the head, but he'd have to wait until he got the item from Gloria, the housekeeper.

Mark also remembered Timmins's remark about using the international database to see if there were any hits on the fingerprints found at the murder scene and Britt's bakery. He buzzed Myrna.

"Good morning," she said in a cheerful voice. "I figured you'd want some answers to that age-old question, whodunit."

He smiled at her bad joke. "It sounds like you got somewhere."

"I certainly have. I was waiting on Timmins, but you're just the guy to see what I've got."

At that moment, Timmins walked in. "He's here now," Mark said. "We'll be down in a few."

As he and Timmins walked into Myrna's lab, the forensics investigator waved at them from the other end of the wide room. "Over here," she called out.

She sat in front of two large computer monitors. Blown up in detail on one of the screens was a fingerprint. On the other monitor were three pictures of a man from the chest up in various mug-shot poses.

"Did you get a hit?" Mark stared at the picture. The man looked to be in his early thirties, with a full black beard and thick curly hair tied back in a ponytail. His dark eyes were unfeeling, bottomless. "Who's this?"

"Now, that's a good question. He has so many aliases, I don't think anyone knows. What we do know is that he's one of the men who broke into and destroyed that bakery across from Ferguson's construction site. His fingerprints were all over the place."

"You don't say." He leaned in to get a closer look. This dude did not look friendly at all. "Did you find an address?"

"No, but here's the interesting part. He had to provide fingerprints for his current job." She hit a few keys, and the picture of a high-level security card appeared, with the suspect's picture and current name. Beneath it was the name of the company he worked for.

"Mighty Big Bakery Inc.?" Mark said, incredulous.

Myrna smiled. "I knew you'd get a kick out of that."

"Do me a favor and print that for me." It was a small step forward, and Mark was cheering inside. "Any other surprises?"

"Why, yes." Myrna pulled up the second set of fingerprints found at Britt's store, then called up the corresponding picture. This second man was younger with a blond crew cut, thick eyebrows and a permanent scowl.

"Hey, that's the jerk who talked to me when I finished my interview with the MBB board of directors," Timmins exclaimed. "Nice, we're getting somewhere."

"And behind door number three…" Myrna retrieved the information on the third suspect.

"That was the other security guard," Timmins told them.

"We could collect their work records, just to see what they wrote down to get a security job at MBB," Myrna advised.

So, one part of the puzzle solved. Myrna provided him with pictures of the men and their prints.

"Thanks, Myrna. Great job."

She got up and offered a curtsy. "My pleasure."

Upstairs, Mark laid the additional information on top of his other papers.

"When are you grabbing the briefcase?" Timmins asked. "Want me to go with you?"

"No need. I'm just getting it and bringing it right back. However…" Mark wasn't sure that Gloria had told him everything. "I think I'll bring the housekeeper in as well for further questioning. Are you going to pick up those three security guys today?"

"Damn right I am."

Mark checked his watch. "I'm going to head out. It should be a full house when we get back."

"Oh, don't forget Jenny's offer."

He swore. "I'm wondering how much we can get out of it. I guess I'd better talk to her first."

He headed toward the jail cell and talked with the officer on duty. "Is Jenny awake?"

"Oh yes, and very impatient to see you. She's in the last cell on the left."

"Did she use her phone call?" Mark asked.

The officer shook his head. "She didn't want to—at least, not yet."

Jenny was pacing the small cell when he stopped in front of it. "Good morning."

She glared at him. "Easy for you to say. You're standing out there."

Mark refused to let her bait him. "My partner told me you wanted to cut a deal."

She smiled, but he sensed an underlying malice behind it. "That's right. You guys want to arrest the protest leader before he does more damage. I know where he's going to be today. Got a text from him before you busted Henry and me."

When she didn't continue, Mark crossed his arms. "And?"

"What do I get?"

He shrugged. "I don't know. I'll need to talk to Captain Fraust."

"Shit, maybe I should have asked for your captain instead." She approached the cell door and wrapped her hands around the bars. "How about a reduced sentence? And you haven't allowed me my phone call. What's up with that?"

"Not true. The officer who brought you in yesterday said you didn't ask for it, despite reading your rights. And I just asked the officer on duty. He said you didn't call your lawyer."

"Fine, I want that and a reduced sentence."

"You'll get your phone call. As for the sentence, I can't do anything. Maybe it'll depend on what you've got to offer." Mark knew she was playing a game, but he was all over that—he had no idea if Jenny's information would be any good.

"Mr. Ferguson's funeral is today, isn't it? At eleven?"

Mark fought not to react, but a cold finger of dread ran down his spine. "What about it?"

She walked to the other side of the cell. "The protest leader is going to show up there. I have no idea how many followers will be with him, but I don't think it's going to be pretty."

"Christ!" Mark ran down the hallway. "Call in every officer on duty!" he yelled at the startled cop. "Find out where Mr. Ferguson's funeral is being held and call it in!"

"Hey, what's going on?" the officer shouted as Mark raced past him.

"The protesters against Mighty Big Bakery. They're going to cause a riot!"

TIMMINS HAD ALREADY left for MBB's head office to arrest the three suspects whose fingerprints were all over Britt's bakery.

Two police cars had already raced off by the time Mark jumped into his car. He got on the radio. "All units, this is Detective Mark Hawthorne. The funeral is at Mount Pleasant Cemetery on Bayview Avenue. Sirens and lights on until we reach Bayview and Eglinton, then go silent. We'll reconvene at Bayview and Sutherland Drive to assess the situation."

He got moving, speeding through traffic as he raced with the others to their destination. Suddenly, his radio came alive. "Hawthorne, it's Fraust."

He picked up and gave her a quick summary of what was going on. "I want us to get there before the protesters," he told her. "Surround the area without anyone knowing. As soon as they show up, we'll take them down."

"This is going to be a large memorial—at least a hundred mourners. You'll need to keep your eyes and wits sharp."

"Yes, ma'am."

"How many officers are with you?"

"I won't know until I get there."

She cursed under her breath. "It may not be enough by the time you pull in. I'll send more but do the best you can." She signed off.

The cemetery encompassed a massive amount of land, surrounded by tall mature trees, condos and large, expensive homes. They parked on Sutherland Drive, and Mark quickly counted his men—nine officers in total. That was all he had to work with. He pulled everyone together into a tight circle. "I don't know what to expect," he told them. "I've heard these protesters wear masks, but they might take them off and try to blend in with the crowd. If you spot the leader, try to arrest them or follow their movements at a safe distance and call for backup."

"That's going to be hard if we don't know what the leader looks like," one of them grumbled.

"He'll be the one up front. I know, it feels like a guessing game, but it's what we've got right now." If they messed this up, the protesters would scatter. "We've got one chance at this. Team up and arrest anyone who endangers the mourners."

Mark instructed them on the go, telling them to sneak toward the church located at the center of the cemetery and to stay hidden. He saw a couple of workers preparing a burial site and went to speak with them. "I'm with York Regional Police," he said quietly to the startled men, displaying his badge. "I understand Edward Ferguson's funeral is this morning. Do you know where he'll be buried?"

"Over there." The older man pointed at a small mausoleum located at the edge of a wooded area. "The service already started." He looked at his watch. "The procession to the mausoleum is supposed to start at eleven—about twenty minutes. What's going on?"

Mark looked around—the officers had surrounded the church at a safe distance and kept mostly out of sight. "We might have unwanted company." At the man's confused look, he added, "Protesters."

"Those anti-MBB bastards." The man spat on the ground. "I'm all for stating my opinion, but they take it too far. Are they really going to show up here?"

"I don't know. I hope not." He scanned around him—no one was in sight.

"You want us to help you with anything?" the other employee asked.

He shook his head. "Just stay out of the way."

Mark hid within the shrubbery close to the mausoleum and talked to the officers via walkie-talkie. No one suspicious had appeared so far, and he surmised the protesters would start something as Ferguson was being entombed.

The mourners had started filing out of the church in small groups. Mrs. Ferguson was in the center, wearing a wide-brimmed hat, a black veil pulled over her face. Two ladies stood on either side while a large man shadowed them; no doubt her siblings.

Mark's radio crackled to life. "Sir, there's a group of people heading this way, moving quickly."

It had to be them. "There's a mausoleum about two hundred feet east of the church," he advised. "Ferguson's to be buried in it. I'm just behind the building."

The coffin was finally brought out, carried by six pallbearers. The priest came next, and Mark watched as everyone slowly proceeded toward the mausoleum. The next five minutes were going to be tense.

As the procession came to a stop, he saw several people marching on the wide path, their faces covered in masks, heading straight toward the mausoleum. Several of the officers appeared from behind, forming a semicircle around the protesters.

As the priest intoned a final prayer, the leader of the protesters started shouting. "Your husband doesn't deserve a funeral—he deserves to rot in hell! He's got a lot to answer for!"

That was their cue. "Move in!" Mark shouted into his radio, then scrambled out of the bushes to confront the protesters. "York Regional Police! Stay where you are and get your hands up!"

Damn it. Instead of everyone holding still, a mass panic ensued. Mourners and protesters alike ran away in several directions, and in the confusion, Mark lost sight of the leader. "Go!" he shouted to the officers.

As planned, they teamed up in twos. Two officers ran west, the next two hurried east, the third pair traveled south and the last two went north. Mark and his partner surveyed the crowd in front of them. Mrs. Ferguson stood by her husband's coffin, with her family flanking either side. Meanwhile, the priest was trying to calm everyone in a loud, commanding voice.

Mark ran the crowd's perimeter, his partner encircling the opposite side, hoping to spot the man who had made the threat. But by the time he managed to find an opening and look around, the protesters were either too far away to chase down or had disappeared among the tombstones and large trees. Masks were scattered across the grass. "Son of a bitch!" he shouted and got on his radio. "All units, report."

"In pursuit of a protester," an officer yelled back, sounding out of breath. "Proceeding south on Bayview."

"Stay on it," he ordered.

The other officers reported in, stating they had lost their targets in busy pedestrian traffic.

"Get to your cars and follow the chase on Bayview," Mark demanded. "Don't lose them." He radioed the officers chasing their suspect. "We have backup coming. Stay on course."

Mark turned to face the mixed emotions of the mourners. He walked straight toward Mrs. Ferguson. "Are you all right?"

"What the hell was that about?" a middle-aged, large-boned man yelled at him. "You've ruined what little peace my sister managed to salvage. When I get back to—"

"Stop." Mrs. Ferguson grabbed the man's arm. "Just stop."

The big man glared at him but backed off.

Mark breathed a mental sigh of relief. "Are you okay, Mrs. Ferguson?"

"Yes. Those are the people who hate Edward?" She shook her head. "Jealousy and anger won't stop the business from running. I wish they would learn that. Now, if you'll excuse us."

"Of course." Mark retreated, silently paying his respects to the grieving family before running to his car. "Status," he commanded as he got in.

"Still in pursuit. Heading west on Moore Avenue. Shit, this guy can run."

There were neighborhoods the suspect could hide in. "You have to grab him before he gets to Moore Park Ravine or we'll lose him. Box him in, mount the curb if you have to." It was too late for him to join in the chase. Glancing at his watch, he needed to get that briefcase from Gloria before Mrs. Ferguson and her family returned to the house.

Mark got the car started and drove off, periodically receiving updates until he heard, "Suspect in custody."

"Yes!" He did a fist pump. "Excellent work. Bring him in."

Mark arrived at the Ferguson house just after eleven thirty. The gates were already open, and he drove up towards the front door. When he got out of the car, Gloria opened the door, as if she'd been sitting beside it. "You're late," she accused. "They'll be back soon."

"The protesters against Mighty Big Bakery showed up at the funeral. We have one in custody."

If Mark only had a camera to take a photo of Gloria's expression. Surprise, mixed with fear—she couldn't be more obvious. "Do you know who?"

"Nope, haven't questioned them yet. Where's the briefcase?"

She headed toward the kitchen. "I haven't touched it after hiding it in the garage."

The housekeeper opened one of the garage doors. "The briefcase was lying here." She pointed at a spot between two of the luxury cars. "I kicked it under the Jeep."

Mark wanted to knock his head against a pole. He'd been

so distracted by Ferguson's corpse and finding certain clues, he hadn't thought to search in other areas beyond the crime scene. He got down on his knees and looked under the vehicle. Sure enough, a silver metal briefcase sat between the front tires. "Do you have a plastic bag?" he asked. "And something with a long handle."

In a few minutes, his evidence was out in the open. As he inspected it, Mark saw dark red stains on one corner— blood. He wrapped it carefully in the green garbage bag Gloria provided him, believing he was close to finding the answers he needed. There was still one problem… "Gloria, why did you hide this?"

That fearful look again. "I'm not sure what you're—"

"You know exactly what I mean. Obstructing a crime scene, hiding evidence and lying to an officer."

She looked around, as if expecting someone to appear. "No, Detective. It's not like that."

"It is, and you're coming with me."

Gloria backed away. "I can't. Mrs. Ferguson will need me when she returns."

"You should have thought of that before pulling this stunt."

THE PRECINCT WAS FULL. Between Timmins's arrests, the officers' capture of one of the protesters and Mark bringing in the housekeeper, Mark didn't know which way was up. On top of that, Britt had left him a couple of voice mails, and he hadn't yet found time to answer her, not with everything else going on.

He immediately took Gloria to an interrogation room and handed an excited Myrna the briefcase and its combination code on a piece of paper. "Give me a miracle," he told her.

"I'll let you know in an hour." She practically ran to her laboratory.

"I think we'd better divide and conquer," he told Timmins when they met up in their office. "I'll question the housekeeper. Who can help you with those security guards and the protester?"

"I'll get Solberg to talk to the protester and one guard. He's in between cases at the moment. I'll handle the other two."

Ten minutes later, Mark sat opposite the housekeeper. "I believe you were read your rights," he told her, setting pen and paper before him. "You refused your phone call, but if you change your mind…"

"I won't. Let's get on with it."

Her demeanor had changed, and now Gloria looked defeated. "Why did you hide the briefcase?" he started.

"I wanted you to think it'd been stolen." Her voice was calm.

"Why?"

"Because I needed to get something out of it."

"What did you think was inside?"

The housekeeper paused. "A contract to buy a business from…someone."

She hesitated on the last word, and Mark pounced on it. "Who? The more information you provide, the better I can help you."

She chewed her lower lip. "A relative. They own a place called Levi's Bread & Bakery on Bathurst and Lawrence Avenue. It's been there for over fifty years."

Mark knew the area. It had been run-down for the past ten years before the city started renovating it, tearing down derelict buildings and putting up condos and multimillion-dollar homes. He also knew the bakery—three generations of the family worked there, fighting against the rapid change of their neighborhood. "Did Mr. Ferguson offer to buy the bakery out?"

"He didn't offer—he threatened. Someone else wanted to buy the business, and Mr. Ferguson wasn't going to give up without a fight. My uncle didn't want to sell."

Mark sensed a *but* somewhere. "What made your uncle change his mind?"

"No one would tell me. I was frantic, worried that something bad happened. I'd heard about those criminals that attacked businesses who refused to sell to Mr. Ferguson." She wrung her hands. "My uncle is a proud man, and he wouldn't give up anything belonging to him. That bakery is his lifeblood."

Mark was still missing a piece of the puzzle but decided to forge ahead. "We need to talk about the briefcase—what's in it?"

"I'm pretty sure the contracts to sign over my uncle's bakery. Mr. Ferguson bragged that evening about how he was going to purchase one of the best properties in the Lawrence and Bathurst area. I knew he meant my uncle's business."

He frowned, staring at the housekeeper. Was it possible…?

She gave him a hard look. "I didn't kill Mr. Ferguson, if that's what you're implying. He's not worth going to jail."

He'd still check her fingerprints against the database to be sure. "What *did* you do?"

"Nothing. I couldn't do anything at all. I went home and called my uncle to try to talk him out of it, but he wouldn't listen, wouldn't tell me what Mr. Ferguson offered. He said it was no one's business but his own." She covered her face with a hand and cried quietly. "That man had no right to destroy my uncle's work, or anyone else's."

Mark waited a few minutes to give Gloria a chance to compose herself. "And you didn't know anything else until you saw Mr. Ferguson's body Tuesday morning?"

She shook her head. "I saw the briefcase and believed it had the contract for my uncle to sign. I kicked it under the Jeep and prayed no one found it. I thought with Mr. Ferguson dead, his company might forget about buying my uncle's bakery."

Well, this was an interesting turn of events. Tampering with evidence usually meant covering up a crime, but the housekeeper didn't hide the briefcase because it was the murder weapon. She wanted to avoid selling her uncle's business.

Man, what a tangled net. Ferguson was like a spider, and anything caught in his web was doomed. "Is there anything else you'd like to tell me?" he asked gently.

"I wanted to know about the protester you caught." She sighed. "My male cousins talked about joining the anti-MBB protests. I hope it's not one of them, but they're adults—they knew what they were getting into." Gloria shook her head. "I'm sorry. I was scared. I didn't know what else to do."

"I'm glad you told me what you know. I have a couple more inquiries. What you've done would normally result in a criminal offense charge, but I'll try to have that rejected. You won't lose your job and you won't have a criminal record."

She smiled through her tears. "Thank you, Detective."

"Oh, and tell your uncle not to worry about anyone destroying his business if he changes his mind and doesn't want to sell." He winked.

Gloria was a smart woman—her look of surprise changed to relief, and she nodded while fighting back tears.

Mark felt better about himself. He hadn't thought she'd

done anything as horrifying as murder, and his instincts proved him right.

She was escorted out while he headed to his office and organized his notes yet again. He saw that Captain Fraust had called and buzzed her. "Captain."

"Tell me you have good news."

He updated her on the housekeeper, the MBB security guards and the one protester they had managed to catch. "We have the briefcase, ma'am, and it's stained with blood. I'm waiting for Walsh to provide me with her results."

A short pause, then she said, "Good work, Hawthorne. As soon as you get something, let me know." She hung up.

He had a few minutes, so he called Britt's cell. No answer, and it went to voice mail. "Hey, it's me," he announced. "Sorry I couldn't call you sooner. The case I'm working on is growing intense, but I'm finding answers. I'll call you or drop by later. Talk soon."

Mark could feel a headache coming on. When this was over, he was going to take a vacation. Maybe Britt would join him.

He let that thought roll pleasantly through his mind as he headed down to the forensics lab. Timmins and Solberg hadn't returned, and he was getting antsy.

Myrna was hurrying from one end of the room to the other when he paused in the doorway. She looked stressed, so he waited a few moments until she sat down in front of a large microscope. "Hey, how's it going?"

"Oh, Hawthorne, you're just in time. Have a seat." She gestured at a chair opposite her.

"What have you got for me?"

"Good news and bad news." She jerked her thumb at the briefcase lying on an examination table, along with a small stack of legal papers. "The good news is, the bloodstains belong to Mr. Ferguson. And there's a good-sized dent in the briefcase, too. The murderer must have hit the CEO hard several times. The bad news, no prints."

Mark swore with a few choice words that had Myrna's eyebrows go up. "What was inside?" he asked.

"A contract for a Levi's Bread & Bakery. I know that place—they make the best bagels in Toronto."

He nodded. "Do me a favor. Keep that contract locked someplace where I can't find it—for now."

She gave him a look. "Because?"

"I want the owner to have time to think about whether selling his life's work is what he really wants to do."

"Well…yeah, I could do that and sort of forget where I've put the documents."

"Thanks." It's not something he would normally do, but Mark knew he'd feel horrible if he didn't at least try to reverse a situation that shouldn't have happened in the first place.

"So, let me provide you with better news," Myrna told him. "The coroner found hairs in Mr. Ferguson's clenched fist and sent those to me for analysis."

Just then the database pinged, and Myrna rubbed her hands together. "Let's see what we've got."

Mark came around the wide table and stood behind her as information flowed onto the computer screen—a name, face in three poses and information he hadn't expected.

"This guy has an international warrant?" he exclaimed. He scanned the charges—domestic terrorism, uttering death threats, aggravated assault, possession of illegal weapons. "How the hell are we going to find him?"

"Like we always do—we have one of the best teams, Hawthorne. We'll get it done."

Myrna's confidence was stronger than his. A tendril of

doubt trickled into his consciousness, but he slapped it away. "Print everything for me," he told her. "After I update the captain, I'm pulling everyone in on this."

She hit a couple of buttons, then sat back. "I heard over the intercom this morning you needed officers. What happened?"

He gave her a rundown of what had occurred at the funeral. "If everyone hadn't panicked at once, I might have caught the leader."

"Well, you caught someone, so it's a start."

He gathered everything and headed out, then stopped. "Myrna, I want you in on the meeting with the captain. Can you make it?"

"I'll come up now." She grabbed some additional paperwork and followed him.

In the office, Timmins and Solberg provided their findings.

The protester knew nothing about the leader and insisted he had only joined because he wanted to impress his girlfriend, which made Mark throw up his hands in frustration. "What about those three heavies?" he asked Timmins.

The older detective propped his hands on his hips. "They couldn't talk fast enough. Said that Ferguson paid them under the table to rough up anyone who resisted his buyout offers." He shook his head. "That dude was a piece of work. The CEO sounded like a mafia leader, for crap's sake."

"Those guys are bad news. Keep them locked up—I'll have them charged and sent to prison for the B and E at least. Personally, I think there's more to them than they're letting on."

Mark buzzed Fraust, who told him to come up. With Myrna at his side, they entered the captain's office. "Ma'am."

"Have a seat."

They arranged their investigative work on the meeting table.

"I don't have to tell you that after the melee at Ferguson's funeral, the media and populace are demanding to know what we're doing, among other things," Fraust stated.

Fraust's words made him unreasonably nervous. She had backed him up on everything he'd done so far. Still... "I'll provide a rundown of our findings, and Walsh can interrupt if I'm missing anything."

Mark condensed his detailed notes into a fifteen-minute speech, summarizing everything that had occurred, up until his conversation with Myrna today in the lab.

"What are your conclusions?"

He nodded toward Myrna. "Walsh has been in contact with the coroner, as we couldn't find any prints on the briefcase. The footprints found in the flower bed are a size 10 for a construction boot. Unfortunately, they're the wrong size. Jenny wears a size 7, so the footprints don't belong to her. Our next best chance was finding something on Ferguson's body. Foreign hairs were clenched in the CEO's fist and provided us with a solid hit." He slid the photo across to the captain. "The suspect is dangerous."

Fraust picked up the photo, her gaze scanning across the page. "Agreed." She looked at him, eyes sharp. "What do you suggest?"

Mark knew his face held surprise—he had expected the captain to provide ideas, especially now with the knowledge that the case had developed into a high-profile investigation. "Originally, I would have said to get this perp's face on all the news channels, but..." He stopped, knowing now that wouldn't work. "It's not a good idea. As soon as he sees that he's on the news, he'll go underground. We'll never find him."

"Very true." The captain paused, waiting, her gaze intent.

"We could advise all law enforcement officers, but I think…" He was taking a big risk on this theory. "I think the perp is still in our area. I also believe he's the protest leader, but that's only speculation."

"But a solid one. Excellent call on making that decision." Her smile was brief, but he noticed it. "I'll put out an all-points bulletin and give the media a general summary of our progress. Like you said, we can't afford the perp seeing his face on the news. Let's catch the son of a bitch first."

Chapter Fifteen

It had only been a day, yet Britt was surprised and happy at the progress made on Konditori. It was as if someone had lit a fire under their butts.

No, that wasn't it—everyone was determined to resurrect the bakery. Her staff had stayed last night, cleaning up and deciding what to keep or toss. Today, Joyce came in with a contractor and a small team, and Britt stayed out of their way as they measured and discussed ideas.

"I want to run something by you," her friend said as she sat down in the other office chair. She plunked her laptop on the desk. "You've been saying how busy it's been, which is never a complaint in my books, but I think a bit more space would help. Have you thought about relocating to a larger building?"

Britt shook her head. "I can't move. I have a lease for another four years. Honestly, I never expected the growth to happen so fast, but I don't want to overextend myself or the staff, either."

Joyce nodded. "Smart. So this is what I'm thinking. Could we make your office a little smaller? The wall between it and the front room isn't load-bearing, so we could knock it down and shave off..." She glanced around the office, her gaze calculating. "About a foot?"

Britt did the same thing, carefully looking about the room. She only used it when she needed privacy, and if she was honest with herself, she wouldn't mind an update, either. "A foot should be fine. It makes the room a bit narrow, but I don't need the built-in bookcase in the corner. Just one set of fireproof metal drawers with a lock, a sit-stand table and a comfy office chair. The window brings in plenty of light, which was always a plus."

"Trust me, sweetie. I'll make this room look nice. The extra foot will also let me add some additional recessed storage behind the cash register. There'll be more space for people to come inside. And you can still have your little area for tables and chairs, but the furniture will be built in a way that'll take up less space. Even the bookcase you used to have out there? The contractor mentioned we can build that into the wall. No more fears that it might tip over."

Britt gave her friend a tight hug. "What would I do without you?"

"That's why I'm here. I'd like to do some last-minute measurements while you and the others continue cleaning, if I'm not in the way?"

"Never."

Just then, someone knocked, and Kevin poked his head around the door. "Hey, Britt, your friend Mark is here."

"Thanks." She glanced at Joyce, who had an unapologetic grin on her face. "What?"

"Girl, if this isn't a hint, I don't know what is."

"Oh, Mark's been throwing clues around." Britt thought of a movie character for her impersonation. "The force is strong in this one, Mistress Joyce," she said in a booming voice.

Joyce rolled her eyes, then laughed. "How do you feel about it?"

Britt got up from the chair. "Let's just say I'm leaning in his direction."

In the front room, Mark walked the perimeter of the space, his gaze taking in their hard work. "Hello, *vakker*," he said softly as she approached, and kissed her on the lips. "You've made some great progress here."

"We did. The staff has been fantastic. I want to give them a bonus or something to show how happy I am."

"You'll think of something."

She mentioned the new layout, and he asked some questions, showing his interest. This feeling of having him in her corner made Britt think she could conquer the world.

"Do you need any help with tidying?" He rolled up his sleeves and glanced around. "Anything heavy that needs moving?"

She opened her mouth when an amused voice chipped in. "Hey there, Detective Romeo."

Oh God, why did Joyce keep embarrassing her? Mark grinned, as if reading her thoughts, then turned to her friend. "Joyce, how are you? Oh, since you're here, I can give you ladies an update."

Britt knew her mouth hung open in surprise when he had finished. "So all the rumors *were* true. Mr. Ferguson hired those creeps to wreck my bakery."

"I'm just glad you got those assholes off the streets," Joyce grumbled. "They were as bad as their boss, except Ferguson didn't want to get his hands dirty. Scumbag." She stepped closer. "I guess you can't say anything about the CEO's murder investigation, can you?" she whispered dramatically. "Clues, updates?"

"Joyce!" Britt exclaimed, but truthfully, she was curious, too.

Mark winked. "All I can say is we're getting somewhere.

My captain held a media conference earlier. It should be on the evening news."

"Thank God for that." Joyce hid a yawn behind her hand. "I'm going to head out. Britt, I'll be here tomorrow morning with the contractor to start the renovations, so it'll be best if you give your staff the day off tomorrow. They should be able to finish the wall in one day, then start installing the display cabinets and shelving."

"Maybe I could hire you to renovate my condo," Mark said with an innocent look.

"As long as you could afford me!" Joyce called out as she left.

Mark helped Kevin with the remaining pieces of the broken bookshelf and took the tables and chairs out back by the garbage bins. "That's done," he said, brushing off his hands. "Anything else?"

"No, thank you. I'm going to close up. Everyone, thank you as always. We'll need to close the store tomorrow so Joyce can work on the wall, but I'll keep all of you up to date via email." She turned to Mark and gave him a big smile. "Let me see if Jacques and Thomas are ready to leave, then I'll get my things."

"I'll be here."

In the kitchen, Jacques was putting on his jacket. "I think another day, *chérie*, and we'll be back in business."

Britt couldn't contain her joy and clapped her hands. "You have been amazing! I can't thank you enough. I admit, I was worried you or the others might have started looking for other jobs."

"Of course not! You treat us very well, Britt. You stood up against that horrible Ferguson man, and with everyone's love and support, you and I shall be ready to give pastry comas to our loyal customers."

She laughed—she loved Jacques's play on words. "Joyce needs to work her magic tomorrow, so you won't need to come in."

"Do you think we'll be in the way if we do?" Thomas asked unexpectedly. "She doesn't need to come into the kitchen. Nothing has been touched."

"Thomas has a point. We'll need all the time required to be ready for our grand reopening," Jacques added.

She pursed her lips. "I don't see why not. I'm just concerned that the dust will get in here. But if Joyce puts a thick piece of plastic over the entrance leading to the front room and tapes all the edges down properly..."

"*Voilà*, that should work. Thomas and I will use the back door, if that is all right."

Britt nodded, her decision made. "I'll talk to her tonight and let you know." She grasped Jacques's arm. "Thank you again."

He placed his hand over hers. "Anything for you, dear boss."

After Jacques and Thomas left, Britt locked up and set the alarm, then returned to where Mark was waiting. "Almost done."

In the office, she grabbed her stuff and made sure everything was secure. She was excited about the plans Joyce had shown her, and she couldn't wait to see how it progressed.

Outside, the early-evening rush hour had already started—the sidewalk was getting crowded. She manhandled the large padlock into place to secure the front and closed it with a loud click.

"What do you want to do, Britt?"

Startled, she looked at him. "I thought you had to get back to work."

"Nah, not right now. I need to clean up some paperwork, but I want to spend some time with my Nordic princess first."

How did Mark always manage to say the right things at the right time? She didn't want to go home yet—she was too excited about reopening the store—but spending time alone was never fun. It had been okay when she started planning Konditori because it kept her busy. But now with Mark in her life, she realized how much she craved having another person to share in her triumphs and challenges. "I feel like celebrating," she told him.

He arched a brow as he moved in close enough to brush against her. "I can think of a few ideas," he said quietly.

Britt couldn't move, couldn't speak. It was as if a bubble had surrounded them and everything else disappeared. She didn't hear people talking or cars honking—it was only Mark. She fought to get air into her lungs.

His hand clasped hers, warm and strong. "Tell me what you'd like to do."

If Mark had started walking, she would have followed him without a second thought. That scared and excited her at the same time. Yet here he was, asking her what she'd like to do, and Britt could feel herself falling for him just a little bit more.

A chorus of screams suddenly caught her attention, and Britt looked around until she spied the top half of a Ferris wheel. She pointed. "Let's go to the carnival."

He looked to where she indicated, then turned back, his expression skeptical.

"What?" she asked.

"Are you sure?"

She gave him a look. "Of course I am! Why are you asking?"

He grinned. "Because I love getting on the wildest, fastest rides they have. You don't have a problem with that, do you?"

She glanced again at the Ferris wheel. It looked like the tallest ride, and she enjoyed riding those. Everything else should be a piece of cake. "Lead on, brave knight," she told him.

Twenty minutes later, they stood in line to get in. The upbeat music and the kids running around in a frenzy lifted her spirits.

"So, what do you want to go on first?" He held up a batch of tickets.

"Let's walk around a bit, then maybe I'll see a ride I'd like to try."

It wasn't packed with people, but children bounced around them like Ping-Pong balls. "I'm scared I'm going to step on one!" she yelled out as another child zipped between them.

Britt paused in front of a ride consisting of huge teacups that sat four people each, and as she watched, they spun in circles. It also stayed on the ground. "How about this one?"

Mark gave her a cautious glance. "Do you get sick easily?"

She looked at him. "No, why?"

He got to the front and handed the employee several tickets. "Guess we'll find out."

There were no seat belts, just a circular bar in the middle.

"Make sure you hold on tight," he warned.

"Mark, it's an oversize teacup spinning on itself."

His grin was evil as he grabbed the bar. "Don't say I didn't warn you."

The ride started out innocently enough, but as it spun faster, she kept sliding around the teacup. Finally hanging on to the bar helped a bit but not enough. "What fresh kind of hell is this?" She had to scream over the suddenly loud eighties music blasting through the speakers around them.

"I said you needed to be sure!" Mark yelled back. "The ride isn't called Mad Teacup for nothing!"

It was a wild ride, all right. While the kids were screaming with glee, she was screaming to be let off. "Oh my God, how much longer?"

"Don't know. Just hang on!"

After what felt like an eternity, the spinning ride finally slowed down. When Britt managed to step out, her vision started spinning like those damn teacups.

Mark grabbed her arm. "Are you okay?"

"I need to sit down." They walked slowly until he grabbed both of her arms and lowered her to a bench.

She covered her face with a hand. "How could a teacup be so menacing?"

He laughed out loud. "I'm a detective, and I view everything with a critical mind. I honestly didn't think those teacups could knock us about like that."

His laughter, so full of life and contagious. She couldn't help but giggle along with him. "Wasn't there a mystery story by a famous author called *Murder in a Teacup*? Did she mean this?"

"Who knows?" He was still laughing as he wiped tears from his face.

Now that Britt knew what to expect, she eyed every ride with suspicion. The kiddie roller coaster looked okay, and it was a snug fit for the two of them. "I think I like this," Mark told her with a wink and sexy smile.

"Until I throw up on you," she retorted.

The highest peak was about twenty feet off the ground, so it didn't gain enough momentum to turn into a heart-dropping dip. But as the ride reached the end of the line, something happened that she'd never have suspected. The damn thing started to go backward.

"Oh, come on!" she yelled out, while Mark busted a gut, laughing beside her.

The ride was more disorienting, since she couldn't see where she was going, and the sudden dips and twists made her body ache in places she didn't know she had.

"You knew about this," she accused him when it was over. She felt like a pretzel, trying to untangle herself from the seat.

"Honestly, I didn't!"

No more rides. Instead, she told Mark they should play it safe with the games and walking through the attractions. One of them caught her attention—a maze of mirrors. "Let's try that one."

Bad choice. She got turned around so badly she had no idea how to get out. Britt tried not to panic as she slowly refocused, managed to get her bearings and finally made it outside.

"Hey." Mark wrapped her in a hug. How he knew she needed one, she didn't know and didn't care. She leaned into his embrace, inhaling his scent. "I guess that wasn't a good idea, either," he said.

"You think? How can this be called fun if all it does is scare people half to death?"

His body shook as he chuckled. "The kids seem to love it."

"The little tyrants have a warped sense of the word *fun*."

They walked through the carnival as the sun set and the bright, colorful lights were turned on. The atmosphere felt electric, and as more people arrived, the air around her came alive as a multitude of voices spoke in different languages.

Britt stood in the midst of this diverse populace and loved every moment.

Although maybe not as much as standing beside a man who accepted her for exactly who she was.

Britt paused on that thought. Was she falling in love? This past week had seen some strange incidents, enough to last her a lifetime. Through it all, Mark had remained her constant rock, despite the unexpected and nerve-racking interview at the police station. He hadn't disappeared when her situation got rough—he'd been there to support, advise and protect. And in her world, that was saying a lot.

"I WANT TO stay with you tonight."

Despite the frantic day he knew he would have tomorrow, Mark didn't want to leave. He stood just inside Britt's condo, his arms wrapped around her waist. He kissed her soft lips, losing track of time within her warm embrace.

She caressed his cheek. "Mark, I want that, too."

Something in her tone made him pause. He'd been absorbed in discovering all he could about his Nordic princess, but he was worried that he might have missed something important. Was he moving too fast? Being too demanding? He searched her face, and it was the small movement of her licking her bottom lip that told him she was nervous. "I'm overstepping, aren't I?"

She frowned now. "I'm not sure what you're talking about."

"I think I'm pushing your boundaries." He'd promised himself that he would let her take the lead between them, but the last few days had been so amazing, spending time with her, just chatting, touching, understanding how she ticked. He'd been enveloped in her scent, drowned every time she looked at him with those ocean-colored eyes, and he had wanted more—so much more.

Yet he kept forgetting that Britt might not be as eager.

Oh, he knew she liked being around him. She hadn't hesitated when they'd made love that first time—in fact, it was as if she couldn't get enough, and Mark had plenty of energy to satisfy her. But her slight hesitation now reminded him that she might want to take things slow, and she was right. With their busy jobs, they needed to make sure any relationship would work.

"No, you're not," she said softly. "Meeting you has pulled me into the light, so to speak. I've had my head buried in the sand for too long with work and ignoring my emotions. It's about time I enjoyed myself with people who want to be with *me*, instead of me using my bakery as a crutch.

"Having said that…" She sighed. "I do have a business to fix, and it couldn't happen at a worse time."

His heart did a funny thump in his chest. It sounded like Britt was ready to take the next step. He wanted to shout his joy but kept a tight leash on his excitement. "Oh, so you're saying you don't mind having me around."

Her smile was sweet. "Yeah, I guess I am saying that. Just…not tonight, Romeo."

He groaned. "Are you going to call me that now? I'm not sure I'm going to like it."

"What's wrong with Romeo?"

"He was a kid with family issues." He bit the inside of his cheek. *Ouch—like me.*

"He was also a romantic. Sort of like you."

"Okay, okay. Compliment it is." Speaking of family, he would have just enough time to see Mom before visiting hours were over. "I'll talk to you tomorrow?"

"You'd better."

He kept their kiss going as long as possible before Britt pushed him away, laughing. "You're stalling."

He waggled his eyebrows. "Of course I am."

That didn't work. Britt firmly turned him around and gently pushed him out. "Sorry, Romeo, but this Juliet needs her beauty rest."

"Like my Nordic princess needs to improve what's already perfect."

She smiled. "Smooth move. Not going to work, though, at least not tonight."

With a final kiss and a glance, she closed her front door.

Mark jogged downstairs, adrenaline flowing through him. Things couldn't get any better between them. He would surprise Mom with a quick hello and a chat before heading home.

Evelyn was off duty, but she had told him she'd updated all the nursing staff who worked on Mom's floor. The envelope she had given him a few days ago didn't get any hits on the AFIS database either. If the letter Mom had received wasn't from Dad, then who?

He stopped in front of the nurses station. "Hi there. I know it's late, but I'd like to see Mrs. Hawthorne before she goes to bed."

Mark had never met this nurse before—he'd never come to the hospital this late. She gave him an odd look that sent chills down his spine. "She has a visitor. But it's not Mr. Hawthorne—it's someone who comes at this time to see her for a few minutes."

He felt his blood start to boil. "And no one thought fit to tell me this?"

He ran down the hallway, the nurse calling after him, but he refused to listen. He slowed down to a stealthy walk as he approached the door, then stopped when he heard laughter.

Mom's laughter.

He pushed the door open without knocking and stopped dead in his tracks at what he saw.

Mom was sitting up in bed, chatting with a man who looked vaguely familiar. When he saw Mark, he stood up quickly, his face flushing red. Mom turned around and gasped, actually raising her hand to her throat. "Mark! What on earth are you doing here so late?"

Not her usual greeting. He stepped inside and let the door swing shut. "I was in the area and decided to come up and visit." He kept a hard glare on the stranger. "I hadn't realized you were entertaining other people."

"Oh, Mark, stop scowling. It makes you look like an ogre." She turned to the man. "Don't you remember Stanley?"

Mark couldn't breathe. It felt like he'd been hit with a baseball bat. Stanley Tucker—coach, mentor and the father figure Mark had desperately needed. This man had saved him from spiraling into a morass of hatred, revenge and depression. Stanley hadn't put up with Mark's shit and had coached him with prompts and a firm hand until Mark became the human being his mother deserved.

"Hi, Mark. Wow, your mom's right—you really have grown into a fine man." Stanley came around the bed, his hand extended.

"Mr. Tucker," was all Mark could manage to say.

"There's no need to be formal, young man." His coach gently grasped his hand and shook it. "Damn, it's good to see you."

Past memories flooded Mark's mind, the ones that meant something, recollections that he'd never forget. Someone else other than his mom had cared for his well-being, stamping their imprint on his conscience. The handshake wasn't enough, and Mark enveloped his mentor in a rough bear hug. "It's so good to see you, too," he whispered in a choked breath.

"Well, there goes my little secret," Mom said out loud, with a sniff for added emphasis.

He released Stanley with a couple of slaps on the shoulder. "Why was this a secret?" he asked, confused.

"Because I wanted to surprise you when I was home from the hospital." Her glance at Stanley was tender.

"That wasn't going to work. I asked the nurses to—" Mark stopped, changing his words at the last moment. "I asked them to keep an eye on you."

"You mean spying. You're letting work take over."

Mark changed the subject. "How did you two find each other?"

"I was scrolling through social media a few weeks ago and found your mom's profile. I was actually looking for yours," Stanley added. "But you don't have anything."

"Too busy to have one."

"I get it. Your mom and I chatted, then next thing I knew, she posted a picture of herself in the hospital." Stanley had a worried expression on his face, but Mark sensed these two weren't telling him everything. The dozen roses sitting on the side table was another hint. "I work late, but I've managed to squeeze in visits."

"Thanks for checking up on her." He meant it. Stanley was a great guy, and Mark felt more comfortable knowing there was someone in Mom's corner he could trust. "I'll leave you two lovebirds alone."

"What—Mark Hawthorne, what's wrong with you?" Mom's voice gave it away, even though her words didn't.

"Oh, nothing." He walked over and planted a big smoochy kiss on her cheek. "I'll try to come visit tomorrow. Work has ramped up, and I've got to be around when an arrest is made."

"I've been watching the news," she said, her voice filled with excitement. "Did you find Mr. Ferguson's killer?"

Mark glanced at Stanley, but his former coach held up his hands. "Nothing will leave this room. To be honest, I don't even watch the news."

He grinned. "We've identified a potential suspect. Now it's just getting our hands on him."

"I knew it! I knew you'd crack your investigation." She held out her arms. "Let me give my detective son a big hug and kiss before he goes."

"Mom," he groaned, but he let himself be fussed over while Stanley watched in amusement.

"Didn't I tell you Mark was doing well?" she said.

Stanley nodded. "Better than well." He grabbed Mark's shoulder. "I'm proud of you."

Mark left the hospital in good spirits. Not only did he manage to see Mom, but Stanley had reappeared at the most opportune time. He had suspected his mentor had a crush on Mom after her divorce, but he couldn't prove it. But watching them just now gave him hope that it was true.

It seemed like his life was filled with second chances, opportunities and love again.

BRITT WAS MENTALLY floating on air, and she couldn't concentrate on anything. Except for a pair of golden-brown eyes that made her feel like she was the only woman in the room. How the heck could she get anything done when Mark talked and looked at her that way? But he'd warned her he would stick around, so she'd have to get used to it.

She made a light dinner and placed that and her work laptop down on the kitchen table. She started to eat as it powered up, then paused while scrolling through some messages. Customers knew Konditori was closed, so she wasn't expecting anything important.

So when she saw the email labeled Please, it's urgent! Britt, can you help?! she hesitated, wondering if it was spam. However, looking at the email in Preview mode, she saw the message was from the very rich client who had sung her bakery's praises to her circle of high-class friends.

Britt, I hope you're well, and I hope you might help me— I'm desperate!

My husband and I are hosting a very important dinner Friday evening for the Defense Minister of Canada. I know, it's an honor for us!

It's only ten guests. I heard your bakery was wrecked during a break and enter—so sorry!—but I wanted to ask if there was any way you could supply some of your delicious treats? If you can't, is there anyone you could recommend? I really hope you can help me!
Thank you,
Angela Weinstein

Mrs. Weinstein was married to a powerful CEO who provided materials to build aircraft. She'd been to the store and asked exclusively for Britt's assistance in choosing the best pastries for her women's club meeting. Ever since that day, Mrs. Weinstein would place an order every week without fail. Even though she knew Britt's business wasn't functional at the moment, she had emailed anyway.

Under other circumstances, Britt would have made the painful decision to say no to the lady's request. However, Britt had to wonder if Mrs. Weinstein was entertaining more than a defense minister. Was it possible one of her guests could also be the prime minister?

"Damn it!" The opportunity was too good to pass up, but it would all hinge on Jacques.

She grabbed her phone. "Jacques, it's Britt."

"*Chérie*, you're calling later than usual. Is there something wrong?"

"Sort of." She hoped he understood her excitement behind this. "What do you think of providing an order for tomorrow evening?"

Silence on the other end. "Jacques?"

"My apologies. Your request stunned me for a moment."

Britt swore under her breath. "I'm sorry, Jacques, but this one is really important. Mrs. Weinstein will be entertaining ten very high-level guests tomorrow." She paused for emphasis. "I think one of them is the prime minister."

"*Merde!* Are you certain?"

"No." She wouldn't lie to him. "But Mrs. Weinstein let it slip that the defense minister will be there."

"That's good enough for me. There are only ten guests, so it will not be difficult to bake some specialties for Madame Weinstein. Thomas and I have finished cleaning and sorting the kitchen, and we've purchased the supplies. As long as your friend Joyce provides adequate protection from the debris, we shall be fine."

She wanted to squeal with delight. "You're amazing, Jacques, you know that? I could kiss you."

He laughed. "I will hold you to that promise, *chérie*. I'll be in the bakery about seven thirty tomorrow morning. I will contact Thomas to come in as well."

"*Merci beaucoup*, Jacques. I'll come in, too, and help keep the contractors' mess to a minimum. See you tomorrow."

Britt didn't know how much better today could be. If

Mrs. Weinstein's guests offered even one compliment about Konditori, she would be overrun with customers. She would seriously have to consider a bigger space if that happened, and more staff...

She got up and grabbed today's mail, then turned on the television. As she flicked through the channels, she stopped on the twenty-four-hour news, listening to a female officer describing the progress on Mr. Ferguson's murder. She kept the information vague, and as reporters clamored for more details, she ended the news conference and walked off. She must be Mark's boss.

Britt flicked through more channels until she settled on an action movie, then slowly sifted through the envelopes. A couple of bills, something from her insurance company—probably a letter formalizing the activation of the renovations—a flyer insisting she vote for her MP candidate in her region. The four nominees, offering their best smiles, didn't interest her, but she guessed she'd better make time to find out what promises they were throwing out to voters.

The last piece of mail was a plain white envelope with her name and address. There was no return address on it. She cut the top with her mail opener and pulled out a single sheet of white paper. As she read it, the air around her seemed to turn ice-cold, and her body trembled, her hands shaking so badly the paper fell to her lap. Britt couldn't tear away her frozen gaze from the terrifying sentences typed in cap letters.

YOU ARE MAKING A MISTAKE THAT YOU'LL REGRET. I URGE YOU TO RECONSIDER.

Chapter Sixteen

Britt didn't sleep for half the night—her mind poked and prodded that elusive message until she thought she'd pull her hair out in frustration. She finally managed to fall into a restless slumber, but her alarm clock rang much too soon.

She got in the shower and turned the nozzle to Cold, letting the icy water wash over her, dissolving the cobwebs in her head. She needed to think clearly, which she sure as hell hadn't managed last night.

The only person she could think of who would send such a note was Mr. Ferguson. His verbal intimidation toward her that past Monday morning was definitely reflected in that letter. What an asshole, sending her another threat after he was dead. Seriously?

She finished getting ready, putting on a pair of flared yoga leggings and a short-sleeved T-shirt. It would be hot in the kitchen, so she packed her duffel bag with three reusable two-liter bottles filled with water for herself and the guys.

At the last moment, she stuck the unknown letter in her purse. It was probably a good idea to call Mark and let him know about it. Not that she thought it would matter—the bakery CEO was dead.

"Ah, whatever," she mumbled. She had other important things to concentrate on.

The bus ride to the bakery was uneventful, but as she stared out the window, that letter came back into focus. The sooner she got rid of it, the better.

She thought she may as well text Mark and let him know. Maybe he could meet her at the bakery and take it off her hands.

Less than a minute later, her phone rang—it was Mark. "Britt, when did you get that letter?" he demanded. "What does it say?"

She repeated its contents. "It was in yesterday's mail. I assumed it was Mr. Ferguson being a jerk and threatening me again."

"What do you mean, *again*?"

She sighed. "Sorry, my mind is… I meant when he grabbed me in the alley and I kicked him."

"And he retaliated by sending those criminals to your store!" His voice rose on each word, but he suddenly stopped. "Damn it, I'm sorry, *vakker*. But you knew what Ferguson was like. You could have gotten hurt, and I'd never forgive myself."

She sighed again. Mark was right—she probably should have handled the situation differently, but Britt believed she gave Mr. Ferguson a very good hint on how she felt about his financial offer. "I'm sorry, too."

The bus arrived at her stop. "I'm at the bakery now," she told him. "I need to help with a special order I received last night."

"That's not a good idea. You don't know if that letter came from Ferguson or someone else."

"Who else could it be?" She blew out a breath. "Look, if you want to grab it and check for fingerprints or whatever, I have it with me."

A pause. "Fine. I'll be there in about twenty." He hung up.

He was angrier than she expected.

She walked around to the back and entered the kitchen, where Jacques was prepping ingredients for tonight's event. "Do you need help with anything?" she asked, then looked around. "Where's Thomas?"

"He's a little late, but he promised he will come in."

"Okay, I'm going to get settled in. Joyce should be here between nine and ten, and I'll make sure the doorway to the front room is taped up tight before she starts the renovations. I'm just waiting for a friend to come by to pick up something first, then I'll help."

By the time she dropped her stuff in the office and got the padlock off the front door, Mark was strolling toward her. "Hi," he said in a short tone.

His stance spoke volumes—he *was* angry. "Mark, there's no need to get huffed up about this," she told him as he walked in.

"Britt, I have to. Do you have proof that letter came from Ferguson?"

She made a face. "Of course I don't."

"Then until I know for sure otherwise, I have to treat that note and envelope as criminal evidence. Do you have them?"

"They're in my office." Britt didn't wait for him, just turned on her heel and headed to the room. She plucked the envelope out of her purse and held it out.

He produced a plastic lunch bag. "Drop it in here for me."

She did as she was told, feeling a bit flustered at his attitude. He was in work mode, which she now recognized after his treatment of her when she'd been questioned about her bracelet being found in Mr. Ferguson's car. "Was there anything else you needed?"

He tucked the evidence and bag into a jacket pocket. Now he looked at her, blinking. "What's that?"

"Do you need anything else? If not, I have a special order to make for a prestigious client." She left the office, but halfway to the boarded door, Mark grabbed her arm, and she stumbled. "Hey!"

"I'm sorry," he apologized. He released her and ran a hand through his hair. "I don't mean to sound like a bastard, but I'm worried."

"About what? The only person that note could have come from was Mr. Ferguson."

He stared at her, his expression growing more concerned. "Has Ferguson ever sent you a threatening letter before?"

"He's—" Britt stopped, uncertain. She let her mind travel back to when she first met the CEO. "No, he hasn't." She looked at him, the fear she fought and won against last night threatening to overwhelm her. "Mark…"

"There's a first time for everything. I won't know for sure until my forensics colleague analyzes the letter and tells me the prints belong to Ferguson. I'd ask you to stay home until I figured this out, but I know you won't." He moved close and brushed his fingers against her cheek.

"Any other time, I'd do whatever you asked, but tonight… It's really important."

"I get it." He took out his phone. "Where are you going?"

She gave him Mrs. Weinstein's name and address and the reason for the unexpected delivery.

"The defense minister will have plenty of security, but I'll be there as well. Find me when you arrive, and I'll drive you home after you're finished."

"Mark, do you really think…?" She stopped when she saw the stubborn expression on his face. "I don't have a choice, do I?"

"Nope."

She nodded, feeling a bit better about having him around.

"Hey." He brushed a thumb across her lips. "Don't worry. If you go in, get everything set up and then leave, things should be okay." He frowned. "You're not catering, are you?"

"No, Mrs. Weinstein hires help for that. We do it exactly as how you just described it."

"As soon as you're finished, come out to the car, okay?"

"Mark…"

This time, he shut her up with a kiss that left her speechless. "You were saying?" he asked, smiling.

DESPITE THE LATE arrival of Joyce and the contractors, and the constant noise they created, the last batch of specialty pastries—a secret recipe from Jacques—was almost finished. Britt helped to get the boxes assembled, labels printed off and pasted on each container, then gathered a small stack of business cards to leave on the table where the pastries would be displayed. This was the adrenaline-induced excitement she loved—cooking, preparing, organizing. She loved fitting the pieces together until they created a masterpiece filled with pride, love and, of course, sweet deliciousness.

Jacques and Thomas even managed to bake a couple of cakes, both covered in icing the same colors as Konditori— they even wrote the store name on each one with blue icing. She looked around in wonder at what her team had created—along with the two cakes, there was an assortment of Nordic and French tarts, Danishes, cinnamon rolls and cream-filled croissants. "Jacques, Thomas, you truly outdid yourselves. Bravo."

Jacques bowed. "*Chérie*, you and Konditori are in a class of your own. I'm proud to be part of your staff."

Thomas nodded. "I really like working here."

"Thank you both. Shall we get going?"

They carefully loaded the pastry-filled boxes onto special built-in shelves in the van. "Thomas, Jacques and I can handle it from here," Britt told him. "Thank you so much again for coming in on short notice. I'll lock up—I think the contractors have already left."

Britt hurried around to the front and went inside to grab her things—the plastic and tape still covered the door to the kitchen. She made sure the boarded-up front door was secure, then walked back down the alley to Jacques. Britt punched in the code for the security alarm and locked the back door. "Ready to roll," she announced as she got into the van.

Mrs. Weinstein's residence, located in the exclusive Uplands, was a twenty-minute drive east. They decided to get on the toll highway because the other routes would be busy with cars coming home from work. As they got off the ramp going south on Bathurst, traffic on this major street was packed.

"We can turn left here onto Flamingo Road," Britt said to Jacques, checking a map on her phone. "Then onto Golfer's Gate to Callaway Court."

Ten minutes later, they halted in front of an imposing set of black iron gates guarded by four security men. The enormous two-story stone mansion within the grounds was ablaze with light. Britt rolled down her window. "Britt Gronlund. I'm with Konditori Bakery," she announced. "Mrs. Weinstein is expecting us."

The guard repeated the information into a radio and was given the go-ahead. "Take your vehicle over there," he said, pointing out the direction. "There's a York Regional officer parked back there, too, a Detective Mark Hawthorne. He informed us that he's here to escort you home afterward."

"Yes, that's right. Thank you."

They were instructed to park next to a side entrance. As Britt got out and looked around, all she saw were luxury cars in front of the five-car garage located beside the home. Others were parked in an empty lot across the street, and surrounded by several security guards.

"Your new boyfriend must be worried about something if he's here," Jacques said.

She turned around, wondering about her baker's choice of words. "I guess he wants to make sure I get home safely."

"*Chérie*, I could drive you home."

"You've been up since six in the morning, Jacques. I'm sure you're exhausted. It just saves you an extra trip."

As she approached Mark's car, he climbed out, smiling. *"Vakker."*

"Hey." She wasn't sure if kissing him in front of security was a good idea.

Mark didn't seem bothered and pressed his lips to hers, firm and insistent. "All ready to go? Anyone else with you?"

The security lights were bright in the parking area, with waitstaff, security and valets jostling around each other to get to their destinations. "My head baker is with me." She turned and pointed out Jacques, standing by the front of the van. "My van is the bright pink one."

He laughed. "Why am I not surprised?"

When she turned back to him, though, Britt noticed Mark's gaze had narrowed as he glanced over her shoulder. "Is something wrong?" she asked.

"Everything's fine." He kissed her again. "I'll be here. Good luck with tonight."

As she and Jacques started bringing in their desserts, uniformed staff surrounded them in a chaotic, but organized manner.

Jacques whistled. "This will be a night to remember, I think."

"Over here!" a young woman called out to them. Her uniform was different from the others, with a name and her position printed on it—Sylvia, Head Caterer. She held a clipboard. "You are?"

"Britt Gronlund, Konditori Bakery." She nodded at Jacques. "And my head baker, Jacques Baudin."

"Ah yes, yours was a last-minute order." She smiled. "Mrs. Weinstein loves your pastries. I'm glad it worked out. This way."

She led them to a small butler's pantry off to one side of the huge kitchen. "The other pantry is being used for the dining ware and service," she told them. "Thank God it's a small number of guests, but it's a very exclusive dinner event. The serving trays are in the cupboards above you— choose whatever you require. You can leave it all in here— the waitstaff will bring everything out when ready. They've just served the hors d'oeuvres, so it'll be about two hours before the desserts are served. You have some time."

"Thank you."

"If you need anything, I'll be in the hallway where you found me." With a bright smile, she was gone.

Britt and Jacques took turns bringing in their foodstuffs until everything was stacked on the wide counters. "I think we should just get our desserts on the serving plates and call it a night," Jacques said quietly.

She nodded. "Good idea. It's not like we'll get close to Mrs. Weinstein to thank her."

They arranged everything accordingly. Britt heard detailed instructions shouted through the back rooms, all timed down to the minute. "You know, I thought about hosting catering events in the future, but if they're going to run it like a military operation, it's going to be a big nope in my books."

Jacques laughed. "For diplomats such as these, there's no choice. They have their schedules, and everything else works around them."

She glanced at him while he arranged the cakes on stands, then covered them with glass domes. "It sounds like you've catered something like this."

"Oui." He fussed over the Danishes. "Back home, my events were all planned. It made things easier."

Britt checked her watch—fifteen minutes to spare. "Looks like we're done. Honestly, I'd like to get out of here before we're descended upon by the waitstaff."

Just as they left the pantry, a contingent of servers hurried in their direction, and they flattened themselves against the wall as the horde went by. "So glad we're not staying," she muttered.

Once outside, Britt inhaled a deep breath of the cool summer air, scented with roses and other flowers. She stretched her arms over her head, looking out into the vast backyard lit with solar lighting and lanterns and bordered by tall hedges and colorful foliage. A stone pathway led from the extensive back porch to a small gate at the opposite end. Britt was curious as to what lay beyond. "Jacques, I'm going to take a walk around the backyard."

He raised a brow. "Do you think that's wise, Britt? What if a security guard finds you out there?"

She laughed. "We're at a party. They must expect guests to come outside and admire the scenery."

"Then let me join you before we leave. I just need to use the bathroom, if you don't mind waiting?"

"Of course not." She wished Mark was here to enjoy such a lovely sight with her..

MARK STOOD JUST within the open door leading out to the parking area. His body was on full alert, adrenaline pumping through his veins as he studied his immediate surroundings. The long, wide hallway before him was filled with staff, and as he tried to angle himself to look at the various faces that hurried past him, he realized it was impossible to pick out an individual person.

But something—or rather, someone—had triggered an internal red flag.

When he had been talking to Britt outside earlier, he noticed a man that looked vaguely like Ferguson's murderer—Mark had memorized every detail from the picture Myrna provided—but he wasn't sure. And if he wasn't sure, he couldn't alert security and cause a panic.

A young woman approached him. "Excuse me, are you a guest? The entrance is that way…"

He pulled out his badge. "I'm here to assist security. I'd like to take a quick look around, if you don't mind."

"Yes, of course." She passed by without another word.

Mark walked casually down the hall, listening to the shouts and clatter of a dining service being prepared. Britt would be in the midst of that, which meant she'd be far away and, more important, safe from anything that might happen.

The end of the hallway revealed an enormous dining room. Everything had been set up, but the room was currently empty. Beyond, he saw several guests in another room, holding champagne glasses as they chatted. That had to be the reception area.

He walked quickly to the other side, his gaze searching. Here, Mark had to be more careful, as his presence would certainly be noticed among the bejeweled women and men in tuxedos. Bodyguards stood at strategic points around the room, their scrutiny taking in everything around them. He stood just behind the grand archway and studied the room, looking for any sign of his adversary. Nothing.

He turned around, intending to backtrack and try another hallway, when he heard several ladies laughing. He wasn't sure why it attracted his attention, but Mark looked over his shoulder...

Damn—it was him.

Before Mark got his wits together, the murderer left the reception via another door. But shit, that was the guy.

He went back the way he came, knowing that discretion was critical. He got outside and hurried to his car, then grabbed his walkie-talkie. "This is Detective Hawthorne!" he said urgently. "Get every available unit to Callaway Court. Ferguson's murderer has been spotted. No sirens and park at the corner of Callaway and Golfers Gate. The house is directly across, with all its lights on. Head for the main gate—I'll meet you there. We don't want to spook him."

He dialed another number on his work phone. "This is Detective Mark Hawthorne with York Regional Police 4 District," he said. "I had a request for the Emergency Response Team to be on standby to assist with the arrest of an international criminal. He's been located."

He gave them the address, and then called Britt, but there was no answer. It was possible she was still busy with setting up, but...

Mark sent her a quick text instead, telling her to get in his car when she was finished and lock the doors. He knew she would freak out when she read the message, but hopefully she'd just do it and wait until he returned.

Now he had to alert security. If the murderer tried anything during the party...

JACQUES REMAINED IN the guest bathroom for a few extra minutes to freshen up. The work he and Britt had done left him feeling sweaty and unfit for such esteemed company.

He checked his clothing, making sure he wasn't dabbed with icing or fruit, swiped away a few flecks of pastry and looked at himself in the mirror, thinking it would do. He needed to hurry as Britt was waiting for him in the gardens. He sighed. This detective was a very lucky man to be dating his boss.

When he opened the door, he stared in surprise at the familiar face before him. "What are you doing here, *mon ami*? I thought—"

Thomas slammed into him, knocking them both into the powder room, and locked the door.

Jacques's brain clicked into overdrive. He held his hands up, palms facing forward. "Now, now, there's no need for this…"

"Why do you have a cop following you?" he snarled.

"An officer? He is not following us. He's here to escort Britt home. He's waiting in his car."

"Not anymore. He came into the house and was hanging around in the hallway."

"I—" Jacques thought fast. If he wasn't careful… "There's no way the police can trace anything back to me. I've played my part leading the Ferguson protests, but I did not expect the police to make a surprise appearance at the funeral. I was lucky to get away. How do I know *you* haven't done something stupid?"

"Because I'm not in jail. But if we're not careful, we will be."

Jacques considered the situation. Thomas was agitated for some reason. "Where is the police officer now?"

"I don't know."

"Mon Dieu." Jacques knew he hadn't been spotted at Ferguson's funeral—he had kept himself well camouflaged. As for Thomas... "We must be very careful as we leave," he warned. "We cannot be seen together, and Britt will ask questions if she notices you."

Thomas stared at him. "I'm leaving the city tonight."

Jacques knew his brows went up at that. "What are you talking about? Why would you go?"

Thomas's expression held a chilling quality that made Jacques nervous. "Because I killed him."

Jacques felt his body grow still with dread at the terrifying response. "You killed an officer? What is wrong with you? Why would you do...?"

Thomas slashed his hand in a downward motion. "Not the cop. I wasted Ferguson."

Jacques's mind couldn't keep up with the horror story Thomas was telling him. The young man had twisted all of Jacques's hard work until he felt like he couldn't escape. "Why?" When Thomas didn't answer, he slammed his palm against the wall. "Why?" he demanded.

"Because he deserved it." Thomas spat on the ground.

Jacques swore. Their plan to terrorize Ferguson into backing off from buying neighborhood businesses had gotten messed up. Somehow, young Thomas had turned it into some kind of personal vendetta, and he didn't know why. "Is that it? Because he deserved it? You need to provide a better reason than that."

"You told me what he's done to you—to other small-business owners. His death could be a warning to Mighty Big Bakery to back off."

"Or it might spur them on, to continue his legacy." Jacques shook his head—where had he made his mistake? His own revenge against Ferguson and Jacques's business partner—who had sold him out behind his back—had gone horribly wrong. It wasn't supposed to go this far...not all the way to murder. He'd have to figure out how to extricate himself from this mess. "*Mon ami*, I think we need to back up and reassess our situation."

"Too late for that." Thomas pulled a gun out from behind his back. A silencer was attached to it.

"Merde." Jacques weighed his options—all of them looked bleak. "There's no need for that," he said gently, keeping his hands out in the open. "I'm not going to say anything to anyone. Just leave—leave the city, the country even. Please, don't hurt a friend."

Thomas hesitated, and Jacques saw his chance, grabbing the young man's weapon and smashing it against the wall. It went off with a muffled pop. Suddenly, Thomas dipped low, and Jacques howled in pain, his eyes watering from the excruciating blow to his crotch. His grip loosened, but before he could regain his balance, hot, searing pain burned in his leg and stomach. Jacques slumped to the ground, his vision darkening as Thomas pushed him out of the way to make his escape.

BRITT GLANCED AT her watch again—Jacques had been gone for over fifteen minutes. Then she realized he must have found an opportunity to schmooze with the guests. "What a guy," she said out loud. She'd take her stroll through the beautiful garden, then head to Mark's car and go home.

She walked down the few steps into the sunken space and stayed on the main path. The grass was a lush green beneath the lights, and on an impulse, she took off her sneakers and walked through it, the soft blades tickling her toes, the earth cool beneath her feet. It felt amazing.

She reached the other end of the garden. Here, the tall

gate led out onto small undulating hills with sandbanks in between—a golf course, and to either side of her, the blackness of a forest.

Odd, the gate didn't have a lock on it. She assumed the course and surrounding area were possibly so secure that a lock wasn't needed. It must be nice to live in this type of luxury.

She heard footsteps from behind. "Holy crap, Jacques, you took your time," Britt called out to him as she turned. "Did you score an opportunity to talk with Mrs.—" She stopped.

Thomas stood a few feet away. "Hey, Britt."

"Um, hey." She glanced at the house. "Why are you here? I thought I mentioned Jacques and I wouldn't need you tonight. We're already finished."

"Oh." He laughed, but it didn't sound right. "Sorry, I guess I thought...maybe you and Jacques would need help cleaning up."

"No, we're done, thank you. You can go home. You've had a long day." She had no idea how she kept her voice steady—her body was ready to bolt because something didn't feel right in this conversation.

"Would you like a ride home?"

Her stomach was turning into knots of fear. There was no reason for Thomas to be out here—none. And the way he was acting in front of her was not the same young man who worked in her bakery. "No, thanks. Jacques said he'd take me home," she lied.

"Oh." Thomas scratched his head. "I thought your detective boyfriend was driving you back."

Thomas couldn't know that—there was no way. Britt swallowed the large lump in her throat. "He's supposed to, but he hasn't come back from wherever he is. Actually, I think I'll go wait for him at the car." Her laugh was forced. "I don't want to have an officer waiting on me."

She almost screamed when her cell phone pinged with a text. She dug it out of her bag and looked at the screen—Mark. He had called and texted several times, but she had turned the phone off when she and Jacques were in the house.

She glanced at Thomas, who had remained still. Something very spooky surrounded him, like a bad aura, and if she didn't get away, Britt was scared she'd be sucked into it. "It's Jacques," she lied again, hoping it sounded convincing. "He's wondering where I am." She started typing a reply.

HELP. IN BACK GARDEN!

"Don't do that."

Startled, she looked up. Thomas was swaying from side to side, as if listening to a song only he could hear. "Come on, I'll take you home."

"No." She backed up until she bumped into the iron gate, slipping her phone into her pocket. "I told you, I have a ride."

"Not anymore." His voice had gone quiet, menacing.

"Thomas, what the hell do you want?" she demanded in a loud voice. Despite the fear coursing through every limb, she had to ask the question.

"I did something bad, and the police are after me." He took a step forward. "If I kept you as a hostage, your boyfriend would back off. I just want to get out of the country."

That was a big OH, HELL NO in her mind.

Britt didn't think, just reacted. She threw her shoes and bag at him, scoring a direct hit in his face, then raced out the gate, turning left and rushing into the depth of the trees.

She immediately slowed down, wincing as her bare feet

stepped on small rocks and stubbed against tree roots. She looked over her shoulder but couldn't see Thomas.

She hunkered down against a tree, her breaths panting out in short gasps. Her instincts had taken over, allowing her to escape a potentially dangerous situation. As she fought to gather her wits, she heard shouting. "York Regional Police! Remain where you are and get your hands in the air!"

Mark's voice. "Oh my God." Britt started crawling in the opposite direction, desperate to stay out of sight until he came for her. Bile rose in her throat, her fear a tangible thing as it wrapped around her ankles to slow her down.

"It's okay. You're okay," she whispered to herself. She used her hands to feel her way around tree trunks and thick bushes. A noise caught her attention, and turning around, the glare of a flashlight wove erractically behind her. Britt heard a shout—was that Mark? She wasn't sure, and decided to keep going.

Britt looked around, hoping to spot something for reference. She knew there was another house beside the Weinsteins' and carefully crawled in the general direction. She needed to gain some distance before attempting to call Mark.

Suddenly, a bright light illuminated the forest in front of her, the trees a stark silhouette of dark angles. Glancing behind her, a portion of the golf course appeared. Several officers ran by, but she didn't see Thomas.

And that flashlight continued to dog her steps. Damn it, was it Thomas? "Shit!" She got to her feet and stumbled through the undergrowth, using what light she could navigate by to get away from the mayhem unfolding behind her.

She desperately wanted to call Mark but was terrified that if she hesitated for too long, Thomas might find her. On that thought, she took her phone out and placed it on

Mute—if Mark called, it'd vibrate instead, alerting her but not Thomas.

Several agonizing minutes later, Britt spied a square of light some distance away—a window. Sobbing quietly with relief, she got down on her hands and knees again to save her feet, and crawled as fast as she dared, occasionally bumping into a tree trunk, or swearing under her breath as she pulled her tangled hair out of an errant bush. She stopped, noticing the darkness around her had receded—it looked like all the security lights at the golf course were turned on. The police should be able to catch Thomas.

Unless he had escaped through the forest like she was doing and was following her. With all the illumination, he could easily find her if she didn't get her ass moving.

Britt focused her waning strength on that square of light, which meant a house, and people inside who could keep her safe.

God, she hoped Mark was okay. Chasing Thomas like that when he could be armed with a weapon…

Suddenly, she stopped and crouched down beside a large tree as crashing noises caught her attention. It was difficult to tell how far away it was, but as Britt listened, she realized it was getting closer.

"Britt!"

She heard her name, but with fear coursing through her body, it could be Thomas trying to draw her out of hiding.

She'd have no choice but to make a run for it.

Tucking her hair down the back of her T-shirt, she worked out a path of least resistance and got moving, trying to be careful where she placed her feet. A couple of minutes later, she slapped her hand over her mouth to muffle a cry of pain—she had stepped on something sharp that pierced her foot. Not missing a beat, she scrambled to find what broke her stride—a piece of broken branch. She bit her tongue as she yanked it out quickly, then half hobbled, half hopped the rest of the way.

Her phone vibrated. *Damn it, could this be a worse time?* If it was Mark, he'd have to wait while she made her last dash to safety. It felt like every piece of plant life was trying to ensnare her, but fear gave her the strength to fight through the foliage that blocked her escape.

And then, nothing. Britt stumbled to a stop in a clearing and looked around, breathing hard. The ground seemed level beneath the faint illumination of the golf course security lights. She took hurried, though careful steps through the knee-high grass. Her foot throbbed in pain, punctuated with sharp stabs that almost had her crying in frustration. She knew it was bleeding, and no doubt infected as well. Sparing a few precious minutes, she stripped off her T-shirt and bound it around her foot, feeling the thick stickiness of blood along her fingers.

Just a little farther—at the edge of the clearing, a thick hedge stood like a sentinel, and there, in the middle, a gate.

"Almost there, almost there," she chanted softly. She used her toes on the injured foot to propel herself forward until her hands brushed against the textured leaves, then moved to her left until cool metal replaced the natural border.

The light from the large picture window was bright, a beacon that called out to her. It stretched far into the backyard, which allowed her to find the gate's latch. She carefully lifted it and looked over her shoulder. No one was behind her, but Thomas would easily see her silhouette from the edge of the forest if he made it this far.

Haunted by the thought, Britt slid inside. She moved to the side so that the hedge hid her from view and looked around. Several feet in front of her, a swimming pool lay covered in a dark tarpaulin. Thank God she hadn't charged straight ahead—she would have fallen in. Around it was a stone patio and beyond, the unbroken darkness of grass—a lot of it. The backyard was huge. She had a lot of space to walk through before getting close enough to yell for help.

She gritted her teeth and started limping, spurred on by the distant shouts behind her. As soon as she managed to get inside, she'd call Mark and let him know she was safe...

Britt hesitated, listening. Above the shouting, she also heard a dog barking. Was it a police dog? Or something else?

When she looked at the window, she froze in her tracks. The large shadow of a canine danced across the grass, and at the window, she spied a German shepherd. It was going wild, jumping up and down, teeth bared, its baleful stare locked on her.

Damn it. Britt needed to weigh her options. If the homeowner released the dog into the backyard before she made it to the door to explain her situation, she didn't stand a chance. It was possible the police had informed anyone living in the area to keep their doors locked and be on the lookout.

"Shit!" She looked around quickly, then took a closer look at a tall square object just beyond the window's light. As she hobbled toward it, she realized it was a garden shed. Perfect, she could hide in there until Mark got her.

A small light winked on when she opened the door. It was a good size, large enough for her to stand in. On the walls, various garden tools hung neatly in rows. Britt grabbed a long-handled aerator, its numerous spikes a couple of inches long. If Thomas opened that door, he'd get a face full of sharp metal.

MARK STOOD IN the middle of a group of security guards and police officers. "I need your help. The police have been hunting a dangerous criminal the past couple of days, and I saw him in this house." Mark gave them a brief summary of the Ferguson murder case. "We can't have a panic on our hands." He pulled out a picture. "This is the man we're looking for."

Several more security guards had hurried over. "I saw that guy," one of them said. "I don't know how he got in, but I saw him hanging around that pink bakery van."

"We have to find him." Mark's anxiety went up with every second that passed without hearing from Britt. "My men will cover the exits. Go inside and take a look around—"

His phone pinged. When he read the message from Britt, his adrenaline skyrocketed. "The back garden! Move!"

He took off at a full run, his officers and several security guards trailing behind him. In the distance, he saw a flash of white and Britt's terrified expression before she bolted. A man was about to give chase.

"Goddamn it!" He ran faster. "York Regional Police!" he yelled. "Remain where you are and get your hands in the air!"

The murderer he'd been hunting sped away, running straight onto the golf course. If they didn't catch him in time, he'd disappear into the darkness.

"Go after him!" he shouted. "Radio for help to block off the course and get some lights on!" Mark turned to the man beside him. "I heard you guys are one of the best ERT units in Canada," he said to Staff Sergeant Victor Moore.

The commander smiled, but it wasn't a friendly expression. "My boys are already circling around the course, detective. I'll follow your men. Don't worry, we'll find him."

As Moore raced off, Mark noticed something white in the grass that worried him—Britt's sneakers, and nearby, her bag. He veered left, following her course. Somehow, she'd already reached the blackness of the forest beyond.

"Britt!" he yelled. He dug a flashlight out of his pocket and switched it on. Thick stands of tree trunks and undergrowth hindered his progress as he pushed through. How the hell did she manage to get through this stuff?

Just then, the remaining security lights at the golf course turned on, illuminating everything in a bright white glare. It didn't quite reach back here, but it offered Mark a little more light to see by.

Several anxious minutes later, his flashlight picked out a gaping hole. The branches were recently broken, still hanging by pieces of bark. He kept going, turning one way, then the other, trying to see through the bush and wondering if she was hiding somewhere.

Something glistened wet on the ground a few feet ahead, and Mark bit back a cry when he realized it was blood—*shit*. "Britt! Where are you?" he yelled out. No answer.

Swearing, he pulled out his phone and dialed her number, hoping she'd pick up or he could hear it ringing in the undergrowth. Nothing.

He continued following her path, shoving at anything that got in his way. He stopped when his walkie-talkie went off. "Staff Sergeant Moore reporting." The ERT commander possessed a thick British accent. "Perpetrator has been captured. Repeat, perpetrator captured."

He hit the send button. "Good work, all of you. Take him to the precinct. I'll be there shortly. The rest of you, get back to the Weinstein residence and make sure everyone's okay. I'm looking for someone—I'll radio when I'm done."

The golf course security lights barely penetrated this far into the forest. Britt must be terrified, hunkered down somewhere and staying quiet until she thought it was safe.

The trees thinned out into a meadow, but before he continued, his trembling fingers wrapped around long, silky strands of blond hair caught on a bush. He was on the right track, but he was frightened for her, wondering what condition she'd be in.

Mark ran across the meadow, following a faint beaten path through the long grass until he stopped at a thick border of hedge reaching almost ten feet in height. As he panned his flashlight, he spied the half-open gate.

Britt must have gone through here.

He opened the gate wider so that he could slip inside. It was eerily quiet, as if the air held its breath.

He jumped at the sound of a dog barking. He looked towards the mansion and saw a large German shepherd thrashing against the glass doors and baring its teeth. The homeowner was nowhere in sight.

Mark started walking the length of the extensive backyard, being careful not to get too close to the edge of the pool. Under his flashlight's glare, he spied a garden shed.

He stopped and looked around. There was nowhere anyone could hide unless they buried themselves beneath the thick hedge.

As a precaution, Mark hunkered down low and swept the flashlight's beam around—nothing.

He rose and blew out a tense breath. With a bloodied foot, Britt wouldn't get too far. And a very angry guard dog would make her think twice about going to the house for help.

He glanced back at the garden shed and started toward it. If he were in Britt's position, he would pick this place to hide and choose a sharp weapon to defend himself.

However, Mark hesitated with his hand on the door handle.

He couldn't hear anything, even when he placed his ear to the cool metal. He chewed the inside of his cheek, thinking.

"Britt, it's Mark. Are you in here?"

Silence.

"*Vakker*, it's okay, you can come out. We've caught Ferguson's murderer."

Still nothing.

If Britt was as scared as he guessed, she wouldn't trust anyone right now. She could attack first without realizing it was him.

He looked at the door, noting the hinges—it would swing outward.

Mark stepped to one side, keeping his flashlight up. "Britt, I'm going to open the garden shed door." Tensing himself for a violent reaction, he yanked the door open.

Suddenly, a garden tool with spikes stabbed the air, followed by a pained scream.

"Britt!" He backed away, dodging as she swung her weapon wildly. "Britt, it's me! *Vakker!*"

She stopped, her green eyes wide and unfocused in the flashlight's beam. "Mark?"

He pointed the flashlight at himself so she could see him clearly.

With a sob that tore at his soul, she dropped the garden tool and reached out for him.

Mark snatched her into his arms, crushing her to him, crooning nonsense words as she cried, loud, wracking sounds that broke his heart. He hid his face in her hair, inhaling the sweet scent that was only hers, then kissed her, hoping she'd forget everything until it was just him in her mind. "Britt, shh, it's okay. I'm here, *vakker*. I'm right here."

He swung her into his arms and cradled her against his chest. She had buried her face into the curve of his neck, and thank God, her sobbing had quieted down—he'd almost become a gibbering mess when he heard it.

Mark carried her through the backyard and to the front of the neighboring house. The dog had continued its frenzied barking while he walked past the home, heading to the Weinstein house so that Britt could get much-needed care before being transported to the hospital.

Chapter Seventeen

The sound of rain.

Britt slowly became aware of other noises, although her eyes remained closed—footsteps, low voices. Her hands touched something cool and soft, and when she moved her fingers, she realized they were bedsheets. Was she at home? Had it only been a nightmare?

She cracked open an eyelid and squinted at the bright light slamming into her eyeball. She groaned softly and raised her hand to block it out.

"Vakker."

His deep voice, strong yet tender at the same time. She took a breath and winced at the various aches and pains. Her right foot throbbed, and in a moment, she remembered what had happened—Thomas's uneasy appearance, the escape through the woods, hiding in the garden shed...

Britt slowly opened her eyes and held still as her vision adjusted to the well-lit room, and the first thing she saw was Mark. He leaned over her, his brown-gold eyes filled with concern. "How are you feeling?"

"Sore." She didn't recognize her surroundings. "Where am I?"

"At the hospital. The way your foot looked scared me,

and you were pretty scratched up. I wanted to be sure you hadn't picked up an infection."

Damn. She moved her limbs, reassuring herself that nothing had been broken.

"Did you want to sit up? Have some water?"

She nodded, not taking her eyes off him as he raised the bed to an elevated position, then lifted a glass of water with a straw to her mouth. "Not too fast."

She took a few sips, the cool liquid quenching her dry throat.

"Girl, what on earth have you been up to *now*?" Joyce appeared in her line of vision.

"Hey. Um, I'd say nothing, except..." She paused, feeling confused.

"We all know that isn't true. You look like something the cat dragged in."

"I certainly feel like it." Britt was relieved that Joyce was here—right now, her friend offered a sense of balance. Mark, on the other hand... Well, he'd been her anchor in a storm of fear and loneliness. But it didn't feel steady right now... More like it wanted to cast off, and she fought to keep it in place. "Joyce, could I have a few minutes with Mark, please?"

Her friend's eyes widened, almost as if she sensed what Britt was thinking. "Of course. I'll be right outside."

As soon as the door closed, she wrapped her hand around his. "What the hell happened? Why was Thomas there?" Her mind snapped on to another troubling thought. "Where's Jacques? I haven't seen him."

Mark raised her hand to his lips, and she gasped at seeing bandages covering her palm. "You need your rest, but let me try to explain it. It seems that Jacques and Thomas were more than just bakers."

"No." Britt didn't want to believe Jacques had anything to do with Mr. Ferguson's murder.

"Jacques Baudin led the protests against Mighty Big Bakery. Seems he owned his own business for a long time with a business partner. Unfortunately, Ferguson convinced the partner to sell and bought it under Jacques's nose. By the time Jacques found out, he'd lost everything." Mark tilted his head. "He never said anything to you?"

"Nothing." Poor Jacques.

"He took matters into his own hands. Raised quite a crowd of rebels, too. Jacques used scare tactics to slow down construction or force employees to quit."

"Jacques, damn you." She squeezed Mark's hand. "Is he going to jail?"

"I don't know. Thomas shot him at the Weinstein house, but I haven't found out why. Jacques is all right, and I'm hoping he can fill in what happened."

Britt nodded. "What about Thomas? What's his story?"

Mark swore. "He's not talking, but we discovered enough criminal evidence against him that will earn him jail time here or extradition."

"Are you saying I hired criminals?" Britt raised herself from the bed as her voice cracked on the last word. "How did— Thomas had all the paperwork!"

"Documents can be deceiving." He gently grasped her shoulders. "It's okay, lie back down."

She rested back on the bed.

"I'm just glad you're all right, *vakker.*" He leaned down, and she felt his warm lips on her forehead. "I'd never forgive myself if anything happened to you."

She looked at him. Mark's eyes were suspiciously shiny. "This wasn't your fault. Why are you blaming yourself?"

He swiped at his face with his other hand. "I should have

caught him before he got to you. If I had been better at understanding the clues, maybe I could have prevented..."

"Hey, hey!" She reached over and grabbed his face, then pulled him down until he was level with her. "You did your job. You caught the men responsible, and that's important. Maybe I shouldn't have run off, but you came after me and brought me back safely. And I adore you for that."

His eyes widened in surprise, and she bit her lip, realizing what she'd just said. But she knew it was the truth, and she shook his head gently to emphasize it. "Did you hear me, Mr. Detective?"

Something changed in his expression, a look that made her skin tingle with goose bumps. Britt shivered, but heat flushed her face until she knew it was bright pink.

"Say it again," he told her, his voice rough.

"What? That I shouldn't have run away from you?" she teased, but the look in his eyes shut her up.

"Try again."

Britt hesitated, feeling suddenly shy. Somehow, her perception of Mark had recently shifted. A part of her recognized a kindred spirit, a man who cared for and had protected her without question during one of the scariest moments in her life. She wanted to tell him her feelings, and she had the perfect way to do it. "Ah, Mark," she crooned in her best French accent. "Do you know how much I adore you? *Mon cher*, talk the language of love to me."

His look had her laughing so hard her stomach hurt. "It annoys me that I know you're imitating that lovestruck cartoon skunk." He groaned out loud. "It annoys me even more that I like it."

She giggled. "I'll have you know I don't talk about my favorite cartoons with just anyone." She paused. "You're pretty special."

He kissed her for a long moment, his mouth insistent and filled with promise. "And you are my Nordic princess."

"MARK, YOU'RE ABSOLUTELY WONDERFUL! Have I told you that?"

He tried not to roll his eyes as he smiled. "Yes, Mom. Several times, actually."

Britt was in the same hospital as Mom, so after making sure she was comfortable, he'd ridden the elevator to his mom's floor for a surprise visit. He'd stopped short when he'd seen Stanley standing over Mom, combing her hair. "Sorry," Mark apologized, backing up. "I'll come back later."

"Don't be absurd." She patted Stanley's hand. "We were watching the news. Congratulations on catching your killer."

He always appreciated her enthusiasm. "How are you feeling?"

"So much better." She looked at Stanley. "And Stanley's been a sweetheart. He's been looking after the house and watering my plants."

Stanley touched her chin with a finger. "It's the least I can do."

Wow, these two. He and Britt were very close to that level of relationship, and he couldn't wait until she decided to take that next step. "Thanks for helping out, Stanley. I really appreciate it."

He waved a hand. "Anything for—" He stopped, his surprised expression flushing a deep red. "You're welcome."

"I gotta run, but I'll come around tomorrow, okay?"

"Where's my kiss?" she demanded.

"Mom." But he obliged her as always, presenting his cheek to be noisily smooched.

He finally managed to escape and headed back to Britt's room, but she was sound asleep.

"She just drifted off," Joyce said quietly, closing the door behind them. "Poor thing's been through a lot."

He nodded, his mind on work, thinking on finishing up some loose ends.

"Are you in love with her?"

Startled, Mark stared at her. Her dark eyes danced with amusement. "We've only been seeing each other a week."

"Okay then, do you care for her?"

He stopped. "I'm not sure why you're so curious about us."

Joyce halted beside him, her demeanor now serious. "Britt is a dear friend, and I don't want to see her get hurt. Emotionally speaking."

"I'm not going to do that." This felt like an interview.

"I mean, she's a big girl and can handle herself."

"She certainly can." He crossed his arms. "Where are you going with this?"

"I just wanted to be sure if you were the right guy for her."

Mark couldn't figure out where Joyce was going with this, but he was going to put a stop to it. "I know you're her friend, and I'm glad you're in her life. I'm mature enough to understand my feelings and how to act on them, but in the end it's for Britt to decide if she wants a relationship with me."

Joyce suddenly smiled, her teeth bright against her dark skin. "Well said." She grabbed his arm. "Gotta run, I have a bakery to finish. Grand reopening is planned for next week, and Britt should be on her feet by then."

This past week had been a roller coaster of tension involving...everything. Now that he could take a breath, Mark collapsed into his car, his body limp and boneless. Captain

Fraust had run with the final points of his investigation at this morning's news conference, sparing him the spotlight and the thousands of questions he knew would bombard him.

He wanted to go home, but he was too wired despite the exhaustion. Joyce's words rang in his head. He assumed she was being protective, and he got that. But her conversation sounded like she had her doubts, which of course didn't make sense. Obviously he cared for Britt; nothing had changed in that department. If anything, his feelings had only grown stronger in the short time they'd known each other.

But he also understood the merit of not rushing into things—he had learned that lesson the hard way in his early twenties. And Britt had displayed that same caution, which he had no problem with. Mark would respect her thoughts and fears, just as he was sure Britt would do the same thing for him. And when it was time for them to talk and take the next step, they would do it together.

Restless, he drove to the precinct and headed for his office. After his computer booted up, he started working, feeling his mind get into the flow of providing proper documentation. About an hour later, he had an organized file folder containing everything he'd collected.

Mark hadn't found the chance to thank Myrna properly for her hard work on this case—it had been nonstop since yesterday. He sent her a text and wished her a good weekend.

Ten seconds later, his cell phone rang. "Hey," she said. "How's it going? Is your girlfriend all right?"

He'd never said anything definite about being in a relationship, but it seemed everyone thought that way. "Yeah, she's fine. I'm in the office cleaning up."

"Seriously? I'm downstairs. I called because I have news for you, so come down and I'll show you."

Curious, he took the stairs and walked down the hallway, his footsteps echoing eerily in the empty space until he knocked on her door and stepped inside. "What's up?"

Her head appeared from behind a screen. "I'm surprised you're here. I'd thought you would take a day off."

"I wanted to finish up." He grasped her shoulder. "Seriously, thanks for all of your help. You've been outstanding."

"We make a great team, Hawthorne. And this was an interesting case." She pressed a few keys. "So, two things. That envelope and threatening letter you gave me to check? Mr. Ferguson's fingerprints were all over it, so it must have come from him."

Mark nodded. "I figured as much, but thanks for confirming it." He watched as information scrolled across Myrna's computer screens. "And the second thing?"

"Cynthia finished working on that other investigation you asked for help with."

What the hell—she was talking about Dad. His body shook with trepidation. "What did she find?" he whispered in a hoarse voice.

Myrna typed something and several photos of fingerprints appeared, along with a picture of Dad's brooding expression. "She's not sure if he was there when your mom fell down the stairs."

"For God's sake." Either way, Dad had breached his bail conditions by entering Mom's home.

"However, with some of her famous ingenuity, Cynthia discovered his workplace." Another moment of typing, and another photo appeared. "He's been working on a farm north of here. He's been arrested for assaulting the farmer and his wife. Cyn made sure to provide every bit of criminal evidence so that he stays behind bars this time." She glanced up at him.

Mark felt light, as if a terrible weight had been lifted off his shoulders. After all this time, he could breathe easier, knowing Mom was safe. Having Stanley in her life again was an added bonus. "Thanks, Myrna. I needed that."

"I thought that would make your weekend better." She shut down the computer.

He had an idea. "I'm starving. Do you want to grab something?"

She smiled wide. "Sure. I've got just the place. You can update me on last night. Man, I wish I had seen the ERT in action."

BRITT STOOD BY the front window of Konditori, looking out onto dozens of customers who had been waiting since the crack of dawn.

She turned in a slow circle, taking in the wonder that Joyce had created. The front room was larger, allowing more guests to come inside. The walls were a pale shade of muted gray, a stunning contrast to the vibrant pink on the outside walls. New furniture that allowed more space, a wider display counter and plenty of hidden storage cupboards made the room look brighter and bigger.

"What do you think?" Joyce asked, standing at the office doorway.

She laughed. "You could tap me with a stick and I would fall over, that's how stunned I am. The bakery..." She paused, searching for words. "It feels like an extension of me."

"That's exactly what I was going for."

Britt watched as her friend unbuttoned and rolled up her sleeves. "What are you doing?"

Joyce gave her a look. "Did you think you could handle this mob with only the staff and you? Betty's going to help Jacques, so I'm helping behind the counter."

Britt shook her head. "Joyce..."

Her friend wagged her finger at her. "No *but*s. I'm happy to help."

The first pastries had already been stocked in the display case. Kevin, Betty, Jasmine and Oliver were all smiles as they approached. "This looks amazing!" Betty exclaimed, wrapping her arms around Britt's waist. "I'm so proud of you."

"I'm proud of everyone. Honestly, without you all, this wouldn't have happened."

"No, *chérie*, all of this is because of your hard work." Jacques, in his usual apron and baker's hat, stood by the kitchen door. Fully healed, he had provided evidence that resulted in a hefty fine but no jail time. He was more than happy to pay that.

"And your delicious concoctions. Which reminds me— we'll need to think of some new recipes."

"But of course. Now, if you will excuse me, there is baking to be done!" He disappeared into the kitchen, with Betty running after him.

Today would be a zoo, but she wouldn't have it any other way. As she watched everyone making last-minute preparations, she wished Mark was here. Maybe work had gotten in the way...

The sudden loud wail of a police siren startled her—it was close. As she looked out the window, two police vehicles pulled up to the curb and three officers stepped out. But the fourth...

Mark.

She ran to the door to unlock and open it, then stood

there, watching as he flashed his badge so that he could get through the crowd. A collective groan emanated from the customers.

"Don't worry, we're here to help. You all look like a hungry bunch," he yelled.

Britt could only stare as he came up to her, a big smile on his face. "I—I assumed you'd be at work."

He wrapped his arms around her waist. "And miss this most important day for you? Oh ye of little faith."

The officers who came with Mark organized the boisterous crowd into a semblance of a lineup.

"Come on, let's get Konditori open for business," Mark shouted.

A collective cheer rose from the crowd, but Britt only had eyes for Mark as he melded his mouth to hers.

Oh, how sweet life was going to be.

* * * * *

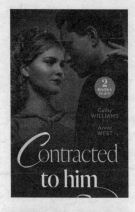

COMING SOON!

We really hope you enjoyed reading this book.
If you're looking for more romance
be sure to head to the shops when
new books are available on

Thursday 9th May

To see which titles are coming soon, please visit
millsandboon.co.uk/nextmonth

MILLS & BOON